KILLER
SUMMER

Also by Ridley Pearson

Killer View

Killer Weekend

Cut and Run

The Art of Deception

The Diary of Ellen Rimbauer
(writing as Joyce Reardon)

The Pied Piper

Beyond Recognition

Undercurrents

Books for Young Readers

Peter and the Starcatchers series
(with Dave Barry)

The Kingdom Keepers series

Never Land series
(with Dave Barry)

Steel Trapp series

G. P. PUTNAM'S SONS

New York

KILLER SUMMER

**Doubleday Large Print
Home Library Edition**

Ridley Pearson

This Large Print Edition, prepared especially for Doubleday Large Print Home Library, contains the complete, unabridged text of the original Publisher's Edition.

PUTNAM

G. P. PUTNAM'S SONS
Publishers Since 1838
Published by the Penguin Group
Penguin Group (USA) Inc., 375 Hudson Street, New York, New York 10014, USA • Penguin Group (Canada), 90 Eglinton Avenue East, Suite 700, Toronto, Ontario M4P 2Y3, Canada (a division of Pearson Canada Inc.) • Penguin Books Ltd, 80 Strand, London WC2R 0RL, England • Penguin Ireland, 25 St Stephen's Green, Dublin 2, Ireland (a division of Penguin Books Ltd) • Penguin Group (Australia), 250 Camberwell Road, Camberwell, Victoria 3124, Australia (a division of Pearson Australia Group Pty Ltd) • Penguin Books India Pvt Ltd, 11 Community Centre, Panchsheel Park, New Delhi–110 017, India • Penguin Group (NZ), 67 Apollo Drive, Rosedale, North Shore 0632, New Zealand (a division of Pearson New Zealand Ltd) • Penguin Books (South Africa) (Pty) Ltd, 24 Sturdee Avenue, Rosebank, Johannesburg 2196, South Africa

Penguin Books Ltd, Registered Offices: 80 Strand, London WC2R 0RL, England

ISBN 978-1-61523-121-8

This Large Print Book carries the Seal of Approval of N.A.V.H.

For Betsy Dodge Pearson.
Have a Killer Summer, Mom.

ACKNOWLEDGMENTS

Thanks to Christine Pepe, Amy Berkower, Nancy Litzinger, Dan Conaway, Dave Barry, Barge Levy, Steven Garman, Ed Stackler, Creative Edge, Storymill, and Mariner software. Thanks, too, to my family for giving me the time and support. But most of all I want to thank Jerry *Femling,* who in real life is *nothing* like the Jerry *Fleming* of this and other novels in the Killer series. I've twisted his character in the name of storytelling, and he's a good sport to go along with it.

—RIDLEY PEARSON, SHANGHAI, CHINA, 2009

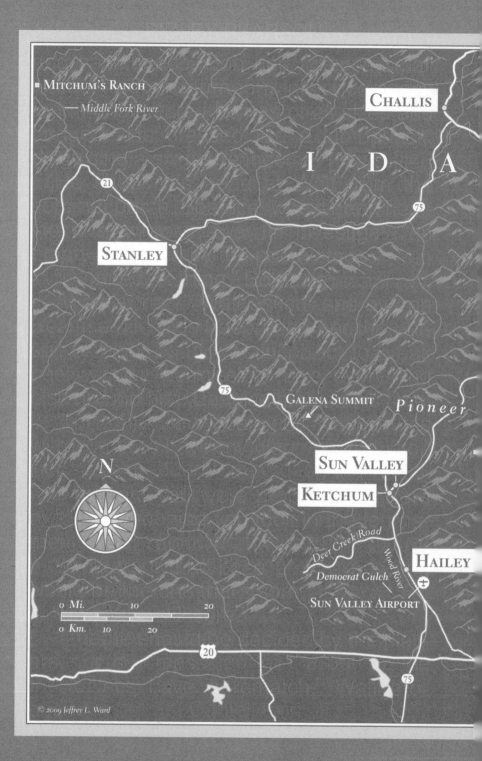

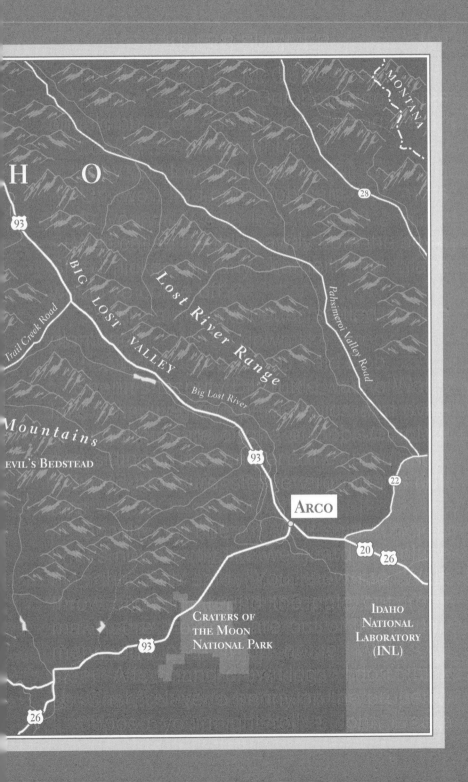

1

Walt Fleming didn't want to be in the river. Any free time away from the office should have been spent applying for a loan of a hundred thousand dollars. That, or risk losing his house, and his daughters, to the divorce. But credit was tight, time short, and so there he was, along with his nephew, Kevin, knee-deep in the Big Wood River. The evening outing was a favor to his sister-in-law, Myra, who could guilt-trip along with the best of them.

Kevin, who would turn nineteen in August, glanced over at his uncle, looking away from the fly he was tying on his own line.

"What?" Walt asked, water gurgling past his waders.

He slipped on a pair of sunglasses to protect against flying hooks, and the glare of an evening sun. At eight-thirty P.M., it still shone brightly in the summer sky. Behind Walt, a rock wall rose out of the gurgling and bubbling river water, reaching two thousand feet nearly straight up into the cobalt sky. Dusk would linger well past ten, during which time the best fishing of the day would be had.

"No uniform."

"Once a sheriff, always a sheriff? You've seen me out of uniform plenty of times. Don't give me that."

"Not recently."

"Then obviously we haven't been spending enough time together," Walt said. "Which is why we're here in the first place."

Kevin remained on the shore, poised as if reluctant to enter the water. A narrow concrete-and-steel bridge crossed fifty feet downstream, carrying the cracked asphalt of Croy Creek Road from downtown Hailey, Idaho, west into rugged terrain. Walt had parked the Jeep Cherokee in a dusty turnout before the bridge. The license plate read BCS-1—Blaine County Sheriff, vehicle 1.

Walt glanced east over Kevin's head, up the slight rise at the town he called home. With a population of three thousand, Hailey was smaller than its famous neighbors to the north, Ketchum and Sun Valley, but larger than Bellevue to the south. The valley was defined by mountain ranges east and west, shaped into an upside-down V, the mouth of which emptied into a great plain of high desert populated by nothing more than rodents, rattlers, and lava rock.

"You hate fishing," Kevin said. "You're all about softball and gliding and your dogs. Besides, that's a radio, right? A police radio?" He pointed to the handheld clipped to Walt's fishing vest. "So it's not exactly like you left the sheriff thing behind."

"Are you going to fish or not?" Walt said, pricking his finger on the hook as he attempted to knot the fly to the line. He sucked the tip of his finger, tasting blood.

"You're doing this because Mom told you to."

"It's true that I suck at fishing, not true about Myra. We're here together, and I want to take advantage of that. It's your call, but if you don't get in the water, we're done here."

"And my job at the lodge? Your idea or Mom's?"

"That one was all mine, buddy boy. Your mom had nothing to do with it."

Kevin waded in up to his knees.

Progress, thought Walt.

"How's that working out, anyway?" Walt asked.

"I'm good with it."

Walt had thought he might get a thank-you. He'd pulled strings to get Kevin on as a bellboy at the Sun Valley Lodge. Better than working as a fry chef.

They moved downstream in tandem, keeping their distance from each other in order to avoid tangling lines. Walt's brother, Robert, had taught his son to fly-fish at the ripe old age of eight. Kevin had taken to it like a prodigy. Walt studied Kevin's technique, hoping some of it might rub off on him. He tried casting his line.

"We're trying to hook them, not whip them to death," Kevin said, sounding just like Robert.

"Ha-ha!" Walt replied, a lump in his throat.

"Less wrist."

Walt stiffened his arm. His second try was an improvement.

"Thanks."

"No charge."

Walt's radio crackled. He and Kevin exchanged a look.

"I've got to monitor it. That's all."

"Promise?"

Walt bit his tongue. Kevin was asking the impossible, and they both knew it.

2

Christopher Cantell couldn't avoid looking at himself in a mirror—any mirror—a window's reflection, a shiny hubcap. Waiting in the Sun Valley Airport's parking lot, he was unaware that he'd turned the rearview mirror of the rented Yukon his direction. It wasn't that he considered himself outrageously handsome. In fact, his attention focused on the flaws: the crow's-feet framing his dark eyes; the fans at the base of his earlobes, the asymmetrical black eyebrows, the smirk on his thin lips that so many found offensive when it was nothing more than genetics, his father having suffered the same slash mouth. But the habit of looking was a tic, a kind of illness he suffered, that he couldn't stop, that he hated so much he lived in constant denial of its existence. It wasn't really him, this vanity. And if not him, then someone else, which implied a case of mild schizophrenia, something more troubling than the vanity itself. The busier he kept, the better: more focused, less self-aware. All his adult life he'd sought out impossible tasks with enormous consequences. Some might call him an everyday thief, but he considered that an insult. He could outsmart the smartest and steal what couldn't be stolen. He thought of himself more as a magician, making valuable objects, including cash, disappear. The bigger the risk, the better. Anything to keep him from seeing those two faces in the mirror.

The courier wasn't much to look at either. He had a purple birthmark on his neck that extended beyond the open collar of his green golf shirt. And he looked a little soft, though Cantell wasn't buying it: couriers with Branson Risk knew their stuff. This guy was certain to put up a fight, if given half a chance. But Cantell's plan eliminated chance altogether. The courier mustn't be allowed to place a call or use a pager. Cantell suspected he was carrying two GPS transmitters—one inside his phone or BlackBerry; the other secreted in the oversized black carbon-fiber briefcase in his custody. Cantell watched as the courier slipped behind the wheel of a Ford Taurus. Cantell had expected a bigger rental: an Expedition, Suburban, or Yukon like his, but neither the make nor the size of the car bothered him. His team was well prepared. He'd spent the past two months and a good deal of money planning and scripting the events of the next few days. He liked to make things complicated. Law enforcement couldn't handle complicated. Theirs was a world of systems, records, and repetition.

He adjusted the rearview mirror—what the hell was it aiming at him for?—to see out the back of the Yukon. He used the Nextel's direct-connect feature to broadcast his report to the others.

"It's a metallic-blue Taurus. Leaving now. Idaho plate Victor-alpha-five-seventwo. I'm the black Yukon, pulling up right behind him. Matt?"

"In position," came the nasal reply.

"Lorraine?" said Cantell.

"The full cycle is two minutes twenty. On my mark we're currently forty-five seconds into green," she said. Cantell tracked the second hand on his watch. "Mark! I'm in position."

"Pulling up to the attendant now," Cantell reported. "Okay, the Taurus is in play." Cantell rolled down his window and handed over his parking ticket to the woman attendant, who clearly didn't catch that Cantell was holding it by the edges to avoid leaving prints. The first half hour of parking was free. The display showed AMOUNT YOU OWE: 0.00.

"Have a nice day," the attendant said.

Cantell rolled up the window. The red-and-white-striped restraining bar lifted. The Yukon followed the Taurus out through a light-industrial park.

The airport access road passed the Hailey Post Office, where the two vehicles stopped for a red light. On the green, they turned left onto Main Street—State Highway 75—with the Taurus now behind a red tow truck. Cantell pulled even with the wrecker, preventing the Taurus or any other vehicle from passing. Traffic was moving at a steady twenty-five miles per hour, just as the posted signs required.

Small towns, he thought.

As Main Street angled north, passing a medical clinic, Cantell got a good look at the town's main traffic light. It was yellow.

Two blocks to go.

"Passing Elm," Cantell announced.

Each of his three team members checked in. The operation was a go.

The light changed to red.

Traffic slowed and stopped. Cantell looked out at the pavement between his Yukon and the wrecker to the left. The evening light made a shadow on the road that came snaking from under the wrecker. It was cast by Matt Salvo, who hung upside down from the undercarriage. Salvo was already moving toward the back of the tow truck. Had the light stayed red only a few seconds longer . . . But it was not to be.

The light turned green, and traffic rolled.

"I've got your twenty," Lorraine announced. "Showtime."

Cantell spotted five feet seven inches of

well-packed California girl on the next corner. She had her hands on a baby carriage
and her eyes on the prize.

He'd met her at the Telluride Film Festi-
val, and had been with her for the three
years since.

She pushed the stroller off the curb and
into the pedestrian crossing. Idaho law required traffic to yield. He and the wrecker
braked. Together they blocked all trailing
traffic. Not a single car horn sounded in
protest.

Small towns.

Cantell watched Matt's shadow move all
the way to the back of the wrecker.

Lorraine, in the pedestrian crossing now,
dropped her bag. Hitting the pavement, it
spilled out Pampers, a baby's bottle, and a
stuffed toy. As she scrambled to reclaim
the contents, Cantell popped his door and
hurried to help her before some other
good-natured soul felt obliged to do so.

Small towns.

He made a dramatic effort to search beneath the wrecker, as if something had
been lost under there. He then stood and
motioned for the driver to back up the tow

truck to where it nearly hit the Taurus. He looked again and came up with one of the stuffed animals—all a ruse.

Beneath the wrecker, Matt Salvo released his harness and dropped to the pavement. He quickly fed a tube through the Taurus's grille and into the vehicle's fresh-air intake. He then turned the valve on a small tank the size of a fire extinguisher that was attached to the wrecker's undercarriage. He freed the tow truck's hook, reached under the Taurus, and found the tow ring with it.

"Hook's on," he announced into his headset.

"Ten seconds to green," Lorraine told Cantell under her breath. She made a show of thanking him for his help.

He hurried back into the Yukon just as the traffic light changed.

Salvo grabbed the undercarriage and clipped himself back into the harness. He worked the hydraulic controls from there as the wrecker's engine labored. The Taurus's front tires lifted off the pavement.

Cantell, once again behind the wheel of the Yukon, stole a look at the Taurus: the driver was slumped against the side window.

"We're a go," he announced into the Nextel. He fastened his seat belt, stretching to sneak a look at his face in the rearview mirror.

The traffic light's left-lane arrow turned green.

Roger threw his hand out the window of the tow truck and made the turn from the center lane. Tethered to the truck in front of it, the Taurus swung left.

3

From thirty-five thousand feet, the two pivot-irrigated parcels of farmland looked like large green eyes above a smile of curving mountains. Summer Sumner peeled herself away from the window of her father's prized Learjet to glimpse him across the aisle, contemplating a laptop open on the collapsible mahogany table that separated a pair of leather club seats, each the size of a recliner. His Airphone was pinched beneath his chin. The Lear could seat eight, including Mandy, the flight attendant. Mandy wasn't on this trip, however, which told Summer more about the family's financial picture than her father, Teddy, probably intended.

Summer relished her father's panic-stricken expression, as he ran his two-hundred-dollar fountain pen across a notepad. He wore his fatigue well; few would have guessed he'd celebrated sixty a few years earlier. The golf tan helped. So did Tanya, his personal trainer. Summer enjoyed hearing the tension in his voice. She turned her attention back out the window, but secretly kept an eye on him in its reflection. *"If you know yourself but not your enemy, for every victory gained you will also suffer a defeat."* And he thought she never listened to him.

"How much?" Teddy Sumner barked into the Airphone. "What exactly are we talking about short-term?" He danced the pen through his fingers, like some kind of circus act. To her, just another example of too much time spent at a desk.

He dared a look in her direction. She hoped he wouldn't say anything. She had no intention of ever speaking to him again.

"Okay, seven's doable," he said. "How soon?" He listened for a moment. "No, not possible. A month at the earliest. Sixty to ninety days, is more like it." He grimaced. "Listen, I would if I could, but this is my last trip on it. Let me get this straight: seven will put a clamp on it. Two-point-two to tie it off?" He ran his hand across his mouth, a gesture signaling pent-up frustration and potential anger. They knew each other all too well.

Summer wasn't about to start feeling sorry for him. He'd explained their financial situation as being "fluid." But she knew more than she should have: he'd cobbled together some television-commercial work to help pay preproduction costs of a feature film that was never going to get off the ground. He owed payments on several loans, all of them large. He couldn't face that he was a one-hit wonder. *Mastermind* had been his only success, and without the foreign box office even it would have failed. Compounding his frustration, no doubt, his wife had started up that film, not him. Summer's mother had been the successful filmmaker, and she was gone now. Gone for good.

She squirmed in her seat, wishing he'd allowed her to stay behind in L.A. She'd given in too easily. He had an Eleanor

Roosevelt quote for that: *"No one can make you feel inferior without your permission."* So when had she given him her permission, anyway?

"I know, I know, I know," he repeated into the phone, his unpredictable temper barely contained. "I will, okay? Listen, we're landing in a minute. I've got to hang up." He paused. "Yeah, okay. You too." He hung up.

She braced herself for what was coming. She became his verbal punching bag when things went south, which, basically, was all the time. He would apologize later, as if that made it all okay.

"So," he asked, "what do you think? Pretty, isn't it?"

She didn't breathe. She'd not expected a tour guide.

"Are we going to go through the whole weekend with you not talking to me?"

He got his answer.

"It's not right, not at seventeen. Somewhere inside, you know that. And *don't* compare it with my meeting your mother because that was completely different, and we both know it. It was at a country club, our parents already knowing one another, having socialized together. It wasn't some twenty-two-year-old *Brazilian* on the tennis circuit. Guys like that, sweetheart . . . that's not you."

But your hooking up with Tanya . . . she felt like saying. *What kind of training was she supposed to be helping with, exactly?*

"You'll like it up here. It's like Telluride, only . . . better. More to do. Really nice people. And, I promise, there'll be all sorts of kids around. Everybody brings their kids along on these weekends."

She hated him calling her that.

"I can still get us into the mixed doubles tournament. You know, we can whip some butt with that serve of yours. It's all for a good cause."

She thought it unfair that silence was her only available weapon. No matter how effective it was—and it *was* effective—she felt robbed of a voice. He treated her like she was still thirteen and that it was still B.C.: before cancer.

"Don't sulk," he pleaded. "Please, Summer, don't do this. I've got enough problems"—she mouthed his next words as he said them—"without you acting like this."

So predictable.

In the world according to Teddy Sumner, she was the cause of everything bad that happened to them. Somehow, he always managed to bring it back around to her.

Her head slipped too close to the window and her breath fogged the plastic. She doubted it lasted long enough for him to see what she traced into the fog with the tip of her index finger.

An *L* . . . for *Loser.*

4

Match the hatch. Walt, closer to the bridge now and still knee-deep in the river's chilly current, tried to fix his eye on any one of the few million swirling insects long enough to snatch it. He swiped his stubby fingers at one and managed to grab it but squeezed too hard and crushed it. *Unidentifiable.*

The idea was to match a live insect to a fly in his kit. He considered using the ubiquitous caddis fly but was afraid Kevin would criticize him for being lazy. The cycle of most flying insects included four stages: an emerging stage, where it rose to the water surface as an embryo; the parachute stage, where it opened its delicate wings to dry; the reproduction stage; and then the spinning stage, where it fell, propeller-like, to its death. Not only was Walt matching the fly to the insect species, but was matching it to the correct life-cycle stage. He found the whole process slightly depressing since it served only to remind him of his own life cycle: he'd risen through the water of his youth, lost his mate, stopped reproducing, ending up with two young bugs—twins, no less—to raise on his own. How far was he from the final spinning stage, he wondered, a thought that didn't preoccupy him but did rear its ugly head occasionally. Like now.

Beatrice, his two-year-old Irish water spaniel, sat patiently on shore, eyeing the river mischievously, wanting to join Walt if for no other reason than out of obstinate loyalty. Walt told her to stay, and she obediently lay down and crossed her paws. With her moon eyes and forlorn expression, she could, and did, play him.

Still studying the swirling insects overhead, Walt was suddenly distracted by the rattling of a tow truck crossing the bridge. It had a Taurus on its hook. But what business did a loaded tow truck have heading west out Croy Creek Road? More to the point, the truck wasn't local—Walt knew both towing services in the valley—which incited his curiosity. There was nothing west of this bridge but a few dozen McRanches and the valley's animal shelter. What could possibly be the point of towing a vehicle *out* of town?

All these thoughts flashed through Walt's mind as he swiped at another insect. Instead of looking into his hand to see if he succeeded, he eyed the tow truck and its catch.

He briefly saw into the Taurus.

It might have been a trick of the evening light, or maybe a reflection in the glass, but the disturbing image lingered: the driver slumped behind the wheel. It was not only illegal but downright dangerous to ride inside a towed vehicle.

Walt grabbed for the radio and checked in with dispatch. "Have we got anybody in the vicinity of Croy Creek?"

He had to wait for a response from the dispatcher, the mountains wreaking havoc with radio reception. He headed for the river's edge hoping to improve communication.

"Hey!" Kevin complained. "You'll put the fish down!"

"Sorry . . . Got to run."

"Now?"

"Now."

"You're leaving me?"

Just then, the radio spit static.

"Negative, Sheriff. No patrols in town at the moment."

"I'll be right back," Walt called out to Kevin.

Kevin moved to the opposite shore. "Forget that," he said. "I'm coming with you."

Walt broadcast over the radio that he was pursuing the wrecker, requesting backup.

"You stay," he told Kevin. "Maybe with me gone, you'll actually catch something."

Walt scrambled up to the bridge, the waders bulky and awkward. Beatrice, seeing this, sat up, electric with anticipation, her eyes pleading for Walt to call for her.

Kevin, moving faster in waders than Walt, reached the Cherokee first.

"No way you're ditching me," Kevin said.

Beatrice trembled at the water's edge.

"Suit yourself," said Walt, grabbing for the driver's door, "but it's only a traffic violation, some yahoo from out of town. You're going to wish you'd stayed here."

Pointing back down toward the river, Kevin said, "You can't just leave the gear."

"I can and I will," Walt answered, stripping off his waders and dancing out of them. He climbed behind the wheel in stocking feet. "We don't have all day."

Kevin stuffed his rod into the back, and climbed in front, still in his waders.

Walt whistled for Beatrice, who raced to the vehicle, throwing dirt in her wake. She jumped into Kevin's lap, pressing up against him.

"That's her spot," Walt said.

"You think?"

The road ran nearly perfectly straight, due west. Walt worked the Cherokee up to seventy miles per hour, the wrecker now nowhere in sight.

"We can't catch a tow truck? You want me to drive?"

"I'm dying of laughter over here. How 'bout you use your eyes instead of your wit?"

Kevin kept his attention on Walt.

"Did you happen to see those pronghorns back at Democrat?"

Walt glanced at his nephew.

"They were moving along real good," Kevin said. "They were up and going before we came along."

"What would a wrecker be doing up Democrat Gulch?" Walt asked. "That makes no sense."

"Chop shop, maybe? Tow it out there and cut it up?"

"A Taurus? Nah . . ."

But a moment later, Walt slowed and threw the Cherokee in a U-turn. He drove off the road and navigated through the scrub.

"We should have seen lots of dust if they went out there," he said, "that's a dirt road."

"Not if they stopped somewhere," Kevin said.

The ride turned loud and shaky as the Cherokee's four-wheel drive bit into the dirt road rising up Democrat Gulch. When Walt took the first rise a little hotly, the fishing rod slapped the window frame, and Kevin's sunglasses flew off his face.

Walt sensed trouble. The pieces of the puzzle just didn't fit together: the wrecker coming out Croy Canyon, the person behind the wheel of the Taurus, the wrecker heading up Democrat Gulch.

Kevin was right: it felt more like auto theft than anything else. But a Taurus? The economy really was tough.

"You're going to stay here in the Jeep," Walt announced, his plan already forming.

"You keep driving like this, there won't be a Jeep," Kevin said, gripping the panic bar.

Walt slowed it down some for the next hill, not for Kevin's sake but because the clear Idaho air was faintly clouded by a shimmer of dust. As the Cherokee crested the hill, Walt cut the wheel sharply, skidding to a stop a few feet short of the back of the Taurus.

The road narrowed here, and though the wrecker and Taurus were pulled to the side of the road they still blocked it.

Walt spotted two men, one working the wrecker's hoist to lower the Taurus, the other on foot already fleeing, heading for an aspen grove. Seeing the Cherokee and its rooftop light rack, the other took off.

The man behind the wheel of the Taurus was either dead or unconscious.

Walt calmly reported the situation to dispatch, then dropped the mic on the seat.

"Stay!" he called to Beatrice. "You too," he added for Kevin's sake. Then he threw open the Cherokee's door and hit the ground in his stocking feet.

He ducked when he mistook a sputter of an engine starting for small weapons fire. Two camo-painted ATVs raced out from the aspen grove and headed away from him. Walt snapped a mental picture, trying to grab any identifying characteristics he could. But the two men had their backs to him, and the ATVs were commonplace.

He hurried back to the Cherokee, climbing behind the wheel before realizing Kevin's door was ajar. The boy was curled in the dirt in front of the Taurus's open door.

Beatrice was pacing nearby, refusing to go closer.

She smells something, Walt thought.

For a fraction of a second—only a fraction—Walt considered pursuing the

ATVs. He then held his breath and approached Kevin, the boy's condition matching the driver's.

A lump in his throat, he dragged his nephew away from the scene. He checked Kevin's pulse and found it steady. He elevated the boy's feet, wondering what he was going to tell Myra.

He called for an ambulance and his ad hoc crime-scene crew, including local news photographer and part-time deputy Fiona Kenshaw.

Far in the distance, a spiral of dust rose like smoke, marking the path of the two ATVs headed north toward Deer Creek Road. He issued a BOLO—be on the lookout—for the ATVs or for a pickup truck carrying ATVs. But, given the few hundred thousand acres of uninhabited wilderness facing him, he understood the ATVs were likely long gone.

He turned his attention to the Taurus and the wrecker, quickly spotting the gas canister, the tubing, and, climbing under and shutting it off, wondering what could possibly justify such elaborate planning. An attempted kidnapping? Breath held, he pulled the driver from the vehicle and searched for his wallet.

Randall Everest Malone carried a corporate AmEx, issued to Branson Risk, LLC. He knew about the private security company, it being one of many repeatedly mentioned by Walt's father as an employment possibility.

A search of the Taurus revealed a black attaché case handcuffed to the frame of the passenger's seat. Larger and thicker than a standard briefcase, it featured a thin slot underneath the handle next to which glowed a red LED.

Government work? he wondered. *Corporate securities?* In all likelihood a delivery to one of the many financial moguls living a few miles north in Sun Valley.

He heard the ambulance sirens approaching. He returned to Kevin's side. The boy's eyes were open. He was coming around.

"What the hell?" Kevin said.

"I told you to stay in the truck."

"I don't think that's going to help me right now."

"What were you thinking?"

"I was trying to help the guy," Kevin said, now sitting up and leaning on his elbows, pleading his case. "I couldn't believe you just abandoned him."

"I—" Walt cut himself off. He wasn't going to explain himself. "You okay?" he asked.

"Head hurts. My stomach feels weird." Kevin rose higher, from his elbows to his hands, and looked over at the car and tow truck. "What the hell, Uncle Walt?"

"I think we interrupted an attempted robbery," Walt said. "Maybe a kidnapping."

"Seriously? Like *Ocean's Eleven*?"

Walt didn't answer. He hurried to the top of the rise to slow down the ambulance, all the while wondering about the contents of the attaché, how much, if anything, Branson Risk would tell him about it, and when, if ever, he'd apprehend the two who had fled.

5

Before disturbing it, Walt photographed the scene—including the wrecker and the Taurus. He then lowered the Taurus, hoping Fiona would arrive before the paramedics left. He wanted as much of a record of this as possible, and she was five times the photographer he was.

Malone was coughing while being attended to.

"Respiratory occlusion," the male paramedic said. "We can't seem to stabilize him. We're going to move him."

Malone's eyelids fluttered, revealing only the whites of his eyes. Even with his mouth covered by the oxygen mask, he was caught in a downward spiral of suffocation.

Kevin was now on his feet and next to Walt.

"Can't they do something?" Kevin pleaded. Tears sprang from his frightened eyes. "Help him! Someone fucking help him!"

The paramedics moved the man to a gurney. Puffs of fine brown dirt swirled out from under him like smoke.

Ashes to ashes, Walt thought.

When the convulsions began, the two stopped the gurney and tended to him. But death was upon him, in its unforgiving way. A series of violent, guttural gasps were followed by an oppressive silence, and he had passed.

Kevin went quiet, looking on in horror, longing for a PAUSE button that didn't exist.

The paramedics, not giving up, finally got the gurney into the back of the ambulance.

Kevin sank wordlessly by his uncle's side.

"God . . ." Kevin finally choked out.

"Let's hope so," Walt said.

6

Cantell heard the insectlike buzzing of the two ATVs approaching the rendezvous. He'd parked the Yukon, engine running, on Deer Creek Road at the intersection with Harp Creek. Their reckless speed, along with the fact that they'd been told to keep a low profile, told Cantell all he needed to know.

Roger McGuiness and Matt Salvo drove the ATVs straight into a thicket of golden willow along the creek and disappeared. They ran out on foot a moment later, frantic and panicked.

The two piled hurriedly into the vehicle.

McGuiness shouted "Go!" too loudly for the confines of the truck's interior.

Salvo climbed into the front passenger's seat and dragged a sleeve across his face, mopping off the sweat and dirt. "Cops!" he said.

"Sheriff's Office," Roger McGuiness clarified. An Irishman of unpredictable temper, McGuiness was a hell of a wheelman. Cantell wished he were driving.

"Did we—?"

"No," Matt Salvo cut him off, "we lost the case." A wiry man of thirty, Salvo could bench-press two-eighty, run a 4.6 forty, and contort himself into ungodly positions. He was their spider, capable of free-climbing anything. "The shit had it handcuffed to the seat frame."

"Resourceful," Cantell said, keeping his disappointment in check.

A vehicle approached in the distance. Cantell slowed the Yukon.

"Get down," he instructed. "Matt, into the far back. Roger, between the seats. Use the blankets."

Salvo scrambled into the back.

Cantell pulled the Yukon over. He was climbing out when McGuiness spoke up.

"What the hell are you doing?"

"My part. Stay put."

He closed the car door, rounded the back of the Yukon, unzipped his fly, and spread his legs. He urinated into the scrub.

It was a Blaine County Sheriff's cruiser. It pulled alongside the Yukon just as Cantell zipped up. "Help you?" Cantell called out to the young deputy, who was just rolling down his window.

"Looking for a pair of ATVs. We got a complaint."

I'll bet you did, Cantell thought. He made a point of keeping his back to the deputy, not allowing him to see anything more than his profile, no face to remember.

"News to me. This is the road to the dump, right?"

"No, sir, that's Ohio Gulch you want. To the left as you enter the highway heading north. It's up the road, then head east."

"East?" Cantell said. "Wouldn't you know!"

"Be safe," the deputy said. He rolled up his window and took off.

If trained well—and he had no reason to believe otherwise—the deputy had made note of the Yukon's license plate.

That meant Salvo would have to steal some plates or they'd have to dump the Yukon, rent another or do without.

And so the challenges began. But rather than resent them, he savored the chance to prove himself.

He climbed back behind the wheel.

"Stay down," he ordered.

"Are you telling me you just stood out there taking a piss with your back to a cop?" Salvo called out from the back.

Cantell said nothing, angling the mirror so he could see himself.

"What now?" Salvo asked. He talked too much. "We got some kind of backup plan? We're going to get the case, right?"

"We'll see."

Only Cantell knew the full plan. He returned the mirror to its center position, and drove on.

7

Walt walked Kevin to the back of the ambulance.

"I'm going to ask you not to say anything about this," he said, "not even to Myra. *Especially* not to Myra."

"If she's picking me up at the hospital, it's going to be kind of obvious, isn't it? I mean, what do I say?"

"You got dizzy out on the river . . . I wanted you looked at."

"Seriously?"

"Whoever did this . . . attempted to do this . . . they don't know the guy died. They don't know the kind of charges they're facing. Thieves, an organized robbery like this, they don't give up easily. They may hang around. That's in my favor. But Myra, God bless her, loves a good rumor."

"Got it," Kevin said. "I'd still rather not go to the hospital."

"No choice in that."

"My gear?"

"I'll get everything together."

"How come it's always got to be something?" Kevin asked. "You and me, this family, one crisis after another? What's with that?"

"It just *seems* that way."

"That's bullshit, and you know it. When do you and me ever get ten minutes together? I saw a lot more of you when Dad was alive . . . Is that it? I remind you of him . . . or something?"

"You're not so much like your dad," Walt said. "We can talk about this later."

"We can, but we never do."

The paramedic was ready to shut the door.

"Not a word," Walt reminded.

"I love you too," said Kevin, climbing down.

Walt called Myra next, relieved to reach

her voice mail. Kevin had fainted but appeared to be okay. He was headed to the hospital for tests. Walt would see her at the hospital or he'd drive Kevin home. Then he tried her cell, got through to her, and endured high drama for five minutes.

Fiona Kenshaw's Subaru crested the small rise. She parked and disembarked, laden with two camera bags. Part-time fishing guide and sometimes wedding and local news photographer, she'd been on her way to Silver Creek for a pleasure fish when located by dispatch. She looked good in her forest green Silver Creek Outfitters polo, the shirt tucked into a pair of brown canvas cargo shorts belted tightly at her waist. Her right knee bore scars, either from an operation or an injury; her left ankle was bruised. A pair of gray Keens kicked up the dusty road. She peered out from under a baseball cap that read KISS MY BASS, several dry flies stuck in the brim. Along with the bags, she carried a grim expression on her face. The sight of the ambulance did that to her—he knew this about her. That, and the latex gloves Walt was wearing. She couldn't be considered chatty. Thoughtful, maybe. And part turtle: if challenged, she retreated inside herself. He'd known her to spend whole days in the Engletons' guest cottage that she called home, alone and content, the world shut out. He never asked about these times she spent by herself. She had enough looks and brains to be doing much more than scraping by working three jobs in Ketchum, Idaho, but that was part of the allure and mystique of the place. Ph.D.s worked as waiters, former CEOs played at being ski bums.

"Hey," Fiona said, tucking an errant sprig of brown hair up under her cap.

"We've got a body on the way to Elmer's," Walt said. "I know that's not your favorite, but we've got to shoot it. Apart from the body, I need close-ups of the scene. All the details. There are some broken tooth-picks on the mat of the driver's side of the wrecker, strapping and rigging on the wrecker's undercarriage, some kind of gas canister attached down there near the back. And get a shot of the plastic tubing leading through the grille of the Taurus, plus interior and exterior shots, along with a shot of that black attaché case that's locked to the passenger's-seat frame.

"The victim's carrying a boarding pass for a flight that just landed," he continued, "so chances are, it came through security, which means it's not an explosive. We've got some shoe and tire impressions. I marked them for you." He pointed.

"We're losing light fast," she said. "I'm on it."

Fiona Kenshaw's ability to separate her social self from her work self was one of the qualities he most admired in her.

She worked quickly and methodically against the fading light of the setting sun. Fifteen minutes into it, she added a flash and a light stand that bounced a strobe off a silver umbrella.

"What was his name?" she asked.

"Randall Everest Malone. He was carrying a loaded handgun in a holster at the small of his back. He had two boarding passes in the billfold pocket of his sport coat. No way he flew with that weapon on him. So it was in his checked luggage—all legal—and he took care of it immediately after landing. That tells me something about him, maybe about the contents of the case, which is high-tech like nothing I've seen."

As Fiona continued shooting pictures of the wrecker, Walt reviewed the contents of several evidence bags he'd kept with him. He'd collected a money clip holding one hundred seventy-seven dollars; three receipts, all labeled SUN VALLEY in pen; a Tul pen; a BlackBerry; and a roll of Tums. In a separate bag was the man's credit-card wallet containing three cards, a California driver's license, a medical insurance card, a vehicle insurance card, a twenty-four-hour health club membership card that, by the look of him, went unused, and six business cards.

"So who is he?" she asked.

"The business card says 'Branson Risk, LLC.' I've worked with them during the Cutter Conference. Personal security, drivers, surveillance . . ."

"Private eye?" she asked.

"They don't call themselves that, but, yes, essentially."

"That makes the briefcase, or what's in it, all the more interesting."

"Doesn't it, though? I'd like to have a look inside before Branson Risk puts their attorneys to work."

"Can you do that?"

"I can try."

They moved to the Taurus. Walt used a pair of bolt cutters from the Cherokee to liberate the bag.

"Boys and their toys," Fiona said. "Looks like something from Sharper Image."

"More like an exhibit at the Spy Museum," Walt said.

"You think?"

"He's not a spook, he's private."

"I'm done with the front seat," she said.

Walt unsealed the freezer bag containing the dead man's wallet and tried each of the four credit cards in the slot beneath the handle. None worked to open it.

He rummaged through Malone's overnight bag. There were no other cards.

Walt tried every zippered compartment, the toilet kit, the pockets of the clothes.

"Judging by the single change of clothes, he wasn't planning on staying long," she said.

"Longer now," Walt said.

"Can you break it open?"

"I'm tempted to try," he admitted, "but Malone took the time to arm himself at the airport before getting into the rental. Maybe he was expecting trouble. Given the sophistication of the case, its contents are either valuable or dangerous or both . . . possibly rigged."

"You're frustrated by this, I can hear it in your voice."

"A private courier delivering something up here? It could be anything. This guy took this job very seriously. That's worth noting."

Fiona spent the next few minutes finishing up the photography and then caught back up with Walt. He was behind the wheel of the Cherokee, Malone's Black-Berry in hand. He was taking notes.

"I'll e-mail you the pictures within the hour," she said.

"Sorry to cost you the fishing."

"Hey, it's a paycheck. Anything there?" she asked, indicating the BlackBerry.

"A reservation at the Sun Valley Inn. An unspecified appointment at nine."

"Who calls his family to tell them?" she asked.

"I'll talk to Branson, and we'll take it from there. But it'll likely be me."

Fiona Kenshaw looked sad and sympathetic at the same time, looked like she wanted to say something more than what she did say. "I'll get these to you."

8

The Sun Valley resort, with its two hotels, outdoor mall, condominiums, golf course, year-round outdoor skating rink, and a two-thousand-seat amphitheater, was situated at the mouth of Trail Creek, a canyon that narrowed as it headed east toward the Copper Basin.

The mile-high air was so clean, it was almost drinkable. Window down, Walt inhaled, savoring his choice of lifestyle. A red-tailed hawk patrolled overhead—predators seldom rested. SUVs bearing bikes, kayaks, and canoes were stacked up at one of the town's five traffic lights.

A bustling porte-cochere fronted the Sun Valley Lodge, a newly redecorated version of the grand hotel that had once hosted Marilyn Monroe, Gary Cooper, and the Kennedys. Ernest Hemingway had written part of *For Whom the Bell Tolls* in Suite 206. Walt drove across the packed five-acre parking lot and borrowed a space reserved for deliveries in front of the modest Sun Valley Post Office. He carried the carbon-fiber attaché case with him, its cut chain dangling like a dog collar. He passed a golf shop, a jewelry store, a bank, and a bookstore on his way to the slightly less prestigious but equally luxurious Sun Valley Inn.

The dark beauty behind the registration desk wore a soft-gray suit, starched white blouse, and a bronze name tag that read SLADANA, and, beneath the name, CROATIA. She had an appealing, provocative accent that also made her difficult to understand. Her eyes so dark, he couldn't see her pupils.

Walt was three inches shorter than she, his eyes level with her mouth. She had nice teeth.

"A Mr. Malone was scheduled to be your

guest," he said, his uniform introducing his authority. "I'd like to see the room, if I may. Any messages or packages. Anything at all you may have for him."

Short, dark purple–polished nails tapped the keyboard.

"Randall Malone?" she asked.

Walt nodded.

"I am show voice mail for Mr. Malone . . . You like?"

"Yes, please."

"House phone across from restrooms, down hall to left. Room two-sixteen."

He had been hoping for a FedEx package containing a card that might unlock the attaché case. His disappointment was somewhat abated by the existence of the voice mail.

He worked his way past designer-label hotel guests crowding the lobby bar—pearl-white teeth and breast implants, golf tans, loafers without socks.

He connected with the hotel operator. The man on the voice mail did not identify himself. He recited a phone number and a time—"nine o'clock"—and hung up. The time matched Malone's unnamed appointment in the BlackBerry.

Walt checked his watch: forty-five minutes late. He had little patience for the cloak-and-dagger that private security firms often embraced. They were wannabe spooks. He doubted the call originated from Malone's office; they'd have phoned his BlackBerry. So maybe the phone number had to do with the attaché. A ransom payment? Was it time-sensitive? Life or death? A kidnapped journalist in Iraq? An oil company employee in Venezuela? Not much would surprise him, given the residents of Sun Valley.

Whom to call first: Branson Risk or the number left on the voice mail? If the person answering the call failed to hear Malone's voice, would that have consequences? Convinced the attaché would disappear behind a wall of attorneys, he decided to hold off contacting the security company until he'd returned the call left in the voice mail.

Concerned that the person on the receiving end of the call might be expecting to see the hotel's caller ID, Walt first picked up the hotel phone and connected to the operator. But he quickly hung up. What if the caller ID from Malone's BlackBerry had been supplied and was part of the verification procedure?

Walt returned to the Cherokee, retrieved Malone's phone, and searched its contact list for the phone number that had been left on the voice mail. It wasn't stored.

He contemplated his options, dialed the number left on the voice mail, and impatiently awaited an answer.

9

Summer Sumner spotted her mark as the black Escalade rolled to a stop in front of the Sun Valley Lodge. The boy's lanky frame wasn't well served by the gray bellboy uniform: the collar was too big, the pants an inch short. But he had an agreeable face that was currently caught in a faraway stare that resonated with her. She doubted he was of drinking age, which put them pretty much in the same boat.

Her father was on the phone—*surprise!*—his face overcome with anguish, the money problems continuing.

She sneaked the second button of her shirt open, a crass but necessary step. A boy like that . . . If her father had taught her anything, it was to take what you want. **"You don't get ahead by waiting for handouts."**

An older bellhop helped her from the Escalade. This wouldn't do. She worked to make eye contact with the boy her age, hoping to provoke him enough to come to her rescue. Instead, he moved toward the doors and pulled one open. She fired off a coy smile that she'd borrowed from a Beyoncé music video. He didn't seem to react, which left her hunting for another easy mark. There was no time to waste. She had to put her plan in motion.

They entered the sumptuous lobby of dark wood and brass fixtures, alabaster chandeliers bathing the space in honey-colored light. Foreign-accented voices of the receptionists mingled with small talk coming from the couches and chairs directly ahead. Beyond the couches was a second set of double doors that she saw led to a patio and an outdoor ice-skating rink.

Her father handed her an envelope with

a card key in it and joined the bellman in the elevator.

"Don't lose it," he said, ever the voice of confidence.

The last phone call had obviously not gone well.

"Gee, I'll try not to," she said. "Tell you what: I'll meet you up there."

They remained fixed in a staring contest until the elevator doors closed.

She scanned the lobby: no one remotely her age. Maybe the pool or tennis courts would turn up a worthy candidate, although she was hoping for a local boy, someone with a car. She hadn't given up on the hotel staff just yet.

"You don't get ahead by waiting for handouts."

10

Hello?" a heavily accented voice answered Walt's call. He wasn't any good at deciphering accents, but just hearing it made him wonder if he'd stumbled into a kidnapping ransom drop.

"Malone," Walt said.

"You're late."

"Complications."

"Three twenty-five Aspen Hollow, Northwood. Twenty minutes." The line went dead.

French or Italian, he thought. He'd been to Mexico a couple of times: it wasn't Spanish.

He called dispatch, requesting backup. The office had eight patrols out at any one time, covering an area roughly the size of Rhode Island. He was told there were no cruisers in his vicinity.

"How about Brandon?" he asked, his stomach turning.

"He's graveyard tonight."

Deputy Tommy Brandon lived close by, two miles south of Ketchum, with Walt's soon-to-be ex-wife, Gail. It had been going on for the better part of the past two years, though Walt had only discovered the affair a year earlier.

"On call?"

"Yes, sir. You want me to raise him?"

"Please."

Ten minutes later, a shiny black pickup truck pulled up beside Walt's Cherokee in front of the Elephant's Perch, an outfitting store in the center of town.

Brandon, a big man with a boyish, rosy-cheeked face, had thrown on his deputy's shirt and gun belt over a pair of blue jeans and running shoes. He walked with urgency to the door of Walt's Cherokee.

"What's up?"

Walt filled him in on Malone's death and

the discovery of the high-tech briefcase, currently in the Cherokee's passenger's seat.

"If it's a ransom drop," Walt said, "maybe it gets tricky when I show up in place of this guy. I'm going to tape down the TALK button on my radio so you can monitor the situation."

"It's just us?"

"There's a possible time element." He checked his watch. "Let's move."

"You get shot up, Sheriff, and I'm the one backing you up . . . Well, given our . . . *situation* . . . how do you think that's going to look?"

"Not good for you. Thankfully, that'll be your problem, not mine."

"You're making jokes?"

Walt indicated his radio handset clipped to his shirt's epaulet. "If you hear it going south, do something."

"Thanks for clearing that up," Brandon said.

Walt parked down the street to keep his Cherokee out of view and walked up a horseshoe-shaped driveway of hand-laid brick pavers, the attaché case in his left hand, his gun hand free. The driveway contained a small aspen grove with a man-made, rock-lined gurgling brook. The aspens blocked any view of the front door from the street. He heard a truck rumble past. Brandon.

The log home was constructed of huge timbers, the gaps sealed with toothpaste-white chinking. Walt rapped the pewter cowboy-boot door knocker twice sharply.

The door opened, revealing a thin man about Walt's height, with a stubble of closely cropped black hair, black eyebrows, Euro-styled green-framed eyeglasses, and rough skin. He wore crisply pressed black trousers, Italian loafers, and no socks. He had a diamond earring in his left ear. His lips pursed in confusion as his eyes settled on the attaché.

"Excuse me . . . Sheriff," he said, reading Walt's name tag. "I was expecting—"

"A Mr. Randall Malone," Walt said.

It took the man a moment to recover.

"I believe this is yours." Walt said.

"The contents, yes. Not the case." He leaned to look down the driveway. "And Mr. Malone is . . . ?"

"Dead," Walt said, adding, "Sheriff Walt Fleming," offering his hand.

The two shook hands—the man's skin was clammy. "Dead? How?"

"Looks like a heart attack," Walt answered. "You are?"

"Arthur Remy." He stepped back and gestured for Walt to come inside. "Good God . . . I'm a houseguest here." He shut the door. "I'm a guest of—"

"Doug and Ann Christensen," Walt said.

"Just so." Remy sounded impressed.

"Sun Valley could just as easily be named *Small* Valley," Walt said.

"Dead?" Remy repeated. "But I spoke to him not fifteen—"

"That was me," Walt said. "We traced him to the hotel."

"But then where? When? Has anyone called the company?"

The living room smelled of vanilla, and from the cut-flower arrangements to the Chinese silk pillows atop the off-white couch it looked like something straight out of *Architectural Digest.* A nineteenth-century seven-foot Bösendorfer grand piano was parked in the corner. It cost roughly the same as Walt's house.

"Branson Risk? No, not yet. We had concerns about the contents of the case. If a ransom drop, then—"

"Ransom? Not hardly."

The living room led to a stately dining room and through to the restaurant-caliber kitchen, off of which was a family room with hearth, four couches, three coffee tables, and a glassed-in breakfast nook. The interior of the log home was Santa Fe stucco, with hand-worked walls sponged with brick-tinted paint. Remy poured himself a glass of red wine from a bottle on the counter, offering Walt something to drink. Walt declined.

"I need to view the contents of the case," Walt stated, "for the sake of the investigation."

"What investigation?"

"The heart attack may be related to an assault and kidnapping."

"Jesus Christ." Remy sat down in an overstuffed chair pulled up to a harvest table beneath a deer-antler chandelier.

Walt set the attaché onto the table, just out of Remy's reach.

"Malone died at the scene."

Remy's hand shook slightly as he worked the wineglass to his moist lips.

"I interrupted the assault, what may have been an attempted robbery," Walt continued. "Because this is now a criminal investigation, Mr. Remy—quite likely a homicide investigation—I need to know the contents of the case."

"So you said."

"My office will do its best to protect your privacy. That goes for your relationship with Branson Risk as well. But we will investigate."

Remy coughed, twisting his face uncomfortably.

"Jesus."

He finished his glass of wine and eyed the bottle on the counter.

"Go ahead," Walt said.

Remy didn't appreciate being so easy to read, but he wouldn't deny himself the refill. He returned to his chair with a full glass.

"You want Andy on the phone?" Remy asked. "I can get Andy for you." He pulled a mobile phone out of his pocket. "Andy Cohen, Branson's director?"

"That can wait. At present, I'm interested only in the contents of this case."

Remy seemed to consider his situation. He looked down at the case, then back up at Walt. He nodded.

"Yes. All right. You will wait one minute, please."

He left the room, returning with a plastic card that fit into the slot underneath the handle and turned the red LED green.

"I've never seen a case like this before," Walt admitted.

"A Branson original," Remy explained. "When locked, the internal GPS is constantly broadcasting its location. If the case is jimmied or violated in any way, a hidden camera transmits photographs continuously. Branson predetermines the route the case will take. The camera also engages if the GPS track varies from that route."

"Were you notified the case was off route?"

"I was," Remy said. "It went west of Hailey."

"That's correct. Branson's reaction?"

"I assume they attempted to contact the courier."

"You didn't hear from them again?"

"There were several calls back and forth," Remy said. "A good deal of concern."

"So, in theory, Branson has photographs that could prove helpful to the investigation." Walt couldn't take his eyes off the case.

"If they exist, I will have them make them available to you." Remy caught Walt staring. "Go ahead, Sheriff. Be my guest. They're a piece of history."

Walt opened the lid.

Inside, packed in custom-molded gray foam, were three dark green bottles of wine.

11

Cantell's team boarded Sun Valley's River Run high-speed quad chairlift at five-minute intervals so as not to be seen sitting together. The views behind them were spectacular: the town of Ketchum in the foreground, then, farther east, the Sun Valley resort, with its hotels and golf course. A second chairlift carried them to the very top, from which one could see for a hundred miles in all directions: craggy mountaintops north, east, and west, and, to the south, a vast expanse of high-altitude desert.

Cantell avoided the busy mountaintop

ski lodge. Mountain bikers and parasailors prepared for descent, while day hikers huddled in groups, trail maps in hand. The grid of Ketchum's streets spread out three thousand feet below, the buildings and vehicles looking like toy models.

Cantell's team hiked down to a location that offered a view both east and south. In late July, the ski slopes were a vivid green broken by flecks of yellow columbine and red Indian paintbrush that swayed in the constant breeze.

The four hoisted binoculars as Cantell spoke.

"First: the bridge," he said. Highway 75's only bridge was a formed-concrete, three-lane span crossing the Big Wood River. "Roger, placement is everything."

"No problem."

"Salvo," Cantell said, "the power pole, to the east, will block the bike path."

"Sure," Matt said, "got it."

"Roger," Cantell said, "you can make out the roof of the new symphony pavilion behind the lodge."

"Yeah."

"The golf course is just to the north," Cantell said, "the row of golf carts."

"Okay."

"That's you . . . *before* the truck. It should look like an overcharged battery or a short. Nothing too spectacular."

Roger smirked. "Can do."

"After setting the charge, you'll meet up with Matt and we enter phase two. You guys will be picked up on the other side by Lorraine, and we'll meet in the Albertson's parking lot north of Hailey."

"Sounds good."

"Lorraine, you'll pick them up in the Starweather subdivision. There's a private bridge there that crosses to a ranch. That's the rendezvous."

Lorraine nodded.

Cantell trained his binoculars well south to his prize, the asphalt shimmering in the heat. "Any questions?"

"What if I can't get the keys?" Lorraine asked. "Has that been considered?"

"Then you need to get yourself invited back to his room," Cantell explained. "Matt will shadow you, as planned. He'll call Roger in if necessary. We need that key, and nothing, no way, can raise suspicion."

Cantell addressed the three. "Remember Fort Lauderdale," he warned. "Timing is everything. These wine bottles fell into our lap. We've done what's necessary. We chummed the water."

"But we screwed it up," Salvo said.

"We can live with that," Cantell said. "It may actually play to our advantage." He considered his next words carefully. "A word of caution to each of you." He looked directly at Salvo. "No screw-ups. Matt, if I hear you're hanging around the hotel pools or trolling the skate parks, I'll cut you out.

"Our success depends on our anonymity," he continued. "None of us can afford to be remembered. And Matt, just for your information, sixteen- and seventeen-year-old girls remember *everything*."

"It's not a problem." Salvo's eyes hardened and his jaw muscles knotted.

Addressing Lorraine, Cantell said, "Makeup and wig aside, you can't be remembered either. And we can't drug him because that'll set them onto us. So it's tricky."

"I know," she said. "Trust me, I'll be careful. I'll have tattoos in all the right places— temporary, but he won't know that. And, trust me, he'll remember them."

Salvo started to chuckle, but she stared him down.

"You want to switch jobs, Matt?" she asked hotly. "Maybe he's into boys. Who knows? That would get me off the hook."

Salvo tried to look confident—a losing effort. "Hey," he said, "I'm going to be the most exposed of anyone. You want to switch? I'll switch!"

"Shut up, Matt," Cantell said. "The risks and responsibilities are as equally distributed as possible."

"I'm just saying—"

"Well, *don't!*" Cantell said. "You take care of yourself. That's enough."

He looked south of the mountain. "People like this . . ." he said, his voice drifting.

Salvo looked ready to brawl. McGuiness patted him on the back. "We cool?" McGuiness said.

"Cool," said Salvo. He was anything but.

12

Lorraine Duisit recognized the man from the photo Cantell had showed her, another of those surprises that made Christopher Cantell such an enigma. It was as if he were two people, one of them so deeply buried even a lover could not penetrate. That was part of what attracted her to him, this mysterious quality that constantly surprised her, but it also put her off, worried her. He could be so difficult to read. How could she ever commit to that?

Michel's Christiania and Olympic Bar and restaurant dated back forty years. It buzzed with conversation and the melodies of a piano man. The split-level layout was divided into a lower-level dining room and upstairs bar. A pair of antique wooden skis was crossed on a wall that rose to a balcony used for private parties. *If walls could talk,* she thought, as she occupied a banquette in the bar close to the piano, with a view of the crowded dining room and out the open French doors to a small patio beyond.

A man belonging to the face in the photo entered and immediately sized up the room, his eyes finding the single women, including Lorraine. She didn't make eye contact—not yet. He took one of two open stools at the baby grand—*exactly* as Cantell had told her he would. It took several inquisitive glances, three songs, and a white wine until she felt the timing was right. She signaled for the check, and took a moment to pull on a sweater that partially covered her metallic-knit halter top. She left her cleavage showing.

"Not leaving so soon?" he said, materializing in front of her.

"The wine gave me an appetite. I'm famished," she explained.

"Then let me buy you dinner," he said. "I

have a table for one that's horribly imbalanced."

"No," she said, blatantly cautious. "It's tempting, but no thank you."

"Because?"

"Again, the wine. I tend to . . . to get myself into trouble."

"That doesn't sound so terrible."

"Not for you." She had a guttural, melodious laugh, and she used it to her advantage. "I have to live with myself in the morning." She looked him directly in the eye.

"I'd love the company," he said. "But I won't push you."

"You just did."

"I'm William. No strings, I promise."

"But it's the strings," she said softly, "that make it interesting. Why brush and saddle the horse if you're not going to ride it?" She paused. "Do you like to ride, William?"

"Fly," he said without missing a beat. "There's an unclaimed stool at the piano. Yours if you want it."

"I want it," said Lorraine. She caught the waiter's attention. "Leave it open," she said, following William to the piano.

"Put it on my tab, Gina," William instructed.

Lorraine glanced over her shoulder catching a glimpse of Salvo. He was sipping a seven-dollar beer at the bar, looking bored.

She ate a big meal: lamb shank with rosemary mashed potatoes and asparagus. Cantell insisted men liked women who ate well. She wanted William to like her.

They skipped dessert for snifters of Grand Marnier.

"Is there dancing?" she asked, knowing the answer. "And I don't mean rock. Something more . . . You know, standards, that sort of thing?"

"The Duchin Room . . ."

"Do you like to dance, William?"

"Let's find out," he said, leaning toward her slightly so the heady scent of alcohol and oranges carried from his breath.

She caught the headlights of the Expedition in the outside mirror of William's rented Chevy. Salvo had replaced the plates earlier in the day and had been outside waiting for Lorraine when she left.

The Duchin Room's lights were low, a

competent trio working through the theme song to *Titanic.* The small dance floor was crowded with white-haired couples. A few trophy wives went through the motions. Thankfully, this crowd would not distract Salvo. He was inclined toward the pom-pom set.

As William searched for a table, he suggested the dance floor, but she declined, wanting another drink in him first. Business before pleasure.

Halfway through their drinks, a table opened up near the band, and they crammed onto a bench side by side. She warmed him up with some affectionate touching, laying her hand on his arm, pressing her leg against his. With the first strains of a slow song, she looked out at the dance floor and said, "So?"

As the two of them stood, she saw Salvo lay a bill on the bar and move toward the dance floor. She appreciated Salvo's ability to stay with the plan.

William was a decent dancer. As he pulled her to him, she let him feel all of her, let him know where she was going with this. His arms now surrounded her and his hands gently brushed her backside. She broke free, spun him around, and pressed herself up against him. As she did so, her hands slipped into his pockets. He tensed with the contact, as she continued to play-fully slip her hands in and out of his pock-ets. She gently urged him closer to a post at the edge of the dance floor and, as Salvo appeared there, released a ring of keys into his outstretched hand, William none the wiser.

Salvo entered the men's room, surprised by the appointments: marble wainscoting, gleaming brass fixtures, lead-cut mirrors, linen hand towels, classical music, oil paintings on the walls.

He closed himself into a stall and worked quickly to take a wax impression of what proved to be an unusual, complicated key.

He arrived back at the Duchin Room in the middle of an up-tempo "Girl from Ip-anema." Lorraine and the pilot were still on the dance floor. She caught his eye and pointed to the floor. Salvo dropped the keys by the post, made a final loop through the bar as if hunting for a friend, and left.

It took William forty-five minutes to notice his keys were missing. The discovery came as he went to pay the check.

"Shit," he said, patting his pants frantically, explaining his loss.

"I'll bet it's my fault," Lorraine said, allowing another of her provoking laughs. "Your pockets," she added, wishing she could force herself to blush. "The slow dance."

They searched the dance floor between songs, interrupted by a waitress. The key chain had been turned in to the bartender.

She accepted a ride back to the Christiania, where they'd started.

"I'm coming off a complicated relationship," she explained from the passenger's seat. "I've flirted tonight and I'm sure I came on a little too strong, and I apologize for that. I'm here for the wine auction tomorrow. I may or may not stay a day or two more. And if I do stay, I'd like to see you again. And this time with no excuses or apologies. But tonight . . . I need to collect myself and not do something self-destructive. Is this making any sense or are you about to scream?"

"A little of both," he said.

"I hope it matters to you that I like you. I hope it matters that if I stay after the auction it will be to see you."

"We're scheduled out Sunday morning," he said. "Back to L.A."

"Oh."

"So, if you'd like to reconsider, I can be very forgiving."

She answered with a kiss, knowing she'd just cost him his job. She slid out of the car without another word.

13

You can pick up the room-service stuff," Summer Sumner told the woman who'd answered the direct-dial.

Her father had abandoned her after his egg whites with salmon, off to a meeting, though he'd booked a tennis court for the two of them at eleven A.M. She'd had a Belgian waffle with mixed berries, orange juice, and green tea. She felt bloated.

The suite was gi-normous, two bedrooms that shared a living room, a balcony with views of the outdoor skating rink and Dollar Mountain—"the kiddy hill." She didn't care one bit about getting rid of the dirty dishes and the rolling cart; it was the room-service boy that interested her. She was crushed when, as it turned out, an older guy with a Russian accent retrieved the breakfast cart.

She waited five minutes and ordered wheat toast, no butter, and another cup of green tea. Fifteen minutes later, a knock on the door drew her to the peephole.

She held the door for him. "Put it any-where."

He might have been the same bellboy she'd seen the day before: about her height and skinny. It looked like his mother cut his hair. He was either her age or a couple years older, which would work just fine. He had an honest face, shy blue eyes, and his Adam's apple bobbed as he spoke.

"Sign here, please."

"You delivered our breakfast too."

"Yeah." He was fighting to remain pro-fessional. "Is there anything else I can get you?"

"When do you get off work?"

"Excuse me?"

"You heard me."

"I'm pulling a double. Seven A.M. to three, and three to eleven tonight. Why?"

"Why do you think?" she asked.

He placed the tray on the coffee table.

"Are there any hot springs in the area?" she asked. It was a loaded question: she'd read in the town paper, the *Mountain Express,* about the hot springs being a magnet for teenagers.

"I . . . ah . . . yeah. There are."

"Could you take me?" she proposed.

"Me?"

She made a point of looking around the room. "Yeah."

"I suppose."

"You *suppose* or you *could*?" she asked.

"I suppose I could. But not until eight. A friend can cover for me. And . . . like . . . I don't have my suit or anything, and I live about—"

"Who said anything about suits?"

"Ah . . ." He'd turned beet-red.

She had him exactly where she wanted him.

"I've got to get out of this hotel," she said. "This place is totally driving me crazy. I'm like a prisoner."

"I could definitely take you," he said. "Are you meeting someone there or—"

"Dude? No. It's just us, you and me,

right? Unless you want to invite some friends along. But I don't bite or anything. It sorta sucks, hanging around here. And my dad's got some private tasting and dinner thing tonight to do with the wine auction, and obviously I'm not invited since the drinking age is twenty-one, which might lead you to ask why he brought me on this trip in the first place since I can't do anything he has planned. And the obvious answer would be how *stupid* it was for him to bring me along and how I did not want to come, but, then again, he is seriously stupid, or can be, and therefore here I am."

"I'm not supposed to interact with guests." He just threw it out there.

"Yeah? So?" she asked.

His eyes ticked furiously back and forth. He was cute enough but immature.

"So, I'll meet you just after eight in the medical-building parking lot. It's over by the inn. You know where that is?"

"I'll find it."

"If you're not there by quarter after, I'm gone," he said.

I doubt that, she thought. "Oh, I'll be there," she said, smiling.

14

But if it's vinegar," Fiona said, standing on a small stepladder in the glare of fluorescent lights, her camera mounted on a tripod and aimed straight down, "then why would anyone bid *anything* for it?"

Walt had set her up in the Command Center, a room laid out like a college lecture hall that sat fifty. There were half a dozen flat screens suspended from the ceiling and an electronic white board. He carefully rotated the first of the three bottles exactly as Remy had instructed. It, along with the others, remained cradled in gray foam. The initials, etched into the glass below the label, came into view:

J.A.

"John Adams," he said. "*The* John Adams. The wine was a gift to Adams from Thomas Jefferson upon Adams's return from Holland, where he'd just secured the financing necessary to save the republic. These bottles celebrate the United States before it existed."

"But a million dollars!?"

"It's an eight-hundred-thousand-dollar reserve. They could go far higher than a million," Walt said. "They sell as a single lot. Remy says his experts claim the wine is still drinkable, but to get that price it doesn't have to be."

"You can't be serious."

"There's ego involved. Since it benefits the center, a nonprofit, the bids get ginned up to astronomical prices. It's all about who gets what, who can spend what, not drinkability."

"The more I learn about this place, the less I understand."

"It's a pissing contest . . . Pretty easy to understand."

Walt continued rotating the bottles. She fired off shots.

"Does he get them back after this?"

"No. It's on us to protect and transport them. A motorcade for a couple of wine bottles. All because they're evidence in a homicide."

"You think other sheriffs deal with this sort of thing?"

It was a question his father might have asked. He reacted defensively, muscles tensing, a spike of heat up his spine, then calmed himself down and said, "It is what it is. We have to assume they may try for them again. Wine is like fine art: there's always a black market willing to pay. These people were obviously well organized, well informed. I'm assuming they have a backup plan."

She climbed down the stepladder. He liked the way she moved, enjoyed watching her . . . hadn't realized how much he enjoyed it, in fact, until that moment.

They were interrupted by a deputy trying to suppress his contagious excitement.

"Sheriff, we've got something."

Thirty minutes later, Walt was riding shotgun in the Hummer, a vehicle anonymously
donated to the Sheriff's Office by a Holly-
wood star. Ostentatious and unnecessary
most of the time, the Hummer rode high
and carried four easily. Its roof rack, light
bar, and the *whoop-whoop* of its siren
cleared the three northbound lanes like a
snowplow in winter.

"It's possible," he told the other three, all
of whom were decked out in SWAT gear,
"that the suspects may possess paralyzing gas. They're to be considered armed
and dangerous. I saw two men out Democrat Gulch. Now we've added a woman to
that. We're going in small. Don't make me
regret it." He could have called up the en-
tire twelve-man Special Response unit,
but mobilizing the squad took time he didn't
have.

Brandon raised his voice to carry over
the roar of the siren. "How do we know any
of this?"

"Evidence," Walt hollered back.

Walt and Fiona had been interrupted by
a hyper deputy named Carsman.

"The traffic cams you asked for," Carsman had said, poking his head into the Command Center. "We've got the wrecker before and after it hooks onto the Taurus."

Walt and Fiona had followed Carsman down the hall to the office's computer lab.

"We picked up the Taurus and the wrecker heading north on Airport Drive," Carsman explained.

The traffic cam archives produced color images shot at two-second intervals. Because of the two-second jumps, cars appeared and disappeared from Main Street.

"We don't pick them up again until the south-facing camera at Croy," Carsman continued. Pointing to the screen, he said, "The wrecker. This is Malone's Taurus. Now, check this."

A woman pushed a stroller out into the crosswalk. The traffic stopped and held as she bent over picking something up.

"Freeze it!" Walt said.

"She dropped something," Carsman said.

"A driver had come to her aid." On any other day, this would have been cause for mild celebration: traffic fatalities at cross-walks were a serious problem in the valley. The fact that traffic had stopped for a pedestrian was a relief to see.

Walt watched the same series several times: the wrecker backing up, the Taurus making the turn attached to it.

"The traffic cams are, what, two months old?" Walt said. "If they scouted this back in June, they wouldn't have known about them. That's probably the only reason we've got them on camera." The system was designed to capture the plates of cars running traffic lights. Within a few minutes, they had the wrecker's registration, and the Yukon alongside it.

"The Yukon's going to be a rental or a stolen vehicle," Walt had informed Carsman. "If it's a rental, it's on a stolen or counterfeit credit card, which won't do us any good, but run anything you get as far as it takes you. The Yukon's our lead for now. Call every hotel, inn, and lodge in the valley. With parking being what it is, most require plate numbers at check-in. Maybe we'll get lucky."

Within twenty minutes, the Yukon had been placed at the Summit Guest House, a sixty-room, midpriced hotel on the north end of Ketchum.

"Room two twenty-six," Walt now told Brandon from the Hummer's passenger's seat. "One night left on the reservation."

"And tomorrow night's the wine auction," Brandon said.

"I guess they aren't sticking around afterward."

Brandon soon killed the Hummer's overhead lights and siren, pulling off Main Street into an office-building parking lot north of Atkinson's Market, well out of sight of the Summit Guest House. Walt and the three deputies climbed out, one carrying a door ram. The three were armed with semiautomatic rifles, "flash and bang" grenades, tear gas, and other hardware. The group held to a tall wooden fence at the end of the parking lot that screened them from the guesthouse. Room 226 faced west, looking out at Sun Valley's Bald Mountain.

Walt put a man on the back door and sent another to the front. He and Brandon addressed the receptionist and then the manager. The sight of Brandon decked out in SWAT gear and the county sheriff in a Kevlar vest startled the man. He was a tightly wound fortysomething, with thick glasses and a high voice.

Walt asked that the second floor be cleared, a process that consumed the next several minutes.

Walt asked for the elevators to be shut down. He and the three climbed the staircase in double time, hurried down the corridor, and regrouped outside of 226. The deputies wore gas masks, helmets, and ear protection.

Walt used a master card key to crack open the door. The ram took out the inside chain as the door flew open. The three deputies swarmed the suite ahead of Walt, calling out loudly, "Clear!," as they quickly determined the status of the bathroom, closet, and bedroom. Walt followed inside, annoyed by his bad luck. Then he looked down and saw wet footprints on the carpet.

He called out a radio code into the room that meant: "Suspect in hiding." It proved a second too late.

A door on the bedroom armoire came open, and a naked woman streaked across the small room, dragging a shirt behind her. She grabbed something off the desk, rushed out the open door to the balcony—left open by Brandon—and jumped.

Brandon was a split second behind her. He leaped over the rail and fell straight down through a canvas patio awning that had supported her weight but failed to support his.

"I'm okay!" Brandon shouted.

Walt watched the woman's bare backside flee across the parking lot. She pulled on the shirt midstride.

By the time the other two deputies took off, she was long gone. An escape route had been planned. Walt was betting she'd grabbed a cell phone off the desk.

No one had seen her face, but Walt thought he had a vague idea what she looked like. It was the woman with the baby stroller.

15

On a manicured lawn, nestled behind the Sun Valley Lodge and cast against a backdrop of rugged, summer-snowcapped mountains, loomed an enormous white tent. In a darkening sky, fiery pink clouds began to melt and dissolve. Vintners put last-minute touches on their tables in preparation for the wine tasting, a preview of the following night's auction items.

The presenters, smartly dressed and deeply tanned, knew one another well. With the preview being as important to them as the rehearsal dinner was to the bride, nerves were on display. It was a matter of honor and company pride to fetch higher bids than the competition, even at a fundraiser. A few lots would sell with reserves. The most famous of these was the John Adams.

Walt, Brandon, and a deputy named Blompier delivered the attaché case without incident. The search for the female suspect had failed, adding to Walt's unease. Although the motel was being watched, Walt didn't expect anyone to return.

With the temperature in the low seventies and expected to drop ten degrees every hour for the next three, the Adams bottles had been transferred to a temperature-controlled Plexiglas viewing case. Brandon stood guard immediately behind the case despite Remy having requested something low-profile.

Guests began arriving.

Seeing the reverence in the faces of the onlookers as they approached the Adams display, Walt understood how rare such a viewing had to be. To him, they were three scratched old bottles of wine, but he overheard the discussions: the story of Remy's discovery of the bottles in Paris, the lengthy authentication, marred by some kind of myth straining to be legend . . . the controversy . . . and always the astronomical reserve price.

Walt had posted several deputies: four in uniform outside, two in plainclothes inside. He had the Mobile Command vehicle, the MC, parked nearby, a thirty-foot RV tricked out with all sorts of communications equipment, all of it donated.

Walt spotted Remy, crossed the tent, and politely ushered him into the grand dining tent, where a sea of bare round tables and a massive stage awaited the following night's festivities. He handed Remy a stack of nine photographs that Branson Risk had e-mailed to him.

"Do you recognize this man?"

The photos were dark, the faces distorted by movement. The man in question had been wrestling with the attaché case, which was locked to the Taurus's seat frame. Two of the nine caught a piece of his face in focus.

"No," said Remy.

"You have to wonder how these people knew what they knew," Walt said. "They went to a lot of trouble trying to steal that case."

"The Adams bottles have been in the catalog for months, Sheriff. Whoever did this has had a long time to plan."

"But as I understand it, Branson Risk contained the delivery details to a handful of people."

"I'm certain of it. But they are in the business of moving valuable art, are they not? Certainly they must establish patterns to their work, no?" He passed the photographs back to Walt.

"It still doesn't explain how they knew which flight Malone would be on or which car he'd rented."

"Someone at the airport . . . a TSA agent, perhaps. The case required all sorts of waivers because of the TSA's ban on fluids. We did as they asked. If you paid off the right agent, you'd know what's moving where."

"You've thought about this, have you?" Walt asked.

"It's my million dollars, Sheriff. A man has been killed. Yes, I've thought about it."

"We are on occasion asked to provide transportation for valuable art," Walt conceded. "As you can imagine, there's a great deal of it in this valley. This kind of thing is not entirely foreign to me. But, honestly, we've met private, not commercial, jets. I've never known of any big-dollar private art arriving on a commercial flight."

"That was at my request, I'm afraid," Remy said. "Your local airport ran out of landing times for general aviation, given the high volume of private aircraft arriving this weekend. That left us the option of landing the bottles privately in Twin Falls and driving them two hours north or flying them in commercially and requiring a nightmare of paperwork. The less they're moved, the better. I opted for the commercial flight, going against Branson Risk's recommendations. So the blame falls on me."

"And Branson Risk," Walt said.

"I'm not convinced this is going to get you anywhere."

Walt tapped the top photograph. "I need to identify this individual. I need to know how they could be so well prepared and ready for Malone's arrival."

"You believe they will try again." Remy made it a statement. "I seriously doubt that."

"Tonight, tomorrow night—they've spent

time and money on this. They'll make another try. It'll be something bold, daring,
and, they hope, completely unexpected.
The way they used the wrecker tells us
that much." He pulled Remy deeper into
the tent, well out of earshot. "What if I
could have a local artist duplicate the bottles? Copy the labels? Replace the real
bottles with fakes?"

Remy's eyes hardened. "Don't be ridiculous. This is an educated crowd, not easily fooled. I guarantee you."

"Just a thought," Walt said.

"And a ridiculous one at that," Remy
said. "Do me a favor and protect my bottles, Sheriff. Don't go getting creative. If
we need to reinvent the wheel, no one will
be knocking on *your* door. So do what
you're good at and be a presence." Saliva
popped from his mouth with the *p* in *presence.* He thumped Walt on the arm play-
fully. "Okay?" he asked. "Okay," he answered
rhetorically.

16

With Lorraine Duisit on his arm, Christopher Cantell entered the wine-auction preview displaying an invitation that had him as Christopher Conrad, owner of Oakleaf Barrels, a manufacturer of casks and distributor of distillery equipment. He wore black silk pants, a white linen shirt, a hand-loomed sweater of burgundy raw silk and forest green microfibers, and lots of gold bling on his hands and wrists. He had donned a medium-length hairpiece and green contact lenses, easy additions that grossly altered his looks. Lorraine wore a copper satin top over tight-fitting autumn-toned linen pants and Ceylon-white, crystal-beaded Bianca sandals. The pair exuded enough nouveau richness to repel any possible interest in them.

Cantell left the photography to Lorraine, who, even though she was a natural brunette, could play the dumb blonde with aplomb. She made a point of giggling and jiggling her way around the tent, speaking a little bit too loudly, name-dropping and snapping shots. She made sure to get shots with the golf shop in the background.

Cantell took note of the large number of drivers and security personnel loitering outside. He was less surprised by the two undercover and four uniformed men, probably from the Sheriff's Office. He and Lorraine confined themselves to the lots of red wines, tasting several cabernets and pinots, sampled the hors d'oeuvres, then pulled away, keeping to themselves and making a point to stay away from the Adams bottles.

"This could get interesting," she said.

"Already is."

"Are you sure it's enough?"

"No," he answered. "It's a bit far, and may not do the trick."

"Then what?"

"I'm considering Fort Worth," he said.

"You wouldn't!"

"Why not?"

"People were hurt," she reminded him.

"Mild stuff. Outpatient material."

"It was a *stampede*!"

"I'm only considering . . . no decision yet."

"Hello!" It was a blond woman whom Cantell took to be in her early fifties, though there was no telling with this set: she might have been seventy underneath all the work. "Susie," she said, extending her telltale hand, her skin like a dried apple.

"Chris Conrad and my friend Laura," Cantell said. "Oakleaf Barrels."

She tried to look impressed but obviously had not heard of them.

"It's like those BASF television ads," Cantell said. "You know, we don't make the wine, we make what makes the wine better. In our case, it's the oak casks. Can't have a good wine without a properly aged cask."

"Oh . . . of course . . . How interesting." She couldn't have cared less. "Do you know anyone here? May I introduce you around?"

"We're just fine, thank you. Looking forward to tomorrow night."

Lorraine burst in. "What a lovely setting."

"It *is,* isn't it?"

"And how do you fit into all this?" Cantell asked.

"I'm in real estate," Susie said. "Along with about half the valley's population." She smiled with her big teeth. "I serve on the center's board. We reap the rewards of all this." She waved her hand. "It's so generous of all of you."

"Happy to do our part. Will the dinner go off on time?" Cantell asked.

"Honestly," she said, lowering her voice, "we typically run about a half hour behind. Ketchum time, we call it."

"So dinner will seat around . . . ?"

"Eight-fifteen, eight-thirty, I would guess. Will you be with us for the dinner?"

"Oh, we're in for the whole enchilada," said Lorraine, "not that you're serving Mexican." She hoped for a laugh. "Chris brought his wallet, if you know what I mean."

"Isn't that . . . delightful," Susie said. She glanced around, desperate to be free of them. "I expect I'll see you tomorrow night, then."

Cantell offered her his hand, and they shook.

"It'll be a blast," Lorraine said.

Cantell flashed her a look. "It sure will be," he said.

Susie worked her way back into the crowd.

17

Fiona entered the tent on the arm of Roger Hillabrand, the CEO of a multinational defense-contracting firm, who'd been a central figure in a recent investigation of Walt's office. He had a Robert Redford thing going: rich, rugged, and ready for action.

Seeing her, Walt wanted to simply disappear. *"Another junior high reaction to an adult situation,"* is how Gail would have labeled it. His relationship with Fiona was not entirely professional, though he wasn't sure she knew that. If forced to say hello, to acknowledge the pair, he might blush or stammer or otherwise give himself away. That was to be avoided at all costs.

He should have realized she'd attend, should have realized guys like Hillabrand didn't give up. He'd gone after her before, during the investigation. Fiona had pushed back, but had now obviously had a change of heart. Walt barely recognized her in the skintight designer jeans, high heels, and red silk, western-style shirt unsnapped to the third button.

They arrived to the party like Sun Valley royalty. Thankfully, they were swallowed up immediately by the social crush.

"Hey, Sheriff, isn't that—?"

"Yeah," Walt said, cutting Brandon off, forcing himself to look away.

"She sure cleans up good."

"I'll be at Mobile Command. Stay on comm."

He headed for the far entrance of the tent.

The tent itself was now crowded with guests, a confusing mix of pretensions and loud talk that went with wine connoisseurs. Overhearing such descriptions as "a buttery nose" and "a chalky vanilla finish," he wanted to laugh. To him, wine came in a box, and eventually went down the toilet.

The more tasting that went on, the louder the voices became, a shouting match with built-in laugh track.

Nearly out of the tent now, Walt overheard a young woman arguing with a volunteer hostess that she should be allowed in the party. The volunteer politely explained it was by invitation only.

"I won't be but five minutes," the young woman complained bitterly. "I promise, I won't drink any wine. I could care less! I just need a minute with one of the presenters."

"Who?"

"Arthur Remy. It's *extremely important.*"

Mention of Remy's name caught Walt's attention. The volunteer hostess said something Walt couldn't hear. The young woman seeking entrance, clearly disgusted, charged past her into the tent.

When Fiona spotted Walt, she gripped Roger's arm more tightly and steered him toward the whites.

"Do you ever play that game where you

make up what other people do, who they are, what they're thinking?" she blurted out before realizing how childish it sounded. "Forget I just said that," she added, embarrassed.

"Heavens no! It's a wonderful game. The only problem is, I know everyone here."

"Everyone?"

"Damn near."

They each accepted a small glass of white wine.

"What about him," she asked, "the anxious-looking guy?"

"You guess first," he said. "I'll tell you how close you are."

"You know him?"

"*Of* him, absolutely."

"Someone intense. A surgeon maybe. Or a broker who lost everything in the crash last year. He's a wannabe, worried sick, by the look of him, at not being the center of a conversation."

"That's Teddy Sumner," Hillabrand revealed. "His wife was the film producer Annette Dunning. You know, *The Last Look, A Farewell to Harm*—"

"I loved that movie!" she gasped.

"She died of breast cancer . . . two years

ago, now. Teddy took over the reins, soon confirming the old adage that there can't be two geniuses in the same bed."

"There's no such adage."

"There ought to be. He's squandered most of the fortune she'd made them—not helped any by the crash, of course—living well beyond his means. Has a teenage daughter, I think, which can't be easy. A nice enough guy who should have been content to live off her earnings rather than trying to prove himself, which rarely works. You want to feel sorry for him, but he was his own undoing."

"Your turn," she said, looking around the tent. She pointed out the Engletons, whose guest cottage she was renting. He was tall, with a wisp of white interrupting his dark hair. She was exotic-looking, wearing a shawl from India or Pakistan.

"I know Michael and Leslie very well. You know that."

"But if you didn't . . . ?"

"But I do . . . That's not how the game is played, is it?"

"Okay, fine. How about the man with the pinup, the blow-up doll . . . Do you know them?"

"Aren't we generous?"

"I don't feel sorry for someone who looks like a teakettle. You don't wear a copper top like that unless you're starved for attention."

"I'd peg him as ex-military. German, maybe something more exotic like Czech or one of the *-zakis.* Extremely confident. Runs his own business, plays by his own rules. Is rough in bed—and she likes it."

Fiona punched him in the arm. His wine sloshed, nearly spilling, and they both laughed.

"*She's* the rough one," Fiona said. "Wants all the attention all the time. Insufferable. Fired from the evening news in some backwater TV market like Bakersfield."

"More like Atlantic City," Roger said.

"Exactly! Skipped college for a shot at showbiz. Failed miserably. Married three times, no kids. Loves dogs."

"Little dogs . . . yappy little dogs she dresses like dolls."

"Perfect!" Fiona finished off the glass of wine. "See? You're good at this."

For a moment, there was something between them, something she found dangerous and seductive at the same time. But the feeling threatened her as much as excited her, and it ruined the moment for her.

"You okay?" he asked.

Just then, there was a commotion at the entrance on the far side of the tent. A woman charged through the crowd, stopping only a few feet from them.

Walt signaled the volunteer hostess and pursued the crasher himself. He reached out for the rushing woman's arm but missed.

The woman was dressed casually, and inappropriately for this crowd, in department-store jeans, a green polo, and brown Keens.

Intrigued by what the woman might want with Remy, he gave her some distance. He knew he stuck out in his uniform, but no one seemed to notice him.

Coming within earshot, Walt was disappointed that the confrontation between the crasher and Remy lasted only seconds. Remy had rebuked her immediately, turning his back on her. But she was determined, pulling a pen out of the purse slung

over her shoulder and scribbling something on a cocktail napkin. Interrupting
Remy a second time, she pressed the
napkin into his unwilling hand.

"Call me," she said.

Remy leaned in close to her and apparently said something disagreeable. Her
head jerking back as if slapped, she turned
and hurried out an opening in the tent's
wall, a move Walt had not seen coming.

He tried to catch up with her but became tangled in the crowd. One didn't
push around members of this set. He politely squeezed his way through the throng,
making for the opening. He was several
steps past one couple before stopping
abruptly to get a better look at the woman's face. Ignoring the hair and makeup,
the outfit that made her look like a copper-
topped battery, he realized she reminded
him of someone. It took him a few seconds
too many to wonder if she wasn't the
woman in the Hailey crosswalk, the woman
caught on the traffic cam. The camera
was too high up the pole and too far away
to get a decent shot at any face, and
yet . . .

His moment of hesitation cost him.

He caught Brandon's eye, hand-signaling him over other people's heads to get going out of the tent.

Brandon, who'd seen Walt pursuing the party crasher, took off.

Then Walt looked back for the woman in the copper top.

Gone.

Not for the first time in his life, he cursed his short stature. In a sea of six-footers, he was forced to lift up to his toes and crane his neck. The Duracell battery and her man were moving away from Walt but in no particular hurry. He took a step in that direction, then heard Brandon speaking in his right ear bud.

"She's getting into a car, Sheriff. What do you want me to do?"

Grabbing the handset clipped to his epaulet, he answered, "Wave her down and stop her, if you can."

"No way."

"Get the plate, then. Take down the registration."

"Ten-four," Brandon mumbled.

Walt glanced back toward his quarry as another volunteer hostess blew into a microphone and began making introductions.

Walt again lifted to his toes, searching for Miss Duracell.

Not seeing her or her escort, Walt hurried back out of the tent. He caught up to Brandon, describing the woman's copper outfit as the two jogged over to the sea of parked SUVs.

The couple was nowhere to be found.

"How's that possible?" a winded Brandon asked.

"Professionals," Walt answered, a sense of dread overcoming him.

He'd had her within arm's reach.

18

Summer was having doubts. Her plan had seemed pretty simple at first, but its execution required a commitment she wasn't sure she could make. *"Easier said than done,"* her father would have lectured. Oddly enough, just thinking of him, whether he was right or not, steeled her to her purpose.

She'd left a note on the coffee table in the suite's living room: *Dad, found a friend. Going out. Back by midnight.*

She assumed the last bit would piss him off, since her curfew was eleven P.M. She had no intention of missing her curfew, but she didn't want him knowing that. He'd get in well past eleven, but she just wanted to give him a little heartburn before checking her room and finding her asleep.

The events of the next few hours were critical to her bigger plan. Her mother, with her many business dealings, had taught Summer how to use strategy. The prize went to the best planner, the one with the foresight to lay the necessary groundwork. To cinch the deal, to make the relationship stick, you had to get the other person to take the bait without knowing what he was swallowing.

She would leave him this message tonight, then obey the rules, and by tomorrow night it would become routine. He'd automatically grant her an extension on her curfew in expectation that she'd never need it. Then . . .

"Hey, dude," she said, sliding into the passenger's seat of Kevin's beater Subaru. The contents of the laundry bag she carried clattered. He looked over at it, curious.

"Whaddya got?" he asked.

She opened the bag, revealing little liquor bottles from the minibar in the room. "Goodies."

"For real?" he said.

"Including four cold beers."

"Sweet."

She pulled the rearview mirror her direction to inspect herself. She then pushed it back into place.

"Seat belt," he ordered.

"You've got to be kidding me."

"You want to get stopped? The cops here . . . well . . . I happen to know they're sweeping for seat belts right now."

"You've got the inside track, do you?"

She clipped the seat belt at her waist, then leaned forward against the shoulder strap, trying to emphasize her chest. She wanted his attention in all the right places, wanted him to be thinking ahead. His cooperation was key to her plan.

"I actually do . . . have the inside track," he said. "My uncle is the county sheriff."

"No way."

"Way."

"So are you cool with this?" She nodded at the laundry bag.

"As long as it's not open in the car."

"You're going to drink with me, though," she said, as if fact.

"If I get too loaded, I can borrow a friend's bike and ride home," he said.

She liked that.

"A planner," she let slip.

"What . . . ?"

"You're a planner."

"Yeah, I guess so . . . sometimes."

"You either are or you aren't."

"You?"

"I'd put a check in that box, yeah," she said. "But I'm no type A . . . not hardly."

"You've got a real thing about your father, don't you?"

"My mother's dead," she said.

The engine sounded rough when their voices weren't covering it, an unfamiliar rhythm under the hood like someone clapping out of time. The silence between Summer and Kevin stretched out uncomfortably.

"My dad killed himself," Kevin said, catching his reflection in the windshield, proud that he could look so emotionless.

"Whoa!"

"At least, I'm pretty sure that's what happened. No one'll say. Mom lost, like, a million pounds after he died and, I don't know, changed. My uncle and grandpa are pissed off at each other most of the time, mainly, I think, because of what happened to Dad. It was ruled accidental, but I'm pretty sure he did it, and that my uncle covered for him, and that the only reason he did that was because Grandpa made him."

"That's *seriously* random."

"I don't know if he did or didn't. He's just dead, you know? You're the first person I've met . . . first person my age and all . . . you know?"

"Yeah. Same here."

The tailpipe didn't sound all that terrific. And there was a low grinding noise coming from the back axle. Just her luck if the car broke down before tomorrow night.

"How much farther?" she asked.

"That's the ski hill. Warm Springs side. Half Pipe's on the other side. River Run. I board. Half Pipe is awesome."

"I've never skied."

"What do you do?"

"Tennis."

"You any good?"

Summer stared Kevin down, though at no time did he take his eyes off the road.

"Yeah, okay, I get it," he said.

"I'm thinking of going pro."

"A friend of mine's on the snowboarding circuit. He has endorsements and stuff like that. But I think his parents basically pay for everything. He hasn't exactly won anything yet." He added, "You won anything?"

"Of course I've won . . . I'm a winner . . . I win."

"Anything big?"

"Big enough."

The road narrowed, evergreens towering claustrophobically on either side. Sunset was fully an hour away, but the sky was all pink and turquoise and full of promise.

"Wow," Summer said about it, not meaning to sound so impressed.

"Yeah, I know," Kevin agreed.

"It's, like, the town just disappeared."

"That's what happens here . . . the outdoors, the wilderness . . . it just kinda takes over. That's what it's all about."

"It's awesome."

"L.A.?" he guessed.

"Is it *that* obvious?" she asked.

"I don't mind, I've got a bunch of friends from there."

"They moved up here?"

"Absolutely."

"Whoa!"

"You and your dad could."

"Ah . . . I don't think so," she said. "You don't know my dad."

She leaned out the window to see the tops of the trees. A pair of birds crossed the sky.

"Almost there," he said. "Another couple of miles."

"Hey, just keep driving and don't stop, as far as I'm concerned."

"Yeah, I know what you mean."

They were quiet again. But there was nothing uncomfortable about it. Silence was usually a contest for her, a weapon. With the window rolled down, the wind was in her face, her hair whipping, and it made her laugh. Her father had been hammering this same message into her for the past two years: *"You're growing up too fast. Slow down and have some fun. Don't be in such a hurry to grow up: it's over-sold."*

"This is *way* cool," she called into the wind.

"Yeah?" he called back.

Not long after that, Kevin parked the car in the beaten-down grass about thirty yards from the hot springs and well off the road. Steam rose from the springs.

He turned the key off and set the parking brake. She got out of the car. Waiting to make sure he was looking, as he climbed out from behind the wheel, she reached down and pulled her T-shirt up over her head while she walked toward the springs. Then she popped the button on her jeans and unzipped the fly. She knew his heart would be racing by now. She knew what she was doing.

Her own heart was racing too, but for a different reason. She didn't want him decoding her embarrassment.

He wouldn't be able to get his pants off without some major awkwardness himself. She thought that might slow him down, give her more time to make a show of her striptease. But despite all her planning, as she wiggled the jeans over her hips and down to her knees, as she sat on a rock stalling for time while kicking off her sandals, her chest felt tight.

She wasn't sure she could go through with this. Only her father's combativeness

and certitude drove her on. If he hadn't
dragged her along on this trip, she wouldn't
be in a position of stripping naked in front of
a virtual stranger.

Now Summer's sandals sat on the grass
alongside the jeans. She stood.

Kevin was looking right at her. He'd
slipped out of his shirt but was taking his
time with his pants. His state of arousal
was apparent from across the steaming
pool.

It's now or never, thought Summer.

She unhooked her bra, taking a deep
breath, hoping for courage, and let it slide
down her arms. Goose bumps raced up
her ribs. She squared her shoulders to
make herself look even bigger than she
was, hoping he was too far away to see her
blush. She slid her fingers into the elastic
of her bikini briefs.

I've gone this far . . .

She pulled down the briefs with both
thumbs, and it was done. Dragging the liquor bag behind her, she slipped into the
water, gasping at the heat.

By the time she looked up, Kevin was in
the pool waist-deep.

"Oh . . . damn," she said, sinking in up to

her chin, hiding herself from his stare. But it was too hot to stay under for long.

"Can you believe this just comes up out of the ground all on its own?" he asked.

"Now I know what a McDonald's French fry feels like."

Hearing herself, she thought she sounded about seven years old. He came toward her, and their legs touched. Terrified, she pulled away and retrieved the bag.

She passed him a beer. It made her feel more in control.

"Just one beer," he said. "A woman died out here last year, getting drunk and staying in the pool too long. So if we're going to get serious about drinking, it has to be out of the water."

She couldn't stop herself from laughing.

"What?" he asked.

"You are, like, way different than most guys."

"Because?"

"Because most guys would *want* to get a naked girl drunk in a hot springs. And here you are, all worried about it."

"I'm not *all worried about it*," he said defensively. "But I also know what's stupid,

and getting drunk in a hot tub is stupid."
He chuckled to himself. "I guess when
your uncle's the sheriff . . ." He let it hang
there.

"Yeah, that can't be perfect."

Chin-deep, she was far too hot. She
felt his eyes search her as she stood up,
the waterline at her waist. To his credit, he
tried to keep his eyes off her chest, but he
strayed.

"You're sweet," she said, gulping some
beer. She moved toward him, kissed him
on the cheek, and made a point of rubbing
her breast against his arm.

She bumped against him below water
as well, just to make sure she had his attention.

Pleased with her accomplishment, she
sipped some more of the beer. He was
right: it went straight to her head.

He rambled on about something to do
with geology, but she didn't hear him.
She'd already moved on to phase two.

She bobbed up and gave him another
look at her front. "You want to take me
down to the airport tomorrow night?" she
said.

"There's a shuttle every—"

"I don't want to take the shuttle," she cut him off.

Summer sank back down in the water. She couldn't have some driver remembering her. She had a plan, and her fake driver's license was part of it, her father was part of it, Enrico was part of it. And now so was a boy named Kevin.

"Yeah, okay, I guess. Why the airport?" he asked. "You going somewhere?"

"I . . . ah . . . I just wondered if you've ever seen the inside of a Learjet."

"Seriously?"

"Totally. I left something in the jet and I want to pick it up, and I don't want to take the shuttle. I hate public transportation."

"Because?"

"Because I don't *take* public transportation," she said.

"And you'd show me around inside the jet." Kevin made it a statement.

"I'd show you lots of stuff." She tried to make it sound sexy but wasn't sure Kevin caught it.

"You mean I could sit in the pilot's seat?"

She bit back a smile. *Boys.* "Whatever . . ."

"How big is it?"

"You won't believe it. And the seats fold flat like a bed."

"No way."

He still didn't get it.

"It'll be *fun*," she said.

That time, she thought he got it.

She didn't know he carried a pager until it suddenly beeped shrilly from his pile of clothes.

Kevin moved to the edge of the pool and clawed for it. "Damn! I'm on call at the hotel," he said. "Got to go."

Relieved, she turned and pulled herself up out of the water, offering him a view of her backside.

No towel.

Summer wasn't about to wait around for a towel and just let his eyes dry her off, but getting into the clothes while wet proved challenging.

"So, Kevin, what do you think, can we do this again around eight tomorrow night?" She tried to load the question with innuendo. Again, she wasn't sure he got it.

He stuffed himself into his jeans and zipped up, his back to her.

"The cockpit?" he said. "Seriously?"

"I'm a hundred percent serious," she

said. "You can definitely sit in the pilot's seat."

She was in her briefs and bra by the time he turned around. Covering herself up gave her back her confidence.

"Awesome," he said.

Her mother would have been proud.

19

Walt had Brandon to thank, and he was not about to do it. Brandon had apparently correctly written down the registration to the car driven by the wine-party crasher. Walt had feared it would come back a rental, but to his surprise it was a Blaine County plate registered to Nick Gilman. The mailing address was a post office box in Hailey, but the residence was in the Starweather subdivision.

Having transferred the Adams bottles to a safe-deposit box in a Ketchum bank following the tasting, Walt headed down valley.

Walt knew Nick and L'Anne Gilman well enough to say hello. He was a builder; she owned an art gallery on Sun Valley Road. They had three kids, the oldest in fifth grade along with Walt's daughters.

The Gilmans had installed a controversial steel sculpture, a nude giving birth to the earth, on their front lawn that had twice been vandalized, requiring investigation by his office. She had also installed a quarter-million-dollar cairn of rocks on the back lawn by a British landscape artist, which had fueled rumors of unexpected wealth. Not just anyone in the valley could afford to fly in British stonemasons to stack rocks. And those stonemasons, being big brutes and not averse to ending the day with a few pints at the local pub, had made themselves known to the Sheriff's Office by putting their rock-hard fists in the faces of some locals who found it necessary to deride them for their thick accents.

It was those brawls—three in all—that had introduced Walt to the Gilmans. And Nick, having a welcoming smile, and L'Anne, having an abundance of confidence and shrewd negotiating skills, meant the masons had been cleared of all charges. By way of thanks, L'Anne had sent Walt a tin of toffee at Christmastime.

The Gilmans lived in a sprawling log home on the Big Wood.

Walt was greeted at the front door by a female employee of the Gilmans', who introduced herself as Betty. He was told the Gilmans were attending one of the wine-auction preview dinners.

Walt asked about the whereabouts of their Toyota Land Cruiser, having its registration number in his top pocket.

"Janet has it," Betty answered, "a friend visiting from California, a grad student at UC Davis. She's staying in the Sheep Wagon. The Land Cruiser goes with the Sheep Wagon."

"Sheep Wagon . . . ?"

"I'm sorry. L'Anne names everything." Betty pointed up the drive. "It's the guest cabin. Your first right, on the way out, you'll see a sheep wagon. Turn there, keep going until you see a cabin . . . Is everything all right?"

A uniform always generated curiosity. People had no right to ask, but they always did.

"Nothing to worry about."

"I'm not sure she's around. I thought I heard her leave a while ago," Betty said, "but maybe I'm wrong. I could tell her to call you." She was fishing for information.

Walt thanked her, told her there was no reason to bother the Gilmans about his visit, and drove off in search of the Sheep Wagon.

He found the Land Cruiser parked beside the cabin, if one could call an eighteen-hundred-square-foot log home a cabin. It appeared to have been dropped into the middle of the aspen grove where it stood, the white-barked trees seemingly glowing in the darkness. It also abutted the Big Wood, the gurgling river reminding Walt of his aborted fly-fishing with Kevin. He owed the kid a rain check.

Walt was about to knock on the cabin's door when a blur of movement caught his eye. He froze, believing it an elk or deer or even a moose watering at the river. He cherished such sights—one of the reasons for living here. But the shadow moved again. It was clearly a human being.

"Hey!" Walt called out, instinctively reaching for his sidearm.

A trespassing fisherman, maybe. But

with a woman in the cabin he couldn't rule out a Peeping Tom, and that required a discussion. A thief would go for the main house, not a guest cabin. Or a transient, one of the dozens of mountain men who squatted in the national forest during the summer, causing his office no end of trouble.

He eased his hand off of his weapon. He might be able to run this guy down, or at least run him off the property.

As the shadow took off, so did Walt, his Maglite in hand. The light briefly caught the man from the back, but it was enough to spot the gloves he was wearing. Gloves in late July.

Walt dodged through the maze of white-barked trees.

"HALT!" he shouted.

Back at the cabin a floodlight came on and the trees made prison-bar shadows.

The man slalomed through the aspens, increasing his lead.

Walt, who prided himself on his fitness, pushed hard but failed to catch up. He broke out of the aspen grove, stumbling over an asphalt curb and falling down hard, and found himself on a neighbor's driveway.

The whine of a car engine starting interrupted the river's growl. By the time Walt made it to his feet, the sound grew smaller.

He took hold of his radio but had nothing to call in—no description of the suspect or vehicle. He stubbed his boot into the driveway's gravel. "Shit, shit, shit!"

Walt wiped his sweating face with a handkerchief and banged on the cabin's front door. The same young woman he'd seen at the wine tasting answered the door, her reaction to his uniform typical.

"Janet . . . ?"

"Yes?"

"Walt Fleming, county sheriff. I was at the reception tonight."

For the moment, Walt held off telling her about the man outside her cabin.

Janet had a sharp Roman nose, some faint acne scarring in her sunken cheeks. Her pale eyes were a remarkable grayish blue. She appeared tired, even drained. He wondered if she might be ill.

"I crashed it, I know. Guilty. Okay? I didn't realize I'd broken a law. Is there a fine, or what?"

"Or what," he said. "I'd like to talk with you about Arthur Remy."

"That's all?"

"That's all."

She waved him inside. The cabin would have qualified as a Native American extension museum.

"Blackfoot?" he asked, looking around.

"I'm afraid I don't know."

"Northern Paiute," he said, correcting himself, identifying an impressive horsehair basket. "Bannock, probably. Uto-Aztecans."

"Are you a collector?"

"I dabble. An uncle of mine—kind of an uncle, not by blood—is a Blackfoot. He got me interested in the culture." He fingered a blanket, wondering if the Gilmans knew it was a fake, and studied two pieces of pottery in a glass case.

"Your interest in Mr. Remy is . . . ?" he asked.

She'd taken a seat in a willow-branch chair on the other side of a walnut-slab coffee table. She motioned for him to take the couch, but he declined and continued studying the collection.

"Arthur Remy," Walt repeated.

"Did he lodge some kind of complaint?" she asked. "What a jerk."

"No complaint. Should he have?"

Her forehead creased.

"I didn't catch your last name," Walt said.

"Finch . . . Janet Finch. What's this about, exactly?"

"My office is providing security for the Adams bottles," Walt said.

"Well, then, you're wasting your resources."

"Because?"

"There are no Adams bottles. Something Arthur Remy does not want to hear evidently."

"Okay. You've got my attention," he said. He took a seat across from her.

"I'm a Ph.D. candidate at UC Davis, Sheriff. Oenology . . . winemaking," she finally said, answering his blank expression. "My thesis concerns the Jefferson collection." She searched his face. "Are you familiar with Thomas Jefferson's obsession with wine?"

"The Adams bottles," he said, "they were a gift from Jefferson, right?"

"Fiction," she scoffed. "That's Arthur Remy's story, but that's all it is, a story."

"I'm listening."

"The so-called Jefferson bottles were discovered by Arthur Remy in nineteen eighty-five and were sold at auction for nearly two hundred thousand dollars, in part because the wine was judged to have survived the centuries . . . no easy feat. Remy claims the Adams bottles are also from Jefferson's Parisian cellar, which is, like . . . totally far-fetched. And quite frankly brings into question the authenticity of the original find."

She made eye contact. "They're fakes, Sheriff. It's a hoax. An elaborate and expensive hoax, but a hoax just the same."

Walt heard the compressor of the kitchen refrigerator kick in. There was a TV or radio playing upstairs.

"I don't imagine that's a popular opinion," he said.

"All I'm asking for is access to the bottles, and the test results. I want to know that I haven't wasted nearly three years of my life. The point is that Arthur Remy is a liar and a cheat, and everyone is so carried away by the story he's invented that they've blinded themselves to this hoax he's perpetrated. He's going to make off with a zillion dollars for some Rothschild bottled as something quite different."

"You've requested access, I take it?"

"A dozen times. And isn't it just a little bit curious that he won't even so much as take my calls?"

"Calling something . . . someone . . . a fake is quite an accusation."

"I understand that. Were the bottles vetted and tested? Of course they were. And by some of the best. But you want to take a guess at how many 'experts'"—she drew air quotes—"there are out there who could authenticate a find like this? Very, very few. And, trust me, he got to them. I don't know how, but that's not my problem. One of those guys is dead, by the way . . . killed. That should interest a sheriff, right? Stabbed to death, in Amsterdam. Has any connection been made to Remy? No. Will it ever be made? No. But how convenient the man who signed off on the authenticity of the engraving—the glass and the method used to cut it—ends up stabbed to death in the doorway of a brothel. And guess what? He was gay. He didn't even belong in a brothel.

"Don't get me wrong," she continued, "I

suspect Remy's Jefferson bottles are legitimate. But these Adams bottles? I'm sure the glass is from eighteenth-century France, the cork is Portuguese, the label is the right paper. I'm sure all the facts support Remy's claims. The bottles wouldn't be on the open market otherwise. But my work on Jefferson reveals no such bottles. Did you get that? The Adams bottles aren't accounted for anywhere in Jefferson's inventory. I think Remy saw a good thing and jumped on it, not fully realizing that Thomas Jefferson was a freak of nature who inventoried every bottle, cataloged every wine he served with every dinner. No one knows Jefferson's wines the way I do. There are a total of three people in the world who've studied his collection the way I have and the other two did so before we had the science we have today—the spectrometers and electron microscopes, specifically. Arthur Remy is not one of those other two, I promise you."

She was red in the face, the veins in her neck protruding.

"But you lack proof," Walt said, "because you don't have access."

"There you have it." Janet Finch drew in a deep breath. "The wine industry is based on relationships. Dealers, brokers, consumers, collectors, and connoisseurs. Those relationships are carefully protected. Scholars like me, we're sought out when authentication is needed and we're thrown to the wolves when we raise suspicions. Remy claims the Jefferson and Adams bottles were found in two different cellars in Paris. Okay, fine, I'd like to know *which* cellars. I know where Jefferson lived in Paris, I know where he cellared his collection. I know when and where he moved the collection. If these are, in fact, authentic— and I'm willing to go there if that's how it proves out—then I need to include them in my thesis if it's to be complete. I've worked forever on this, Sheriff. I'm not going to give up now."

"The killing in Amsterdam . . . ?" Walt said.

"Investigated and closed. A random act of violence." Janet studied him. "You actually believe me?"

"If you're right, you'd cost Remy a heck of a lot of money."

"It's his reputation he's worried about,

believe me, not the money. If I'm right, he's ruined. And I *am* right."

"Ms. Finch, I think you'd be well advised to seek other lodging."

"No thanks. The price is right. L'Anne's a friend from grade school."

"When I approached your cabin just now, I scared off a prowler."

"You what?"

"I pursued, but the individual fled and escaped."

"There was some guy out there? Are you serious?"

"In light of what you've told me, I think it would be smarter if you stayed in the main house, or took a hotel room, or even left the valley."

"Remy? Are you kidding?" She mulled this over. "Good God! You are totally freaking me out. It could have been someone fishing or just walking the river. Right?"

"Maybe," Walt said, not sounding convinced. "But still, you might consider staying over with the Gilmans for a few nights."

"I can't do that. I gave Remy the phone number here at the cottage. He'll either call or he won't. And if not, I'm gone by Sunday morning."

He didn't like the idea of her staying here alone but was powerless to do anything about it. "The bottles would be heavily insured," he said.

"Of course."

"And if stolen"—*En route to the wine auction,* he thought but did not say—"the insurance would pay out, and the bottles, as well as any questions of their authenticity, would disappear."

"I suppose. Why?"

"Call-forward that line and stay in the main house," Walt said. "And I'm not asking."

20

As Walt pulled up to the picket fence that fronted his house, a house he wasn't sure he'd live in much longer, because of the divorce, he flashed the Cherokee's brights, flooding the porch and signaling his guest.

Fiona Kenshaw waved at him from the Smith & Hawken bench by the front door. He'd given Gail the bench on their tenth anniversary. He wasn't sure anyone had ever sat in it before. It was more a monument to his picking the wrong gift. Gail had gushed over it, unwrapped it on the porch, and had left it there, never to look at it again.

"Hey there," he said, climbing the steps.

"Hey there yourself," she said playfully, in a voice he didn't recognize.

She looked beautiful despite the glow of the yellow bug light overhead. He tried to think of her only as a professional—a part-time crime-scene photographer, an associate—but failed miserably.

Seeing her with Hillabrand had caused him a moment of unease. He hadn't processed it at the time but recalled it now, feeling squeamish. There had been a time, not long ago, when he'd have felt awkward having a woman other than his wife on his front porch. But it was just the opposite: he wanted to wake up the nosey Mrs. Merimer, and all his neighbors, and show them he'd picked himself up. Like Gail, he too could move on.

"This is a surprise," Walt said.

Fiona patted the bench beside her.

"Would you like to come in?" he asked. He pulled open the screen door and held it with his foot.

"No. It's a gorgeous night." She patted the bench again.

Walt sat down beside her. She smelled

like lilacs, or maybe the bench was scratch-and-sniff.

Her hands—they were rough from all her hours in rivers as a fishing guide—twisted in her lap. He'd never known Fiona to be the nervous type. Single-minded, independent, socially cautious, to be sure. But agitated and uncomfortable?

"How was the dinner?" he asked. "I'm assuming you did one of the private dinners."

"Surreal," she said. "Six courses. Too much wine. *Way* too much."

Then he saw it: she was drunk. "Did you drive yourself?"

She put her arms out. "Cuff me." But her eyes sparkled, and he felt tempted to kiss her wet lips.

"I'm driving you home," he said.

"Party pooper," she said. "Do you know what the Brits used to call spirits? Maybe still do, for all I know."

"I've never been good at trivia," Walt said. "Unless the chosen topic is forensics, dogs, or wildlife."

"Courage," she answered.

"Okay," he said. He clawed at the knees

of his pants, suddenly extremely uncomfortable.

"So I'm just going to say this whether
you want to hear it or not, because I may
never be like this around you again. Feeling my courage, that is. *Carpe diem,* and
all that."

"And all that," he echoed.

Then she said nothing. His throat had
constricted to the width of a cocktail straw.
He was afraid to try to talk for fear he'd
merely squeak.

"You listen, but do you hear?" She
turned her head to face him, and he felt a
jolt.

"I definitely hear," he said. "I promise, I'll
hear whatever you have to say."

"You were jealous tonight," she said.

"Guilty." Gail had complained he was
never honest with her. He had vowed to
not repeat that mistake. "I'm not exactly
sure why."

"It's because we both feel this thing between us. You know that's true. I feel it too,
Walt. I'd love to go on pretending I don't,
because I don't want to feel it, acknowledge it, but I do. And so do you, whether
you'll ever admit it or not, because I saw it

on your face tonight at the tasting. It made the whole rest of my night a lie because it was all that I could think about. You . . . were all that I could think about, which was hardly fair to Roger."

"You looked like you were having a good enough time."

"You're a better judge than that. I have no idea what Roger must have thought. But the point is . . . Well, that *is* the point, isn't it? I don't know what the point is, and there's something sad about it taking way too many glasses of the best wine to convince me to say something about it. Especially when I don't know what exactly it is I'm trying to say."

Walt looked away from her, out to the empty street and the porch light on Mrs. Merimer's cottage. He had a resuscitation kit in the back of the Cherokee. He wondered if she'd know how to use it on him. He felt as if he was going to blow a valve.

"You are going to say something, right?" Her voice sounded terrified.

He nodded, hoping that might do until his pulse leveled off.

"Say something, Walt." She sounded dangerously close to being angry.

"I'm trying," he managed to choke out.

"Don't leave me hanging here. I don't think I can take it. Tell me I didn't just make a complete ass out of myself. Oh my God," she said, leaning over with her head between her legs.

He tentatively reached out and rubbed her back. She was hot and damp.

She rushed forward then, grabbed the rail, and threw up into the lilacs.

He hurried to her and again placed his hand on her back.

"Okay?" he said.

"Do I look like I'm okay?" Fiona sounded as if she was crying. "Could I bother you for a paper towel?"

He hurried inside, composing what to say in order to rescue the moment. He did feel the same as she but hadn't known it until she'd confronted him. He wasn't sure he knew how to explain himself. Gail. Brandon. His two girls. The house.

He heard a car engine start.

He ran to the porch, the damp paper towel in hand.

Taillights.

A swarm of bugs were circling the porch's yellow light, a light that was supposed to repel them. A dog barked a block away. A drip of the water fell from the paper towel striking the toe of his boot. A feeling of remorse overcame him, of loss, of missed opportunity. More water hit his boot, and he caught himself having squeezed the paper towel in his fist.

He turned and headed inside, straight to the phone.

The scent of lilacs was gone.

21

Squinting through the blinds of her hotel bedroom, Summer Sumner watched a Zamboni crawl across the ice of the lodge's outdoor skating rink, leaving behind a wide swath of clean ice like a glistening silver ribbon, mirrorlike in the morning sunshine.

The bedside CD/iPod/clock radio read 10:34. A fairly typical rising time for her, but—and she was certain of this— unacceptable to her early-bird-gets-the-worm father. He'd have been up since five A.M. negotiating some deal with someone five time zones away. She felt sorry for him: he could never turn it off. She as-

sumed that, even at the wine tasting the
night before, he'd been talking up some
film or television deal, a deal that would
never get off the ground.

She wondered what he'd thought of the
note she'd left him. Certainly, he'd seen it:
she'd placed it front and center on the table
just inside the door. Impossible to miss.

As she crossed the bedroom, she happened to glance into the living room and
see her father's laptop up and running
on the desk, alongside a pile of papers
and his BlackBerry. There was also some
pocket change lying there and . . . *his
keys.*

But he was nowhere to be seen.

She heard the toilet seat clunk down,
the rustle of newspaper, and knew he'd be
a while.

Wearing nothing but a T-shirt and briefs,
she hurried across to the desk, nervously
glancing back toward the suite's powder
room.

His key chain required unscrewing a tiny
sleeve that sealed it shut. She squeezed
and turned the sleeve, but it held tight.
She tried again, and this time it gave. She
spun the sleeve out of the way, then sorted

quickly through the keys to find the strangely shaped one to the jet. She freed it and was screwing the sleeve back in place when his BlackBerry rang.

Summer heard the toilet flush.

Impossible! she thought, panicking.

"I'll get it!" she called out, trying to buy herself an excuse for being caught hovering over his things.

He came out the door, fastening his belt.

"I've got it," he said.

But she answered it.

"Hello?" she said.

Silence.

"Hello?"

Her father crossed the room.

"I've got it, Summer."

"I'm calling for Teddy Sumner," said a man's voice.

She'd heard the caller's voice before and tried to place it. Her father would be proud if she presented herself correctly.

"This is Summer speaking. Whom may I say is calling?"

Her father stood there, his hand out, wanting his phone.

"Is your father there?" The voice was vaguely familiar, but she couldn't dredge up a face to go along with it.

She handed her father the BlackBerry.

"Thank you," he said, though he didn't mean it. He didn't want her answering his calls.

"Sumner," her father said into the phone, sliding down into the chair.

Summer stood there, her eyes on the key chain, which she'd set down, but not where she'd found it. She shuffled closer to her dad, putting herself between him and the keys, wanting the chance to slide them back toward where they belonged.

"This is a business call," he said, cupping the phone, clearly wanting privacy.

Her hands behind her back, she moved the keys back in place.

"Sure," she said, wondering what was up with him. He was constantly on the phone. He never gave a damn about what she overheard.

"We have a court in twenty minutes," he said, wanting her out of the room.

"I know, Dad," she said, heading back to her room, glancing at the keys on her way out to confirm that she'd left them where she'd found them. Gripped in her right hand was the key to the jet. As she shut the door to her room behind her, she was already celebrating her triumph.

22

Tell me again why I'm awake at this ungodly hour?" Fiona asked. It was five-thirty A.M. A melon-colored light graced the ridgetops of the eastern mountains, as seen from the asphalt of the small Sun Valley Airport. She wore a down vest zipped snugly over a blue jean jacket, the July dawn registering only forty-five degrees Fahrenheit.

She'd reluctantly accepted Walt's invitation to a predawn flight in his glider, an olive branch he'd offered via voice mail following the debacle of the night before. She didn't love the idea of the flight—her

last flight with him had landed her in federal custody—but his voice mail had left
her smiling, and here she was. She nursed
a slight hangover with a cup of green tea.

The glider was towed to ten thousand
feet and released, the tow plane banking
sharply away and leaving them to the
whine of wind over the wings and the orange sun rising over the horizon.

She sat directly behind him, her camera
around her neck, brought along voluntarily
this time. She took a series of pictures,
working with the play of morning light as it
caught the western spine of mountains
framing the Wood River Valley, the ridges
aflame with a yellow light that sank slowly
down the slopes toward the valley floor.

"Outstanding," Fiona said into the headset's microphone.

"This is my form of meditation, where I
come to find myself . . . whatever that
means."

"I can't believe all the planes at the airport," she said, looking down. A lower
ramp packed with parked aircraft revealed
itself from the air.

"The wine auction."

"There must be fifty jets, or more."

The glider bumped and shook as he found and caught a thermal uplift. They spiraled higher, approaching eleven thousand feet.

"We're going to dive lower in a minute," Walt warned. "There's nothing to worry about, okay? I want to get a look out Democrat Gulch . . . where we found the wrecker."

"This is a business trip?" she complained.

"I can't pass up the opportunity."

"Do you want me to make pictures?"

"Your call. If we see anything, sure."

"Such as . . . ?"

"Tents . . . a campground. But I'm not expecting to see anything. Those two fled north, and we never saw any hint of them. That's been bothering me."

"Have I been shanghaied?"

"Camera work is optional. Honestly, I thought you'd enjoy the view. No ulterior motives."

"None?" she said, regretting it immediately.

"I was an asshole last night."

"Yes, you were."

"I will work on being less of one."

"I saved your voice mail." She regretted he couldn't see her smiling. "Evidence," she added.

"Here we go," he said, dipping the left wing slightly.

The view of the terrain from above was wondrous. The rugged landscape of ever-larger mountains and more dense wilderness rose in a progression of deformities like shark's teeth. North and east of Croy Canyon, where Democrat Gulch lay like a dirt ribbon on the valley floor, there was not a structure to be seen. The barren floor of waxweed and rabbit bush gave way to aspen groves, intermingled with fir and lodgepole pine, from where a blanket of green conifers rose toward the jagged rock and the lifeless realms of gravel fields and ice—all that remained above the tree line.

Sunlight drew a sharp, brilliantly bright line across the rock, reminding her of a scratched negative. A pattern of shadows moved in unison—deer or elk on the run—then vanished, absorbed by forest.

Fiona struggled for words to convey her awe, or at least her appreciation, without sounding stupid or overly spiritual. But failing to find any, she raised her camera and recorded the moment instead.

The glider rose. As her insides pressed through her feet and out through the floor, she rested the camera on her chest and shut her eyes, holding on to the cold frame of the seat for a sense of security.

"Holy shit!" she said.

Walt lifted the glider higher in ever-widening circles. It gained over a thousand feet in a matter of minutes.

"One more pass," Walt warned. "I saw some shapes in the willows below those mine tailings."

She collected herself and pressed the TALK button. "Shapes?"

"Might be tents or something."

"I'll make pictures."

The glider dove. Even the headphones' noise-cancellation feature couldn't hold back the roar. She ran off a series of pictures.

The glider began its lazy climb.

"There!" he said. "Two o'clock!"

She aimed and saw the dark shapes, zoomed in.

Click. Click.

Fiona listened as Walt contacted the

airport tower and asked for a message to be relayed to his dispatcher. He requested a patrol explore the area.

When Walt was off air, Fiona pushed the button and spoke.

"I got a pretty good look at those shapes. Smaller than tents."

"ATVs?" he asked.

"Why not?"

"Parasailors," he said, pointing through the canopy. "Off the ski mountain."

Three colorful parachutes—red, green, and blue—hung in the air, with their ribbed foils bulging, just below the top of the Sun Valley ski mountain, the silk caught in the glare of the morning sun. They were too far away for her to see the nylon cords, the jumpers appearing to float beneath their chutes.

"Beautiful," she said.

He steered the plane north, flying directly above the parasailors, and she took more photographs. To the east, the butterfly-winged canvas roof of Sun Valley's new outdoor amphitheater caught her eye, and, nearby, the enormous white tent that would shelter the wine auction later that evening.

She thought he might overfly this venue as well, but instead he looped south and soon returned to the airport. In a matter of minutes, they were on the ramp near the hangars.

"You're good at your job. You know that?" she said.

"I'm a hack," he said.

"Why do you do that?" she asked, shaking her hair out. "Why can't you accept a compliment?"

"My father makes a point of it when the *Express* covers my men chasing a bear out of a backyard or arresting a man for riding a lawn mower down Main Street. You say I'm good at it, and I want to agree, believe me. There's a jazz standard called 'Compared to What?' You hold my job up against even a rookie cop in Los Angeles or New York and it looks like I'm sleepwalking."

"But we're not in New York. And I meant it as a compliment." She paused.

"Okay. So, thank you."

He was dancing on ice. It made her uncomfortable.

"I'll e-mail you the pictures," she said. She could sense his impatience to get going.

"Okay. Thanks."

"Don't hide from me," she said.

Walt looked at Fiona curiously, and she wondered if she'd gone too far. *Again.*

"I've known you for, what, two years? I barely know you."

"You know me better than most," he said.

"Then that's a shame."

"What are you looking for?" he asked.

"I plead the Fifth, Sheriff."

He fought back a grin.

"I need to hangar the glider," he said.

"I'll help you."

"It's light. One person can do it."

"Consider this: maybe it's easier with two. You think that's possible?"

Their eyes met.

"I'd appreciate the help," he said.

"That's better," she said, moving behind the wing and awaiting instructions.

23

As Walt left the hangar, he heard a radio code spoken over his handset and decided to respond himself. Another day, another weekend, he would have left the call for others—he tried hard to avoid micromanagement—but with his patience worn thin awaiting word from the patrol he'd sent out to Democrat Gulch, he knew the short drive down to Bellevue would keep his mind on other things. Besides, he'd known Bob Parker, the owner of Sun Valley Log Homes, for years.

A round-faced man, with clear blue eyes

and hard hands, Bob had taken a small lumberyard and turned it into a company that manufactured homes of all sizes and budgets. He dressed like a lumberjack, disguising a six-figure income.

He shook his head at Walt from the summer porch. Beatrice, who'd been heeling nicely, broke away to investigate an empty dog bowl by the porch steps.

"Damnedest thing," Bob said.

"What's that?" Walt asked, one eye on Beatrice. He didn't begrudge her the pursuit of food, but it was incorrect to break heel without permission. Like everything else around him, Beatrice needed his time.

"The only way I can get five minutes with you is to have my place busted into," Bob said.

"I thought you were probably still sore over the whooping you took in the tournament," Walt said.

"A different third-base umpire and you would be the one that's sore."

"So you're still sore?"

"A game should be decided by the players, not the umps."

"So let's have a rematch," Walt proposed.

"For the trophy?"

"I didn't say that. But bragging rights should be good enough for a losing team."

"*Losing team?* You think?"

"Why don't we find out?"

"Oh, we'll find out," Bob said. "Or, more likely, you will."

Walt called Beatrice away from the bowl. She'd licked it any harder, the glaze would've come off.

"Such claims are better settled on the diamond."

"I couldn't agree more," said Bob.

Sheriff's Deputy Bill Tuttle was to Walt's left, consulting two paramedics and over-seeing their care of one of Bob's employees, sitting on the bumper of the ambulance, a blood-pressure sleeve around his left arm.

"So why am I here?" Walt said.

"It's not exactly like we guard this place at night," Bob said. "You know me, Walt: throw a chain around the gate out front, make sure the keys are out of the equipment, and pack it up home. What's to steal? A few hand-drawn logs? I don't think so. Cash? Never a penny on the property. I suppose you might roll a John Deere mower into the bed of your half-ton, but it's never happened."

"Isn't that the Dodge kid?"

"Morgan? Yeah. Looking to get a jump on his college loan."

"How's that?" Walt asked.

"College loan," Bob repeated, as if Walt hadn't heard. "He's been working nights for the past month. Starts over in Moscow middle of August. Wanted to get a nut under him, and I said fine. Why not? If he wants to spend his evenings sharpening mower blades and swapping out air filters, who am I to stop him? I didn't know that that would mean working 'til one in the morning. Good God, talk about initiative. Walt, the kid's got a battery in him that won't die."

"So Morgan was here late last night?" Walt said, hoping that might encourage the *Cliffs Notes* version.

"He was. Wishes he hadn't been now, I want to tell you."

"Kids?" Walt asked. "Vandals?"

"Who the heck knows?" Bob said. "Whoever it was fried his ass with a cattle prod or Taser or something. Knocked him flat on his ass, I'll tell you that."

Walt looked around the yard: five acres of piled logs, mountains of split wood, and stacks of scrap. There were a half dozen badly worn-out Caterpillar tractors and forklifts.

"Damned near stopped his ticker, from what the ambulance boys are saying," said Bob.

Walt didn't like the sound of it. The break-in itself wasn't all that unusual. The Wood River Valley had seen a sharp increase in vandalism and burglaries over the past few years. But a cattle prod didn't knock a person unconscious, and a Taser wasn't exactly a common weapon in the valley. His department had two—the only two he knew of up here.

"Anything missing or messed with?" Walt asked.

"Not as if I've kicked every tire or anything," Bob said, "but nothing sticks out."

"I'm going to ask him a few questions before they get him out of here."

Bob didn't object.

Morgan Dodge had an intense face, with brooding dark brown eyes peering through floppy hair. He was trying to grow a mustache, which wasn't going to work out. He looked like a hundred hungover kids Walt had interviewed the morning after a DUI.

"You okay?" Walt asked.

"It's kind of like a migraine," Morgan said, "only worse."

"Tell me what happened," Walt said.

"Not much to tell." The boy—he couldn't have been over nineteen—averted his eyes. "Other than I was in the shop, minding my own business, and some asshole zaps me and drags me outside and leaves me there."

"You see him? Get a look at him?"

"No, sir." Head down, boots swinging forward and back, reminding Walt of his girls on a swing set in the backyard.

Walt took a second to look around, specifically over at the back door of the shop where presumably Morgan Dodge had been dragged.

"You didn't see who did this to you?" Walt repeated.

"I said I didn't." Defensive, a little too adamant.

The boy's reaction fed Walt the way a biscuit rewarded Beatrice, who currently was sniffing Morgan's right ankle.

"Give us a minute," Walt told the paramedic.

Morgan's head came up, worry in his eyes.

Walt sat down beside him on the ambulance's bumper. He allowed a good deal of silence to settle between them, waiting to fill it.

"Let me guess," he finally said to Morgan, "it was beer."

Morgan looked over at him, puzzled. "What was beer?"

"No one dragged you anywhere, Morgan."

Another long silence, not strictly for effect. He wanted to give the boy a chance to rethink the situation.

Walt lowered his voice. "A girl? You have a girl here keeping you company? Afraid of what Bob might have to say about that?"

"No, sir, no girl. What do you mean, I wasn't dragged? Was too."

"Careful, son. It's dangerous territory, okay? I'm the sheriff. There are actually laws against lying to me. *Serious* laws. You can get yourself into some big trouble. So I'm going to start again and pretend your headache got the best of you and that you weren't yourself, okay? You understand?"

Walt dreaded the day he would need to have a similar conversation with one of his daughters. *"I'm your father. You don't lie to your father."* He wished his girls could stay young forever and not grow up only to make the same stupid mistakes everyone else makes. He missed his girls. The freedom that summer camp had promised turned out to be much harder on him than he'd imagined. The house was too quiet, and all he did was think about what they were doing. The not knowing drove him nuts.

"Look down there," Walt said. "Right there, in the dirt. What do you see?"

"Wood chips?" the boy asked.

"Don't ask me," Walt said, "tell me. What do you see?"

"Wood chips . . . sawdust . . . dirt . . ."

"Very good. Now, what about them?"

"I don't get it," the kid said.

"See how scuffed up things are? That's because this yard is about six inches deep in wood chips and sawdust. Everywhere you go, you disturb it. Like walking through a light snowfall or something."

"So?"

"So look over at the back door of the shop."

Morgan turned his head.

"You see any disturbance?"

"No," the boy said, a little too quickly.

Walt toed the ground in front of the ambulance's bumper, drawing a perfect line.

"If someone had been dragged out that door, son, we'd be able to see it."

Morgan did his best imitation of a bobblehead doll. "But I—"

"Don't worry about it," Walt said, "it's what I do. What you don't want to do is lie to me anymore. Don't try telling me why there're no lines in the dirt because I know why there're no lines in the dirt and so do you. No one needs to know anything about this, no one but me, understand? There's no public record here. You're not under oath, and I'm not taking notes. But you lie to me again and I'll punish you for it, son. The state of Idaho will punish you. Now, listen. You've got a heck of a year ahead of you. The first year of college is something special, believe me. You're working hard to make it happen. I respect that. Bob respects that. Don't screw it up."

The boy was breathing hard and fast. Walt thought he might start to cry.

"Not beer, not a girl . . . then, what?"

Morgan Dodge spoke so softly that Walt had to lean down to hear him. The boy's chin was flat against his chest.

"N . . . smok . . . in," he mumbled.

"Didn't catch that."

"No . . . smoking," he said deliberately. "It's a lumberyard."

There were NO SMOKING signs mounted everywhere.

"Bad for your health," Walt said.

"Tell me about it."

"Tobacco or something else?" Walt asked. "And remember, don't lie to me."

"A cigarette, yes. I'm not a hempie."

"And if you tell Bob . . ." Walt said, leaving it hanging there.

"I need this job."

"So you were outside."

His head bobbed, chin still close to the chest.

"And you saw someone," Walt said.

"A guy jumped the fence over there." He pointed without looking up.

"Dressed how?"

"Hard to see. It was dark, man. I don't

know. All black, maybe. He was dark, that's for sure."

"He see you? Or did you call out, or what?"

"You kidding me? I freakin' panicked. The cigarette and all. I'm like GI'ing the thing and trying to stamp out all the sparks and shit. I was so . . . stupid, GI'ing it right into the chips. I couldn't tell if it was smoke or dust, but the more I stamped, the more of it there was. I could see myself setting the place on fire and trying to explain it to Bob. And then there's, like, this noise behind me. I mean, this guy was one fast dude."

Or there were two of them, Walt was thinking.

"Coming up behind me like that. I turned. He had a balaclava over his head. Like a ski mask, you know?"

"I know what a balaclava is," Walt said. Inside, he was churning. This was sounding worse and worse. The Taser. The balaclava. A professional. Again.

"Guy does this Zorro move, and I'm, like, gone, fried. No idea what hit me. I woke up, lying there. No frickin' clue how long I'd been there. God . . ." He rubbed his eyes. Walt had been right: he'd been crying. "I mean, I'm not out here, I never would have known anyone was messing around. Probably could have gone right on with my work and nothing would have happened. There are houses behind here, right? Nice homes. I figured that's what he was after. Not this place. He was just cutting through, trying to rip off one of those houses. But, I swear to God, Bob hears this and I'm gone."

"Doesn't have to hear it from me."

"Seriously?"

"You get a look at his face?"

"Nah. Nothing. It was the balaclava, you know? It was just so out of place. That was all I saw. And then he nailed me. It nailed me, whatever *it* was . . ."

"They'll want to run some tests," Walt said. "Just procedure. Nothing to worry about."

"And the . . . you know . . ."

Bob was approaching.

Walt patted the kid on the thigh. "I've got what I need. How you deal with it, that's your choice. But you're asking the wrong guy if you want me to tell you to lie. Rule of thumb: it never helps anything. My call: it's better to man up and deal with reality. Lies tend to self-propagate. You know what that is?"

"Yeah, I got it."

Walt hopped off the ambulance and took a long look around the yard. The kid's theory about the houses down along the river was an interesting one, but he wasn't buying it. One of the Caterpillars? One of the two tractor trailers? He tried to see a use for the split wood or any of the hundreds of stacked, limbless trees. There were several splitters that ran off diesel-powered hydraulics. How did stealing wine involve hydraulics?

For the first time, there was a tingle at the back of his skull. What if it isn't about stealing wine?

Across the yard, he heard Bob blowing a gasket at the kid. Morgan caught Walt's eye from a distance, clearly blaming him for him being on the wrong end of a rant. Bob steamed off toward the office.

Beatrice came to a heel and sat down obediently, as if Bob was angry at her.

Walt was going to have to try to make things right.

24

Her father had returned from a massage, and the sound coming from his room of the shower running caught Summer in the gut. A stock-market update was running on the flat-screen television in his room, the female anchor talking about "puts and calls." For whatever reason, Summer thought about Enrico.

If she was going to do this, it had to be now, and just the thought of it flooded her with both excitement and dread. Despite being a moron and a loser, her father did his best. She was pretty sure he bent the rules and broke his word from time to time, but only because he was desperate to keep her happy. If it had just been him alone, he'd have bought a Barcalounger and surrendered himself to ESPN for the rest of his days. He sucked as a producer, but as a father he looked after her and cared about her, and would not approve in the least of what she was about to do.

Enrico, on the other hand, made her feel like she was already out of college.

She kept one eye on the suite's living room as she began repacking her suitcase. She left the closet open so that if he happened to come into the room, she could hide the suitcase, hide her intentions.

She was sweating despite the room's air-conditioning. Her head throbbed and her stomach felt squeamish. She'd never done anything like this. He would go ballistic. She had no idea what he'd do to her, but she knew it wouldn't be pretty.

She flashed back to the voice on the BlackBerry call she'd taken for her father. There was a name attached to that voice— a face, even—but she couldn't remember it exactly, couldn't make a name stick to the face. She shook off her wondering and

continued stuffing her delicates in the suitcase.

She trusted he was too consumed in
the wine auction and his deals to notice
any change in her, because she knew
she wasn't going to pull this off perfectly.
She didn't lie to him and he didn't lie to
her: this was an oath they'd made after
her mother died. They were in this together.
Only now she was deserting him. It made
her feel a little crazy in the head. He didn't
deserve what she was about to do to him,
no matter how much he tried to keep her
being a kid instead of allowing her to be
the woman she was.

Her hand hesitated, about to deliver a
T-shirt to the suitcase. She could have un-
done this before it ever got started. He
begged her all the time to talk, to tell him
what she was thinking. But she put the
shirt in the suitcase, continuing her packing.

There was no turning back now.

25

Walt heard the aspen leaves overhead, clattering like playing cards raking bicycle spokes. He watched Beatrice zooming around in the leaves on the ground, chasing phantoms and kicking up dust. This was where his heart was, he was reminded, away from town, away from his badge, on a walk with his dog in the backcountry. Gail's abrupt departure from the marriage had driven him deeply into his work. In an instant, here in the sweet-smelling air, with the wind whistling past his ears, he realized he'd used his work as a place to hide.

Leave it to Beatrice to reveal this truth to him.

Yellow police tape ran tree to tree, enclosing a thicket of golden willow. At the center were two camo-painted ATVs, the geometric shapes seen from the glider.

"So?" Fiona said, watching Brandon and the two deputies, Tuttle and Blompier, cut back the willows to make a path to the vehicles.

It was nice to see Brandon do some hard labor. Tuttle, on the other hand, worked like a maniac, going at the willow with lopping shears like a man possessed. Tuttle had spoken to a man peeing by the side of Deer Creek Road, a man now of interest to the investigation, and he was taking out his anger and frustration at having not written down the Yukon's plate number on the willow stalks.

"We want a record of the scene," Walt answered her, "including the boot print Tuttle found." He pointed. "Same for the tire tracks. Everything to scale."

"I was actually asking what you're hoping to get from this," she said, attempting to clarify.

Walt checked his wristwatch. The second hand seemed to be moving much faster than usual. "Evidence. Something to follow? The auction begins in a little over eight hours. Basically, I'm hoping for a miracle."

"You had them on the run. You think they wiped them down?" she said.

She'd been around his office enough that she was beginning to think like an investigator. He suppressed a smile.

"We'll find out," he said.

He pulled her aside as a car pulled up behind them.

Walt lacked a forensics team. On those rare occasions when he needed one, he'd call the Nampa crime lab. But when in a real hurry, he called Barge Levy, the principal of the valley's Silver Creek Alternative School. Levy held a master's in science from MIT, and he was something of an amateur lab technician, as close as Walt could get to a local forensics expert. Levy could perform basic tasks, such as fuming, dusting, and lifting prints, as well as the Nampa team.

Levy walked stiff-legged, the result of two hip replacements. He had salt-and-pepper hair and piercing blue eyes. He used his contagious, self-aware laugh to his advantage, a means to politely interrupt.

"What goes, boss?" Levy asked.

"Hate to take you away from summer vacation."

"No you don't." He let loose a laugh, startling some birds out of a nearby tree. "You want the rest of us to suffer right along with you."

"You two know each other . . . ?" he said, gesturing in Fiona's direction.

"Fiona's been kind enough to help us out on Professional Day at the school," Levy said. "And she works with some of our girls."

"I didn't know that," Walt admitted.

"You don't have to sound so surprised," Fiona said.

Levy let rip another of his laughs. Fiona knelt and rummaged in her bags, switching camera lenses.

"These may relate to an open investigation," Walt told him. "If they were wiped down, it was in a hurry. Fiona will record your work, if that's okay."

"No worries. But I've got to tell you, they're dust bombs," Levy said. "I doubt I'll be lifting any prints."

"Whatever you can do."

"Got it."

"Try the gas cap, and the valve caps to all four tires."

Levy nodded. "Nice. You must do this for a living." He barked out yet another laugh.

Walt said, "Before you start, I've got a riddle for you."

"Riddle-iculous," Levy said.

"Let's say I've got a group trying to boost a couple of bottles from the wine auction."

"Okay."

"And I suspect one or more of them pulled a B and E at Sawtooth Wood Products last night."

Levy cocked his head curiously. "Yeah?"

"The lumberyard has a couple of tractor trailers, some Cats of various sizes. A pair of wood splitters, both hydraulic. Some John Deere lawn mowers, some chainsaws. A few hundred logs, and mountains of slash and piles of split firewood."

"Okay."

"They've got a hell of a shop to maintain all that gear—maybe the best shop in the valley." He paused, allowing Levy to take it all in. "How does any of that fit into a plan to steal a couple bottles of wine?"

Levy pinched his chin. "Where are these bottles now?"

"In a vault, a bank safe."

"Hydraulics might help open a vault. A Cat could take out a wall."

"True enough. But the bottles are more vulnerable once they're at the auction, right?"

"And if they're pros, they know that's just the way you'd think."

"Okay," Walt said, "I can buy that."

"House plans," Fiona said. "That company has built some of the premiere houses in the valley. We did a profile of them in the *Express.* They must have plans on file for some of the biggest."

"Brilliant!" Walt said. "I hadn't considered that."

"Maybe they need some lumber to build themselves a Trojan horse," Levy teased, chuckling to himself.

Once again, Walt thought back to fly-fishing with Kevin, his attempt to match the hatch. "A Trojan horse," he muttered.

26

Listen, Sheriff, my bikini's a lot more revealing than this bra is," said Janet Finch, "so don't feel you're embarrassing me. Please, stay, so we can talk this through."

She pulled off her T-shirt, her back to Walt, while Deputy Sheriff Wilma Karl pinned a tiny Bluetooth microphone inside the bra cup, ran a wire along the right strap and over the collarbone to a small credit-card-sized transmitter taped to the skin beneath the bra's hooks at the back.

On the table lay a mobile phone to take the place of Finch's. Whether on or off, the Motorola CABO would transmit whatever the microphone picked up, enhanced by a Bluedriving kit, with an extended range of nearly two hundred yards. Even if Finch's phone were taken from her, switched off, and placed in a room at the other end of the house, Walt's guys in the MC would still be able to eavesdrop on her conversation with Remy.

At her request, Walt stayed in the room. It had been a while since he'd seen a woman's bare back, and Janet Finch's was taut and smooth-skinned. He suffered the physical tug of being male, the emotional whiplash of a betrayed husband, and the self-righteousness of always wanting to remain professional. He felt a little sick, in fact.

"Why would Remy suddenly agree to see me?" she asked.

"He's protecting his investment, I imagine. Doesn't want a repeat of last night, your barging in on the tasting. He's hedging his bets."

"But not to hurt me?"

"I can't see that, no," Walt said. "He's a guest in that house. And if he tries anything, we'll hear what's going on, anyway, so not to worry."

"Easy for you to say."

"It was you who called me, not the other way around."

"Because he called me! Okay, so I'm curious. I want to do this," she said. "I admit it."

"You're nervous. That's good. If you weren't, I'd be worried."

With the deputy's help, Finch pulled the T-shirt back on.

Deputy Karl asked Finch to speak, to test the equipment, which Finch then did.

"All set, Sheriff," Karl said.

Walt thanked Karl and dismissed her.

"If you can get him on the defensive," Walt said to Finch, reminding her of what they'd discussed only minutes earlier.

"Yeah, I know: trip him up."

"No, actually, I wouldn't go there. He invited you. You're not going to plant any land mines that he isn't prepared for, that he hasn't seen coming. But if you engage him intellectually, you might get an emotional reaction. You might get him off his game."

"I'm listening . . ."

"We use these same techniques in interrogation. The idea is to get the subject in his own comfort zone, whatever that is. Then engage him on his own terms, not yours. Speak his language. Act as if you're his guest, not the other way around. If he has a one-syllable vocabulary, keep with one syllable. Pull him out slowly and then challenge him, again on his terms. Don't back him into a corner until you've led him out into the middle of the room. It's an outgrowth of differential reinforcement. People allowed to win early will later defend their positions. People challenged from the start will shut down. The catch is, it requires you to forfeit your own ego. It's tricky stuff, but I promise you it works."

"Which means I do what?" she asked.

"Basically, let him do the talking as much as possible. Be aware that he may try the same techniques on you. One thing I wouldn't do is state anything as fact. Questions are fine. Statements tend to backfire, and, in your case, may shut him down."

"But I know what I'm talking about!" she protested.

"That's exactly what you have to leave behind: that attitude. Someone may have been stalking you, maybe or maybe not related to Remy, but, from where I stand, it only makes sense. He may have wanted to scare you out of the valley. When that didn't happen, he moved on to plan B, fraternizing with the enemy, dismissing your claims. If nothing else, by questioning you he finds out how to be prepared for you. He knows he has to come up with acceptable answers in case you try to crash the auction like you crashed the tasting. He's playing you. If the bottles are forgeries—"

"They are!"

"Then he's fooled a lot of people already. As you said, that means he's already got a lot of time and money invested in this. So a lot is riding on the outcome, including his reputation. And you are the Antichrist."

"If this was supposed to be a pep talk . . ."

"It wasn't," he said.

"And if he does try something . . ."

"He won't. If he does, we're two to three minutes away, tops." Walt scooped up the CABO phone and handed it to her. "We're recording everything. Go in and get what you can."

Janet Finch stood at the front door of the Christensens' house on Aspen Drive, the doorbell chiming, her heart in her throat. She took a deep breath to settle herself. It didn't work.

Remy answered the door, his übercool glasses and stubble haircut, silk pants and linen shirt lending him a moneyed look.

"Ms. Finch." He stepped aside, admitting her.

She entered the home, admiring the furnishings, including the piano in the living room. He pointed to a couch. She was swallowed by it. Remy took a sturdier armchair to her left. She found him intimidating.

"I would like to think you've come here of your own accord, Ms. Finch—what a lovely name, incidentally: a practical and decorative bird, the finch—that your thoughts are your own. Because I fear it is more likely that your so-called research is really an effort on someone else's part to devalue or invalidate my historic find, either out of penurious underhandedness or scholarly jealousy."

He had taken the high ground, attempting to drive her back on her heels.

She resisted the urge to defend herself.

"I appreciate your time, Mr. Remy. I'm delighted you called."

"You are aware of the due diligence a find like this is put through?" he said. "The rigors of research and testing involved in verification? I remind you: these bottles were discovered nearly eleven months ago, shortly after the Jeffersons, and have been undergoing authentication and verification ever since. The best experts have examined, reviewed, and analyzed this find, and yet you, a graduate student who originally majored in animal husbandry, believe the experts got it all wrong. Don't you find that the slightest bit presumptuous?"

She took a deep breath. "I may have given you the wrong impression, Mr. Remy. Yes, I have some questions for you, it's true. And, yes, they are of a scholarly bent and for my doctoral thesis. I did not, do not, expect to be compared in the same breath with such experts as Shilling, Partuuk, and Hamlin. I was hoping, however presumptuous it may be of me, to help you, not to challenge you; to prevent you from making what I believe would be a horrible mistake and thereby safeguard your incredible reputation . . . a mistake that would be bad not only for you but for our industry."

He studied her, squinting suspiciously through his thick glasses. She felt violated, and crossed her arms high on her chest.

"That would presume I give your claims any credence," he said.

"Indeed."

"And I assure you, I do not. We have documentation and certification confirming the authenticity of this find. What is more problematic is the damage your dogged determination to prove me wrong can inflict on the auction price. If you are trying to make a name for yourself, Ms. Finch, you may want to rethink your strategy. I promise you, it's not my reputation that's going to suffer if you persist, it's yours."

Again, she fought the urge to do battle with him. "Ha! I see you figured me out," she said sarcastically. "How clever you are, Mr. Remy." She stood up from the couch. "Believe it or not, I didn't come here to entertain you. If at some point you're interested in keeping yourself out of the tabloids and maybe out of jail, you might study microfractures, especially as they pertain to glass of a wood-ash composition. You have my number."

He came out of the chair with a remarkable agility, a catlike quickness that surprised her. He had her by the upper arm, his strength considerable. "I've insulted you," he said. "How foolish of me."

"You are a legend, sir. A broker that has put his name in the history books multiple times. You must have plenty of money. So I just don't see the point of this . . . charade. You may believe me out of my element, and you're entitled to your opinion, but in fact this is my element. I am a student of the very experts you've used in your verification. My interest is to complete the research necessary to finish writing my thesis."

"Microfractures?" he said.

"Glass is a supercooled liquid," she said. "As a result, there is no order to the molecules. They've been caught in a state between liquid and solid, and won't achieve a solid state for aeons. Because of this random distribution of molecules, glass, when it is cut with an engraving tool or

ground with a grinder, produces microfractures aligning away from the tool or
grinder. Modern engraving is done with
diamond tips spinning at phenomenal
speeds, far faster than the tools of two
centuries ago. Today's tools produce microfractures aligning *into* the glass, not
away from the tool.

"Dr. Weisling was not stabbed to death
by a madman. He was stabbed to death
because his microfracture research un-
covered your bottles as fakes. Either you
knew that going in or it was too late to stop
what you'd started, but either way your
reputation is on the line."

Remy's eyes had grown even bigger
behind the distortion of his glasses.

"What . . . do . . . you . . . want?"

She hesitated. "You won't believe me."

"Try me."

"To prove that Jefferson inventoried every bottle, damn-near every glass from his
cellar, and that these Adams bottles were
never a part of it. In short: the truth."

"You're right, I don't believe you. Is it
money?"

"I want you to withdraw the Adams lot

from the auction," she said. "I want access—full access—to the bottles for further analysis. I want a thorough description—which you have yet to give—of exactly where and under what circumstances you discovered the bottles. And I want any documents that show any mention of these bottles as having been in the possession of Jefferson, John Adams, or John Quincy Adams, as I've been unable to verify the existence of any such gift between the families."

"That's all?" he said sarcastically, gasping as he ran a hand through his hair stubble. "Jesus! You . . . are . . . a . . . piece . . . of . . . work."

"What did you mean by money?"

"What do you think I meant?"

"I think you were offering me a bribe."

"Nonsense. I was suggesting you *wanted* a bribe. That's a far different thing."

"I have to wonder about the attempt to steal the bottles," she said, finally finding her way into the line of discussion the sheriff was hoping for.

"That was a horrible thing. A man died."

"A man—a good man—was killed in

Amsterdam as well. These bottles have blood on them."

"If you're accusing me of something, just say it."

"Very well . . ."

She studied him for a minute. She wanted to make him wait.

"Dr. Weisling's murder put you in a bind. You expected someone like me would show up. You're smart enough to know that would happen. Sun Valley was already arranged. If you could have withdrawn the lot, I believe you would have. But that would only focus more attention on Dr. Weisling's tragedy. However, if the bottles never made it to the auction, having been authenticated and properly insured . . ."

"If only I was so smart as all that . . . since you have me as a murderer and a crook already . . ."

"If not you, then who? An investor? Someone put you up to the Adams bottles? Brought you the idea? Forced it on you maybe? It's no time to be defending someone like that. Unless you plan on killing me too?"

"I had nothing to do with the attempted theft," he said. "Would I have profited? I suppose so. The bottles are well insured, it's true. Do I plan on killing you? Why would I invite you to this meeting if that were the case?"

"To find out just how serious a threat I am."

He winced and pursed his lips. "You are a graduate student, my dear. The bottles were vetted and authenticated. You value yourself a little too highly, I'm afraid. How should I know who killed Weisling, if it's as you say? I don't believe a word of it."

"Then you have nothing to worry about," she said.

"The reserve on this lot is seven hundred and fifty thousand dollars. I have plenty to worry about. If you cost me that reserve, I'll sue you so that any paycheck you earn for the rest of your life goes to me. I'd consider that, if I were you."

"No you wouldn't," she said. "Not if you were me. I studied under Weisling. I worshipped that man."

He laughed. "God, you are impossible."

"Now you're catching on," she said. "Think it through: whoever buys these bottles is going to have them vetted by their own people, and you can be sure I will

make myself a part of that process. Microfractures, Mr. Remy, it will all come down
to microfractures. What you want to be doing is getting yourself out in front of this
thing, ahead of it. If it wasn't you behind
Dr. Weisling's death, then you know who
was. Speak up. Say something. Save yourself while there's time."

His eyes danced behind the magnifica-
tion.

"So dramatic," he whispered harshly.
"Perhaps you missed your calling."

"Don't bet on it."

She left, hoping she could find her way
back to the front door. She began roaming
from room to room.

"'Before God, we are all equally wise,'"
he called out, "'and equally foolish.'"

"Albert Einstein," she said, turning.

She'd knocked the wind out of him.

"Microfractures," she said, pulling the
door shut behind herself.

27

Walt sat at his desk, looking at printouts of three e-mails, each a criminal record, while Tommy Brandon tried to look comfortable in the small room's only other chair. His six-foot-four frame made the chair look like something from *Alice in Wonderland.*

"You don't see a sheet like Matthew Salvo anymore," Walt said. "A second-story man, is what they used to call a guy like this."

"I guess he's an ATV man now," Brandon said.

"He's a bridesmaid," Walt said. "All his arrests are as an accomplice. No assaults.

Two charges of statutory, both pled out, so he obviously likes them young. Nothing else here to get him more than medium time and a pair of reduced sentences. He's Matt Damon in those *Ocean's* movies."

"So, who's George Clooney?" Brandon asked.

Walt wanted to say: "You are." Because Brandon was undeniably handsome. He had piercing dark eyes, a strong chin, and perfect teeth. It was hard for Walt to look at him and not imagine Gail straddling him. There was nothing to break Walt's spell, the grim porn movie running through his mind involving his soon-to-be ex-wife and his deputy.

"I doubt it's this guy," Walt said, tapping Roger McGuiness's face. "He's the wheel man. We can bet he drove the wrecker. One arrest, six years ago, no time served. He's kept himself clean, which I imagine appealed to Clooney."

"We issue a BOLO?" Brandon said. *Be on lookout.*

"Yes, for both. Ketchum and Sun Valley PDs need this. Ask them to walk these sheets around to the bars and hotels and property managers. Where do young girls hang out? The pool at the Y? Tennis courts? I'd put those on the list too. Let's hope Matthew Salvo has been trolling during his free time."

"Got it." Brandon stood.

"Tommy," Walt said, stopping him halfway to the door.

"Yeah?"

"The girls come home Monday."

"Yeah." It wasn't exactly an *I couldn't care less,* but it was close enough that Walt felt a stab in his chest. Brandon would never care about his kids the way he did.

"It's been two weeks, the longest they've ever been away. I was thinking, it might be nice if Gail and I took them out to dinner. You know, just her and me. What do you think?"

"I think you're asking the wrong person."

"But you're okay with it," Walt said.

"What are you asking?"

Walt hesitated. "You think she'd be good with it?"

Brandon crossed his arms tightly. "Listen, Sheriff . . ."

"We sign the papers next week."

"Yeah," he said softly. "I imagine that sucks."

Walt realized he should have kept his mouth shut. What was he doing talking to Brandon about any of this?

Neither man spoke. Walt's silence was the result of countless sleepless nights spent on the couch or in one of the girls' empty beds, anywhere but in the bed he and Gail had once shared. He silently suffered such heartache and physical pain that he'd sought a doctor's opinion, not just once but several times, only to be told it was all in his head. Walt's silence was the silence of defeat, regret, shame, and disgust.

"Well, hey, I ought to notify Ketchum and Sun Valley." Brandon was blocking the doorway.

"Yeah," Walt said, "go."

28

Arthur Remy stepped out of the shower and reached for the monogrammed towel. The initials on it belonged to his hosts, currently hiking a trail on the ski mountain.

His hand swiped the air where the towel should have been.

"Jesus!" he barked, his voice ringing off the imported Spanish tile. He quickly covered his groin.

"What were you thinking?" the man asked.

"What the hell are you talking about?"

"Talking to the police, initiating inquiries within Branson Risk."

"Oh, Christ!"

"Did it not occur to you we would be keeping an eye on our investment? That we would be watching you? Did it not occur to you that if you started turning over rocks, something vile would come out from underneath?" He indicated himself. "Voilà!"

"The sheriff came to me, not the other way around."

"And this theft? An attempt at insurance money?"

"That wasn't me."

"Lying won't help you, believe me."

"It wasn't me!"

"Insurance adjusters . . . is there a lower life-form? Like a dog with a bone. You get them involved . . . And now, thanks to you, they *are* involved. What if they decide to look at this more carefully?"

"You're jumping to conclusions. I had nothing to do with attempting to steal the bottles."

"That's what I was told you would say. I said you weren't that stupid, that you could be reasoned with."

"It was someone else . . . a third party . . . has to be . . ."

"It was very, very stupid."

"IT WAS NOT ME!"

"I've already told you, it wasn't us. You panicked. You were afraid that after what happened in Amsterdam . . . that a closer look . . . that the insurance would cover it. It was a decent plan, had it worked. You should have come to us. But look where you are now." He passed Remy the towel. "Look where it leaves you . . . where it leaves us."

Remy wiped the shower water from his eyes and then wrapped his waist. "Let's just calm down, okay?"

"I am perfectly calm. This is me being calm."

"It's a misunderstanding," Remy said, "a fuckup."

"*Your* fuckup."

"No . . . no . . . no . . ."

"Let me explain." The man stepped closer. "We have two concerns. The first is that you might try to flee, to shirk your responsibilities."

"No! That won't happen."

"The second," he said, "is that you understand the degree to which you've *fucked this up*." He placed his hands on

Remy's shoulders, his arms locked. "The bottles will be sold, our investment re-couped. End of story."

He kicked Remy's left knee, snapping it as loudly as a tree branch breaking. Remy screamed and fell back into the shower.

"More people break a leg or a hip in the bathtub than on ski slopes," the man said. "Did you know that?" He picked up the fallen towel and tossed it onto the writhing man. "No more reminders. Next time . . . if there is a next time . . . You don't want a next time."

29

The persistent squeak of the room-service cart's errant wheel created a counterpoint rhythm to the whoosh of Kevin's rubber soles on the hotel hallway's carpet. A good-looking woman in her thirties, with wet hair and pool water clinging to her tan skin like pearls, strode toward him in a tiny bikini.

"Down, boy," came a girl's voice over Kevin's shoulder. He slowed the cart. The woman passed by, offering him a sideways glance that told him she'd caught him staring and that she enjoyed the attention.

"Get a room, why don't you?" Summer said.

"What's up?" he said, trying to act casual.

"I have an answer to that, but it's too dirty to say in a hotel hallway. Dude, she's ancient. Give it a rest."

Kevin pushed the trolley forward. "I've got to deliver this," he said.

"We're still on for tonight?" she asked, walking side by side with him. She showed him the key to the jet. "Fifteen minutes. Right?"

"I'm off at seven," he confirmed. "But I owe a friend big-time."

"Where do we meet? I'll have a bag with me and don't want to drag it all over the place."

"A bag? What's with that?"

"It's just clothes and stuff. No big deal."

"I don't know about this," he said.

"Are you kidding? I am, like, totally looking forward to this," she said. "It is so boring here. You don't even know how much fun you're going to have. You thought the hot springs were fun?" She took a step closer. "You don't have a clue, do you?" she said in a raspy voice. She'd seen her mother tease her father this same way.

"Yeah?"

"I told you, you can sit up front," she reminded. "It'll be so awesome."

He glanced over at her, and she offered him as much reassurance as she could muster.

"Yeah, I guess."

She relaxed. "Awesome. So where do you want to pick me up?"

They made arrangements to meet in back of the hotel a few minutes past seven.

Her plan saved, her face brightened. She kissed him on the cheek, the same way her mother would her dad when she got her way. Kevin flushed and looked away.

"You're running away, aren't you?" he said, speaking down to the cart.

Her brain seized.

"What happens to me when it turns out I'm the one who drove you, huh? Have you even thought about that? I'll bet you have. And I'll bet you don't give a crap, do you, because you'll be long gone?"

"I'm eighteen, Kevin. I can do what I want."

"Nice try," he said. "I'm the one who's eighteen. I'm the one gets in trouble for this."

"I thought we were going to party in the jet? I promise, that's happening. The flight I'm on is the last one out, at ten o'clock. You think I could get on a plane by myself if I wasn't eighteen?"

"Maybe with a fake ID you could."

"You've been hanging around your uncle too long, dude. This is not *Without a Trace,* you know?"

Kevin looked at her, remembering the hot springs.

"You never drove me down there, okay? All we're going to do is hang in the jet until my flight, and if anyone ever asks I'll say I took the shuttle bus, I promise."

"So, then, why don't you take the shuttle bus?" he asked.

"I thought we were friends," she said, pouting and disappointed. "I thought we were going to party."

Kevin slowed the cart and stopped in front of a room door.

"I've got to do this," he said.

"Come on." She pressed against him. "Please, Kevin . . . seven-ten, at the circle out back," she said, confirming their plans. She hurried off before he had a chance to answer.

30

The door to the Incident Command Center in the Blaine County Sheriff's Office was closed, a MEETING IN PROGRESS sign on the wall alongside.

Walt addressed Barge Levy, as Fiona took pictures of Janet Finch's inspection of the Adams bottles.

"One thing you didn't explain, Sheriff," Finch said, never taking her attention off the bottles, "is how you talked Arthur Remy into allowing this."

"Who said I did?"

"You have the access card. You opened the case."

"True. And true."

"Go ahead, be that way," Finch said.

"Every once in a great while, blind luck plays a hand in an investigation."

"You *stole* it from him?"

"Remy showed up at the emergency room earlier," Walt said. "Slipped and broke his knee, he claimed. I was contacted because the on-call orthopedist and his radiologist judged the fracture to be blunt-force trauma—a baseball bat, maybe a martial-arts kick, to the knee. We ask them to report that kind of difference of opinion, primarily to head off domestic violence against women."

"And?"

"He left his pants."

"Excuse me?" Finch said.

"Remy left his pants in the emergency room. Was driven home in a pair of hospital scrubs. One too many painkillers, and he spaced out and forgot his pants. The pants, and their contents, were turned over to me. I'm required to do an inventory, and, as it happens, the card was in his pocket. I'd seen it before. This office has every intention of returning Mr. Remy's belongings. We have been in communication with him, and it was agreed I would pass along his things when I see him tonight at the auction."

"Holy shit! Did he ask about the card?"

"Not a word. I'm sure he didn't want to attract my attention to it."

"Who says there's no God?" Finch said.

"Other than the photographs, we can document the test results, right?" Walt said.

"Of course," Levy said, still making adjustments on what appeared to be some complicated electronics.

"I'd rather have a spectrometer," Finch said. Wearing cotton gloves, she viewed the labels with a loupe, and, as she did, she made noises like she was in the throes of really good sex.

"Trust me," Levy said, "the piezoelectric effect is just as conclusive. We can measure density, size, clamped capacitance, and low-field dissipation."

"English?" Walt said.

"She can determine the pattern of any microfractures," Levy said. "Listen, we wouldn't have this gear if I didn't know what I was doing. It was donated by the father of one of our students after we found those pottery shards out at Muldoon. Remember? The mine cave-in? The piezo-electric effect was the cheapest way to determine if it was authentically Native American without sending the shards out to a lab, which would have cost aplenty." He laughed one of his laughs. "Turned out they were common gardening pots. But, hey, I got the equipment donated, so who's complaining?"

"The results will have to be verified," Finch reminded. "No offense, but they're not going to take the word of a grad student and a school principal."

"Alternative-school principal," Levy corrected. "And I taught science for twelve years. And graduated from MIT, don't forget."

Finch didn't comment.

"Do you know someone?" Walt asked.

"I can ask one of my professors to examine the data we collect," Finch said. "There will definitely be someone on campus who can do this."

"But not before the auction?"

"Doubtful," Finch said, "it being a weekend and all. But, who knows? These bottles are famous. I can think of a couple people who would jump at a chance to examine them."

"I can try Lowry, at MIT," Levy said, "there's always a chance . . ."

"Dr. Lowry would do it," Finch told Walt. "If he signed off on this, no one would dispute it." She flattered Walt with a look. "Thank you for doing this."

"Don't mistake this as benevolence," Walt said. "Those bottles are evidence in a homicide. If they're fakes, that impacts the investigation. It's something I need to know."

"I would *so* love to see you bust Arthur Remy," Finch said.

"That's not how it works," Walt said. "But if Remy is pawning off fakes . . ." He didn't finish the thought.

"We're ready," Levy said.

He ran nearly the exact same test five times. The glass near the engraving was exposed to ultrahigh sound frequencies that were then measured from different places on the bottles. A laptop computer crunched the data, displaying it as a color-coded graph that Levy studied and then saved before repeating the test.

At the conclusion of the tests, Levy

looked up from the laptop, wearing a grave expression. "The microfractures are random," he said.

"I knew it!" Janet Finch looked as if she'd won the lottery.

"That's good?" Walt asked Levy.

"They're fakes," said Finch, smiling widely.

31

As Summer heard the television switch off, she braced herself for the confrontation. Like a heavyweight fighter before the bout, she lowered her head, closed her eyes, and visualized her opponent's weaknesses, his soft spots, knowing all along that he had the weight advantage.

First, she wanted to see if he would remember that he'd invited her. Supposedly, she was to be his date at the wine-auction dinner, but he tended to forget his offers to her, especially if a better offer came along.

If he did remember, then she intended to incite his anger, exploit his sense of social punctuality with her wet hair and the towel wrapped around her. Seeing her like this he would make impossible demands she couldn't meet and would then desert her, telling her to catch up—and that was all she needed.

"Summer, are you ready?" he eventually bellowed from the other side of her door. "We don't want to be late."

She drew a deep breath and strode into the living room just in the towel, knowing how uncomfortable it would make him. He could barely look at her at the pool. Perhaps he saw her mother in her, or maybe he couldn't face his daughter as a grown woman, but whatever it was it momentarily gave her the upper hand.

"I'm running a teensy bit behind."

His face registered horror.

"Sorry. Is twenty minutes okay?"

"Twenty minutes? NO! That's not okay. I told you ten of seven. It's already five 'til."

"Hey, I don't get all dressed up that often," she said, changing to a tone of voice she knew he didn't care for. "Besides, I thought it starts out as a cocktail party, right? So, what's the big deal? We can be late."

"We cannot be late! Cocktail hour's more important to me than the auction." He drew a deep breath—a bad sign; he was struggling for patience. "You're important to me. I wanted to show you off." He sounded so hurt, she loved him for it. "Once we're sitting down at dinner, we're stuck with whoever we're stuck with. But at the cocktail party . . ."

"Please, go ahead," she said. "I'll hurry."

"I'll wait."

"NO!" she barked out too loudly and too quickly.

His parental radar switched on, and she chastised herself for the outburst. He could read her far better than she was willing to admit, and he cared more about her than she let herself believe. His look conveyed all of this, and the guilt it caused her ran up her spine in an icy shiver.

"You're trying to put together a deal," she said, "right?"

"I'm always trying to put a deal together, sweetheart."

He sounded defeated. She resisted feeling any sympathy for him. He had denied her the opportunity of watching Enrico in the semifinals. He had made her come to

Sun Valley with him instead. He'd made her play tennis with him in the mixed doubles, had humiliated her with his poor playing. He deserved what she was about to do to him.

"You go on," she said. "I'm not real big on cocktail parties, anyway. I mean, what's the point?"

"I'm sorry if this trip hasn't lived up to its billing," he said. "I really thought you'd have a better time than you've had."

"I'm okay."

"No. I should have had you bring a friend or something. I wasn't thinking right."

"I'm fine, Dad." The guilt now traveled to her throat, where it balled up in an unforgiving knot. She was not going to change her mind about this. She was not going to cry.

"Fact is, things are not going real well moneywise. I think you know that. I think you know I'm going through a rough patch. Times like this, I know we both miss her. Miss her a lot more than we talk about—"

"Don't."

"We should talk more, you know? Figure this stuff out together."

"Dad . . ."

"We've only got each other, you know? None of the rest of it matters to me, Sum. I know you probably don't believe that, but it's true. You're it. You're all I've got. The meetings, the deals . . . they're just a means to an end, a way to keep us going, keep you going, give you the best shot I can give you. Your pal, the tennis guy . . . Eric—"

"Enrico!"

"He was not the way to go. He . . . you know what that's all about. You know what he wants from you. And it's not happiness. It's not safety and security. It has nothing to do with any of that. My job, whether you like it or not, is to help you make the right decisions. Not run your life. That's not what I'm talking about. Just to make decisions with a clear head and your eyes wide open. That's all. That was not the case here. You can be mad at me, that's okay. Pissed-off? Absolutely. But please know that, in my heart of hearts, I have your best interests first. Not mine, yours."

"Violins, Dad."

"Yeah, okay. So get dressed."

"I'll meet you there."

"If you aren't there in ten minutes, I'm

sending the Texas Rangers after you. I don't want to do this dinner alone. I need you, okay? We're a team tonight."

"*O-kay.*" Her voice cracked, and she looked to the carpet. "I'll hurry," she choked out.

She pushed the door shut behind her, then held her back to it, as if blocking out all that she'd just heard.

Why tonight? Of all nights, why tonight?

Teddy Sumner's antennae were sparking. He knew she was up to something secretive. Either it was something she was doing for him, or against him, and, given the past two weeks, he was betting on the latter.

He left the suite and headed directly to the concierge in the lobby, a blond-haired woman in her late forties, with an agreeable face. He kept his voice low.

"Your house detective, as quickly as possible."

"Of course, sir. If you'd like to have a seat." She indicated a wing chair with Queen Anne legs.

"I don't need a seat, I need your house

detective. Right now!" He could be a real bastard when he needed to. This was one of those times.

She pulled a walkie-talkie from a drawer. "Chuck," she called into it.

Sumner spent the next five minutes watching the door to the patio swing open and shut. The bar on the terrace was active, and dinner was already under way for the Saturday-night show on the outdoor ice rink. But all he saw was the world moving on without him.

The concierge caught him looking. "Scott Hamilton's All-Stars," she said, "best ice show of the summer. Would you like tickets?"

"No thank you," he said, "just the house detective." He didn't want to make conversation. He checked his watch instead.

Chuck Webb filled out his navy blue sport coat to the point where it wouldn't button. He had an agreeable face but a drinking man's complexion.

Teddy Sumner passed him a hundred-dollar bill as the two shook hands. Webb gripped the bill but didn't pocket it.

"There's no need for that." He pretended

to hand it back, immediately cut short by Sumner's raised hand.

"I have a seventeen-year-old daughter who thinks she's twenty-six. She's up in the suite, three twenty-seven. I wish I could say I trust her but I don't. You have kids?"

"Two boys. A little younger than yours. We use an outfit called Super Sitters. The hotel, I'm talking about. Good people. Patricia can arrange it." He looked back toward the concierge desk, a yard or two away.

"She's supposed to join me at the wine auction," Sumner said. "I'm betting otherwise. I need someone to keep an eye on her. If she leaves the room, I'd like to know about it. And if she doesn't head over to the dinner, I need to know about that too." He pursed his lips. "How about it?"

"I'm spread a little thin tonight," Webb said. "I wish I could help out but—"

"You got cameras? If she doesn't leave the room in the next fifteen minutes, I need to know. And if she does, then maybe you or one of your guys could just keep an eye on her long enough to make sure she's headed to the dinner. Please?"

He fished for another bill but Webb stopped him.

"Room three twenty-seven," Webb said. His left hand slid in his pant pocket and came back out empty.

"I appreciate it," Sumner said.

"I'll need a cell number."

32

The Cherokee took the final turn, pulling past the golf shop and up to the entrance to the inn, where Walt stopped to collect himself.

The tent, set to seat six hundred for dinner, glowed like a giant white lightbulb fifty yards ahead of him. He viewed that distance as a gulf, an open and exposed area where he was a target.

The bottles were fakes. Remy's best bet was to have them stolen prior to the auction and collect the insurance. Salvo and McGuiness were part of the team hired to steal them, Walt felt certain. But proving intent was impossible.

"You want to run that by me again?" Brandon said.

"Taking the lead guy into custody is more important than the bottles at this point."

Brandon snorted. "Whatever you say, Sheriff."

"I know that doesn't feel right," Walt said, "but the only way to link this back to Remy is to have George Clooney in custody. Arresting Salvo or McGuiness may not do it, but it would be a start. They probably don't even know who Remy is, and it's Remy we want."

"But I don't know how to be incompetent," Brandon complained. "There's no way these guys get these bottles."

"We've got to make it look convincing. If they take the bottles, the bee will return to the hive."

Walt had replaced the GPS device belonging to Branson Risk with his own. Branson's was in the back of the Cherokee. The MC was tracking Walt's, and he hoped to follow it to whoever was running the heist.

If there actually is a heist.

He waited for word from the MC that they had a good signal on the GPS. He was still trying to fit together the connection with the kid getting Tasered at the lumberyard in Bellevue. He couldn't make sense of it but somehow believed it was connected to the heist.

"Here comes trouble," Brandon said.

"Not now," Walt said, spotting Gail storming toward the Cherokee. He knew that stride of hers, knew that look on her face. Was it for him or Brandon? He hoped like hell he hadn't got the date wrong for the girls' coming home.

"This is for me," Brandon said.

"Well, send her packing. We don't have time for this."

Walt felt relieved. But he also understood the power Gail still wielded. How was that possible? How had he allowed such a thing to happen? For all his strengths, this woman's reach was suddenly his glaring weakness. It just leaped out at him.

"You hear me?" Walt said.

"I get it, Sheriff," Brandon snapped. His hand rested on the door handle, but he had not opened it.

Over the radio, the MC dispatcher said, "All set."

Walt tripped the handset. "Roger that."

"We're rolling," he said to Brandon. Gail was five feet from the car.

"Yes we are," Brandon said.

Walt drove ahead. They both watched Gail in the rearview mirror as she threw her hands in the air and followed.

"I need you, Tommy. Don't get caught up in this."

"Ten-four," Brandon replied hotly, his eyes never leaving the mirror.

Walt's cell phone rang. The caller ID read CHUCK WEBB.

"I've got to take this," Walt said, slowing the Cherokee to a stop, still a few yards from their destination alongside the tent.

"Shit!" Brandon snapped. He popped his door and climbed out. "Give me a second. I'll handle this."

Walt power-locked the car doors behind Brandon and answered the call, his eyes lighting on a dozen different locations. He felt absurdly vulnerable. The wine case, strapped in the backseat, suddenly felt like a bomb.

"Chuck?" Walt said into the phone.

"Listen, I know we've both got enough on our plates, but I've got a situation here."

"Can it wait?"

"I don't think so."

"Okay."

"It's Kevin," Webb said. "We've got a seventeen-year-old female guest who just left the hotel premises carrying a suitcase. She was picked up by Kevin, Walt. *Your* Kevin. His car, out back by the circle. Reason I know this is the girl's father is over at the auction. He asked me to keep an eye on her. Considered her a flight risk. And now she's flown. She's a minor, pal, and that puts Kevin smack in the middle of aiding and abetting. And, beyond that, statutory—if you catch my drift. And this is one hot babe, so I doubt I'm really that far off."

Blood pulsed so loudly in Walt's ear, he switched the phone to the other side, thinking it might help. It didn't. He could hardly hear.

Once again, he glanced at the attaché in the backseat.

"You there?" Webb asked.

"Yeah," Walt answered.

Kevin would be nineteen in a few weeks.

That was how the courts would see it. Webb was basically right.

"He drove off our property, or I'd offer to help," Webb said.

"You have helped, Chuck, big-time. Thanks. I'll get back to you."

Walt ended the call. He caught sight of Brandon. Gail was tearing into him, one of her rants that could peel paint off the walls. Four of his deputies had formed a gauntlet into the tent.

He speed-dialed a number on his mobile phone. He waited. There was no answer.

He speed-dialed a second number, and was boiling mad by the time Myra answered.

"Myra? Goddamn it, Myra!"

"Walt, what is it?"

"What do you think it is, Myra? It's Kevin. Again. He's not answering his phone, and I need to speak to him."

"Because . . . ?"

"Because he has an underage girl in his car. Underage and carrying a suitcase, Myra. The girl's father thinks she might be running away, and that puts Kevin square into the middle of it . . . as in, a felony count. Do I have your attention yet?"

"I'll call—"

"He's not answering," Walt said, "which makes me all the more sick to my stomach. Did you do as I asked? His phone service? Did you do that, Myra?"

"That location thing?"

"Yes, the Web tracking," Walt said. "The GPS . . . did you sign up for that?"

"I signed up, but I've never used it," she said. "It seemed kind of like . . . spying, or something."

"I need you to go on the Web and find him, Myra, now. Right now."

Tonight, of all nights, he thought. Kevin had a knack for bad timing.

"I don't have a clue how to do this, Walt. You know me and computers."

"Figure it out," Walt said. "Call someone. Do something. But figure it out. And call me back. We've got an hour, maybe less. The father's going to want answers. Kevin has got to bring that girl back here and right now."

"Oh, God."

"It's up to you, Myra. This is something you've got to do. Right now, not a minute to lose."

"Me?" Since the death of Walt's brother,

Myra's mothering duties often had been passed to proxies.

"We're lucky to have gotten the tip. Find him, and then we'll deal with it."

Walt hung up. He climbed out of the car. Gail was halfway across the lawn, heading away from him. He felt her receding fury as a wave washing out to sea. No longer directed at him, he celebrated that burden lifting.

Brandon was pale. He looked disoriented. Walt knew that feeling, savored the fact that it belonged to someone else.

"Stand ready!" he ordered his men as he opened the Cherokee's back door and removed the seat belt from the attaché's handle. "Chances are, something's going down."

33

Fiona studied herself in the mirror. She was wearing a black tea dress. She wore it well. It wouldn't be considered sexy or daring, just "right."

Her cottage had warmed with late-afternoon sun. If she stayed too long in-doors, she'd break into a sweat. She gathered up her camera bag and her purse, pulled her only black sweater from a hanger, and deposited everything into the passenger's seat of her Subaru, then headed next door.

Leslie and Michael Engleton had offered her a ride to the auction, but she'd decided to drive herself and wanted to tell them in person. Their house sat atop a secluded hill overlooking a teardrop-shaped pond. It faced the slopes of the Sun Valley ski mountain to the west.

She heard children playing as she entered the house through the kitchen—a niece and two nephews from Carmel, here for two weeks—and wished she'd thought to bring them presents.

Leslie would not be ready on time. She knew she'd find Michael somewhere close by the children, and there he was, dressed for the auction and on his knees, playing pick-up sticks in the house's main living room, one of three.

Michael was a handsome man, with a shock of white hair in the black that rode above his left ear like a feather. She loved the way he looked at her, like there was no one else in the room—one of his many gifts.

"Perfect," he said when he spotted her. "She'll be down in a minute."

She wondered if he meant the way she looked or the fact that she'd arrived on time. To his credit, Michael never flirted. But she secretly wished he would try just once.

She explained her decision to drive herself, that it was a job for her. Though disappointed, he didn't act surprised.

"We'll see you there, then," he said. He rolled his eyes to the ceiling. "Maybe by dessert."

She allowed herself a smile, at Leslie's expense, and was turning to leave when she remembered to say something to the children. She had looked after them on several previous visits and liked all three very much.

It was only then she paid any attention to the pick-up sticks. She stepped closer to the game, looking straight down at the pile of colorful knitting-needle-length wooden sticks interlocked in a jumbled mess.

Perhaps it was flying with Walt, the bird's-eye view. Perhaps it was her photographer's eye. Whatever it was, she saw something in that pile of sticks that ran a spike of adrenaline through her.

She was in her car, speeding out the drive, before she realized she'd been rude. She'd forgotten to say good-bye.

34

With the open attaché displaying the Adams bottles inside the air-cooled Plexiglas case, Walt kept an eye on the crowd at the cocktail party. An ATKINSON'S MARKET bag containing Remy's pants and belongings rested on the grass at Walt's feet. If the bottles were stolen without the attaché and its GPS, then Walt's plan to follow it to George Clooney would fail. Convinced he had not seen the end of these people, he watched for the woman who'd been wearing the copper-colored blouse, the woman who'd pushed the baby stroller across

Main Street and stopped the wrecker, the woman who'd run naked from the motel room. He believed she was the one in charge. She was the one he was after.

Arthur Remy hobbled in on aluminum crutches. Approaching Walt, he looked like a man on too many painkillers.

"Sheriff . . ."

Walt handed Remy the bag. Remy rummaged through his belongings, his pants, his wallet, found the security card, stuffed his pockets. He then dropped the bag and pants into the grass.

"You have quite a few officers here this evening. I counted four outside."

"Deputies, yes. An ounce of prevention . . ." Walt said.

He had five total, Brandon and four others. The radios were live, the MC parked nearby, its dispatcher maintaining control over the team. Walt had three roadblocks set up, if needed.

Remy shuffled over to the case containing the Adams bottles, like a mother hen checking her nest. He glanced at the bottles, then up at Walt, and for a moment Walt sensed Remy knew the bottles had been handled. But Fiona had photo-graphed their position, and Walt believed they had been returned exactly.

"We need to talk," Remy said.

"Anytime."

"Give me a minute."

A crowd was gathering. Remy turned and raised his voice so they could hear him.

"An historic evening! A piece of history will end up in a private collection. It's not every day that happens."

Walt stepped back. Remy was sur-rounded at once. Condolences over his knee mixed with questions about his dis-covery of the bottles. He caught Walt's eye briefly, but if he intended to convey anything it was lost on Walt, whose atten-tion was galvanized by a woman just then entering the tent.

Fiona hurried toward him.

"Wow!" Walt said, eyeing her.

"I know what it is," she said breathlessly.

Her present state—flushed and panting—excited him.

"What *what* is?" he asked.

"Sawtooth Wood Products . . . the kid getting zapped."

He drew her away from the display tables.

"What about it?" he said.

"Pick-up sticks. The kids, at Michael and Leslie's, were playing pick-up sticks. The people doing this—the thieves—they're going to use the logs to block a road. They were after one of the logging trucks. You spill one of those logging trucks . . . you dump logs on the road . . ."

"It would stop traffic for hours," he muttered, realizing she'd seized upon the escape plan.

He grabbed for his radio but dropped it, pulling Fiona close to him and throwing her to the ground beneath him, as the walls of the tent briefly flared yellow and an explosion ripped through the cocktail party's peaceful chatter.

There were screams, and immediate panic, but no more explosions. Walt rolled off Fiona and sprang to his feet.

It had begun.

35

In one ear Walt heard the calm voice of the MC dispatcher report the explosion. "To all units in the vicinity of the Sun Valley Golf pro shop . . ." her report began. She was broadcasting a 10-80, the radio code for an explosion, over the secure frequency monitored by the valley's police departments and all on-duty sheriff's deputies.

Walt immediately returned over the same frequency. "Code nine," he said, ordering the roadblocks established. "All units outside a half-mile radius, hold your current positions."

Three months earlier, there had been a

shooting in downtown Ketchum. In and of itself, that was a rare event but not unheard of. It being a slow night in the valley, what made things interesting was that every patrol from Bellevue to the North Shore responded, seventeen police officers and five sheriff's deputies in all. Walt could see it happening again, despite a review board organized by him, following a front-page article in the newspaper ridiculing local law enforcement for overreacting.

Fiona's theory about spilling logs on the highway entered his decision making. What if the thieves had read that same newspaper? What if they expected and were trying to orchestrate the same overreaction?

Within seconds, he heard a siren approaching. Then another. And another.

While four of his deputies hurried toward the fire in the golf shop, Walt and Brandon secured the Adams bottles in the attaché and made for the Cherokee, parked alongside the tent.

Emergencies instilled a certain calmness in Walt. His hearing was heightened. He saw things more clearly. He loved this shit.

Guests had scattered. Some had hit the deck like he had, others had fled to their cars. Still others had been rescued by their own bodyguards. But as the confusion settled down, so did the remaining crowd, and surprisingly quickly. Wineglasses were refilled. They all seemed to be enjoying themselves again.

Fiona was by the tent entrance, camera in hand, getting shots of the distant fire.

Another siren, and yet another. It quickly became apparent that, once again, the action-starved police were turning out in droves.

Now behind the wheel of the Chero-kee, Walt called his own deputy, who served as the Bellevue marshal, to ask him to recheck the lumberyard for logging trucks.

"There should be two of them," he told the man.

"Got it."

"What's that about?" Brandon said from the passenger's seat, the attaché in hand.

Walt quickly explained Fiona's theory, tying it to all the sirens and responding fire trucks and patrol cars.

"So they're shutting down the highway?"

"Makes for an easier getaway."

"But they don't have the wine," Brandon said, patting the case.

"Not yet, they don't," Walt said.

He drove off, negotiating all the well-dressed people gawking at the fire.

"If they didn't get the rig from Sawtooth, that hardly matters. There are plenty of logging trucks around. All that work on the ski mountain . . ."

"True enough," Walt said. "First, we get these bottles back into the bank."

"Why didn't they rush the party?" Brandon asked. "Why blow that golf cart and then not rush the party?"

"Yeah, I know, that's bugging me too."

They passed five patrol cars—two from Hailey, three from Ketchum—heading toward the fire.

"We screwed this up . . . again," Walt said. "That's probably half our resources heading the wrong direction."

Brandon grabbed for the radio and, on Walt's instruction, reiterated the order for dispatch to recall the patrols. But as he did, two more cars zoomed past, lights blazing.

"*Shee-it,*" said Brandon, his face lit by

the colorful lights. "Like kids in a candy store."

"Entirely too predictable," said Walt.

They drove through their own roadblock, then moved traffic out of the way with their lights and siren. Ten minutes later, the bottles were returned to the vault, courtesy of the manager, who had agreed to be at their disposal all evening.

"Not exactly what we wanted," Walt said, back behind the wheel, the Adams bottles now safe.

"We're missing something," Brandon said.

"Yup."

"I don't get it."

"Nope."

"They should have gone after the bottles."

"Yup."

Beatrice stuck her wet nose between the seats and licked Walt, who reached back and petted her.

"Why block the highway if you don't steal the wine?" Brandon asked.

"Roach Motel," Walt said, yanking the car into gear and racing out of the bank's parking lot. Brandon clipped his seat belt.

"What the hell, Sheriff?"

"They check in, but they never check out."

"Yeah, I remember," Brandon said. "But, what the hell?"

"They set off the explosion. We respond. They use the logs to close the highway. We're all trapped."

"They aren't after the wine," Brandon said, grabbing for the vehicle's support handle.

"They aren't after the wine," Walt echoed.

36

Summer signaled for Kevin to pull over next to a chain-link fence that separated the tarmac and hangars from the airport access road. Beyond the fence, a dozen business jets were parked and tied down. Kevin killed the engine, his palms slippery on the steering wheel.

"Sun Valley Aviation's up there," he informed her. "Why here?"

"Yeah, but we aren't exactly going there."

"Because?"

"Because of the small technicality that I am underage and neither of us is a pilot.

You're not a pilot, are you?" she added as an afterthought.

"No, but my uncle owns a sailplane, a glider. I'm sure they'd let me show it to you. I know most of the guys in there."

"That's the point. I'd rather just jump the fence."

"That's insane."

"No, it's not. It's easy. Look around, dude. It's not like anything's happening around here."

"Hello? It's illegal."

"We can be over in, like, two seconds."

"But why bother if I can get us through the FBO? Fixed Base Operation," he added, answering her puzzled expression. "Sun Valley Aviation, we don't have to jump any fence," he said. "Maybe I should just go."

"No way!"

"You're here. You wanted me to drive you here, and I did. We're good."

"I'm *way* early for my flight," she complained. "The inside of the jet is *way* cool. That's it, right over there." She pointed. "I'm telling you, you're going to totally love it."

"I'm not jumping the fence, that's nuts. It's, like, a federal crime or something."

"Are you afraid?"

"No. I'm just not going to do it."

"Because you're afraid . . ."

"No. Because I can just walk through Sun Valley Aviation and get to the same place."

"At some point," she said, "my father's going to look for me, we both know that. Tonight, tomorrow? When he does, he's going to check everywhere. He doesn't do anything halfway. If you and me go through Sun Valley Aviation, we've been seen together. And then, when I'm suddenly not around . . ."

"Which is why this is where you get out."

"That's not going to happen."

"Yes, it is," he said. "Seriously, I've got to go. Have a safe flight."

She yanked the keys from the ignition, popped open the door, and sprinted for the fence. She climbed the fence like a cat. Through the chain link, she grinned playfully, dangling Kevin's keys from her finger. She glanced furtively to either side, wondering if she'd been seen, then was all the more obnoxious when she realized she was in the clear.

"If you want 'em, you're going to have to come and get 'em." She slipped the keys into the tight front pocket of her jeans. "Throw my suitcase over, while you're at it."

He left the suitcase in the car and climbed the fence, landing flat-footed on the tarmac.

She backed away, her right hand still guarding the keys in her pocket.

"Your bag for the keys," he said, looking around hotly, terrified of being caught.

"Come and get it," she said.

She sprinted toward one of the jets.

He caught up to her just as she was slipping a key in the jet's lock. The top half of the jet's hatch lifted up as a set of stairs simultaneously lowered with the bottom half.

She grabbed Kevin by the front of his shirt and pulled him toward her. Then, as their lips were about to touch, she spun around, placing her backside against his crotch, and pulled his right hand down around her, his fingers inching into her pocket.

It was warm inside the pocket. And *terrifying.*

"They're yours, if you want them."

His fingers touched his keys. She forced his hand lower, deeper into the pocket. It was like a furnace down there.

He grabbed his keys, pulled them out, stuffed them in his pant pocket.

She pulled his now-free hand against the skin of the jet.

"Now that you've touched it," she said, confusing him, "don't you want to *see* it?"

"I . . . don't think so," his voice cracked. He looked back at his car.

"One beer," she said. "Have a look around. Stay or don't stay. Whatever you want. But I've got time to kill, and we might as well kill it together."

Her warmth lingered on his fingertips.

Now that you've touched it . . .

He followed her up the stairs.

37

Having set the charge in the golf cart, Roger McGuiness had met up with Matt Salvo, who'd had a much easier time stealing the logging truck than on his first try.

McGuiness dropped the semi into a low gear, and they drove off, leaving behind Sun Valley Company's Cold Springs base camp, an area of collected construction equipment and material.

"We're good?" Salvo said.

McGuiness replied, "I must have passed a dozen patrol cars headed north."

A siren *whooped* from behind them.

"Heads up!" McGuiness said, his attention on the truck's wing mirror.

Salvo checked the opposing mirror and he pounded the truck's dash. "Shit!"

"Chill. We've got this," said the driver.

The GREENHORN/EAST FORK traffic light was just ahead. Less than a quarter mile past the light, and slightly downhill, was the highway bridge, a three-lane concrete span.

Salvo reached over and picked up the fat black electric cable that lay between the seats. The rest of it ran out of the cab's sliding rear window to the load of logs chained to the truck bed. Attached to the cab end that Salvo held was a black button switch.

The cop car had pulled to within a few feet of the red safety flags stapled to the ends of the longer logs.

"Not yet," McGuiness said.

"The fucker is right there!"

"And what's he going to do, run us off the road? Do not detonate those charges, Matt. Hold off."

Salvo's thumb hovered over the button.

The truck ran the light, speeding toward the bridge.

"Timing is everything," McGuiness said. "I set those charges. I know how this thing is going to work. Don't freak out over some cop car."

The cop car jerked out into the turn lane and pulled up alongside. Oncoming traffic swerved to avoid it.

A hundred yards and closing.

Salvo's thumb loomed over the button.

"You strapped in?" McGuiness said, double-checking.

"Yeah."

"Good. Hold on."

McGuiness tugged the steering wheel sharply left, quickly corrected, and then applied the brakes. The tires squealed and smoked as the cab and trailer drifted in slow motion, first in unison, then like the tail wagging the dog, as the truck jack-knifed into a graceful skid. The move got the cop's attention—one second, alongside the rig; the next, about to be crushed by it. He veered off the highway, spewing a rooster tail of dust and crashing head-on into the berm that supported the bike path.

McGuiness had landed the cab and trailer squarely between the bridge's opposing guardrails. A thing of beauty.

"Now!"

Salvo pushed the button.

A great cloud of gray smoke arose from a series of small explosions along both sides of the trailer. The giant logs tumbled from the trailer in both directions.

It happened exactly as Cantell had proposed—a nightmarish tangle of enormous logs, rolling and bouncing off the truck. The truck shuddered to a stop, complaining steel squealing. McGuiness had jackknifed the truck into the mouth of the bridge like a cork in a bottle.

"Nice," Salvo said, as he grabbed the chainsaw at his feet.

"See you at the rendezvous," McGuiness said, sliding down out of the cab.

Salvo made his way through the fallen timber, and, keeping an eye on the damaged patrol car, climbed to the bike-path bridge, dragging the chainsaw with him.

He tugged its cord and the saw sputtered to life. He planted its blade into a power pole.

He looked away, avoiding the spray of wood chips and sawdust, only to see cars everywhere. In both directions, traffic had come to a stop, causing a few rear enders, and leaving the highway in chaos.

He made a second cut with the saw. A wedge of wood broke loose and fell out. He started a third cut.

The driver of a pickup truck climbed out and started shouting at him. The man ran for the wrecked police car.

Sirens called from the north. He looked south. No sign of cops coming from there, just as Cantell had planned.

He leaned his weight into the chainsaw. The power pole popped and splintered. Then it teetered and fell.

Overhead, wires sparked and flashed. Salvo had failed to remember he was bringing down a few thousand volts with the pole. A half dozen wires now sparked and jumped on the ground. He dropped the saw and took off south across the bridge. Car horns sounded. He took them as applause for a job well done.

He sprinted across the highway, jumped down an embankment, lost his footing, and rolled to the bottom. He got to his feet and took off running.

Some hero had left his car and was

coming after him. "Hey, ass-hole, hold up!" the man shouted.

Salvo reached for his knife. He stitched his way through a thicket of aspens and found himself in a yard next to a tool shed. He ducked around the side, silently begging his pursuer to give it up.

But the hero came crashing through the aspens a moment later, and Matt, who'd grown up in Sparks, Nevada, in a neighborhood where survival required a degree in viciousness, timed the blow perfectly. He swung around the corner of the shed just as the hero arrived, delivering the hilt of the knife to the man's forehead.

The guy dropped like a rock.

"Nice try," he told the hero.

He then looked around to get his bearings, wondering how long Lorraine and McGuiness would wait for him.

38

As Walt's Cherokee approached a string of taillights, his mobile rang. Seeing the caller ID, he answered it.

"What'd you find out?" he asked Myra.

"He's at the airport," she said. "I used the tracking thing. Best I can tell, he's there, or right around there."

"That's not good," he said. "She was seen getting into his car with a suitcase. If he's seen as having aided her flight . . . Myra, he's in trouble."

Brandon looked out the side window, pretending not to hear.

"I'm on my way there," she announced.

"He's still not picking up?"

"No."

"Can you text him?"

"Me? I have no idea how to do that. And I'm in my car."

She was about to cry.

"I'll call Pete. Hopefully, he can find him and put a cork in this."

She thanked him and hung up.

A flash of brake lights. He flipped on the light rack and took the empty middle lane, reserved for vehicles turning either direction.

Walt quickly called Pete, head of operations at the airport, and filled him in on Kevin's situation. Pete said he'd head down to the terminal and take a look around.

"I'll call over to Sun Valley Air as well," Pete said.

"Appreciate the help."

"Back to you shortly."

As they passed the entrance to the Rainbow Bend subdivision, Walt got a better look at the chaos up the road: a long line of taillights ahead of him, no headlights coming at him. A patrol car off the road—Ketchum police, maybe. A second later, he could make out the truck blocking the road.

"Are those logs?" Brandon asked.

Drivers were out of their cars. A few had gathered around the wrecked patrol car.

Walt and Brandon hurried to the patrol car. Brandon moved the onlookers aside. Walt wrenched open the door and determined the driver was dazed but otherwise seemingly okay.

He looked around, focusing first on the spilled logs, then the power pole lying across the bike-path bridge, the downed wires still spitting sparks.

He handed Brandon the keys to the Cherokee. "Get the power pole cleared first. No civilian traffic is to use the bike bridge, but get me a couple of our guys across if you can."

"Got it," Brandon said. "You?"

"Stay on comm," Walt said, running for the bridge.

39

With the jet door shut, Summer encouraged Kevin forward.

"Come on, I want to show you," she said. She squeezed past him, making sure to rub up against him, not wanting his interest to lag. "Seats eight. All eight can sleep flat. Each seat has its own TV, and there's the big TV on the wall." She pointed. Light shined weakly through the oval windows.

She handed him a cold beer. There were two microwave ovens, a built-in coffeemaker, a stainless-steel sink. A fire extinguisher was clamped to the wall. Beyond the kitchen, a folding door gave way to a padded seat over a toilet. It faced an emergency exit door. Just over the toilet was a partially open roller panel that accessed a sizable storage area.

Kevin drank some beer, impressed and overwhelmed.

A rechargeable flashlight hung next to the toilet. There was a first-aid kit on the wall.

"All the comforts of home," he said.

"That's the idea. Including a satellite telephone." She pointed to her father's seat.

"Are you okay?" he said.

"I love this thing. I never tell my father. I don't want him knowing what I like and don't like because sometimes I feel like anything I mention liking means he has to buy or get it for me. Believe it or not, I don't love that. It's love/hate with this plane. He's so into it, it actually bugs me. But I love flying it."

"TMI," he said, "too much information."

"Whatever . . ."

"It's very cool," he said.

"You should feel it take off. Oh my God, it's *so* totally random! Like a rocket or something. My dad . . . he puts his head back, you know? During takeoff. Shuts his eyes, and it's like he's getting off or something." She blushed and giggled again. "Forget I said that," she spit out quickly.

But Kevin couldn't forget it, and he thought she probably knew it. The more he thought about it, the more she seemed to be acting, and he wondered what that was all about.

"So, you ready?" she asked.

"Depends what you're talking about."

"Don't do that," she said. "Don't try to sound cool. Guys do that all the time, and I'm telling you it's a complete turnoff, okay? Just be you. You're cute; live with it. But don't try to sound like James Bond or something, because you're not."

She squeezed past him again and headed toward the cockpit.

"What is it with you and your father?" he asked, trying to strike back. He didn't like being lectured to.

The question stopped her. She didn't turn around to face him. "I explained that," she said. "It's just father-daughter stuff."

"And your taking off like this? Running away, coming here when you shouldn't? That's just you getting back at him?"

"What are you, my shrink?"

"I'm just curious, that's all."

"Well, lose it. You're a buzz kill."

"I don't think you should go."

"No one asked you."

"I wish you wouldn't go. I wish you'd stay. Why don't you just tell him whatever it is you want to tell him? Then we could hang out some more."

Her face brightened, but her look was patronizing. "That's so sweet," she said.

"I'm serious."

"I'm leaving," she said, her voice deeper and her eyes darker.

"Because of the tennis guy you told me about?" he said.

"Men's finals are tomorrow, Sunday. He's playing. I'm going to be there."

"But then he's gone, right? To some other tournament? What's with that? Are you going to follow him? You think he's down with that? You're seventeen. They'd arrest him."

"So, what, you're suddenly my father? Lose it, would you?"

"If you stay, you get props from Dad, right? Coulda run off but didn't? He's got to appreciate that."

"He doesn't appreciate anything about

me. Believe it and leave it. I'm serious. I'm going down to L.A. and don't want to be talked out of it. So just let me, would you please?"

"The thing is," he said, "and we know this better than anyone else, it's a lot harder when they're gone, no matter how much of a pain in the ass they are when they're around."

"Do you want to see the cockpit or have an *Oprah* moment?"

He followed her to the front of the jet, and she stepped aside to allow him to pass. He hesitated.

"Go on. It's why you came along, isn't it?"

He thought about it. "I don't know. Maybe."

"To sit in that seat."

He remained standing.

"I understand wanting to blow him off," he said. "I've asked my mother, like, a thousand times to move. Everything here reminds me of him. I can't stand living in the valley anymore. I'm done. How my mom does it, I have no idea. She's like trying to hold on to something that isn't there. She is so lost."

He slipped into the pilot's seat. He could hear her breathing.

"You could come with me," she said.

"That would go over big."

He sat there. She said nothing.

"We can turn on some music," she said. "See those battery switches? Flip the second one."

"I need the key, right? Are you sure this is cool?"

"There is no key. Not for this part."

"No way."

"*Way.* The key's for the door."

"You're bullshitting me!"

"No key, no shit."

He double-checked her instructions and then pushed the buttons as told. Lights came on in the cabin, and she turned them off. Then she pulled down all the window blinds.

The dash had come alive, the number of lights and instruments overwhelming.

"Have you ever flown it?" he asked.

"I've steered it a couple of times, sure. My dad can land it. He took instruction and stuff. He's a complete safety freak. There's a case in the closet," she said, "with an extra radio, a portable GPS, charts, flashlight. Extra everything—that's my dad. He'll probably wish he had an extra daughter by this time tomorrow."

Kevin's phone chirped, signaling a text message. He slipped the phone out of his front pocket.

Kev? Walt is looking for you. Where are you?
I'm coming to the airport. Mom

He stuffed the phone back in his pocket.
"Gotta go!" he said. *How the hell does she know I'm here?*

Someone must have seen his car.
"No way! We just got here."
"I've got to go," he repeated.

40

Cantell, McGuiness, and Salvo entered Sun Valley Aviation wearing flight uniforms. They approached the reception counter with an air of confidence, their caps pulled low.

ON DUTY: REBA KLINE read the plaque.

Cantell placed a small key on the counter, along with a pen and some paperwork.

"I'd like to settle charges for Lear tango-alpha-niner-five-niner."

"Absolutely," Reba said. She worked the computer, found the account, and printed out a statement for him to review.

Cantell paid her eleven hundred seventy-five dollars in cash.

"Something wrong?" he asked.

"Cash is king," she said. "We just don't see a lot of it here."

She printed out a receipt.

"Where's William this evening?" she asked the pilot. "Wasn't that his name?"

"William the Conqueror?" the man teased. Salvo and McGuiness laughed with him. "He's picking up the flight in the morning. We're the maintenance crew."

"There's that pesky little requirement of TBO," said McGuiness. TBO was an aviation term for time between overhauls. McGuiness had spun that into time between drinks. Reba Kline got the joke and laughed with him.

"There is *that,*" she said.

Cantell scribbled a physician-style signature on the paperwork.

"Did you happen to cater?" she asked, already checking a card file.

McGuiness produced a tin of Altoids. "This is our food service," he said, winning another laugh from her.

"We're bringing it down to Boise for a

DVD issue," Salvo said. "Can't have the DVD malfunctioning."

Cantell shot Salvo a look.

"We've got some good electronics guys here," Reba said.

Cantell smiled at her weakly. "Boss wants it done in Boise."

"I hear that," she said.

"Should be back around nine A.M. tomorrow," McGuiness added.

"So, we'll see you tomorrow, then," she said. "Safe skies, gentlemen."

Cantell checked his appearance in a mirror behind her that had been frosted to look like clouds.

Reba Kline experienced a slight tinge of unease as the three men left and headed for the Lear.

It wasn't the pilot's vanity—*Lord knows, pilots are full of themselves.* It wasn't him paying cash, not exactly, though maybe that was part of it.

She'd gotten plenty of dirty looks in her time, but she'd come to accept the egos of flyboys. So the little guy had made a point of undressing her with his eyes, big deal.

What pissed off and confused her was the wake of debris they left behind. Bark chips, sawdust, dried mud: it was like they'd been climbing trees or cutting firewood minutes before coming in here.

What was with that?

She turned back to the keyboard and closed out the sale.

41

Walt clambered over the logs, already on the radio trying to identify possible high-stakes, south valley robbery targets. The first thing that came to mind was the cache of arms and vehicles housed at the National Guard Armory. Every kind of weapon, half a dozen Hummers, the theft could be catastrophic. There were other prizes locally as well: art collections, famous and wealthy kidnapping targets. When he looked at the valley from that point of view, he was all the more aware of how vulnerable it was to an organized attack like this one. The thought drove him over the final log all that much faster.

It was then, through the obnoxious beeping of car horns, that he heard someone falling and cursing behind him, someone following him over the logs. He turned, prepared to give Brandon an earful.

Fiona stared back at him, holding her black dress well above her knees. She released the dress's hem, and it fell.

"I told you," she said.

You can't be here," Walt said from the driver's seat of a Toyota Prius he had commandeered. Thankfully, the driver hadn't put up a fight.

"But I am, so live with it."

"You're a civilian. I'm dropping you off in town."

"No, you're not. I was the one who figured this out. You obviously need me."

He smirked, resenting that she could win this from him.

"I also happen to be a woman," she said, "which is something that has apparently escaped your attention. If you take custody of this runaway, then you're going to need a woman as part of your team."

"How can you possibly know—?" He cut himself off, answering himself. "Myra."

"No, it wasn't Myra," she said. "I may have run into Chuck Webb, but I'm not saying I did."

"I can't deal with Kevin or the girl . . . not now."

"That's why I'm here."

"You followed me."

"You really are a brilliant investigator."

"Why would you follow me?" he said.

"You ask too many questions."

"That's not an answer."

"I'm conflicted," she said.

"What does that mean?"

"*Some* detective you are."

42

Kevin scrambled down out of the pilot's seat. He pushed her back into the body of the plane.

"What?" she said.

"Three guys heading this way."

"No," she said. "To a different plane. Chill, dude."

"I swear."

She eased into the cockpit and sneaked a peek.

"Not us," she whispered but not convincingly. "First, it's not William or Jack. Second, we don't have three crew with us."

But as they drew closer, she stepped back alongside Kevin.

"I don't get it. They are not our crew."

"I don't think that really matters at the moment. What the hell do we do?"

"The power's still on!" she said, diving forward and crawling on her knees to toggle the switches.

A loud electronic *clunk* came from the cabin door as it began to open.

"Shit! Shit! Shit!" Kevin said. "My mother's going to kill me!"

Summer hurried him up the aisle and into the storage area over the toilet. She slid the partition shut behind her but not all the way, her eye to the crack.

Both jammed into the small space; his heart was beating too hard and too fast.

The cabin door came fully open.

Summer pressed her index finger to her lips, as she whispered at him, "I don't know these guys. It can't be anything much. Prep for tomorrow's flight maybe. Who knows?"

She returned her attention to the passenger area.

As the three men came on board, they

barely said a word to one another, which struck Kevin as odd. He could hear noises up in the cockpit. They were doing stuff.

Lights came on, the air system hissed.

When he finally heard the mumble of a voice, it was someone reading.

Summer's hair tickled his face. "That's the checklist!" she said. "I think they're starting it up."

"What? They can't do that!"

"Shut up and let me think." For the first time, she looked as scared as he felt.

Cantell read off the checklist just as he and McGuiness had practiced dozens of times. McGuiness had nine months of training invested in the next twenty minutes of flight, and though he ran through the run-up with authority his anxiety permeated the cockpit.

Cantell's responsibilities were limited to the radios and GPS navigation. He set the proper frequencies, double-checked the destination he'd keyed into the GPS, and held his index finger over the transponder switch.

"Transponder off, yes?" he said.

"Off," McGuiness said, busy with other switches.

Cantell's action prevented the broadcast of a radio signal that would allow ACT, air traffic control, to track the Learjet's flight. Above fifteen thousand feet, the Lear would be visible on most radar. But McGuiness had no intention of flying above fifteen thousand feet. He'd keep it at ten thousand or lower, once out over the desert. It was only mountain flying that presented problems. That, and the fading light.

"Nice and easy," Cantell said. "No rush."

"Call the tower."

Cantell had practiced his few lines to the point of impatience. McGuiness had warned him that it wasn't just a matter of saying the right words—there wasn't all that much to say—but it was the cadence, the indifference, that would sell the call to the Hailey tower.

Cantell announced their tail number, then requested, "Taxi to takeoff."

The unusual wind direction meant a northbound takeoff. The tower reminded TA959 that noise abatement was in effect.

Cantell acknowledged.

McGuiness shook his head in disbelief. "We would have preferred three-one," he said, meaning the southbound runway.

"C.C.?" Salvo stood in the gap behind them. He'd been instructed by Cantell to keep back and allow them to do their jobs.

"I told you to stay out of the way!" Cantell looked over his shoulder.

Salvo was holding a Heineken.

"Jesus, Salvo, throw that thing out. . . . Not now!"

"It's not mine!" He raised the can.

The Lear jerked into a taxi.

"Pre-takeoff checklist," McGuiness said to Cantell, ignoring Salvo.

"It was in the cup holder, C.C.," Salvo said.

"What do I care where it was?" Cantell complained, grabbing for the laminated checklist. "Toss it, and take a seat."

"It was in the cup holder," Salvo repeated, "and it's *cold.*"

That won looks from both pilot and copilot.

Cantell reached out and touched the beer can. He glanced over at McGuiness.

"It's not like we can back up," McGuiness said. "We're cleared to taxi."

"Search it," Cantell whispered to Salvo.

"Let's roll," he said to McGuiness.

One of those guys sounds so familiar," Summer whispered into Kevin's ear, "but I can't place it. Maybe . . . I think . . ." She didn't complete her thought. With the jets rumbling, she had to press her lips to his ear, contorting them both in the small place and causing Kevin to practically lay atop her.

"I'll take care of it," she said. "It's probably better if you stay here until I get it straight."

Kevin reached to stop her but she shook him off, as she slid the partition open and slipped out of the storage compartment. Kevin blocked her from shutting it completely, wanting to see out.

"Excuse me!" she then called out.

She was met with three dumbfounded expressions. The copilot pulled off his headset. In five quick steps, she was standing behind the short guy, her back to Kevin.

"Where's William?" she said, getting a

look at the pilot's face and realizing she didn't know him. She stood erect, trying to assert her importance. "Who are you guys, anyway?" She then addressed the copilot, having identified him as the one with the familiar voice. "I know you, right? I'm Summer. You know me. You've got to take me back to the FBO."

"We've not met. What are you doing on this plane?" the copilot said. "You can't be here."

"You think? My father *owns* this plane. Take me back to the FBO, please."

"Can we turn it around?" the copilot asked the pilot. It seemed an odd question for the copilot to ask. Of course they could turn around, and would, right now.

"You can and you will," she said, reminding them who she was.

The pilot shot a confused look over at the copilot.

"Where's William?" she repeated.

The pilot didn't seem to hear her, but then he hadn't pulled off a headphone cup as the copilot had.

"We'd have to explain things to the tower," the pilot said. "You really want to do that?"

"I need to go back. I can't fly with you,

even if it's only a short flight!" Summer said. "I don't have the time, okay?"

The copilot checked her out. Then he looked out the plane's windshield at the blue lights of the runway to their left.

"Is anyone listening?" she said.

"Step back a moment, miss, would you please?"

The copilot's demeanor had changed. He was suddenly the one in charge, which was not the way a cockpit crew worked.

She kept her feet firmly planted. She wasn't going anywhere.

"Take me back," she said.

The copilot had been ignoring her, but now he faced her and raised his voice. "TAKE A SEAT!"

The reprimand turned her stomach. "I . . . am . . . not going with you. You will turn the plane around now!"

The copilot flicked his head, and suddenly a pair of arms wrapped around her. The third guy had her.

"Go!" the copilot instructed the pilot.

The jet rolled forward. It swung left, taxiing north onto the runway.

The engines screamed up to a high-pitched whine.

"No!" she said, kicking and trying to break free. But the man holding her was seriously strong, and his hands were all over her.

Kevin caught pieces of the confrontation. At first, it appeared that, true to form, Summer had taken charge, or tried to. Hands on her hips, back arched, she'd tried to come off older than she was.

He heard her ask—demand, was more like it—to be taken back to the FBO.

But then it went wrong. The small, wiry guy had grabbed her, and Kevin's first instinct was to run to her defense. The man pinned her arms behind her back and held them at the wrist with just one hand, pushing her to the floor with the other. He did it like he'd done it a hundred times before. He tied her hands with a seat belt, then touched her face in a lecherous, disgusting way. He glanced hotly toward the pilots, saw they were occupied, and ran both hands over her chest.

Kevin sat up furiously, thumping his head against the plastic ceiling.

The guy looked back. Kevin hoped he'd

backed his eye away from the opening in time. He reached for his cell phone as the jets screamed louder, his thumb searching out the correct string of numbers.

43

Walt pulled the borrowed Prius up to the reserved parking at the Blaine County Sheriff's Office. It was his prize, this long-sought-after, newly constructed headquarters and county jail. It had taken him three failed referendums to raise the bond before finally convincing the public of its necessity. Erected in the light-industrial zone adjacent to the airport, it was thirty-six thousand square feet of state-of-the-art law enforcement, and he was as proud of it as he was of his daughters.

"The airport's right there," Fiona said,

pointing out the obvious. "Let me just run over there and look for him."

"If you want to, sure," he said, climbing out of the car. "Check with Pete." He tossed the keys into her lap. "I've got to stay on point."

"Happy to do it," she said.

"Hey!" he said, stopping her as she hiked up her dress to climb behind the wheel. "Pick-up sticks. That was a good call."

Caught!

She nodded, wiggling and tugging her dress down.

He shoved the car door shut and headed for the entrance.

His cell phone vibrated.

The caller ID read KEVIN CELL.

Walt pressed the CALL button.

"Where the hell *are you*?" he said by way of introduction.

The line crackled and spat.

"Unc . . . alt?" Kevin's voice was nearly unrecognizable.

A roar erupted in the background.

". . . got . . . her," he thought he heard. He missed everything else.

He didn't want to hear the true confessions of a teenage conquest. Playing Kevin's surrogate dad required they both walk a fine line.

The roar grew ever louder. It dawned on him that it wasn't static but background noise.

A plane—a jet—took off to the north, and he glared at it.

Maybe the background noise hadn't come over the phone after all.

It took him several seconds to connect it with the jet. Even allowing for the delay over the phone, the two were inseparable. It meant Kevin was close by. Maybe at a hangar party, some rich kid throwing a rave.

"Where . . . are . . . you?" Walt hollered into the phone.

"I'm on—" Kevin's voice stopped mid-word.

Walt checked the phone. It had lost its connection.

On? he wondered. It was the operative word that lodged in his thoughts.

He waved for Fiona to hold up, rushed to the car, and motioned for her to lower the window.

"Kevin just called. Have Pete check the north hangars. And see if Teddy Sumner owns or operates a private jet, and, if so, have Pete check that out as well. I think Kevin's right here, somewhere ridiculously close." He realized he was ordering her around like he would a deputy. "That is . . . if you wouldn't mind?"

"I wouldn't mind at all," she said.

He looked up. The jet's lights blinked in the gray of the evening sky.

"Aren't you glad I came along?" she said.

"If I'm overstepping . . . There are people here . . ."

"Shut up, Walt. I'm happy to do it. This, and . . . *more.*"

She backed up the car. Her hair caught in the window when she put it up.

Amused, Walt stood there a moment wondering how long it had been since anyone had told him to shut up.

44

Dave McCormick's gloved hands gripped the parasail's plastic handles, sensing the amazing control he maintained over the ribbed fabric overhead. Before him, an astonishing waterfall of red-and-orange light cascaded into the craggy horizon. Without referencing the altimeter on his wrist, Dave could tell by his shortness of breath and the sudden bite to the air that he'd exceeded eleven thousand feet. He didn't want to go any higher or stay aloft too much longer, it being far darker on the ground than in the air, making for a difficult landing.

He spilled some wind from the sail and

began a descending spiral. He spotted a dark V, coming from the north, aimed directly for him. It was several hundred geese.

He glided lower, hoping to join the formation, and descended into the twilight incredibly fast. He arrived within yards of the lead goose, startling the formation and scattering their symmetry. The V quickly reformed, Dave McCormick suddenly a hundred yards in its wake.

A blinding strobe won his attention.

A jet. Coming fast, at an absurdly low altitude.

He saw what the pilot could not: the jet was on a collision course with the geese.

And quite possibly with him.

He tugged on the parasail's controls, trying to drop down and outrun the jet's blowback. The plane hit the geese like a dart, the V scattering as orange flares rose from the jet's engines.

Smoke streamed thickly from the port jet.

He reached for the portable two-way radio strapped to his chest just as a blast of engine thrust hit him, driving him upside down and away from the plane like a seed. He struggled to control the fall.

45

Bird strike!" McGuiness called out, leaning back to look at the wing, his right hand searching out toggles overhead.

Cantell grabbed for the dash.

"Mac," Cantell said, "tell me we're all right."

McGuiness studied the instruments.

"Starboard's producing three-quarter . . . check that . . . *fifty percent* power."

"Mac?"

"Not good."

McGuiness reached for the buttons on the GPS.

"I've got that," Cantell said.

"Known airports," McGuiness said.

"Known airports," Cantell acknowledged. "Mac . . ."

"The GPS can show us all—"

"Nearby airports. I got it. But we can't put down at an airport, Mac."

"Fuck that! We've lost our port engine. Starboard's currently on fire."

"So put out the fire," Cantell said, eerily calm.

"I hit the extinguishers and I extinguish combustion. We go down like a rock."

"Fix it."

"We're *not* going to reach the Nevada field. We need to put this thing down now, and it can't be some grass strip. We need length."

He'd worked the GPS without Cantell's help.

"Stanley. That'll work. Fifteen miles. Look it up in the book. How long's the strip?" He kept his eyes on the instruments. "I need the length of that runway."

"I'm on it."

"I need it now! And here . . ." He tossed a set of laminated pages at his copilot. "Emergency landing checklist."

Cantell had not moved.

"Read me the goddamned checklist!"

"We're not putting it down in Stanley," Cantell said. "We do that, we walk away."

"We don't do that," McGuiness said, "and they'll be shoveling us into body bags."

"We're flying. It's flying, right?"

"It's on fire. Forget about everything else, damn it." His eyes searched the various instruments. "Forty-five percent and falling. We are losing that engine. We are going down. We need to put this bird down! I am *not* trained for this. This is not good. Now, are you going to read the goddamned checklist or not?"

"What's *that*?" Cantell asked, pointing to a black-and-white screen on an instrument labeled MAXVIZ, a night-visioning system designed to help spot deer on runways, among other things. At this altitude, the screen showed the whole of the Sawtooth Valley before them—mostly black, representing cold, but intersected by a thin white ribbon, heat emanating from the warm asphalt of Highway 75 running north from Galena up through Stanley. The streets of Stanley showed as well. The highway then curved right toward Challis.

Cantell was pointing to a perfectly straight white line about an inch long in a sea of black well northwest of the spotty glow of Stanley.

"That's nothing, an anomaly. It's in the middle of nowhere," McGuiness snapped. "Now, read the goddamned checklist, Chris!"

"But if it's white like that," Cantell countered, "it's asphalt."

"I doubt it. The signature is weak. See how faint it is?"

"No, no, it's almost the same heat signature as the highway. It's got to be asphalt. A private strip."

"Out there? Starboard engine's at forty percent and still burning."

"That's where we land," Cantell said. "That strip. We can make that."

"You're suddenly the pilot?" McGuiness stole another look at the MaxViz. He glanced over at Cantell.

"We can do this," Cantell said. "We put it down there. We make the call. Not so different than what we had planned."

"*The checklist,*" McGuiness shouted.

The nose of the jet slowly moved away

from the lights of Stanley and pointed northwest.

"Thata boy," said Cantell.

He then flipped the laminated sheets and began reading aloud.

46

The periodic updates from his dispatcher began to weigh on Walt. He put two patrols on the armory. He had his deputies there in vests and with shotguns.

Connected with the MC from the Incident Command Center, using a video uplink, he was apprised of the damage and informed of the overwhelming response from law enforcement—eighteen officers in twelve patrol cars were currently on the scene. Including his own deputies, that put the number at well over twenty. By his estimate, that left four or five officers total

in the Hailey area, four his, two already
guarding the armory.

It was another screwup of epic propor-
tions by valley police departments.

He had finally identified George Clooney. He'd popped out on a federal sheet
of "known associates" of the wheelman,
McGuiness. A picture of one Christopher
Cantell was in the upper-right-hand corner
of the OneDOJ sheet that lay in front of
him. It listed arrests, not convictions, and
noted that Cantell had a reputation for creating feints for his heists. He was "a master of deception, calm to the point of
sociopathic," and "a person of interest" in
four open investigations.

Whatever Cantell's plan had been for
the wine, Walt now believed it too was a
feint, a second robbery attempt planned
south of the blocked bridge. His patience
stretched thin, still reeling from Cantell's
success with the Roach Motel bait-and-
switch tactic, Walt took a call from Fiona.

"Not north of the terminal," she said.
"South. Sumner's jet, a Lear. No one's seen
the kids."

"Okay."

But it wasn't okay, and they both knew it.

"The Lear . . . Sumner's Lear? It just took off. That was the plane you saw. Tail number T-A-nine-five-nine."

"What?" His head spun. "Hillabrand's at the auction dinner?" he asked.

"What has he got to do with anything?"

"Yes or no?"

"Yes, but—"

"Call him, please. Tell him it's an emergency, that we need him to find Teddy Sumner in the crowd. Sumner needs to call my office ASAP. Can you do that?"

"Of course."

"Is Pete there with you?"

"Yes."

"Put him on please." Walt waved off Nancy as she entered his office to tell him something. She leaned over and passed him a note. *Armory clear. Standing guard.*

He acknowledged it with a nod.

A gruff voice answered the phone.

"Pete! Have you got a flight plan for the Lear?"

"I'll look into it."

"I think Kevin's on that plane. If and when that jet lands in another state, he's looking at a felony. Transportation of a minor. We need to contact the pilot and turn that plane around for everyone's sake."

"I understand."

"Call me."

"Done deal."

The phone rang less than five minutes later. It was Teddy Sumner. Fiona was proving herself invaluable.

"What's this all about, Sheriff?"

Walt could hear the auctioneer prattling in the background.

"Your plane," he said. "I need you to tell your pilot to turn it around."

"My pilot's at the Best Western, running up movies and room service on an expense account, Sheriff. What do you mean, turn it around?"

Walt held the receiver to his ear but said nothing. The bidding price in the background was up to seven thousand dollars.

"Your Lear took off from the Sun Valley Airport less than ten minutes ago. I believe your daughter and a companion are on board."

"Summer's due . . . Oh, shit—"

There was a long pause on the other end. The bidding had reached eight-five.

"I suppose it's possible William needed

a maintenance run," he continued. "I don't always hear about those things. Maybe Summer talked him into a joyride."

"We need to reach the pilot."

"I can call."

"Anything you can do to confirm the location of your plane and whether your daughter and a friend are on board would be appreciated."

"To confirm you're mistaken?" Sumner sounded dubious.

"Yes."

"That would be a first. What kind of cop are you?"

"Elected," Walt answered.

Sumner barked a laugh.

"One other thing, Mr. Sumner. Can you tell me how much a plane like yours costs?"

"The general rule is, if you have to ask, you can't afford it."

"Millions." Walt made it a statement.

"Seventeen-five."

"Get back to me as soon as you can. And thank you again for your cooperation."

The bidding stopped at nine thousand five hundred. Going once . . . going twice . . .

Walt grabbed his cell phone from its charger on his way out the door.

Seventeen-five.

He stopped in front of Nancy's desk.

"Call Myra," he said. "Get the details of how to track Kevin's cell phone. We'll need her user name and password."

Nancy reached for the phone.

Walt moved around to behind her desk. Within a minute, she had accessed the website and had the GPS location for Kevin's phone, which was north of Ketchum.

Walt checked the map's time stamp: seven minutes earlier.

"Oh, crap," he said, his eyes jumping between his watch and the time on the screen.

"Click 'History,'" he said.

Nancy moved the cursor and clicked. The screen refreshed to Kevin's location of ten minutes earlier.

"The airport," Nancy said. "That can't be right. Hailey Airport to Ketchum in a couple of minutes? I don't think so. No one can drive that fast."

"He isn't driving," Walt said.

47

As the call went dead, the plane shook, and to the left Kevin heard a series of loud pops followed by silence. The roar now came only from the right.

He checked his bars: zero. He powered down the phone, saving the battery for when they landed.

He looked at the phone cradled in his hand. If they caught him—and they would—they'd confiscate it. The trick was to hide it, come back for it later. He tried slipping it under the pad he was lying on, but it made an obvious bulge. Just outside the sliding partition, he spotted a hand-towel dispenser. With the pilots busy and Summer and her captor facing forward, their backs to him, Kevin reached out of the storage compartment.

His finger deciphered the dispenser's front panel and he opened it, slipping his phone inside.

The challenge was to think like his uncle. For all he knew, these guys were planning a 9/11-style suicide flight into some skyscraper in Seattle or Salt Lake. Or maybe they were hijacking the Lear to pick up some criminal, like on *Prison Break.*

He relived all that he'd seen on his brief tour of the jet: a fire extinguisher next to the galley, knives and a corkscrew in the drawer, a flashlight above the toilet, a first-aid kit.

He assumed there would be cleaning supplies, possibly beneath the sink or in one of the larger drawers in the galley.

The wiry guy had taken down Summer with one hand. Kevin wasn't going to let that happen to him. He'd seen enough movies to know the good guy never got a second chance. He'd get one shot, if he was lucky. He was Bruce Willis in *Die Hard,* Matt Damon in *Bourne,* Daniel Craig as 007. He had plenty of reference material to draw upon.

But could he actually stab a guy? He convinced himself not to think about it. *Just do it,* all the Nike ads told him.

One factor in his favor was the element of surprise. His Uncle Walt was not a hunter but was an expert marksman and one of the best trackers in the country. Kevin had been on overnights with Walt when he would locate an animal or herd and then see how long and how far he could stay with them. Hours, sometimes days, and many, many miles. What he'd learned on those outings came less from watching his uncle track—although he picked up some pointers—and more from the late-night stories told around the campfire. It was then that Walt had talked about Kevin's father. And he learned about the use of the element of surprise.

Remaining hidden made him feel like a coward. What would Bruce or Matt or Daniel do?

He pictured himself going through each motion. Then, with some sixth sense alerting him, he sneaked a peek out into the plane's main compartment.

The wiry guy was coming up the aisle straight for him.

Trapped, Kevin thought it better to show himself than to surprise a guy like that.

He reached to push the partition back just as the creep stopped and opened one of the window shades that was pulsing yellow and orange. The man pushed his face against the window, turned around, and ran toward the cockpit, shouting, "WE'RE ON FIRE!"

Kevin slid open the partition. He climbed down into the galley, his back to the emergency exit. The door's small window revealed the source of the guy's anxiety: the engine was on fire.

Kevin's heart leaped into his throat.

He peered around the panel to see Summer looking back at him. Her face was blotchy. He wasn't sure she saw him. She was staring off into space. She seemed to be in shock.

He undid the clasp that secured the fire extinguisher and pulled the ring pin. To him, it felt like pulling the pin on a hand grenade. Time began counting down in his head.

If Kevin was going to take a run at the wiry guy, it was now or never.

What if he was the last line of defense between them and another 9/11? What if these guys planned a suicide dive into the Sun Valley Lodge or the wine auction? A guy once had tried to bomb the Cutter Conference. Anything was possible.

The cabin went dark, and the jet banked to the left. His eyes adjusted to the green glow from an LED on the flashlight.

His inner ear crackled, telling him the plane was descending rapidly.

He had to get himself strapped into a seat. He had no choice about that. He raised the fire extinguisher, rounded the corner, and charged.

The guy, facing forward, was swearing a blue streak at the top of his lungs. The pilots didn't seem to hear him. Kevin continued down the aisle. The guy looked much bigger up close, strong and dangerous. He had a birthmark or tattoo on the side of his neck.

"Ahhhhh!" Kevin shouted.

The guy's head came around, his hands lifting defensively.

Kevin pulled the trigger.

48

It took Walt three minutes to reach Sun Valley Aviation. Pete was already there, speaking to a woman that a counter plaque identified as REBA.

"No kids," Pete said as Walt entered. "Just a flight crew of three."

"T-A-nine-five-nine?" Walt said.

"Yes," the woman said. Her upper lip was moist. "It wasn't the same flight crew that flew it in, but that's not all that unusual."

"Video?" Walt said, pointing to a camera high in the corner.

She led them into the back office, where a dedicated computer screen showed four camera angles. It took her only minutes to match a time stamp on the fuel receipt with the time stamp on the video and play back the images of the flight crew.

The first two guys wore crew caps down low, obscuring their faces. The third guy wore a baseball cap backward, and managed to stay off camera most of the time. Finally, he happened to look up.

"That's Salvo," Walt said.

The receptionist froze the image. Matthew Salvo was looking right at the camera.

"And Salvo is . . . ?" Pete said.

"A person of interest," Walt answered.

Cantell was no longer after the wine. He'd stolen Sumner's private jet worth seventeen million dollars.

"I want to confirm T-A-nine-five-nine is not on this ramp," Walt said.

He walked briskly to the FBO's door and pushed out into the cool evening air, taking in the large number of jets and the gaping hole in the back line where Reba was pointing.

"See?"

But Walt didn't see. His eyes were fixed on the beat-up Subaru parked outside the chain-link fence.

49

A spray of noxious yellow powder huffed from the fire extinguisher's nozzle, coating the man's face. Kevin swung the extinguisher at him, striking him with the butt end in a roundhouse blow that sounded like a ripe melon hitting concrete. The man went down, bouncing off one of the seats and convulsing to the carpet.

Freed, Summer kicked the man twice, before Kevin pulled her away and wrapped her in his arms.

The pilots, consumed with the complexities of landing a damaged jet, were unaware of anything going on in the back.

Kevin and Summer stood there several long seconds, their uncertain faces flashing green and orange, frozen in place, unable to speak.

Kevin finally blurted out, "We've got to get buckled. This thing's going down."

"His cap," she said, bending down and feeling around in the dark. She found it and handed it to Kevin. "In case they look back here . . ."

Kevin moved the man so his legs didn't stick out in the aisle. Summer took her seat again, while Kevin donned the cap backward and sat in the unconscious man's seat. Facing toward the back of the plane meant the pilots wouldn't see his face, if they bothered to check.

Kevin glanced over at Summer in the inconsistent light and caught her looking back at him inquisitively. He had no answers for her, wondering if he should make a move for the galley's knife drawer. But the jet was losing altitude fast, wobbling as if dangerously out of control.

White light washed the cabin when the landing lights came on at the last moment. Kevin bent forward and grabbed his knees. Summer followed suit.

In a flash of absolute certainty, he knew what came next. It was as if his uncle were telling him what to do. He signaled Summer, motioning aft and to the left, to the emergency door.

She nodded.

He pointed at her.

You go first.

She nodded again.

Progress, he thought. *Now, the knife, the flashlight, the phone—in that order—while we're still moving.*

He and Summer could do this.

The Learjet landed hard, bounced, bounced twice more, then shook hard as if about to break apart.

With the impact, the man at Kevin's feet shifted and groaned. He was coming to.

Everything suddenly went dark.

Kevin signaled Summer.

It's now or never.

Summer released her seat belt and ran for the back of the plane.

50

Walt should have been looking at a team of twenty trained deputies at his spanking-new Incident Command Center. Instead, he was looking at four, two of them civilian clerks. Five on-call deputies were on their way, but still twenty to thirty minutes out. Overhead displays, satellite links, the Ethernet—all seemed to be laughing at him in almost empty space.

The Subaru was Kevin's. The Learjet was gone. They had a parasailor's 911 report that a low-flying jet had hit a flock of geese and, when last seen, its engines were smoking or on fire. The timing of the sighting matched the cell-phone-following GPS program that placed Kevin over the town of Ketchum.

Walt attempted not to show the despair he felt, but this last bit of news had sent a wave of panic and dread through him— recalling the US Airways jet that had taken less than two minutes to crash-land in the Hudson. He caught himself staring at the phone, expecting it to ring. He'd lost his brother several years earlier. He couldn't bear to lose his brother's son. He reached to loosen the top button of his uniform, but found it unbuttoned already.

He was not a man to shrink from re- sponsibility, yet, for a moment, he just wanted to walk out the door and keep go- ing. No more phone calls, no more bad news. He watched the clock on the wall's second hand jerk around its face.

Walt caught Fiona staring at him from a seat in the otherwise empty front row. She grimaced and cocked her head silently, checking that he was okay. He returned an indifferent shrug, his eyes revealing the dead space inside. He so did not want the phone to ring.

"Okay," he said, getting the attention of

the four other people in the room, including Fiona. "Pull together Search and Rescue. Apprise Joaquin up in Stanley of the situation. Update the Challis sheriff. And we'd better at least notify the Forest Service to prepare for a fire response. If the plane goes down . . . well, it's mostly forest up there."

The speakerphone beeped.

"Sheriff?"

Walt steeled himself, resolving not to fall apart in front of this group.

"Go ahead."

"The MC has a Theodore Sumner trying to vid-chat with you. Do you want to take it?"

Walt worked the laptop. The screen came alive, as did an overhead monitor. Walt didn't want the man's face overhead but didn't know how to shut it off.

Teddy Sumner's stress could be measured by the sweat on his upper lip and the pain in his eyes.

"I've got it," Walt said, punching the phone and slipping on a headset. "Go ahead, Mr. Sumner."

"Good evening, Sheriff," Sumner began. "As I suspected, my pilot is in his hotel room, watching television. But I asked him to call for the plane, and, of course, you're also right that it's gone. It took off right around the time you said it did, which, I can assure you, it did without my permission. The only conclusion to draw is, my jet's been stolen. Why? I have no idea. With proper notification, it will be seized the moment it lands anywhere, although, fully fueled as it is, it could reach Mexico. If that happens, I'll likely lose it. I asked my pilot about the key—there are only two— and he has his. When I looked for mine— I'm loath to admit this—it was missing. As is my daughter, which, I'm told by Mr. Webb, you're aware of. Putting two and two together, my daughter took my key and got someone to fly my plane, though, for the life of me, I refuse to believe it."

"That's not how it went down," Walt said.

He briefed Sumner on the Sun Valley Aviation security video, and allowed how they had three suspects, all known for participating in major robberies, though he did not name them.

"It's possible that one of the three

convinced or coerced your daughter to take your key," Walt continued. "It's also possible—probable—that your daughter and a companion are on the jet. Circumstantial evidence supports that theory: a phone call made to this department."

Sumner's reaction was immediate: stunned breathlessness. Then a father's fury filled his eyes, and he choked out, "Not possible . . . That can't be right."

"In the spirit of full disclosure, her companion is assumed to be my nephew, Kevin Fleming. Kevin's employed by the Sun Valley Company and works in the lodge, where, as I understand it, you're staying."

"Your nephew?"

"And your daughter, yes. Believe me, I want them to be anywhere but on that plane. We have a report, sir, that it may have suffered some damage while in flight."

"Come again?"

"Geese . . . a flock of geese. We have an eyewitness report that both engines were smoking and on fire. We're organizing a Search and Rescue."

"Good God, on fire? My jet? How certain are you Summer's on board?"

"It's not all speculation. We've got the phone call, some mapping software. And the times match. The evidence is fairly conclusive but not definitive. I would like to stress that point."

"What's she doing on that jet?" He looked as though, if he could have reached through the screen and grabbed Walt by the collar, he would have. "Your nephew put her up to this! Christ Almighty, I'll have his hide."

"We know nothing about what led up to this. What little we do know, we're acting on by deploying Search and Rescue. Beyond that—"

"Beyond *that . . .* ?"

"We're of the opinion that the theft was not an act of terrorism. We have, however, notified the proper federal authorities, as mandated by law. They will scramble fighters and force the jet down—"

"Jesus, stop!"

"Unless this was meant to be a robbery, as I believe, likely an insurance scam, in which case the thieves never intended to fly very far. The mountains block tracking radar, Mr. Sumner. And seventeen million makes for a very attractive target," Walt added.

"And they lured Summer into this scheme somehow?"

"We can't confirm your daughter's or my nephew's involvement, only that the evidence suggests they're aboard that plane."

"What a cock-up!" Sumner shouted. His spittle flecked the camera lens and Walt's screen. "On fire?" His face seemed to melt down to his chin as belief slowly registered.

Down to his heart, Walt was thinking, feeling the same thing in his own chest.

"Let's hope not," he said.

51

Kevin watched out the small window in the jet's emergency door, his face pressed against the glass, as the ground beneath them raced past illuminated by the orange flames coming from the engine.

He held fast to the door's handle as the brakes squealed. The plane shuddered, then slowed. A cloud erupted from the engine, followed by darkness. The fire was out.

There were no runway lights, no outbuildings visible.

"Ready?" Kevin said, the plane rolling to a stop.

Summer didn't answer, paralyzed by all that had just happened.

"Matches!" he said. "I forgot the matches."

Despite herself, Summer pulled open a drawer in the galley and grabbed a pack of matches. She wasn't as far gone as he thought.

He yanked on the handle, pushing the door open and grabbing a suddenly un-willing Summer.

"It's still moving," she protested.

"We're going, anyway," he said.

Holding the squirming Summer around the waist, he began lowering her to the ground.

"Tuck and roll," he said, and let her go.

As an afterthought, he tossed out the knife. He couldn't jump with it in his pocket.

He lowered himself, getting his feet go-ing in the direction of the plane, and let go. He slammed to the surface and rolled, surprised to find it was a dirt-and-gravel strip, not a paved runway. He stood up and took inventory—both elbows were scraped up, as was his right knee, but otherwise he was intact—and then ran back to find Summer. Risking use of the flashlight, he located Summer sitting up but in shock. She had a pretty bad raspberry on her right temple, and the hair on that side of her head was bloody and matted.

"You okay?"

She nodded.

"Anything broken?"

She tested her limbs, then shook her head.

A loud crash came from the direction of the still-rolling jet. It had hit something. A final screech of the brakes was followed by silence—total, utter silence—the kind of silence Kevin knew from his time in the wilderness. He switched off the flashlight. The sky was filled with a million stars piercing the rich blue glow, another sign of their isolation. They weren't anywhere near the lights of civilization.

The starlight was enough to see shapes by. There was a small plane, a piece of its right wing missing, pushed off to one side of the runway about twenty yards behind where the jet had come to a stop. That explained the loud crash.

"Come on!" he said, trying to help Summer to her feet. But she just sat there like a sack of cement. "Summer!"

"I can't do this," she sobbed. "I give up."

"No, no, no—no giving up."

He pulled her to her feet, took her hand, and hurried her down the runway, all the while searching for the knife. He flicked on the flashlight, revealing sticks, a couple fist-sized rocks, and a glint of metal. It was the blade of the knife. He flicked the light off, then ran in the direction of the knife.

"Hey!" a man shouted out.

Kevin couldn't risk using the flashlight again. He dropped to the dirt and felt around with his hands. Summer was at his side also searching.

"What are—"

"The knife," he said.

"They're coming!"

"Got it!" he said, adding, "We're out of here."

They ran for the woods.

"We're going to be okay," he said. "Just don't slow down. And don't look back."

"Okay."

More shouting came from behind, as a faint beam of light cast their shadows in front of them. Kevin led Summer off the dirt strip, grass whipping their ankles. They passed a shed, then jumped a small stream. An imposing hill rose up darkly in front of them.

"Stairs!" she said, tugging him to the left.

"No! That's what they'll think," he answered, pulling her to the right.

The light from behind grew brighter, their pursuers gaining on them.

Kevin and Summer fled through the trees and up the hill, their footfalls quieted by pine straw. They headed right, away from the stairs, but climbing, always climbing, dodging the black tree trunks, weaving around opaque outcroppings of rock.

A voice called out from behind, followed by the pounding of their pursuers' feet on the stairs. The faint glimmer of white teeth appeared on Kevin's dark, sweating face. He was smiling.

52

Walt couldn't remember the last time he'd spoken to his father. There had been a brief cease-fire a few months back, but neither party had followed up with negotiation. Stagnation had given way to rot, a return to normalcy. He had once hoped that his marriage and the arrival of grandchildren would help heal things between them, had held on to the belief that family was a bond that transcended petty problems that cluttered other relationships. But hope could not compete with reality, the ideal collapsing under the glare of practicality. He'd begun to doubt they would ever be friends again. In the end, his brother's death had taken three lives, not just one.

"What are you doing here?" he said to Fiona as he entered his office.

"You said I could use your computer."

"Did I?"

"Are you all right?"

"No," he answered. "I have to call my father. He has to be told."

"I've got something for you." She motioned for him to sit by her, but he remained standing while viewing the screen.

"Ears," she said.

"Ears," he repeated.

"As individual as fingerprints."

"I'm aware of that."

"You wanted proof it was Cantell."

Walt moved closer. "Yes . . ."

"Behold the magic of digital photography."

From a mug shot of Cantell taken from a scanned image of his OneDOJ sheet, she cropped the right ear, then enlarged it, made it transparent, and laid it over a video still from Sun Valley Aviation's security camera. It matched Cantell's ear exactly.

"I can do the same thing with Roger

McGuiness," she said, "although the angle is not as absolutely perfect as this."

"So we've got them dead to rights," Walt said.

"You don't have to sound so excited," she snapped sarcastically.

Walt snatched up the phone and barked out an order to arrest Arthur Remy "on suspicion of fraud." He added, "Three-quarters of my deputies and every cop in the valley are up there. Find Remy and hold him for questioning."

Hanging up, he explained himself to Fiona. "We know the bottles are fakes. We can tie Cantell to the attempted theft of the bottles and Remy, by association, to the theft of the jet and the kidnapping of two teenagers. It gives us someone to question, an actual suspect. *You* gave us that someone. Maybe we can catch a break."

"Then I'll save my work?" she said.

"By all means." He glanced at the phone.

"Just take the punches, if he throws them," she said.

"Oh, he'll throw them all right."

"It's all in how you respond."

"Yes, *dear.*"

"Jeez," Fiona said, coming out of the chair—his chair, "you're welcome."

"I'm sorry," he called out after her. Too late.

Walt sat down, let out a long breath, and reached for the phone. He started punching in the numbers he knew by heart. But he did it more slowly than usual, his index finger hovering over the final button, refusing to punch.

He then sat up straight, elbows on his desk, and pressed the button.

"Well, look what the dog drug in," Jerry Fleming said.

"Been a while."

"Has it? Hadn't noticed."

"I've got a situation here. Kevin may be involved, may be in way over his head. I need your contacts at Air Force."

"Kev? What kind of situation?"

Walt talked him through the attempted theft of the wine, the explosion at the auction, the blocking of the bridge. Chuck Webb's seeing Kevin's car behind the lodge and the theft of the jet he saved for last. When he brought up the engine fire, his father cut him off.

"Kevin's on board?"

"We haven't verified that, but that's what I believe, yes."

"Jesus H. Christ, what kind of Mickey Mouse outfit are you running over there?"

"I'm told the Air Force may have radar that reaches up here. The FAA believes they do. Since you have friends over there, I thought—"

"You'd get me to bail you out."

"Not exactly how I saw it."

"I'll make the call."

Walt outlined the window of opportunity as he understood it, impressing upon him that they needed to make every effort to locate the Learjet.

"You're in over your head."

"Thankfully, your opinion doesn't matter. By now, they're likely well beyond my county, well out of my reach."

"Not if that second engine was burning out. Any pilot with a beating heart would put that jet down in a matter of minutes if one engine had been lost and they were losing the second. It couldn't have flown very far."

"We're on it. We're contacting every airfield."

"Takes a good deal of runway to land a jet."

"We're on it," Walt repeated.

"The right kind of satellite might pick up a flare out. I can check on that as well."

"Anything you can do . . . The sooner we can track that jet—"

"I'm coming over there."

"That's not necessary."

"Did I ask? I said I'm coming over there. If you find Kevin, then call me. Otherwise, plan to pick me up in . . . ninety minutes. I'll call you from the plane."

"The company jet?"

"You could have had this, Walt. This was your choice, not mine. I'll call from the jet and give you a number where you can reach me. See you shortly."

Cringing, Walt hung up the phone. He had ninety minutes to save himself from certain hell.

53

The forest floor was interrupted by choke-cherry and brambles, slash and deadfall. Often impassable, the changing terrain required Kevin to traverse the hill instead of climbing vertically. Summer not only stayed with him but occasionally took the lead. While the forest's darkness made for slow going, using the flashlight would have been suicide, revealing their position in the same way the glow of a light below them told them where the chase was coming from.

Still a good distance away, there was no question that at least one of the three men had followed them into the woods.

"I don't get it," he whispered, huffing a bit. "Why bother with us?"

"What do you mean?" she asked.

"They obviously stole the plane, right?"

"Okay . . ."

"We were never part of that, so why follow us?"

"Because we saw them?" she suggested.

"No," he said. "We can't be the only ones who saw them. That doesn't make sense. I think it's you."

"What about me?"

"I think they want you. The jet's wrecked. You're the prize. And me? I'm nothing but . . . an inconvenience. I'm disposable."

"I think you're wrong."

"I hope I'm wrong," he said, now picking up the pace.

Summer suddenly passed him and leaped onto one of the huge boulders they'd been avoiding.

"Come on," she urged.

She led the way up and over the rock.

"Don't scuff the ground," she hissed. "Don't give them anything to follow."

She led them nearly straight up the hill.

Light played in the overhead branches,

then dimmed and moved left. Summer and Kevin headed higher, though considerably slower, in total silence. The next time Kevin checked, the beam had moved well away.

"Awesome," he said.

Summer shushed him.

The ground leveled off. The trees thinned. The moonlight shone brighter.

"Check it out!" she said.

They faced a rambling lodge cut into the rocky hill, making it look as if its log walls grew right out of the cliff. Bluish light glowed from the windows nearest them. Less light came from the far end of the lodge, where Kevin now spotted a tall, white-haired man on a path leading toward some stairs emerging from the forest, stairs that led down to the airfield. A pair of floodlights shone from the corner eaves of the lodge, casting a halogen glare across a field of wild grass.

The lodge was landscaped on three sides by a clearing. Summer stepped forward obviously wanting to call out to the man, but Kevin pulled her back.

"We have two choices here," Kevin said, his lips to her ear, "the forest or the house."

He pointed to the treetops. The flashlight beam had turned yet again and was once again coming up the hill from behind them.

The tall man—he looked like an old cowboy—wore blue jeans, boots, and a light-colored long-sleeved shirt. He stopped at the top of the stairs.

"Over here!" he called out loudly in the direction of the flashlight beam.

The beam froze, illuminating the tops of trees. Then it began to advance again up the hill, directly toward Kevin and Summer.

Kevin tugged on Summer's arm, making sure he had her attention. He pointed to a pair of doors cut into the rock at the base of the lodge, either a garage or storage area, by the look of it.

He drew her close and whispered. "Follow me, fast and low, straight for those doors."

"He'll help us!" She meant the cowboy.

The crunching of undergrowth grew ever louder. Whoever was following them was close now.

"Over here!" the cowboy called out. He headed down the stairs.

The lawn was now empty.

"Trust me," Kevin said to Summer.

He pulled her, and she followed. Together, they ran toward the lodge, reaching
the shadows sheltering the two doors.

"Okay?" he asked, panting.

She nodded.

He felt for the door latch. It engaged,
and the heavy door sagged open.

"There are stairs over here!" the cowboy
called out. The flashlight beam paused
briefly.

"It's going to be dark in there," Kevin
warned.

Summer nodded.

"No noise," he added.

"So, shut up!" she said.

"Whatever . . ."

Kevin slipped inside, Summer followed.
He took one look around, then eased the
door shut, blocking out the light, and gently lowered the latch in place.

The space smelled of cedar and grass,
oil and dust. He slipped the flashlight under his shirt to mute its beam, then quickly
flashed it on and off to get his bearings.
They saw a pair of sawhorses, a work-
bench, trash bins, tarps, a small tractor, a
skimobile or ATV—maybe both—and extension cords, ropes, and tools hanging

from a pegboard on the right wall. There was a stack of firewood against the back wall. Steps at the far left of the room led to a door. He determined a route for them to follow.

"We should have stayed in the woods," she said in a hot whisper. "Or said something to that guy."

"We've got to get word to someone," he said.

He pulled out his cell phone, turned it on, silenced its ringer.

"No bars," he said, angrily jamming the phone back in his pocket.

"I've got to pee," she said.

"You've got to hold it," he said.

"There is no way I'm going to hold it."

"So, pee."

"Yeah, right."

"I'll turn my back."

"I am not peeing in the dirt."

"I am not dealing with this."

"There's got to be a toilet in the house."

"Why don't you go ask if you can use it?"

She huffed at him.

"We're somewhere near the Middle Fork," he said. "There're a half dozen of these places, max, in a couple thousand square miles of wilderness. There could be a neighbor a half mile away. But it might be forty miles or more."

"That's impossible. We were in the air, what, like ten minutes? Fifteen? How far could we have gone?"

"At three hundred miles an hour, you do the math. The point is, all these places have radios. Maybe that cowboy dude lives here all alone. We need that radio. So, come on."

Kevin reached out for Summer in the dark and found her arm. She didn't resist him as he led her along his newly memorized route. He moved slowly, inching his feet out ahead and avoiding knocking over any of the objects he encountered. As the toe of his running shoe connected with the first step of the stairs at the back of the room, he pocketed the flashlight, trading it for the steak knife. He tested the step. It accepted his weight without creaking. They then climbed slowly, eventually reaching the door at the top.

He tried the handle. It wasn't locked.

He couldn't see a thing, but he could feel Summer trembling. She squeezed his arm, wanting him to reconsider.

He found her ear and whispered, "Better odds if they don't catch both of us. There's a tarp in the corner. Hide under it." He tried leading her back down the stairs.

"No way," she hissed, resisting.

"Way," he said. "I may need you to save me."

"Right . . ."

"Remember, you're the prize, not me. We can't let you get caught."

He eased her down the steps, found their way along the stack of firewood, and reached the tarp. It smelled pleasantly of oiled canvas, triggering memories of his father and camping trips.

He sat her down. "Stay here until I come back for you."

"And what if you don't?" She sounded angry.

"If we get separated," he said, not answering her directly, "then we meet at the far end of the runway near the jet. You still have your key. There are radios on the jet as well."

He pulled the tarp over her head before she could reply. He tucked it around her. He flicked the light once to make sure she was covered, then waited a few seconds for his eyes to adjust to the dark again.

"... ud ... uck ..." Her voice muffled by the tarp. She'd either said "Good luck" or "Get fucked."

Kevin headed back to the door that led into the lodge.

54

Walt paced the Incident Command Center. His father had come through with the last-known whereabouts and vectors for the jet. The Mountain Home Air Force Base refused to admit they had radar capable of seeing into the mountains, so none of the information that Walt was given was official. And, since it wasn't official, Walt wasn't supposed to know that a pair of fighters had been scrambled to find the jet and shoot it down, if necessary, because it had been stolen. Walt reminded his father that he'd delayed reporting the jet as stolen in order to avoid what to him was a predictable response. His father had told him he couldn't have it both ways, and to meet him in sixty minutes when he landed.

Evelyn Holmes, a civilian employee of Walt's who typically ran numbers, approached Walt.

"Evelyn," he greeted her. He had no time to discuss budget but didn't want to seem dismissive. As a civilian, she had no business being in the Incident Command Center, but he wasn't about to throw her out.

"Word is, you're looking for someone to calculate a flight path."

"As it's been explained to me," he said, not wanting to insult her, "it's complicated stuff. Speed in the air, speed over ground, rate of descent, the fact that the engines are constantly losing thrust . . ."

"May I take a look at the data?"

"Sure. I don't mean this the way it sounds, but, from what Steven Garman says, it *is* rocket science."

"I was awarded my Phil-D in astrophysics from Imperial College, London."

"You have a Ph.D.," he said.

"And a master's in material sciences."

She was working for him for just a few dollars more than minimum wage.

"This valley . . ." he said.

"My son wanted to compete at the national level in snowboarding. His father and I made some sacrifices."

"But you've been here—"

"Six years, yes. He broke his ankle and blew out his knee in his second season. His snowboarding career was over. But we all fell in love with this place. No way we were going back to southern California."

He showed her what little information they had on the Learjet.

"I need to predict possible airports and landing strips," he said.

Evelyn gave a cursory look at the data and grunted. "Okay, I'm on it," she said.

A deputy knocked and entered the room. He hesitated at the threshold under the glare of everyone's attention.

"Well?" Walt called out.

"EOC has a report of a UFO . . . That's right, Sheriff, you heard me right . . . Seen south, southeast of Stanley. A yellow light, not running lights, that just hovered there in the sky for about a minute, then sank slowly over the horizon and vanished. EOC thought it might be your jet."

"Give what you've got to Evelyn," Walt said.

"The guy making the call is retired Navy. Made a big point of that. Didn't want to be taken as a quack. He gave us his location in lat/long."

"In order for it to appear not to be moving," Evelyn said, accepting the note from the deputy, "he would have had to have been directly behind it, looking in its exact line of flight. I can work with that."

Walt referenced a map that was projected on one of the overhead screens as Evelyn drew a line north, northwest across Stanley.

"There's nothing out here," he said. "No airports. There aren't even roads."

"Given the jet's rate of descent, it went down somewhere here," Evelyn said. She drew a line perpendicular to the first line, like crossing a T. She glanced at the wall clock. "Twenty to twenty-five minutes ago."

"Went down?" Walt said.

55

Kevin opened the door that led from the garage/storage into the lodge, listened for signs of life, and, hearing none, sneaked inside. Adrenaline-charged and terrified, he hoped to find a phone or a radio. Since the death of his father, he'd manipulated his mother, banked on friends' pity, bargained for better grades from his teachers, and underperformed for his employers. Only his uncle wouldn't cut him any slack. And now, of all the people, it was his uncle that he found himself emulating.

Coats hung on pegs to the left, boots

were lined up neatly next to a rough-
planked bench. The coats were all big, the
boots all the same size: large. Kevin worked
his way down the hallway, past the kitchen,
and into a living room. It was furnished
with couches, overstuffed chairs, and a
dining table and chairs. In the oversized
fireplace, the remnants of a summer night's
fire glowed.

The room was unintentionally shabby
chic. The furniture didn't match; there were
wrought-iron lamps with cowhide lamp-
shades, a deer-antler chandelier over the
table. There were no bright colors or flow-
ers. The tone was more hunting lodge than
family getaway.

While the cowboy appeared to live
alone, this notion was contradicted by a
better view of the kitchen, with its eight-
burner range and twin refrigerators.

He was the caretaker, was more like it.

Searching for a phone and not finding
one, Kevin didn't panic. Summer had told
him about the radio and portable GPS in
her father's emergency bag on the jet. If
Kevin struck out here, with the right distraction he might be able to return there.

Just when he was about to give up, he spotted a radio atop of a walnut cabinet. Its face was dark, and a handheld microphone on a spiraled black cord was hanging from it that reminded him of the CB radio in his uncle's Cherokee.

Kevin heard deep voices rumbling through the wall, and he looked out the window to the top of the stairs, where the cowboy was talking to the copilot from the jet. The two men turned toward the lodge.

He now rushed to the radio, switched it on, grabbed the microphone, and hit the TALK button.

"Mayday! Mayday!" he whispered. "I'm at some lodge . . . on the Middle Fork, I think. Our plane went down . . . a jet. There are guys after me . . . the guys who took the jet."

He heard the cowboy's boots and the pilot's shoes clomping up the steps of the lodge.

Replacing the microphone, ducking down, and making for the nearest door, he looked back to see he'd left the radio on. At that moment, the front doorknob was turning. Only then did he spot the open gun case to the far right of the door. It held at least five rifles.

He hurried through the door and found himself in the study, with its two-person couch, beat-up recliner, and flat-screen television mounted on the wall. There was a cowhide under the harvest-table desk, and on the walls a pair of snowshoes, a brass clock, and some old black-and-white photographs. The fireplace was con-structed of river rock, with a wide hearth for sitting close to the flames, and nearby was a closet with sliding doors. The room smelled sweetly of pine sap and pipe smoke, and it felt like it would be a cozy place to spend a long snowed-in day.

Kevin had his ear to the study's door while searching for a way out—the door and a casement window immediately be-hind him.

". . . basically, a ten-acre island in the middle of God's country," a man's heavily accented voice was saying on the other side of the door. It was the cowboy. "The river is down there by the strip, with gorges at either end. Amazed you made it in. We extended that runway a year ago, but the boss's pilot took three weeks of simulation before daring to try it."

"What do you mean 'an island'?" asked the other man, the copilot.

"This cabin's on Shady Mountain. It's four thousand feet. Between it and the river . . . It's the isolation of this place, the privacy, that the boss finds so pleasing. Original cabin was built eighty years ago from logs cleared from the land. Major redo when the boss got it ten years ago. You can fly in, float in, but you don't get hikers knocking on your door like at some of these ranches . . . Can I get you something?"

"I'm okay, thanks . . . So, you take care of it by yourself?"

"That I do."

"Must get a little lonely."

"Not that I've noticed—"

"Come back. Didn't copy," a nasally thin voice broke in.

"Ah! The radio," said the pilot.

"Huh?" the cowboy said.

"Didn't copy your call," the radio voice clarified.

"I didn't call." The cowboy raised his voice for the radio.

"Is this John?" said the radio.

"It is. Ernie?"

"Get yourself off the channel, would you, John?" said Ernie. "You're clogging the airwaves. Someone was calling on this frequency."

"Keep your britches on," John said.

There were a couple pops, then Ernie's voice was no more.

"Not sure who we should contact first," said John. "I've got a satellite phone. I'm thinking you might want to call your boss before I go getting the Custer County sheriff all in a froth."

"You're right about that," said the pilot.

"I've got to call it in, but I sure as shit can wait ten minutes if that'll keep you your job."

"It might."

"I'll chase down that sat phone for you."

"Sounds good."

The cowboy's boots sounded as he crossed the room, then stopped abruptly.

"You must have made a shout-out to ATC once you caught fire," the cowboy said.

The pilot stuttered with his answer. "Ah . . . of course we did."

"Well, hell, there's no putting it off, then.

They'll be organizing searches. We had something similar last year—a Beechcraft Bonanza gone missing. Radio's probably the way to go. Call off the dogs, you know . . . not fair to them."

"I know what you're saying, but I'd sure appreciate contacting my boss first. That phone would be a big help."

"Timing won't make any difference," the cowboy said, his voice suddenly cautious and reserved. "How many souls did you say were on board?"

"I didn't say," said the other man. "But it was three of us: me, my pilot, and one crew."

A loud knock caused Kevin to jump.

"Yeah?" the cowboy hollered. "Come in."

The door opened, then banged shut.

"Whoa!" said the cowboy. "You took quite a hit."

"That'll teach you to tighten that seat belt," the copilot said, "won't it, Bobby?"

Bobby . . .

Kevin knew the newcomer. He'd hammered him with the wrong end of the fire extinguisher.

Kevin hoped the cowboy's change in tone meant he'd reasoned through the radio being found switched on. The discovery had to be weighing on him, had to have prompted the question about the number of passengers.

One thing became clear to Kevin: the cowboy wasn't part of the team. He and the copilot were strangers to each other, each testing the other. Distrustful of each other, it was beginning to feel like.

"Let's do hold off on the radio," the copilot said, a little too insistently, "until I can reach my boss and let him know what's going on. He's a low-profile kind of guy. He's not going to want a lot of attention over this."

"Who'd you say the owner of the jet was?"

"I didn't say. He keeps a pretty low profile," the copilot repeated. The tone between him and the cowboy had turned chilly.

Kevin, glancing again at the window, then the closet, was riveted by what he was hearing. He knew he should run, but his eavesdropping had him glued to the spot.

"A plane that fancy and all," the cowboy said, "surprised it don't have its own sat phone. Most do, right?"

"You know what?" said the copilot, his voice less antagonistic. "Of course it does.

I didn't even check before coming up here, the power being down after we fried that panel. I didn't think anything was working. Let me go check."

"Not a problem," the cowboy said, also sounding less tense, "you can use mine. Now, about keeping a low profile around here? Not possible, I'm afraid. It's big news when a bear rips into the trash. But a private plane—a jet, no less—hell, if this is handled wrong you'll have Boise news choppers getting aerial shots by sunup. And let me tell you something: *my* boss wouldn't appreciate that. So I'm thinking, maybe we're of a like mind here. First we'll call your boss, then mine. We've got to call off the search somehow, but let me set on that for a minute. We best go about this with kid gloves. Let me get me that satellite phone. I just remembered, it's not upstairs."

The *clomp-clomp* of boots was now coming Kevin's direction as he frantically glanced around the study on his way to the closet. He spotted a small green light on the bookshelf. It was the satellite phone. It had been there all along, just five feet away.

He was late getting to the closet, his

hand on the sliding door as the cowboy entered the room.

They locked eyes.

Kevin's eyes must have looked fearful. The cowboy's eyes widened at first, then softened.

"Won't be but a minute," the cowboy called out to the others. He then shut the door.

The moment the door closed, the copilot's footfalls hurried toward the study. He wasn't having any doors shut on him.

The cowboy stabbed at the air, directing Kevin to hide in the closet.

Kevin got in the closet but didn't shut the door in time. He let it go rather than chance making any noise shutting it. Just then, the pilot, not the copilot, charged into the room behind the cowboy. He hit the cowboy on the head with a lamp, dropping him with the single blow. He was about to deliver a second blow, quite possibly fatal, when the copilot stopped him.

"No!" said the copilot. "That's enough!"

"He's a big son of a bitch," said the wiry guy. "Let me give him another."

"He knows this place . . . he's our way out of here. Tie him up."

The wiry guy, "Bobby," raced over to the phone and grabbed it. "Got it!"

Kevin, behind the closet door, peered through a crack.

A second light came on in the room.

"We're out of here, right?" Bobby asked. "Same plan?"

"Get real," barked the copilot. "The airstrip and the river are the only ways in and out of here. The jet's not going anywhere, Matt. We smashed up his Cessna, something he doesn't even know about yet. Maybe we could float the river . . . Or maybe we could contact Lorraine and just sit tight."

Lorraine, Kevin noted. *Matt, not Bobby.* He now had two of their names.

"What about the girl?" Matt said. "She's worth something to someone."

"Trust me, I'm aware of that. The ranch is an island, is how he described it. Those kids aren't . . ." His voice trailed off.

With his narrow view of the room, Kevin couldn't see anyone. But he hadn't heard them leave the room. The silence stretched out.

"I don't have time to play games," said the copilot.

"What the hell are you talking about?" said Matt.

"Shut up, Matt."

When he spoke again, he was immediately on the other side of the closet door.

"There are two ways to play this," the copilot said through the door. "You come out of the closet with your hands where we can see them or you stay in there and it plays out worse for you."

Kevin held his breath. The copilot was talking to him. But how—?

Then he spotted his own wet shoe print on the floor outside the closet, the toe pointing in. His black Reeboks were soaking wet from the dew.

"Okay, have it your way," the copilot said. He then slid the closet door shut.

Kevin was overcome by the darkness of the space.

"Find a broom handle," the copilot said to Matt, "and hammer and nails."

"Jesus!" said Matt, as he took off out of the room.

"What are you, kid, a size nine? Too big for her. And you're in there alone, which means she's alone too. Or hurt. Or whatever. If you want to help her, you start talking."

Kevin heard Matt's footfalls returning to the room. Then he heard wood crack. The sliding door nearest him wobbled as the broken broom handle was jammed in place. Then there was more wobbling as the copilot tested the doors.

"Bad decision, kid," the copilot said through the door. "Find the girl," he then said to Matt. "She's probably close by."

"Roger is not going—"

"No names!" the copilot shouted.

"Search the house first. Radio our friend at the plane. Tell him the girl's alone. We're going to be fine."

Kevin finally exhaled. His head was spinning. *Roger.* Three names.

"But get me those nails or some screws or something first," the copilot said.

The storage room!

Speaking to the closet door, he added, "You had your chance, kid."

56

Summer squeezed her legs together, her swollen bladder making it impossible to think. Kevin, who'd said he would hurry, hadn't returned. How long was she supposed to wait? Only moments earlier, she'd heard noises and voices coming from inside. Scary noises, angry voices.

Despite her sense of security beneath the tarp, she had to get out of the garage, both to relieve herself and to escape the claustrophobic panic spreading through her. But she was no fan of the great outdoors; the closest she had gotten to wilderness was Orange County, a wasteland without a decent shopping mall in sight. The idea of fleeing alone into the woods at night made her have to pee all the more badly.

She slipped from beneath the tarp, ducked behind a combination ATV-trailer, and kept still. In the colorful, eerie light of power tools recharging, she searched the pegboard above her. There, she found a chisel with a razor-sharp blade about the width of her little finger. She leaped to her feet, slipped it in her pant pocket, and instantly cut a hole first in the pocket and then nicked her thigh. Noticing the leather sheaths on other chisels, she stuffed hers into one and put it in her other pocket. She then pressed her pants against the wound—only a scratch.

Armed, Summer made her way to the shed door, paused, then slipped out into the chilly night air. She pulled the door behind her, ensuring it was latched shut, and sneaked a look at the yard.

Empty.

The woods were incredibly dark and more than a little terrifying. How had she let Kevin get away with the flashlight? There was probably one in the shed, but she wasn't about to go back there. She tasted freedom in the crisp air. If they were after her, as Kevin had claimed, they were going to have to find her.

57

With the fallen telephone pole and wires cleared from the bike-path bridge, an hour and twenty minutes after the log spill, two vehicles carrying half a dozen Search and Rescue volunteers, including two canines, were the first allowed across.

Vocal citizens, demanding to be allowed to cross, kept Tommy Brandon and four deputies busy.

"I need to get across," said yet another man from behind Brandon.

"You and everyone else, buddy," Brandon said.

A group of twenty to thirty volunteers

was working to clear the bridge, using a combination of chainsaws, four-by-fours with hitches, and even a team of draft horses from out Green Horn Gulch. A third of the fallen logs had been removed, and now efforts were under way to tow the semi clear.

"Give it another hour and we'll have it open again."

"I'm the girl's father," the man said.

Brandon turned.

"Excuse me?" he said.

"The girl who's believed to be on the plane with the sheriff's nephew. Teddy Sumner," he said, then introducing himself. "I need to get to the sheriff . . . now!"

"Yeah, okay," Brandon said. "You parked back there somewhere?"

"That's right."

"Problem is, Mr. Sumner, there are about a hundred cars in front of yours, and no one's going to take kindly to someone jumping the line."

"I'm going across that bridge, Officer."

"It's *Deputy*. And, no, you're not. Not unless I say so, *sir*. Right now is not a good time, as you can probably see."

"*Those* cars just came across . . ."

"They're Search and Rescue. We just about had a riot on our hands when we allowed that to happen. So we've got to let things cool before trying it again."

"One of your patrol cars . . . someone could drive me."

"I'm not exactly long on deputies here. I've got four men to see that the bridge is cleared and to hold back a couple hundred very pissed-off people, all of whom have a better reason than their neighbor for getting across. I'm sorry, sir, it'll be maybe twenty minutes."

"I can walk across," he proposed.

"Of course . . . as you can see."

People on bicycles and motorcycles and on foot were crossing the bike-path bridge in both directions.

"How far to Hailey?"

"Four or five miles."

"I demand to be taken to the sheriff."

Brandon looked at the man, dumbfounded. "You *demand*?"

"Call him, tell him I'm here."

"I respect your situation, Mr. Sumner, and I really wish I could help . . ."

A tricked-out pickup truck rumbled off road through the sage just then and gunned for the bridge. Brandon hurried toward it, waving the driver back.

"A little busy here!" he called back to Sumner.

The man was clearly frustrated. "Call Fleming. Tell him I'm on my way."

Sumner charged across the bridge with overemphasized strides.

Who?" Walt said. "You're sure?"

"Yes, sir."

Someone had called in some of the office's civilian employees. Walt had borrowed three deputies from the jail. He recognized the woman he was speaking to but couldn't recall the department she was with.

"Here?"

"Front-door desk. Wants to see you."

"Send him back. Absolutely."

Teddy Sumner wore attitude on his face as he entered the Incident Command Center. But as he saw the nearly dozen deputies and civilians at their laptops, as he sensed the orchestrated effort led by Walt who stood behind a central lectern, his brow furrowed and he looked as if he might cry.

"Down here," Walt said.

Sumner made his way through the room slowly, taking it all in.

"Jesus," he said.

"Your tax dollars at work," Walt said. They shook hands. Walt reintroduced himself. "We don't usually allow civilians in here while we're running an operation. I'm happy to have you look around, but you'll have to wait in my office if you want to stay."

"She's my daughter."

"Which is exactly the point," Walt said. "I make decisions here that affect the investigation, the search, and hopefully the outcome. This is not a democracy."

One of the deputies looked up, about to say something, then went back to his laptop.

Sumner looked around. "How certain are you that they're on my jet? Before you even think about trying to get me out of this room, I suggest you share some of the circumstantial evidence you spoke of."

Fiona, sitting in the front row, met eyes with Walt, hers showing concern. He motioned her over, and she produced the OneDOJ sheets.

"We believe three individuals—a Christopher Cantell, Roger McGuiness, and Matthew Salvo—stole your Learjet after creating a diversion at the auction and by blocking the bridge with logs."

Slack-jawed, Teddy Sumner stepped back. "You've already identified them?" He sounded far more surprised than impressed. "How's that possible? Are these positive IDs?"

"Confirmed. Ms. Kenshaw can walk you through the evidence later."

"My daughter . . . ?"

"Was seen leaving the lodge with my nephew. That's also confirmed. My nephew's phone has a tracking feature called SPOT. Are you familiar with it?"

"No, never heard of it."

"It uses the phone's GPS, and, through a subscription service, allows parents to keep track of their children. My nephew's mother is a bit overprotective, and his phone is equipped with a similar device. He's not aware that it's been activated. The point here is, we were able to map a number of locations for him over the window of time provided and have confirmed he left the lodge at a rate of travel consistent with a car and arrived at the airport. He then leaves Hailey at 9:07 P.M. and heads north at an accelerated rate that can only be a fast plane like a jet . . . *your* jet."

That bit of information knocked the wind out of Sumner. "And where is he now?" he finally asked.

"That's the thing: there's no cell coverage north of Galena Summit. The tracking locator, although it's called GPS, it actually works off cell-tower triangulation. A portable cell transmitter, being flown up here from Salt Lake City as we speak, may light up Kevin's phone if we can get the transmitter airborne. We're working every angle we can think of."

Sumner looked around the room.

"I'd like to put our guys in touch with your pilot," Walt said, "to see if there's any equipment aboard the Lear we might be able to use to locate the jet."

"Summer's on the plane?" Sumner asked, still winded.

"We think so, yes."

He looked around, found a chair, sat down. He rolled the chair closer to Walt, looking somewhat pitiful in the effort.

"Something you could help us with. First, we need you to keep your phone turned on and ready. We'd like your permission to monitor and record any calls you receive. Same with the landline to your hotel room. I'd rather you hadn't come down here, frankly. We need you in that room when that call comes."

"Well, I'm here, reroute the call. Insurance? You're thinking extortion?"

"Extortion would be welcome news, Mr. Sumner."

The two men stared at each other.

"Kidnapping?" Sumner coughed up a laugh. "This is *not* a kidnapping!"

"At first glance, I'd agree. There's nothing on any of these sheets to suggest anything more than robbery . . . large-scale robbery. But given your daughter and my nephew being on that plane, we can no longer make that assumption. Our chief suspect, Christopher Cantell, is no dummy. If he has your daughter, whether by design or not, he knows he's facing kidnapping. And that changes everything."

Sumner stared at him blankly. "No, no, you're wrong." He said it with a father's certitude. "It's not a kidnapping. A heist, maybe—I can see that. But, as you've said, their records . . . nothing suggests kidnapping. It's not possible."

"First thing is, locate the jet and determine its condition and the condition of those aboard."

Sumner looked at the map on the screen overhead. A line drawn on it terminated in a T with a fairly large circle drawn around it.

"I know you made an effort to get down here," Walt said. "But, honestly, you're of more value to us, and to your daughter, waiting for that call back in your hotel room."

"Forget that. Like I said, reroute the call. Do what you have to do, but I'm not going anywhere. Who's in on this, Sheriff, besides you? Who's on this investigation?"

"It's a big operation, at this point. Prior to this, we had issued a BOLO for the suspects. Law enforcement for the five-state region are on alert—the FAA, the Air Force, Homeland Security, the FBI. Given recent events, this country doesn't take lightly the commandeering of jets."

"The FBI, Homeland? I don't want them on this. They'll screw it up, shoot it down without regard to who's on board."

"Everyone's apprised of our suspicions . . . it's a fluid situation."

"Fuck that, she's my daughter! Do you have kids, Sheriff?" Sumner asked.

"I do. Two daughters, a little younger than yours."

"And if they were your daugh—" He caught himself.

"My nephew," Walt reminded. "Believe me, I don't want anyone else on this case any more than you do. But the only way to keep that from happening is to find that jet tonight before the Bureau or other agencies get their act together. It's all about timing. Nothing much is going to happen on their end tonight. It'll take them a while to even get here."

Reminded of arrivals, Walt checked the wall clock.

His father's plane was due.

58

Summer zipped and buttoned her pants, releasing a pent-up breath of relief. She peered around the tree trunk, having chosen a spot in the woods with a decent view of the lodge, partway down the hill and well away from the stairs. A tendril of gray smoke rose from the lodge's chimney.

Her mother had been an expert problem solver, getting from A to Z in as straight a line as possible. Priding herself on being like her mother, Summer had resolved long ago to show her father that she need not depend on him for her every thought and deed. Pushing away her panic, she would think her way out of this on her own.

Kevin had yet to appear. He was either hiding inside the lodge or had been caught. Not only was he of no use to her, he probably needed her help. He'd made a big deal out of her being the prize these men were after. Could she use that to her advantage? Offer a trade she then wouldn't honor? She owed him, there was no doubt about that. He'd saved her from that creep with the wandering hands, had messed up his face pretty badly. He'd gotten her out of the plane and into the woods when she was, like, a zombie. She now saw how hard it must have been for him to stay with her rather than just taking off and leaving her.

Was she supposed to leave him in that lodge, or what? She needed to think clearly.

It was growing colder by the minute. Dressed as she was, in jeans and a T-shirt, Summer wondered how long she could last. She certainly couldn't make it through the night. If she could get up the nerve to hide under the tarp again, she'd be relatively warm. But going back inside the

lodge felt all wrong. It had eaten Kevin up.
She wasn't about to let that happen to her.
That left . . . *the plane* . . .

Would they be watching the plane?

Kevin had suggested they intended to
steal the jet . . . that seemed possible.
They'd picked the right target: her father
loved that Lear more than he loved her.
He'd have paid anything to get it back,
if he'd had two nickels to rub together. But
now that it was out of the picture, was she
their target as Kevin had suggested? If so,
why weren't they looking for her out here?

Or are they?

She began to fall apart. Her sole focus
for the past fifteen minutes had been to
pee, but with that taken care of she was
faced with too many unknowns and not
enough choices, and no one to help her
figure it out. That brought her back to Kevin
and whether she should or even could actually abandon him.

And then she saw the woodpile to the
right of the shed and heard a voice as
plain as day. It was her mother's voice.

Make a signal, the voice said.

If anyone was searching for the jet, it
was from the air. There was far too much

wilderness to cover on the ground. She needed to make something big so they could see her.

Smoke from the chimney . . . *Fire!*

If fire drew the attention of the three men and the cowboy, it might buy her time to get to the jet, where she'd find food, water, blankets, her father's emergency kit, its radio and GPS. She even could picture his sacred Airphone next to his seat. "I can call anywhere in the world with this thing!" he had told her proudly so many times. The best thing she could do for Kevin was to get both of them rescued.

She reached into her pocket, found the key to the jet alongside the chisel. It warmed in her hand.

No longer cold, suddenly she was burning with anticipation.

59

The whirring of an electric drill, followed by the crunch and crack of a screw biting into wood, prompted Kevin to call out.

"No!" he shouted, banging on the closet door.

They were sealing him inside.

As the drill cried out, screws splintered the doorjambs, first one, then the other.

Kevin pounded.

"LET ME OUT!"

Nothing, not a word. Just the grinding whir of the drill, now affixing the doors to the floor.

Kevin had the knife from the Learjet,

something they didn't know about, as well as the flashlight. If only he could get them to open the door, he could fight his way out. But that wasn't going to happen.

The minutes passed, and there was even more drilling nearby, the window perhaps, or the door to the room, or both. They were sealing him up in a tomb.

"Listen to me, kid," now came a man's voice from the other side. The copilot spoke in a hushed, confiding tone.

Kevin took a step back, hit the wall, and sank into a squat, his heart racing. The man's voice also had an unmistakable note of finality about it.

"We're doing you a favor here," the man said. "This doesn't involve you or Sam Elliott here, and let's keep it that way. By morning, you're out of here, alive and well, got that? So give it a rest. Don't be stupid, don't fight it, you're safe. Stupid will get you hurt, hurt bad. Be smart, sleep it off. By tomorrow, this'll be just a nightmare you had."

Why hadn't the man mentioned Summer?

Kevin thought this through from several angles.

Because they already have her.

Footfalls receding.

"This doesn't involve you and Sam Elliott here . . ."

For Kevin, the operating word was *here.* Did *here* mean that the cowboy was tied up in the study? That gave him some sense of hope. Isolation scared him more than claustrophobia.

His eyes lighted on the closet's old-fashioned plank ceiling. The rough lumber probably had been taken from the property. The ceiling, casement, and walls were all constructed of one-by-six pine boards. None of the joints fit together perfectly, having withstood decades of deep winter snow and the unforgiving climate. The gaps between the boards were about the thickness of . . . *a steak-knife blade.*

Kevin stood, slipped the flashlight out of his pocket, and switched it on. A pair of metal filing boxes were stacked in the corner. He gingerly climbed atop them to inspect the ceiling. He slipped the tip of his knife into a gap between the boards and gently began to pry them apart.

60

Roger McGuiness, lathered in sweat from having spent the past hour cutting pine boughs to disguise the Learjet, delivered Cantell's satellite phone to the lodge's living room.

"It rang, but I didn't answer it," McGuiness said.

Cantell stared at the bulky phone. He'd left it behind on the jet, having seen lights on in the lodge while landing and wanting to have an excuse, if necessary, to get inside the lodge. He'd been expecting a call from Lorraine to tell him she'd arrived at the remote Nevada strip, but to his surprise the caller ID showed a different number.

He knew who it was and was thinking about when to call back as the phone rang in his hand. With McGuiness and Salvo watching, he hit the POWER button and shut the phone off.

"I'll deal with that later," he said.

"What now?" McGuiness asked, mopping his face with his shirt sleeve. "FYI, we're maybe eighty or ninety miles from Hailey. We flew damn-near directly over Stanley, so we've got to assume we were spotted. A jet flaming out is a pretty spectacular sight, so we're made."

"What's the plan?" Salvo said anxiously. "We're out of here, right? You said the idea was to get away from the plane. 'Radioactive': isn't that what you called it? All we need are the GPS coordinates to find it, right? Let's not forget we were going to be a hundred miles away from here before we even made our demands, right?"

McGuiness feigned disinterest by flipping through a pamphlet.

"And we will be," Cantell said. "The schedule is changed but not the plan."

He lifted a framed topographical map

from the wall and laid it on the coffee table in front of the oversized stone fireplace. The map covered an area of roughly fifty square miles, a red star stuck on the lower half of the glass next to a light blue line designating a river.

"We're not flying," Cantell said. "And the cowboy told me that if we float the river, it's four days minimum"—he pointed to the map and shook his head—"mostly in a very long canyon through very steep terrain. After the first day, there are a few dry tributaries, but if you hike any of them you're looking at thirty to fifty miles of total wilderness without trails, which would take longer than floating out on the river. And if we do that, we're sitting ducks: they'll be waiting for us."

"So we're screwed . . ." Salvo said.

"No, we need to be resourceful," Cantell said. "Behind this cabin is Shady Mountain, part of the river canyon's walls. It surrounds this part of the ranch, sealing it off from unwanted hikers, the Grape-Nuts crowd. Now, there's rock-climbing gear in the garage, and my guess is, there's a route set in the face of the mountain. If it's there, it should be easy to see in daylight.

But first things first: we need the girl. We need to find her fast. Then we put Sam Elliott and Shia LaBeouf in one of the rafts and send them downstream."

"But—"

"They're the biggest threat to us, Matt. We eliminate the threat by getting rid of them. We have to close the deal. We're going to need time to do it. Once they're on the river, we've got four days—"

"Unless," Salvo interrupted, "they run into somebody on the river who has a phone—"

"Trips on this river are strictly controlled," McGuiness broke in, holding up a dog-eared Forest Service pamphlet from the coffee table. "They're not to spoil, and I'm quoting here, 'the natural sights and sounds that campers deserve in a remote-wilderness experience.' In other words, this is no Disneyland." He pointed to sites on the map. "We're just about halfway between these two camps, a full day's journey. If we put those two on the river about sunrise, they're not running into anybody. The only way they would would be to stop and wait for the next group floating downriver, and then they might not have a phone. If they have a radio, it's a day and a half before the terrain allows it to transmit. There's a big warning in here about that. The cowboy knows about it. He won't sit around waiting for other campers to show up. That gives us at least a couple days."

"Screw that, it's too risky. We should just lock them up here."

"Good plan, Matt. Just let them dehydrate and die. Or maybe we should give them the run of the kitchen. The cowboy is our number one threat. He knows this place, the woods. He knows what our options are. We need him gone. But, last I checked, we're not in the business of killing people."

"Tell that to the wine currier," Salvo protested.

"All the more reason to get out of here. Think about it, Matt: who turned on the gas valve?"

That silenced Salvo.

"The girl?" McGuiness said, usually the silent one. Cantell noted this change.

"We tell the insurance company they have to pay up. We tell them that without payment in full, the jet will blow with the girl in it."

"No way!" McGuiness shouted.

"Hang on, relax. She's with us the whole time, not on the jet. But we need to give them an incentive to speed things up because we don't know how long we've got."

"But if the two somehow manage to make that call . . ." Salvo protested.

"We have the girl," Cantell repeated. "Let them find the jet."

That silenced Salvo and McGuiness both.

"Once we've rendezvoused with Lorraine at a new location we're free and clear. We leave the girl behind. No harm, no foul."

"But the beauty of the original plan," McGuiness said, "was that we weren't going to call the company until we were long gone. If they didn't pay up, then we wouldn't give them the coordinates and there'd be no way for them to find the plane. We could then go back four months later and fly the thing out of there, sell it in South America. That was our backup. All of that's gone now. We're not exactly in the Nevada desert, and no one's flying that jet anywhere, probably ever. So if we're going to play the girl card, why not start there?"

"I'm open for suggestions," Cantell said, throwing his arms out.

He searched the faces of the other two. Salvo appeared to be brooding. McGuiness reeked of impatience.

McGuiness said, "What if we can't find the girl?"

"We'll find her. If necessary, we use the boy in her place."

"We don't take hostages," McGuiness said. "We don't kill people."

"We broke one of those rules already," Cantell said. He looked directly at Salvo. He wanted the man motivated. "It's a work in progress."

"We could put all three of them in the raft," McGuiness suggested.

"We could," Cantell said. "But I'm voting to bring her along as insurance, and, given her age and looks, how do you think Matt's going to vote?"

Salvo grinned. "Give her to me for an hour and I promise you she'll do whatever we ask."

"You disgust me," McGuiness said.

"Like I should care," Salvo fired back.

Cantell stepped in. "Girls!" He could ill afford such dissension. "We'll make a lot of noise like we're going off to look for her, then one of us stays here while the other two keep an eye on the jet. Temperature's dropping fast out there," he added. "She's not ready for that. She won't last an hour."

61

I'm not going back in the garage, Summer told herself repeatedly. But a little voice at the back of her brain told her otherwise. The woodpile would need fuel of some kind to light it, and she remembered seeing a beat-up cooking grill and a lighter wand on her way out. A row of jerrycans next to the ATVs suggested gasoline or diesel fuel. So while she had no problem connecting the dots, she just couldn't muster the courage to go back in there and get the wand and fuel.

And, if she could, then what? What if all

three men responded to the fire? Did she head for the jet and try to phone out or did she head for the lodge and look for Kevin? What if only two men responded? Or only one? What if they just let it burn?

She stood there, shivering. More than anything, she just wanted all this to go away. She'd dragged Kevin into this, taking his keys and forcing him to follow. What a jerk she'd been. And now she'd gotten him kidnapped, or worse. A big part of her just wanted to take off, to convince herself that it was in everyone's best interest for her to save herself and somehow get word to her father.

Her father! How she had betrayed him, abused his trust. Having argued her own case so many times that she actually had come to believe it, now she saw the absurdity of her logic, the product of her mistakes. She now could see it all through her father's eyes, could feel his anger. He wouldn't know where she was, probably didn't even know the jet had been stolen, and by the time he figured it out any concern he had would fester into rage. He didn't lose his temper often—she should have been more grateful for that—but when he did she'd be on the receiving end. Dread now joined the cold, and she felt like all the life had drained out of her.

62

Balanced atop the file boxes, the knife wedged between the boards and prying, Kevin at first thought his efforts looked promising as the boards began pulling loose. But then an unwilling nail cried out, sending a chill through him that was like biting down on an ice cube. He moved the tip of the knife closer to the nail and tried again and again it squealed. If he kept this up, the sound would bring them running.

Discouraged, he pounded his fist on the closet door.

"Let me out of here!" he shouted.

It was a futile, childish outburst, but the

longer he remained inside the dark closet, the greater his growing sense of panic. He was no lover of confined spaces, and the closet felt ever smaller by the minute.

His father—or had it been his Uncle Walt?—once told him that "everything happens for a reason." He dismissed the platitude at the time the same way he dismissed anything an adult said. But now things were different. With the words reverberating in his head, he tried to clear his thought. He had a spark of realization. Now he understood.

Everything happens for a reason . . . even childish outbursts.

He stuck the knife between the boards again and kicked the closet door.

"LET ME OUT OF HERE!" he hollered even louder, yanking the knife down, the nail crying out and the board coming free, the sound covered by his petulant plea.

"PLEASE!" he screamed, grabbing the board and pulling down, his cry timed perfectly.

The board came loose in his hands.

63

Painfully aware that the Avicorps jet carrying his father was scheduled to touch down
in fifteen minutes, Walt leaned over the
Incident Command Center's first row of
tables and found Steven Garman's cologne a little too much.

The pilot was stocky, with an Irishman's
florid cheeks and the kind of handsome
that found its way onto the labels of soup
cans. He had spent the last several minutes proposing to fly the portable transmitter on the same vector as Sumner's
jet. The plan included some sophisticated
flying that would allow the wireless carrier

to locate the phone, if Walt could win their cooperation. That seemed unlikely to Walt, but he wasn't going to squash Garman's optimism.

Walt moved another foot or two away. The cologne had to have a name like Brute Force or Demon's Mist.

"I can tell you where I'd have aimed for," Garman said.

"Please."

"Some big guns have been buying up ranches along the Middle Fork. There are, what, maybe half a dozen grandfathered deeded properties up there, right in the middle of national forest? Those money guys love to have what no one else can have. They also love to break the rules. Any one of them could have made improvements to their strips—I mean, they're not supposed to mess with the landscape but no one's going to know whether they have or haven't, right? And let me tell you something: if you've got one engine flamed out and another not producing power, you're not going to be real picky about where you put it down." He stood, moved over to Walt's electronic map, and drew on a pad with a special pen, circling a shaded-out area. "Given the route you've predicted, that's my bet: Mitchum's Ranch."

"That's at least a mile or two past where the math puts them," Walt said. A yellow circle had been drawn around a sizable area on the map. "The trajectory would put them here." He indicated the center of the circle.

"And if they crashed, that's probably right," Garman said. "Listen, we're always hearing about pilot error. What no one talks about is pilot terror. No one wants to crash. You'd be surprised what you can get out of a plane when it gets hairy up there. Given their rate of descent and the fact that Mountain Home's radar lost track of them somewhere in here . . . If they had a bead on a private strip out here, they could have been skipping right along the treetops," he said, his voice excited: he was enjoying this! "They bank it into the canyon"—his big hand, thumb and pinky extended, became the plane—"and now they're off radar, keeping maybe a hundred feet off the water. Full power, because that engine's down to thirty percent or less. All they have to do is squeak out another mile or mile and a half." His finger now followed the river's twists and turns. "They're down inside the canyon, having executed this final turn and put it down hard. Hope for the best. Whether it's in one piece, I don't know. But I'd start my search somewhere here."

"That's miles off of where we're planning," Walt said.

"All I'm saying is, a pilot doesn't follow math, he tries to stay alive. I'd have tried for Mitchum's. Anything short of that, with a full load of fuel, you're in a thousand pieces and burning. No thanks." He added, "And that's another thing: the national forest is full of people this time of year. If that Lear crashed, it would have produced a massive fireball. You'd have heard about it by now."

"I'd like to take that to the bank."

"Send up a chopper."

"I'm trying to avoid that," Walt said. "If this is a hostage situation, God forbid, the last thing we want is to broadcast that we know their location. We want this done as quietly as possible until we know what we're dealing with. Keep that in mind when you're up there."

"Okay, but let me tell you something: we have to face facts that the odds of hitting a strip are not good. First and foremost, we need to search for the wreck and for survivors. Thinking we've got a hostage situation here, I'm afraid, is nothing short of optimistic."

Walt anxiously checked the clock, dreading his father's arrival.

"So if you were conducting a ground search ahead of first light . . ." Walt said.

Garman nodded thoughtfully. "Mitchum's Creek was their best shot."

"The wireless repeater will tell you if there's a phone logged on?"

"It will. But I'll need to be well past Stanley to eliminate any *touristos* who've left their phones on."

"You can contact me on either of these numbers," Walt said, scribbling them down and handing them over.

The room phone beeped, and a woman's voice filled its speaker.

"Sheriff? I have Special Agent Barlow for you, line one."

The news of a call from the FBI won the attention of everyone in the room. Walt's office was to be gently pushed aside in the name of national security. All eyes turned to him. He hesitated before answering.

"Tell him I stepped out for a minute."

64

Summer stuck her nose to the jerrycan's cap and sniffed. She couldn't tell the difference between gasoline and diesel, but the can clearly contained some kind of fuel, so she dragged it out of the garage, having spent less than a minute inside. A moment later, she faced the large pile of split firewood. She circled the pile, dousing the wood, then drizzled a fuse of fuel some twenty feet away.

She wasn't sure how big the fire would be, but big enough, she hoped, to bring them running. And, if all else failed, she at least would have created a signal that might be spotted by planes, although she hadn't seen or heard any.

She stood there, with the empty jerry-can in one hand, the lighter wand in the other, thinking she wanted the can well away from her before she lit the soaked ground.

She screwed the can's metal lid down tight and ran it back to the woodpile, launching it up on top.

She hurried back into the grass and found the lighter where she'd left it. The grass stank of fuel.

A trapezoid of light played across the lawn in the distance. Voices!

She fumbled with the wand, its safety feature requiring both thumb and index finger working in concert to light.

She pulled the trigger: *click, click.*

A silhouette stretched across the light-painted lawn as a man filled the doorway.

The wand sparked, a tiny blue flame dancing at the end of its chrome barrel.

She lowered the wand to the grass, expecting the flame to creep along. But what happened was nothing like that.

Whoosh!

In a fraction of a second, the woodpile

ignited, black smoke spiraling up from it. She fell back, off balance, and then scrambled to her feet and made for the woods.

"FIRE!" she heard someone shout.

She raced down the mountain, dodging tree trunks and tearing through bramble and shrub.

Behind her, the men were shouting frantically now as the woods glowed yellow from the fire.

Then there was an explosion, as the jerrycan blew up, sounding like a bomb going off. She stopped and turned around in time to see a ball of orange flame rising forty feet into the smoke-black sky. Sparks rained down like fireworks.

She continued her way down the mountain, made easier by the light from the fire. She reached the level airstrip, the sound of the river not far off. Turning to admire her handiwork, she saw the orange glow now lighting the rocky face of Shady Mountain.

Keeping to the trees, Summer hurried toward the jet at the far end of the strip, its wings and tail covered with pine boughs.

Feeling in her pocket, she took the Learjet's key firmly in hand.

65

Jerry Fleming, all business from the moment his son had picked him up at the airport, looked straight ahead out the Cherokee's windshield as he spoke, as if it were twenty years earlier and he was teaching his son to drive.

"How certain are we?" Jerry asked.

"At this point, I'm convinced. Until something comes up to suggest otherwise . . ."

"Is Sumner prepared to play along?"

"With a ransom call?" Walt asked. "No. He's in denial. Says kidnapping is out of the question."

"Nothing strange about that."

"No. He seems able to reconcile someone stealing the jet but not kidnapping his daughter."

"What happened to your mentoring the boy?"

"Well, that didn't take long," Walt said, adding sarcastically, "This is all my fault, you know."

"Myra has no control over the boy. We've discussed it."

"We've discussed nothing, Dad. Not since Robert."

"Don't bring that up." Jerry stared out the side window, Hailey's amber streetlights flashing across his face. "I knew you would. Why aren't we going to your shop, this new shop I've heard so much about?"

Walt had not told him about the new headquarters. Either Myra was playing both sides or he'd read about it in the paper.

"Since when do you keep up with anything I'm doing?"

"You'd be surprised," said Jerry.

"Believe me, I am."

"I thought you'd want to show off."

"Yeah, that's me all right."

"No need to get defensive."

"We're not going back to the office," Walt said.

He'd stopped at his house and was loading in some extra camping gear for his father while his father remained in the passenger's seat, never offering to help.

"So, you're in charge, are you?" Jerry said. "Is that right?"

"I can't go back to the office without dealing with the Bureau. At this point, if we're going to avoid their intervention, then we've got to outrun them. You and I are going to connect with Brandon, and the three of us are going on horseback into the Middle Fork."

"Are we, now?" Jerry said.

"We've got a plane aloft with some cell gear that may help us pinpoint Kevin. It's up there sweeping now. We're fairly certain the jet got down in one piece. It was fully fueled, so if it had gone down hard there would have been a fireball, and nothing like that has been reported. There are some private strips, some grass strips, maybe a few better than grass. All I'm saying is, it's possible—probable, even—that they got down, that they walked away. If we get a hit, we can narrow this down . . . maybe even talk to Kev."

"Am I supposed to be impressed?"

"You're supposed to listen," Walt said. "Your former employers would love nothing more than to take over this case. For the time being, my phone is off. And, if you noticed, the radio's off too."

"Of course I noticed. I notice everything. Don't test me, son."

"This whole thing is going to test you, Dad, because it's my way or the highway this time. You can follow or you can stay behind, but you can't lead. There's a system in place, a system I put in place. The arrangements have been made. You can badger me all you want, guilt-trip me . . . Have at it. But I won't budge. We're going into the backcountry. All your criticism about me being a hick sheriff, well, welcome to Hicksville, Dad. You get to see it up close and personal now. I'm going in and I'm getting Kevin back. We're getting him before the Bureau even hits the ground, because, once they do—"

"I know. I know," Jerry said. "I was the

one warned you about the SAC, remember?" He looked tempted to say more, to challenge Walt, but he didn't.

Then the silence set in, a wall rising between them. And where once Walt would have done anything to tear that wall down, including acquiesce, this time he did not. Instead, hands gripping the wheel, he bit his tongue.

They stopped by a buddy of Walt's and loaded a raft onto the roof. They bypassed a mile and a half's worth of traffic backed up from the bridge by going off-road, arriving at the bike-path bridge that still remained under Brandon's control.

"How long?" Walt asked his deputy out his window.

"Another fifteen or twenty. Almost there."

"Good. You're coming with me," Walt said. "Turn it over to someone."

They stopped for five minutes at Brandon's trailer.

"She inside?" Jerry asked.

"Probably," Walt answered. "But please don't . . ."

Jerry climbed out of the Cherokee and went inside the trailer to speak with Gail. Walt felt like driving off and leaving his father in the company of the woman he thought of as his ex-wife and the deputy she now was sleeping with.

Instead, he waited it out.

Brandon threw some stuff in the back of the Cherokee, and, when Jerry returned, offered his hand over the backseat. But Jerry wouldn't accept it. Brandon caught Walt's eyes in the rearview mirror. Walt aimed the mirror at the ceiling.

"Did you call Willie?" Walt asked Brandon.

"He'll have three of his best saddled and waiting for us, a fourth with a pack saddle. We can borrow his Dodge, a dually that can haul an eight-horse, no problem."

Walt passed a topographical map back to Brandon. "I've circled Mitchum's Creek Ranch. You will figure a route while I speak to Remy. I left Sumner at the office. He's not going to like my bedside manner of leaving him in the lurch. But it is what it is."

"And Remy?"

"Is worth a half hour. Maybe we'll learn something."

Jerry glanced in his son's direction. If he had something to say, he kept it to himself. Walt hoped some of his father's toxic anger might transfer over to Brandon for breaking up his marriage, although that was asking a lot.

"So, Brandon . . ." Jerry finally said.

"Yes, sir?"

"What if she'd been your wife?"

Walt wished he hadn't moved the mirror. Sometimes he loved his father.

66

Walt took a seat opposite Remy on the brown velour, horseshoe-shaped bench at the far back of the Mobile Command RV. A collapsible table separated the two, but to Walt it felt as if they were sitting too close. On the table were a digital voice recorder, a legal pad, a stack of Post-its, and two paper cups of Tully's coffee. There was a black-and-white sticker on the cups advertising KB'S BURRITOS.

Walt spoke into the recorder, providing time, location, and both their names. The formality won Remy's full attention. He seemed ready to say something but didn't.

"Do you understand why we're here, Mr. Remy?" Walt asked.

Remy adjusted his left leg, bound in a straight position by the cast, sticking it out to the point where it rubbed against Walt.

"I've been detained. Believe me, it will all be straightened out shortly."

"My nephew's gone missing, along with a hotel guest. A plane has been stolen . . . a private jet."

Remy cocked his head. If he was acting, he was doing a good job of it: he seemed genuinely surprised to hear any of this.

"Let me just lay it out for you," Walt said.

"I'm not talking without a lawyer present."

"So noted. And, yet, here we are . . ."

"Yes, here we are . . ."

Walt stared at Remy's leg, then looked him in the eye.

"Slipped in the shower," Remy said.

"Yes, I'd heard that. Your possessions were passed along to me by the hospital. I returned them to you, as you'll recall."

"And I never thanked you properly."

"You're welcome."

Walt looked down at the man's cast again.

"Must hurt."

"Comes and goes." He winced a grin. "The painkillers help."

"We're a sports-oriented community," Walt said. "Skiing in the winter, all sorts of stuff in the summer: biking, hiking, tennis . . ."

"So, you're the Chamber of Commerce, all of a sudden . . ."

"We see an inordinate number of broken bones here, have some of the best orthopedists in the country . . . A little town of five thousand . . . Amazing, really."

"Guess I was lucky I slipped here," Remy said, "but sure doesn't *feel* that way."

"We know it wasn't an accident. Your doctor and your radiologist confirmed that it's blunt trauma. We know someone did this to you."

"Not true."

"And I know you're lying."

Remy stared straight at Walt.

"We know the Adams bottles are forgeries . . . fakes . . . counterfeit . . . whatever term applies to wine. You can feign shock, continue to issue denials, but the fact is, we have conclusive scientific proof."

"Impossible!"

"We conducted tests on the bottles earlier this afternoon."

Remy grimaced. Perhaps he had known all along. "Ms. Finch . . ." he began.

Walt didn't comment.

"She's a reckless, overly ambitious amateur, Sheriff. I wouldn't go taking her word—"

"Some kind of sound-wave test can determine the alignment of the fractures in the glass. It wasn't performed by Ms. Finch."

Remy didn't appear to be breathing.

"Fakes," Walt said. "I'm operating under the assumption you knew as much. That, in fact, you're responsible. Ms. Finch is evidently quite the researcher. She believes she can help the FBI connect the dots."

"A *graduate* student." Spoken with a convulsive disdain.

"Makes my theory of insurance fraud all the more credible. Which brings us to the death of Mr. Malone and the attempted theft of the bottles, which brings into question one Christopher Cantell and his associates, one Roger McGuiness and one Matthew Salvo. You with me?"

Remy pursed his lips.

"Here's where it gets a little dodgy for you, Mr. Remy . . ."

Walt drank half the coffee in two swigs. He was starving, couldn't remember the last time he'd eaten.

"Cantell was not only behind stealing the wine, he stole the jet . . . the missing Lear-jet with two teenagers aboard, a young girl and *my nephew.* That means you, Mr. Remy, are in all likelihood not only con-nected to the death of Mr. Malone but also to the theft of that jet and the kidnapping of those kids. You, Mr. Cantell, and the others are all in serious trouble."

For a third time, Walt looked down at Remy's leg.

"Let's say," he continued, "just for spec-ulation's sake, that you had nothing to do with the jet . . ."

"I had nothing to do with *any* of this."

"When this all comes unraveled—and it's already started to—you'll be charged. And you'll need to dig yourself out."

"Innocent until proven guilty . . ."

"Yeah, right. I'm not talking about our legal system."

Walt bumped his leg into Remy's cast, and Remy flinched and gasped.

"You'll need to dig yourself out," he re-peated. "You know the rule of thumb about the first person to confess, the leniency shown by the courts. Which leaves you in that dodgy position I just mentioned. Be-cause when your attorney arrives, he's go-ing to shut this interview down, shut you down. And he has every reason to do so. Nine times out of ten, it's the smart move.

"But this isn't one of those times. In fact, you and I are preciously short on time."

Walt called out to the front of the bus.

"How long?"

"He's about five minutes out," came back the reply.

"See how on top of things we are?" Walt asked Remy, who was struggling to look at ease. "We have only your best interest at heart."

Walt pulled back his sleeve and looked at his watch.

"Go on . . ." Remy said. His eyes ticked toward the front of the bus.

"Me? I've got nothing more to say. Should I keep the recorder going?" He reached for the device.

Remy glanced toward the front of the bus once again.

"Decisions, decisions," Walt said. "Maybe they'll stop with the knee."

Walt's hand touched the OFF button.

"Stop . . . Leave it running."

Walt sat back. At times he found the work boring and tedious. Then there were times like this.

"I had nothing to do with the theft," Remy said, "either one. I knew nothing about them."

Walt kept his face expressionless, but inside he was churning. Remy seemed so self-righteous.

"The bottles will not go to auction," Walt said. "They've been pulled."

Remy searched the bus as if looking for an escape.

"In that case," he said, "I need protection . . . tonight . . . going forward."

"We're not in the protection business."

"Then arrest me, Sheriff."

"How can I? You deny being involved with the bottles or the jet." Walt made it a statement for the recorder. He rapped his knuckles on Remy's cast.

"The Adams bottles are fakes," Remy said, head down, "forgeries. My doing, it's true."

"You have to convince me, Mr. Remy. You have to provide details that, as an investigator, I can substantiate. I have to bring something to my prosecuting attorney. Facts are often a good place to start."

"The Jefferson bottles are authentic."

"I don't remember discussing the Jefferson bottles . . ."

Walt looked Remy in the eyes. *Tick, tick, tick,* he thought. *The lawyer will shut us down.*

"I did very well off of that sale," Remy said, his eyes devoid of light. "Then the economy tanked, and people weren't exactly beating a path to buy wine. Up here in Sun Valley is different, I don't need to tell you. 'What recession?' people are saying. But, still, the rest of the world is broke. So I decided to find some new bottles, something to tide me over. It didn't come cheap. Neither did verification. I had to find an investor, which I did, who put up a substantial amount of capital. But then there were questions from one of the verification experts—"

"Amsterdam," Walt interjected, wanting Remy to know he was ahead of him, thanks to Janet Finch.

Remy could not contain his surprise, though he recovered quickly.

"The theft . . . the attempted theft here . . . I'm being blamed for that?"

"Makes sense to me."

"But it wasn't me."

"What's done is done."

"It wasn't my investors either. But they think it was me. It's a mess."

"Tell me about your relationship with Christopher Cantell."

"Never met him." He waited for Walt to say something. "You don't believe me!"

"Don't sound so surprised," Walt said.

Tick, tick, tick.

Remy had gone ashen. He ran his hand through his stubby hair. He couldn't stop looking toward the front of the bus.

"Have I *heard* of Christopher Cantell?" Remy said. "Of course I have."

"That's better."

"No, you misunderstand . . . Have I met him? No. Spoken to him? Never. But he had his fifteen minutes. You're aware of that, right?"

Walt's head swooned. He cursed not eating. He should have looked more deeply into Cantell.

"You *do* go to the movies?" Remy asked.

"Apparently, not often enough."

"Christopher Cantell," Remy said. "That movie. *Italian Job*? No, that was a different one. Mark Wahlberg, right? Was it that one with Hanks? No, no, that was a con man, I think . . . I don't know, I forget . . . But they made a movie based on this guy Cantell, a heist movie. Above average, nothing great. But I remember the press: they played up the real-life side of it . . . That's as much as I know about him."

"A movie," Walt said. He felt the rug going out from under him.

"Look it up," said Remy, "IMDb it. What do I care?"

"And you think Cantell just happened to go after your wine?"

"Ask him!"

A fine line of sweat pearls had formed on Remy's upper lip. They both sensed the imminent arrival of the attorney.

"How should I know?" Remy continued. "There was lots of publicity, advance press—believe me, I saw to that. Churn up the market, you know? And part of that is churning up the rumor mill. The trades have been covering these bottles for the past six months."

A man came onto the bus. Walt recognized Terry Hogue, one of the valley's best attorneys. The Christensens had helped their friend out indeed.

"I forged those bottles," Remy leaned forward and whispered harshly. "So, charge me."

"A movie?"

"Charge me!"

"That'll be enough, Sheriff," Terry Hogue called out to Walt from the front of the RV. "We're all through here."

"Charge me!" Remy pleaded.

67

Ranches gave way to national forest, and soon there was not a structure in sight. The pale moonlight played off the towering blue-gray boulders to the right, the rolling carpet of evergreens to the left. A pair of amber eyes suddenly glowed at the side of the two-lane road, a black-tailed fox darting across in the glare of the headlights just barely in time to reach the other side.

"Sixteen miles on horseback," Brandon reported, "four to five hours, if we can stick to the trail. If we're lucky, we can cross to the east side of the Middle Fork by dawn."

Jerry checked his watch. He'd been doing so often, far more than necessary. Walt
was pushing seventy-five miles an hour
with the light rack flashing.

"You understand, it could get ugly," Jerry
said to Brandon in the backseat.

Brandon looked up from the map and
the handheld GPS, which he was pro-
gramming, but didn't speak. He and Walt
met eyes in the rearview mirror.

"There are times to wear the badge and
times to put it in the drawer," Jerry said.

"That's not the way we do it," Walt said.

"If anyone survived, if anyone's holding
Kevin, it's going to get wet. I just want both
of you prepared for that."

"Rescuing the boy and the girl is our
first priority," Brandon said. "I've got no
problem with that."

"The FBI gets hold of this . . ." Jerry cau-
tioned. "I happen to know the SAC out of
Salt Lake, personally. He's a shock-and-
awe advocate. Loves the heavy-handed
approach. He'll get them both killed. We're
not setting up comm lines, we're not negotiating. We get our sights on these guys,
we'll drop them just like that. We've got to
hit them hard without warning. We've got

one chance. After that, they take control, and we oblige them. But we're not going to let it get to that. Kevin is going to walk away from this."

The whine of tire rubber on road filled Walt's ears.

"I'm just saying," Jerry continued, "that that's the way it's going to be. I need to hear you say it too, Brandon, or you can stay behind when we switch to the horses. I've got no problem with your doing that. It's either all in or not in at all. An operation like this, it's just the way it's got to be."

"We get it," Walt said.

"I gotta hear him say it."

"I'm in," Brandon said.

"We might face charges," Jerry said, "Walt and I . . . That boy's our blood. It's not fair to ask that of you, but I've got to lay it out the way I see it."

"I'm in," Brandon repeated. "And, just for the record, they fired first."

Jerry turned to face Brandon for the first time.

He was grinning.

68

Cantell futilely sprayed the garden hose on the burning pile of wood while McGuiness shoveled dirt on it. Salvo was trying to flatten the pile and spread out the logs with a rake. For all their efforts, the fire continued raging, throwing sparks and smoke high in the sky. Leaning against the rocks behind them were a loaded rifle and a loaded twelve-gauge over-under shotgun. Cantell had no desire to use the guns but understood the authority they represented.

Other thoughts competed in his head. The fire had been deliberately set as a signal. The girl's doing. She had a brain and a lot of nerve—information useful to him, but unwelcome.

"Matt, take over here!"

Cantell passed the useless hose to Salvo and took off for the front of the lodge. Throwing the door open and looking directly toward the study, he could see that its door remained screwed shut.

He hurried outside behind the lodge and double-checked the window to the study. Plywood was screwed down tight.

Back inside, he stood in the middle of the living room listening to the boy banging around in the closet like he'd been doing for the past ten minutes. It was driving Cantell nuts, but he had no way to quiet the kid, to warn him.

Cantell didn't see the girl, but she could be hiding anywhere.

He pushed the front door shut.

"First and last chance, Ms. Sumner," he called out.

The kid's banging stopped.

"If you give yourself up," Cantell said, "we'll treat you okay. If not, you'll be dealt with . . . well . . . it won't be pretty. Your call . . . I need your answer right now!"

He waited.

It was only when his eyes alighted on the destroyed radio that his head cleared. The radio reminded him of the jet.

The girl has a key.

Preoccupied with trying to copilot McGuiness's emergency landing, he hadn't considered how his stowaway had gotten on the plane. But now . . .

He'd had to deal with Sam Elliott and the boy, ad-libbing as he went. But now . . .

He ran to the fire, shouting as he went. Salvo and McGuiness had gotten some control over it.

"The girl has a key," he announced. "Watch the inside of the house!" he called to Salvo. "You're with me," he ordered McGuiness.

69

Kevin had heard someone shout "Fire!" and then people stampeding out of the lodge. This was followed by silence.

He sniffed the air, didn't smell anything. But he wasn't about to stick around to find out if the place was going up in flames. He pulled the boards free from the ceiling as fast as he could. Two split and broke, three others came out cleanly. He now had a hole big enough for his head.

He shone the flashlight into dead space between the ceiling and the roof. Pulling free several more boards, he pushed the flashlight through. He climbed up into the attic.

Again, he smelled for smoke. He got dust and an overwhelming putrid odor.

He now shone the light in both directions. He could see the full length of the building.

The cowboy was tied up in the study below. He was a big guy, an adult. He knew the ranch. He'd be a good ally. Kevin *needed* him as an ally.

The attic floor was covered with a mix of sand and what looked like shredded newspaper, a decades-old attempt at insulation. It took Kevin a few tries to get the knack of placing his knees successfully on the crossbeams. Protruding from the sand-newspaper insulation was the occasional electrical wire. Following one, he dug down until he reached a junction box.

If he could get to the study and untie the cowboy, it would be two against three—decent odds. Once he got Summer out of the garage, it would be three against three—even better odds. He kicked the study ceiling hard but the boards held.

He thought he heard a man's voice so

he stopped and listened. It was coming from the general direction of the living room.

A few agonizing moments passed. Had they found the closet empty? The sound of someone leaving the lodge allowed him to breathe again. He waited. There was no more shouting.

Kevin drove his heel down on the junction box and it gave way, opening a small gap between it and the ceiling boards. He put his eye to the hole and could see the cowboy lying on the floor on his side. He was gagged. His hands were tied behind his back, his ankles tied with what looked like electrical cord with the leg of the desk between them. His blue eyes were staring back at Kevin.

Kevin knew he wasn't getting through the ceiling without a chainsaw. The thought he might have to go it alone overwhelmed him. He wondered if the hijackers had found Summer or had the fire been Summer's doing? That thought charged him with purpose.

Leaving the cowboy wasn't right. If the lodge was on fire, he had no choice. And he needed him.

He aimed the flashlight around the attic, hoping to see another way down. Dust filled the beam. He lit on a paper wasp nest in the far corner, some sagging spiderwebs. Then he lit on a row of upside-down bats. Stifling a reaction, he now knew the source of the putrid smell.

He wanted out of there—now! He lifted his knees from the crossbeam and squatted on his feet, ready to move. Nothing he could do about the cowboy . . .

His knife poked him, nearly cutting him. His only weapon, maybe the only way he had to defend himself, it was crucial to his survival. He reached down and adjusted it.

But the cowboy was down there staring up at him.

Holding the knife, Kevin forced his arm through the gap. He trained his eye through the same hole. The cowboy nodded at him and bounced his way off to one side of the desk, out of the way.

Kevin sniffed the air again. Still no smoke.

What if he dropped the knife and the cowboy couldn't reach it? But he had to try. It'd be cruel not to.

With the cowboy's legs bound to the desk, it was doubtful he could reach the knife if Kevin just let it fall. He had to throw it.

Swinging his arm, Kevin signaled his plan. The cowboy nodded. Kevin hoped like hell they were speaking the same language.

As Kevin leaned lower to tell the cowboy to look out, there was a bang to the right.

Someone had entered the lodge.

"Boy? You hear me, kid?"

It was Matt, the one Kevin had hit with the fire extinguisher.

Kevin let the knife drop. It landed quietly on the rug, which was good, but well out of the cowboy's reach, which was bad.

"Be that way!" Matt shouted from the living room.

Even if the cowboy managed to reach the knife, he was still locked in the room. Kevin began crawling quietly toward the opposite end of the long attic.

70

The hijackers had closed up the Learjet and camouflaged it well. Summer used her key. The Lear was dark inside, suggesting it was empty, but she stood there a moment before climbing the stairs and then shut herself inside.

She hadn't thought through any of this. Everything for her was minute to minute, and she feared her lack of planning would backfire. Her mother would have worked it out logically step by step. Her father, on the other hand, would have tried to talk his way out. She was some hybrid of the two, a stranger in her own strange family.

The jet's soundproofing made the drumming in her ears all the louder. This was the first chance she'd gotten to stop and think and she couldn't think. She felt removed. She felt numb.

She headed straight for the battery switch. The batteries had to be engaged in order to use the CD, the TVs, or any of the outlets. Next, she headed for her father's seat. She slid back the wood panel and nearly squealed with glee when she saw the red LED on the Airphone flashing. It had powered up.

"Come on!" she encouraged the red to change to green, signaling a connection to the satellite.

She counted backward from ten.

Had the antenna broken off? Had they covered it with pine boughs?

On the count of four, it changed to green.

She snatched up the receiver and dialed.

For a moment, there was nothing on the other end. Then came static and soft pops that went on far longer than she thought appropriate.

Finally, the phone purred in her ear. It was ringing.

"Hello?" her father's voice said.

She'd meant to speak, to say something—*anything*—but the sound of him choked her, and she couldn't get a word out.

"Dad . . ." she gasped, but far too softly.

She could see him clearly: his face, his smile. She had a mental picture of him in the hotel suite. She thoroughly regretted every ounce of grief she'd ever given him, felt so badly for making him pay for her mother's death when he'd only tried to help her understand it. She loved him so much but never expressed it, always taunting him to fill the void, an impossibility. Her accusing tone, her reckless blaming him for her problems, the bitterness with which she dealt with him: it all washed over her in a wave of self-loathing.

"Sum . . . ?"

Her vision blurred.

Just the sound of his voice . . .

"Yeah . . ." she choked out. "It's me. I'm on the plane."

A very long pause. "Oh, thank God!"

She thought he might be crying as well.

"We landed . . . kind of . . . crashed into something. There's a river. There's three of them . . ."

She rambled through a quick, disjointed explanation, laced with apology and begging for forgiveness.

"I don't know what to do," she finally said.

"You . . . Jesus . . . Listen, they won't hurt you."

"You don't know that! They've got Kevin, I think . . . I'm pretty sure . . ."

"I won't let them hurt you," he said.

It wasn't so much what her father said as the way he said it that gave her pause. She knew better than to interrupt. She needed him to talk, and to just keep on talking.

"I want you to . . . You've no idea where you are . . . none?"

"No. The woods, a big river. Kevin said it was the Middle Fork, but he doesn't know that for sure. There's a log cabin on top of the mountain with a huge cliff. We took off the same direction we landed the other day, so that's toward Sun Valley, right? I don't know, we could be anywhere. I lit a fire . . . a big fire. Someone should be able to see it. But it won't last long. Can you get someone to look for it?"

"A fire! Of course I can. You lit a fire? That was good thinking, Sum."

"What do I do, Dad? What am I supposed to do?"

Static on the line interrupted them.

"Isn't there some kind of locator or something on the plane?" she then asked.

There was no answer. She pulled the phone away from her ear, making sure the light was still green.

"Dad?"

"I'm here. I need to talk to them, Sum. I need to start a dialogue."

"Forget it! I am not going there. Doesn't the GPS know where we are?"

"The GPS?" He sounded distracted. "Yes, of course. Are you on the Airphone? Is the panel lit? There's a color map in the middle of the panel with a readout for latitude/longitude. Can you see it?"

"I don't want to let go of the phone."

"Put the phone down, Summer, write down the coordinates, and read them to me. It's important." He added that last bit in the same condescending tone he used to use to let her know how stupid she was. She resisted her immediate reaction of turning against him.

"I can't," she whined.

"Summer . . . please . . ."

She pulled the receiver away from her ear, but even a few inches made her feel alone. She smacked it back against her ear and stretched the wire instead. Making it to the aisle, she squinted at the illuminated instruments panel.

"You've got to do this for me," he said.

"I'm trying."

"And don't forget the bag in the closet. There's a GPS in there as well, a portable. And a radio, handheld, an aviation radio. Planes continually monitor the frequency. They'll be able to hear you. Get me the coordinates and read them into that radio. Listen, go get that bag right now and then give me the coordinates over the phone."

"I can't!"

"You have to, Sum. You need that bag, I need the coordinates. It's easy, you can do this. Stay in the plane, turn off the batteries to conserve power, and use the handheld to broadcast. Everything you need is in the plane: food, water, blankets. You're there alone, right?"

"Yes. Can I lock the door? I couldn't figure out how to lock it."

"No, it doesn't lock from the inside. You could probably hold the handle, which would keep the key from turning. The thing is . . . Now, listen to me . . . I need those coordinates, okay? You've got to do this for me."

She looked to the front of the jet. It seemed impossibly far away.

"I want to go home," she said. "I'm so sorry, Dad. I am so, so sorry."

"Summer Sumner, you listen to me. You've done incredibly well. There is nothing to be sorry about. We'll come get you and your friend. This is going to work out okay. But I need to speak to the men who flew the plane. I need to speak to the guy in charge, the guy with the dark hair. You've got to figure out a way to get him on this phone. In the jet. I can call back."

"Forget it," she said.

"They'll listen to me, Sum. We've got to make this happen."

"They've got Kevin! They're not listening

to anybody. For all I know, they killed the cowboy."

"What cowboy?"

"Wait a second . . ." Her heart raced even faster, as if that were even possible.

"You didn't say anything about any cowboy," he said. "What cowboy?"

She tried to focus, but her thoughts were like a scratched CD: they kept jumping back, playing a riff, then leaping forward again.

"I need to speak to the guy in charge, the guy with the dark hair," she was repeating in her head.

"Summer? Are you there?"

She'd frozen. She couldn't speak. The copilot had seemed so familiar—especially his voice—and now she could place it: he was who'd called her father's BlackBerry.

"SUMMER! I NEED YOUR COORDINATES! PUT DOWN THE PHONE AND GET ME THOSE COORDINATES!"

Pause.

"Summer? Sum . . . ?"

"I need to speak to the guy in charge, the guy with the dark hair," repeated again in her head.

She dropped the phone, spun a full circle, and marched, trancelike, into the cockpit. She looked to the right, saw a logbook with a pen shoved in its spiral spine. She tore out a sheet of paper, wrote down the string of numbers, double-checking them against the navigation screen.

She returned to the Airphone.

"Sum? You there? Sum . . . ?"

"I'm here."

That shut him up.

"Do you have them?"

"I've got them."

"Read them to me."

"What did you mean, 'the guy with the dark hair?'" she asked.

"What are you talking about?"

"No, Dad, I'm the one asking *you* what *you're* talking about? Who said anything about dark hair?"

"You're imagining things. I didn't say anything of the sort."

"You just said it!"

"Read me the coordinates."

"What's going on, Dad? He called you, right? In the hotel. Your BlackBerry. The call I answered. I know him . . . Who is he?"

She had it, then. She slumped in his chair.

She recalled him sitting there on the phone as they were about to land. He'd said, "Listen, I would if I could, but this is my last trip on it."

How could he have known that? He'd said nothing to her about giving up the Lear. He had a trip to New York planned, another to Toronto. He'd talked to her about going with him *on the jet.*

"I need the coordinates, if I'm going to help," he said. "That, and I need to speak to whoever's in charge."

"The man with the dark hair."

"If he's the one in charge, sure."

"You said he was."

"Summer, you're in shock. You're not thinking clearly. Come on, sweetheart— *kiddo*—you've done amazingly well. Phenomenal. Keep it up. Just read me the coordinates, would you please? Sweetheart . . . ?"

The torn piece of paper trembled in her fingers.

"What have you done?" she gasped into the receiver.

The static hissed and popped. There was a snake in her ear, the devil's tongue.

"Now, you listen to me, Summer, you're

in shock. It's completely understandable, expected. You're inventing things. It happens. But you've got to clear your head, okay? I want to help you."

"You . . . *asshole*!"

"Now, you listen to me, young lady . . ."

She pushed the END button. Tears began flowing as she stared at the receiver in her hand. It represented him. It represented everything wrong with him. She beat it against the seat's console and threw it against the fuselage. Pieces of plastic broke loose.

She stood and moved toward the closet, but in a drunken, disconnected way. These weren't her feet, her hands; this wasn't her. She stumbled, fell into another seat, and buried her face in her hands.

She didn't remember coming to her feet again. She found herself facing the closet. She fumbled in the dark for the case and found it. It opened by twisting two metal tabs. She rummaged through the case and withdrew two devices. She couldn't see well enough to know what they were, but both were small and electronic.

A loud noise came from the front. The door was opening.

The jet was so well insulated, she hadn't heard anyone approaching. Only now, as the key activated the opening mechanism, did she know.

She hurried down the aisle, only to slip and fall. She banged her head against an armrest and dropped both devices. Leaving them, she crawled ahead on hands and knees and reached for the door handle just as it was raising up and the stairs were lowering.

She threw her body on the handle, forcing it back down.

From the other side, a mumble of men's voices.

Seconds later came a rustling from the jet's right wing. She kept her shoulder against the lever, preventing it from moving. She squatted down to get a better look out the right side. She couldn't see anything, but someone was out there crawling around the fuselage. Then she heard two loud snaps, one directly beneath her, the other directly overhead.

The shattered Airphone's LED changed from green to blinking red. They'd snapped off the antennas, rendering the satellite phone and no doubt the plane's other instruments useless.

The door lever pushed against her. She kept her shoulder against it. It was the last place she wanted to be.

More banging around outside. With each sound she flinched.

He was out there on the wing.

There was more sound: metal on metal.

Something was going on out there. She focused. It was coming from the rear of the plane. From . . .

The emergency exit.

The same hatch through which she and Kevin had fled the plane.

Again, the front door's lever attempted to move. Again, she braced against it.

But her attention remained on the rear of the plane, where obviously someone was opening the door *from the outside.*

She spotted the handheld GPS and radio she had dropped on the carpet. She stretched out and kicked the GPS beneath the first seat. She then hooked the radio with the toe of her sandal, noticing for the first time how scratched up her foot was.

Keeping her shoulder to the door handle, she saw things get light at the back of the plane.

Paralyzed with fear, she left the radio on the carpet a few feet from her.

The plane's captain stepped into the aisle. He aimed a small but blinding light at her.

"We're not going to hurt you," he said. "Don't do anything stupid."

The flare gun.

Her father kept a flare gun for emergencies somewhere on the plane; she'd heard him mention it to William before. The closet briefcase? Had she been so eager to find the radio that she'd missed the gun?

"Step away from the door and keep your hands where I can see them," the pilot said.

"Or else what?" she called out. "I thought you weren't going to hurt me."

"Don't be a smart-ass."

She kept her shoulder against the handle.

"Too late," she said.

If she could get past the pilot, if she could get her hands on that case in the closet, maybe, just maybe . . .

"I'll hurt you, if necessary. I saw what you did to . . . to my associate. Now, keep your hands where I can see them and step away from the door."

Her knees wobbled, her arms and legs shook, tears threatened once again. She hated herself for it.

"Do not test me," the man said, his voice ominous and chilling.

Summer stepped away from the door.

71

Willie Godfrey, a third-generation trust funder who could trace his lineage back to William Brewster, sported a mane of white hair even though only forty-odd years old. Tall and movie-star handsome, he had a larger-than-life persona that was even bigger than his oversized, overaccessorized pickup truck.

"I can shave a good hour off your route," he said loudly, drawing Brandon to his side. The two men studied a map under the glare of a mercury light mounted on an outbuilding.

Walt watched things play out between

the two through a kitchen window. Cell-phone and radio coverage having died passing Galena Summit ninety minutes earlier and wanting to preserve every watt of the satellite phone's battery, he was taking advantage of the Godfreys' landline.

He was brought up to speed on events in the valley: the bridge was open to traffic again; no further attempt had been made on the wine, or the armory, or half a dozen other potential targets. Things were returning to normal. His biggest concern, he was told, was the barrage of phone calls from the FBI and Homeland Security, and a growing anger because of Walt's silence.

"Sumner?" Walt asked.

"Hanging around, miserable. He cursed you a blue streak when he found out you'd left."

"Remy?"

"He's booked and in jail. Since when do we actually lock up a guy like that? Don't they usually make bail?"

"It's complicated," Walt said. "Back to Sumner . . . His hotel phone . . ."

"Is forwarded and under surveillance, and his wireless usage is being tracked in real time. We can't hear conversations, but we know—"

"The caller ID, incoming and outgoing," Walt said.

Sometimes his own staff treated him like he didn't understand his own requests.

He considered the delicacy of the Sumner situation.

"Where have you got him?"

"He's turned the break room into an office."

"Leave him there. That's okay."

"I have Fiona on hold, waiting to speak with you. Do you want to take it?"

Walt said to put her through.

"Hey," Fiona said.

"Everything okay?" he asked.

"I answered your phone," she said apologetically. "Your office phone. I figured that with you gone and me using your office, if they put through a call it was probably you."

"And who was it?" Walt asked, bracing to hear she'd communicated with the FBI or another federal agency, digging him into an even deeper hole.

"A guy named Bremer."

"FAA," Walt said. He'd dealt with Charles

Bremer earlier when trying to make sense of Sumner's missing jet. "Makes sense. I gave him my direct line."

"A plane, a Frontier jet, spotted a fire from thirty thousand feet."

Walt caught his breath. "Wreckage?"

"Just what I asked . . . Too small and organized. More like a bonfire."

Kevin? The boy was smart enough to start a signal fire.

"They eyeballed the coordinates . . . It was definitely in the backcountry. Could have been a rafters' bonfire on the Middle Fork. But it was big . . . very big . . . maybe too big for that."

"A signal fire," Walt said, thinking aloud.

"Who do I tell this to? What do I do next? My first reaction was to jump up and tell someone, but then . . . That was something, like, twenty minutes ago, and I've been going crazy since trying to figure out who you'd want me to tell. Do we send up a search plane? Does the FAA do that for us? How does any of this work?"

"You didn't ask me that," Walt said.

"Excuse me?"

"The reason I took off without telling anybody . . . My father knows the SAC

who will take this one. The guy's a wannabe Rambo. We don't want Kevin caught
in the middle of that."

"Ah, okay. So . . . ?"

"You don't approve of my dodging a potential disaster," Walt said, hearing it in her
voice.

"When it comes to you and your father?
It's not exactly like there aren't issues
there, Walt, you know?"

"I'm not doing this for my father," Walt
said, "I'm doing it for Kevin."

"And you know for a fact that this SAC is
who your father says he is?"

"No, but—"

Walt saw his father out the window. He
was on the truck's tailgate, checking out a
rifle and a handgun. Would his father lie in
order to hold off the FBI and give himself a
chance at some fieldwork? Would he put
Kevin in the middle of his own ambitions?

"Christ," Walt muttered inadvertently into
the phone.

"What do you want me to do?" came
her voice.

"It has to be reported. You'd better tell
Brad. But if it takes you thirty minutes or
more to get down the hall . . . If you told

Brad to call back Bremer and determine the veracity of the report . . ."

"You want us to stall."

"We're still several hours from the ranch" Walt said. "I'd like to hold off the helicopters and jump squads until I know the situation out there."

"I can understand that."

"You think it's a mistake. I can hear it in your voice."

"I'm new to all this," she said.

"Don't give me that."

"It's your father," she said.

"Yeah," he said, still watching him through the glass.

"I'll do this however you want."

"Okay, then," he said, not changing his instructions.

The line went silent. Neither said a thing.

Walt didn't want to be the one to end the call. He felt like he was fourteen.

"It's Kevin in trouble, not me," he said softly.

"Doesn't exactly feel that way from here."

"About the other night—"

"What's interesting," she cut him off, "is that it's important to me. *You're* important to me."

"I handled that all wrong," he said.

"Shut up, Walt, I'm not talking about the other night."

"But I am. If you were in my position, with Gail and Brandon, the need to protect the girls . . . It gets so you don't trust anybody or anything."

"You can trust me," she said, he thought rather boldly.

"I'm beginning to figure that out."

"Yeah? Well speed it up a little, would you?"

"I shouldn't be smiling with all that's going down," he said.

"Give it a rest. It won't kill you."

Kill you hung on the line between them. He knew what she was thinking and she knew what he was thinking.

"Okay, then," he said.

To her credit, she didn't get maudlin or overly dramatic, which he'd half expected.

"Okay, then," she said, just before hanging up.

72

Kevin discovered an attic access hatch at the opposite end of the lodge from the study. Given the change in framing, he believed he was somewhere over the kitchen.

Whoever had entered the lodge only minutes before was still there. He'd heard an occasional footfall as he'd crept from one crossbeam to the next. The overall silence was uncomfortable. He couldn't help but think that each might be listening for the other.

Now the silence was broken by a tapping sound coming from the study. It continued

until provoking a response from the hi-
jacker.

"Whatever you're doing in there, stop it,"
a man shouted. It wasn't the copilot's voice;
maybe the guy who'd grabbed up Summer. "Any more of that noise and I put a
couple rounds through the door."

So, he had a gun.

Kevin used the noise of the man talking
to cover the sound of his own lifting of the
hatch. It came up easily, issuing a pale
light into the attic. He found himself looking down into a pantry closet, its shelves
loaded with cans and dry goods. Just inside the closet's louvered doors, he spotted a bucket filled with cleaning supplies,
and next to it a broom, a mop, and a canister vacuum cleaner. There were boxes of
lightbulbs and boxes of tape, extension
cords, a stepladder, and a toolbox. On the
opposite wall was a soapstone sink and a
clothes washer.

Tap, tap, tap.

"LAST WARNING!" shouted Matt.

The cowboy was the one doing the tapping, meaning he'd managed to use the
knife to free himself. It was either an intentional distraction, trying to buy Kevin time

by keeping the sentry's attention, or it was an effort at escape.

Kevin had to take advantage of it. He lowered himself down through the hatch, swinging from the opening and catching the toes of his shoes on the lip of the sink. Hands on the walls, he quickly lowered himself.

He eased the louvered doors open just as the sentry shouted again.

"I SAID, BACK OFF!" He cocked his shotgun.

Kevin grabbed a spray cleaner from the bucket. He slipped out into the hallway, crept down it, and looked around the corner and saw the sentry by the smoldering fireplace with his shotgun aimed at the door to the study.

The ensuing seconds stretched out uncomfortably as Kevin was knotted by a dozen what-ifs, tortured by not having a clue what to do. Finally, his mind made up, he backtracked to the pantry and found a bottle of cooking sherry. He snuck back down the hall, took two steps into the room, and launched the bottle at the fireplace.

"NOW!" Kevin shouted.

The shotgun misfired.

Kevin dove back into the hallway, scrambled to his feet, and ran like hell for the garage. He saw a flash of orange light on the walls that signaled the sherry igniting in the fireplace.

The shotgun fired a second time. He heard wood peppered right behind him. Some of the shot rolled past his feet, tiny balls no bigger than BBs.

Salvo narrowly missed being set on fire when the fireplace erupted. He jumped out of the way as flames spit out of the hearth. The rug caught fire at his feet, and he discharged the shotgun wildly in the direction of the kitchen. But then the fire died out as quickly as it had exploded.

Salvo reacted a split second too late to a noise coming from behind him, and as he turned around he saw the study door open—*Impossible!*—and a coffee table coming at him at full speed. In an instant he understood that the tapping sound had been the cowboy pulling out the door's hinge pins.

Salvo hoisted his shotgun while backing away from the table coming at him. He fell

over an ottoman and the shotgun discharged a second time. Dropping it, he
then was able to deflect the table to the
right and toward the fire, and he rolled that
same direction.

Whoosh!

A wrought-iron fire poker missed Salvo's
head by inches. He sprang to his feet and
grabbed a nearby lamp.

Another swing of the poker demolished
the lamp and broke the index and middle
fingers of his right hand. He screamed,
jumping back out of the way of a third
blow. Retreat was his only option.

He turned. A wet mist struck his face,
rendering him blind and in even more pain.
Screaming again, he fell to his knees. He
wiped his face with his sleeve but it was
no use.

He heard the cocking of the shotgun.

"You so much as twitch and I'm taking
the side of your face off," said the cowboy
in a low rumbled twang.

"My eyes!" Salvo wailed. "Help me!"

"What was that stuff?" the cowboy
asked.

"How the hell would I know?" Salvo
shouted. "Fuckin' help me!"

"Toilet-bowl cleaner," said a second voice.

It was the kid. But Salvo couldn't see him, couldn't see anything.

"Hands out," said the cowboy to Salvo, "flat on the floor."

Salvo sagged forward.

"Get a wet towel," the cowboy said to Kevin. "There's some rope in the shop . . . not the climbing rope. Bring it here—"

A few minutes later, Salvo was gagged and tied on the study floor. The cowboy tied the last knot and led Kevin into the living room. He extended his hand, and Kevin took it.

"Kevin," he supplied.

"John," said the cowboy. "Your friend?"

"Gone," Kevin said. He yanked back the tarp in the shed only to find her missing.

"I know the season, son."

"Her name is Summer. We were on the plane together. It's complicated."

"Gone where?"

"Dunno. Just gone. It's her jet . . . her father's. She was supposed to wait here for me."

"Mistake number one: don't ever expect a woman to do what you think she's going to do. Mistake number two: don't ever tell her what to do because that's a surefire way of making sure she doesn't."

"You're making jokes? She's out there . . . They could have her."

"If they had her, then who lit that fire? Ever shot a rifle, son?"

"Yes, sir."

"Follow me."

Five minutes later, Kevin and John were armed with the shotgun and the rifle, respectively. John got them flashlights, two-way radios, and a large handgun for the small of his back.

"Pulling the door like that . . . You could have gotten yourself killed," Kevin said.

They had gone out a back window of the lodge and up the rocks, a route John knew from repairing the roof. They had a bird's-eye view of the dying fire and the flickering orange woods beyond. They tucked in behind a stone chimney that Kevin immediately recognized as an elevated, well-fortified, defensible position, something that obviously hadn't just occurred to John on the spur of the moment.

"You ever play poker, son?" John asked.

"No, sir, not so it counts."

"When they showed up, they were un-armed. If there was any time to produce a weapon, it was then, and they didn't. So by the time that one was in the living room and I heard him cock the shotgun, I fig-ured it had to be my twelve-gauge pump. And I knew something he didn't: because we'd had some guests up to the ranch not two weeks ago with three kids under nine, none of them three rifles was loaded. I'd emptied 'em all myself. We keep the ammo in the study, so I had it in there with me. They had the big guns, leaving the two pellet pushers: the over-under twenty and the twelve-gauge pump. Both were loaded with bird shot. Did that myself. We had a murder of crows waking up guests at five in the morning with their damn squawking. Flying garbage men, is what they are. Been using the bird shot to discourage them . . . Not that I'd shoot a crow, be-cause that's illegal."

"But bird shot—"

"Would sting a bit but wasn't going to kill me."

"But if it didn't turn out to be your shot-gun?"

"But it was. That's where gambling

comes in, son. Chance is nothing but a balance of risk to reward."

In the silence that followed, they both heard voices filtering faintly through the trees.

"That's coming from down below," John whispered.

"The jet."

"They wouldn't be shouting at each other, not unless they're short a few cells."

"Summer."

"Yeah."

"I'm going—"

But John had him by the arm. His grip was like a vise.

"Number one: this is my ranch, in a manner of speaking. So let's get straight right off the bat that I'm calling the shots. Number two: I served my country, served it well, so experience is on our side. I promise you, the only war these guys have seen is in movies. Number three: they got my sat phone and busted up my radio."

"They busted up more than that," Kevin said. "They took most of a wing off that little Cessna down there."

Hearing that, John seemed all the more mad.

"They're guarding the jet, which is smart," he said. "But I'll bet good money that they haven't thought much about the Cessna's radios. Mind you, they will before long, but so far they haven't had the luxury of time, something we owe your girlfriend a debt of gratitude for."

"She's not my girlfriend," Kevin blurted it out, his patience running thin. "Do you always have to talk so much?"

The cowboy surprised him with a grin. "I go long stretches out here all by my lonesome, kid."

"How 'bout we *do* something like find Summer."

"You gotta learn to strike a balance between your pecker and your brain, boy. Number one: we don't know they've got the girl. Number two: I know this ranch well. Come daylight, I'm going to find her. At the moment, we got one of 'em tied up and two of 'em on the loose. They took two of the rifles, but they're not loaded. They heard that shotgun go off, you can count on that. They know their boy up here has got problems. I've got a loaded thirty-aught with a night scope and you've got a twelve-gauge pump with seven shells holding twelve thirty caliber balls each and another seven in your pockets. That's enough round ball to stop a bear in its tracks. Those boys are outgunned and on unfamiliar ground, and I imagine the silence is killing them. At some point, they've got to come to us, they've got to find out what happened. That's just human curiosity. The best weapon we've got right now is patience. We put our curiosity on hold. So do exactly as I say, and it'll all work out. Start improvising and you put me, the girl, and yourself at risk. Got that?"

"We can't just sit here."

"Not exactly. But nobody's ever going to find you up here. You've got a rock cliff behind you and a rock chimney in front of you and fourteen shells to stop anyone from trying to pay you a visit."

"What do you mean by 'find me'? You going somewhere?"

"You catch on real quick."

"No way!" Kevin said. "I got you out of there. You need me."

"Exactly. In case something goes wrong, you're my backup. I'm going down to the Cessna and make a call out before they figure out that the radios still work."

"And I'm supposed to just sit here?"

He set the volume control on both radios, slipped Kevin's radio into the neck of his T-shirt, and explained how to keep from announcing themselves to the others. They'd use two different signals: one to talk, the other to announce that Kevin had spotted either of the men headed for the lodge.

"There's no way they're going to find you up here," John said. "But if they should, you're going to have to shoot them, and you're going to find out that it's just about impossible to pull that trigger. So what I want you to do is aim low, for their feet. The gun will kick when you shoot, and likely you'll hit them closer to the knees. But you won't kill them, you understand me? You will not kill them. Don't think that way . . . Don't think at all. Just hold the gun tight to your shoulder, aim at their feet, and squeeze."

"I'm a wicked shot," Kevin boasted. "My uncle, he's like the best there is, and he taught me."

"There's a big difference between a rifle and a shotgun, son."

"Yeah, okay."

John asked Kevin to repeat the instructions for the radio, which he did flawlessly.

"I could give you a pep talk," the cowboy said, "but the fact is, we're looking up the wrong end of the horse here. As long as we don't do anything stupid, maybe we'll get through this. You want to do right by this girl, then do as I've told you."

"I got it," Kevin said testily.

John gave him a look in the dim yellow from the slowly dwindling fire. Kevin nodded. John laid his hand on Kevin's shoulder, then worked his way down the rocks. A moment later, he disappeared.

73

John Cumberland had his pride. Three men had taken over the ranch where he was caretaker, wrecked his Cessna, lied to him, smashed his skull, tied him up, threatened the lives of others. His own life had been defined by a failed war, a failed marriage, a brush with the law, then the successful stewardship of the ranch. Now he had failed in that as well.

A man's handshake means more than his signature and his word more than that. John had offered these people a helping hand and look how they had answered.

He would put an end to it. Had the boy

and girl not been in the picture, he would have gone on a shooting spree. Instead, he would approach things in a slightly more civil manner.

He silently worked his way down the wooded slope, his body pumping with adrenaline, breaking a keen sweat despite the chill in the air. He followed a familiar game trail that switched back repeatedly until reaching the airstrip. He moved slowly and carefully among the trees as he approached two hulking shapes—his Cessna and the Learjet.

There were lights on inside the Lear, the aft door open. He couldn't see the other side, but light on the ground suggested that the main door was open as well.

Drawing closer, John saw two shapes in a window. He wondered if one was the girl. If he could account for her and confirm she was safe, he would be free to deal with the others as he saw fit.

He considered a surprise attack. He could catch them unawares, wound them, and greatly improve his odds. But if they had the girl, his advantage was compromised. Smarter to make the radio call first to get help on the way. Timing the call was important. Given the narrowness of the valley, the Cessna's radio would likely reach only planes flying directly overhead. Plus, it was late, approaching eleven P.M. No small aircraft would be flying now. His only chance was a commercial flight, and few flew over at this hour.

He made his way to the Cessna, keeping his eyes on the Lear.

Always account for the enemy.

Reaching the Cessna, he quietly popped open the passenger door and leaned across the pilot's seat. He activated the battery, set the radio to 121.50, an emergency frequency monitored by all commercial aircraft, and put the headphones to one ear.

While it was possible that the hijackers were monitoring the jet's radio, John felt making the call was worth the risk. Nonetheless, he stealthily aimed the barrel of his rifle through the Cessna's partially open door at the jet.

He pushed the TALK button.

"Mayday! Mayday!" he said in a husky whisper. "Aircraft down. Hostage situation. Request immediate law enforcement at Mitchum's Ranch on the Middle Fork of the

Snake River. Repeat: Mayday! Mitchum's Ranch on the Snake."

He released the TALK button and listened.

If anybody was out there, the response would be immediate. The crackling static in his ear suggested he'd not been heard.

He repeated the call, listened anxiously for a response. Again, nothing.

He waited several minutes and tried yet again.

This time, the headphone popped with a male voice breaking through the static.

"It's summertime. I know you can hear me, cowboy. Summer . . . time! No more prank calls. Get off this frequency. NOW!"

Summer. Time.

Two silhouettes appeared in the jet's aft door, one unmistakably female. It appeared the girl had a knife held to her throat.

John sighted the man's head through the scope and considered the tight shot. The man changed angle, putting the girl between him and the Cessna. John lowered his rifle and put it on the ground.

74

Three to four hours to go," Brandon said to the other two men, slipping his GPS device back in his pocket. He was riding a chestnut filly with a blond mane, a showcase quarter horse with a gait as smooth as a Cadillac's. All three riders wore headlamps, a bluish glare illuminating the narrow trail ahead.

"How long can the horses keep up this pace?" Walt said. He was not a regular in the saddle.

"Longer than you can," Brandon said. "They can trot for hours, they're fine. But it won't be too much longer now before we have to walk them, anyway. Terrain's not getting any better."

"We'll ride them 'til they drop," Jerry asserted.

"No, we'll walk them," Walt corrected. "And we'll hike the last half mile without them so they don't give us away. They're our way in. They may be Kevin's only way out."

Jerry was turning in his saddle to object but nodded instead. "Yeah, okay."

The sudden agreement silenced all three.

Brandon consulted the GPS.

"Looks to me like the trail runs out pretty soon," he said.

"First light," Jerry announced.

They'd agreed that their best odds of reaching Mitchum's Creek Ranch unseen was to cross the Middle Fork before sunrise, before four A.M. Daylight diminished any element of surprise considerably.

Walt thought unlikely they'd meet this worthy goal. They had to hobble the horses, inflate the raft, and make the crossing—all very time-consuming.

"This guy Sumner," Brandon said, "he made *Mastermind,* right?"

"He produces movies," Walt said.

Something sparked at the back of his tired brain. A voice was shouting at him. But whose was it?

"You think if we get his daughter out safe and sound he'll make it into a movie?"

"Put a sock in it," Jerry said.

Walt tried to focus on the voice in his head. It wasn't Fiona's voice, it wasn't his own. It definitely was a man's voice . . . Something about movies . . .

"What about *Mastermind*?" Walt said, trying to stimulate whatever had prompted the mental itch.

"It was so-so," Brandon said. "Fairly predictable."

"It was a heist movie," Walt said.

Flickers of an earlier conversation . . . The voice belonged to Arthur Remy.

"Absolutely. Horse racing, hitting up the track on the day of the biggest race of the year. The bad guy stole the movie, the *Mastermind* guy. He was the best thing about it."

"But he had his fifteen minutes. You're aware of that, right?"

Walt had it. He reined his horse to an abrupt stop. Brandon reined his horse but Jerry's kept trotting.

The satellite phone rang as he was reaching for it. His mind was elsewhere as he answered.

"Dad!" Walt called out to Jerry, who still rode on.

"Stay with him!" Walt said to Brandon. "Stop him if you can. We ride together."

Brandon passed Walt the lead rope to the pack horse as Walt spoke into the phone. The bluish hue of Brandon's head-lamp disappeared into the curtain of tree trunks.

"It's me," Steven Garman answered back, his voice just audible above the growl of an engine "I'm at nine thousand feet, directly over the river."

Walt had heard a small plane not twenty minutes earlier. He'd switched on his phone and had caught a signal briefly. The phone had buzzed repeatedly with incoming mes-sages. The connection was lost before he could check them.

"I've got the repeater on board and up and running," Garman said. "Damn, if the thing didn't light up about five minutes ago."

"I had reception about twenty minutes ago. Didn't last long."

"I'm talking five minutes ago. I'm well north of you. Didn't last for me either."

"Kevin?"

"Could be one phone . . . could be ten. I had the hit only a few seconds. I came around and headed upriver, throttling back to limit engine noise. I'm now a mile west of my earlier route. I'd like to get closer and try again."

"Only one pass," Walt said, "as quietly as you can, directly over the ranch. See if the repeater gets a hit. If it lights up, then circle and try to hold the connection. I'm going to start calling Kevin's cell from the sat phone and hope I get through."

"Copy that," Garman said. "Turning for the ranch now."

Walt was about to punch in Kevin's number when he realized that it would take Garman a few minutes to get in position. That gave Walt time to make another call first.

He punched in the numbers and hit SND.

75

Come down from there, boy," a man's deep voice called out.

Kevin shuddered, cold and scared and unsure what to do. The cowboy had told him to shoot if he were discovered in his rooftop hiding place, and yet by all appearances, the cowboy had led them to him.

As if reading his thoughts, the cowboy spoke.

"Forget what I said, son. They've got Summer. I surrendered my weapon. We need you to come down."

Kevin's back to the stone chimney, he replayed the message, focusing on *weapon* and *need you.* Was there a subtext to the cowboy's message? Was Kevin supposed to come down shooting? Was he supposed to hide the shotgun for later? He was shaking so badly he couldn't keep his hands still.

"We're not going to hurt you . . . or anyone." He recognized the voice as the copilot's. "We're only interested in the plane."

The plane?

"We know you've got a shotgun. I've got Summer in front of me. Lower the shotgun down to me, and then we'll get you off of there.

"This is no time for heroics, Kevin," the voice continued. "No one's getting hurt unless you start something. You hear me?"

If the copilot had Summer, that left the two others with the cowboy. They likely had his rifle and pistol.

Can I get a shot off, maybe two? Maybe even drop one of them? With Summer as their only bargaining chip, would they dare hurt her?

"Do as he says, boy," said the cowboy with resignation in his voice. "They don't mean no harm to us."

He and Summer had gone through too much to surrender now.

"Kevin, they mean it," Summer called out.

He felt for the extra shotgun shells, slipping one in each sock. Doing it made him feel like this wasn't surrendering.

"Okay!" he called back.

The copilot came around the side of the building, his left arm slung over Summer's shoulder and tightly across her chest. In his right hand was the cowboy's handgun.

"The shotgun first," he said.

Kevin wasn't about to provide them with another weapon. He swung the gun against the chimney like a baseball bat, busting it at the hinge. That left the three men with the over-under shotgun *loaded with bird shot,* and the cowboy's rifle and handgun.

"That was unnecessary," the copilot hollered, his voice brimming with anger.

Kevin climbed down. The small guy took Kevin by the arm, roughed him up as he took away the flashlight and knife.

"Easy," the copilot chastised.

"I owe this kid," Matt said.

As Kevin was led away along with the

others, he glanced surreptitiously up at the chimney. No one had thought to check up there.

If they had, they would have found his cell phone, tucked onto a high chimney rock, its red NO SIGNAL flashing.

High above, a shining star flickered, then disappeared in the black velvet backdrop of space. A moving object had blotted it out. Farther along, another star flickered, disappeared, then reappeared.

Unseen by any human eye, the phone's LED began blinking green, just as it had done ever so briefly only minutes before.

76

The impenetrable coal-black sky bled to the color of a fresh bruise as it surrendered to the first photons from a faraway morning sun. It held a luminescence not unlike the ocean depths where the last vestiges of sunlight mingle and fade. Soon the ashes of the Milky Way would shrink to a mere brushstroke, leaving only named constellations and the planets battling for recognition.

At four-thirty A.M., Fiona should have been in bed, savoring a final few hours of sleep. Instead, she, along with Teddy Sumner, had hung around the Sheriff's Office, awaiting word of Walt's rescue attempt, her stomach in a knot. When asked if she would fill in for the videographer, she agreed solely because of the subject matter: Teddy Sumner. Walt had requested an interview with the man.

The interview room, directly across from Walt's office and one of three down a long hallway, had a metal table bolted to the floor and metal chairs. Two fluorescent tubes lit the room too brightly. Fiona and her tripod-mounted camera kept to the far corner, a close-up of Sumner's tortured face on the screen.

Deputy Gloria Stratum read from a card, declaring the date, time of day, location, and who was in the room. It was noted that Sumner was submitting to the interview voluntarily.

Sumner was nodding. Fiona saw an acceptance on his face that she didn't understand.

"You understand this interview is at the request of the sheriff," Stratum began, reasserting what had just been said.

"Yes. I'm aware that timing is critical. You people have no idea what this is like for me."

Fiona watched the close-up of his face as his pain intensified. She braced herself, realizing this was no simple Q&A.

Stratum shifted uncomfortably in her chair.

"You understand: I know what's going on," Sumner said.

"The sheriff . . . I realize this is a bit unorthodox . . . but the sheriff asked that I say just one word to you. He wanted me to add that the best chance he has to rescue your daughter requires full disclosure . . ."

Sumner pursed his lips until bloodless white and nodded solemnly.

"*Mastermind,*" Stratum said.

She then waited for some kind of response.

"That was it," she finally said. "The one word he wanted me to say. *Mastermind.*"

Sumner was flash-frozen by what he heard. Then his lips twisted and a wave of relief seemed to melt his agonized expression.

"I . . ." he started, then trailed off. "The point is . . . No one knows what it's like . . ."

His eyes flashed at the camera angrily. He was addressing it, not Stratum.

"Trying to hold this together without her mother, trying to reinvent the wheel and get something going . . . In this economy, no less. Are you kidding me?"

Stratum said nothing.

"But, here we are, right?" he continued. "I want to help her. If I don't do something now and it's later determined that if I had . . . If it gives the sheriff an advantage . . ."

"It comes down to money, right?" he continued. "Love and money. How fragile it all is, how quickly it all changes. All you ever want to do is protect her, take care of her, keep her out of trouble. Steer her away from the things that are only going to make it harder and push her toward the things that make it easier . . . college, good friends. Build her a solid foundation to stand on. Am I right?"

He jerked back in his chair so abruptly that he went out of frame of the camera. Fiona widened the shot, noticing in the process that her finger was trembling.

"Mastermind," Stratum repeated.

He looked up at Stratum, up at the camera, and winced.

"They say I'm a one-hit wonder, did you

know that? You know what it's like to hear that said about yourself?"

He closed his eyes slowly, shook his head, opened them, managed another smug grin.

"To stay in the game . . ." he continued. "There's a level of play that I don't expect you to understand, but it's critical if you're going to see the A scripts, if you're going to have a chance at the big projects." He leaned forward across the table, the camera laboring to keep him in focus. "A bridge loan, that's all." He was shouting by now. "'Nothing to it!' he said." Sumner snorted. "Nothing to it . . ."

He exhaled and looked around the room anxiously. "He's a clever man, your sheriff."

"He's a keeper," Stratum said.

Sumner put his hands behind his head and stretched. His neck made a popping sound. It wasn't fear in his eyes but anger, a man pitting himself against the world. Fiona cowered into the corner.

"Okay," he said. "Pay attention."

Again, he was addressing the camera directly.

Fiona pushed herself farther into the

corner, her back flat against the cool wall.

"I first met Christopher Cantell when we were developing the script for *Mastermind*. He was brought in as a paid consultant."

Fiona threw her head back and it hit the wall with a thud. Sumner's eyes ticked in her direction but only briefly. He looked back into the calm, unresponsive face of Deputy Gloria Stratum and said, "Ransoming the Lear . . . That was my idea."

77

As the sky passed from faintly maroon to sapphire, the forest interior remained dark as night. Kevin and John were being led down the log steps to the airstrip and river beyond. Kevin had never known such darkness, his heart heavy with regret, his limbs jangled with frustration. He and the cowboy walked along in silence, the rush of the river constant and growing louder like ringing in his ears.

He assumed the plan was to lock the two of them in the Learjet. He didn't know what they had in mind for Summer, but just the thought of that made him angry at the cowboy. They should have put up more of a fight than they had.

They reached the flat, graveled plain of the riverbed. Kevin spotted the pilot on the riverbank with a raft and some gear. As they walked closer, he could see it was an established put-in.

Upstream and down, towering cliffs formed a gorge through which the river churned, opening only briefly here at the ranch. Kevin saw it for what it was without an explanation from John, whose body language was becoming increasingly agitated.

"You'd better provision us well," John said. "The first take-out is four days downriver."

"We're well aware of that," said the pilot. He was holding John's handgun.

"And a snakebite kit and a water filter—"

"Enough! You'll have what we give you. Be happy we're not leaving you tied up here to starve. That option was seriously considered."

"Without sunblock and a tarp, what you're offering will be worse than starving—"

"I said shut up."

The two hijackers exchanged a look that, even in the dark, Kevin understood.

"They don't care," Kevin said. "They just want us out of here. They'd rather the river kill us. That way, maybe it won't be called murder."

"Shut your trap."

"Y'all plan to scale the face of ol' Shady," the cowboy said. "I saw the climbing gear all laid out."

"None of your business," the copilot said.

"Taking the girl?" the cowboy said.

"You're not getting the point," the copilot snarled.

He struck with lightning-quick speed, a single blow with the gun to the back of the cowboy's head. He was shorter than the cowboy, and the blow connected just above the neck.

The cowboy lurched forward but remained conscious and retained his balance.

"What I was trying to tell you," the cowboy struggled to say, "is that you want to take the north route if you're going with the girl." He caught a breath. "There are two routes up that face, and although the south route appears easier from the ground it's far more difficult at the top. The girl won't make it unless she's an experienced climber. In fact, none of you would. And watch out for the hawk nest on the north route. Half the time, those damned birds are in that nest and will come after you like they mean business. The other half of the time, they're in the air and will attack from behind. This time of day, they're in the nest. And you ain't seen nothing angrier than a hawk when its nest is disturbed."

The copilot clearly wanted to stop him from speaking but was too taken by what was being said.

"Okay, then," the copilot said, "get into the raft."

"Our hands? We won't make it around the first bend with our hands tied. We'll come up against the Widow Maker, and that'll be all she wrote."

"You'll have your hands free."

The raft was eased out into the current. The copilot motioned the two into it and they waded out and climbed in awkwardly. The pilot waded out with them and untied their hands while the copilot kept the gun on them. Kevin wondered if the copilot had the nerve to shoot them, if he could aim well enough to hit them at fifteen feet. The cowboy was probably thinking the same thing.

And then, with a push, they were off, into the churning current, into cooler air and a slight breeze not felt on shore.

They moved downstream quickly, coming up even with the camouflaged jet sitting at the end of the airstrip. The pilot and copilot watched them.

"Have you ever rafted?" the cowboy asked, climbing past Kevin, immediately all business.

"Couple of times."

"I'll take the stern and steer. You do as I say the minute I say it. You got that?"

"Yes, sir."

"Stay on the right for now. They'll be two commands: paddle forward, paddle back. I'll do the rest. There's a number four ahead. Won't be so bad this time of year with the low water and all, but it's no picnic . . . especially in this light."

"We can't leave her," Kevin said.

"Well, we have. First real chance at getting out is two days downriver, and that would mean a forty-mile hike. They were smart. We're stuck on this river for the next couple of days."

"There's got to be a way back to the ranch."

Then the cowboy barked some paddling instructions, and Kevin responded. The last glimpse of the jet slipped past, the rock wall rising quickly.

"I'll jump," Kevin said. "I'm not leaving her."

"Settle down, kid. This river is nothing to mess with."

"What if I climb the wall?"

As he said this, he saw how quickly and steeply the wall rose.

"We're not doing anything with them watching us. Now, paddle forward!"

"And when they're not watching . . . ?" he said over his shoulder.

"There is one possibility. It's called Mitchum's Eddy, but we call it the Widow Maker. The river swings left up ahead. Mitchum's Creek dumps into it there at the Maker. There's a waterfall made by the spring creek running off the ranch. But the eddy, even in slack water, is nothing to mess with. You get a raft in there and you'll get thrown into the wall, as it makes that bend, and the raft'll wrap, be pinned to the wall. And that's that. We'd have to swim for it or drown."

"So, I can swim," Kevin said.

"The currents, boy, are wicked. A couple died there about ten years back. It's nothing to mess with."

"But if we made it, if we could do it, we could follow them. Catch them."

"They won't leave any climbing gear behind, count on it."

He barked more instructions.

Kevin saw the bend in the river looming before them, maybe half a mile downstream. White water foamed at the base of the rock wall where the eddy pounded into it.

"What those fellas apparently don't know, or didn't think about, is that there's a zip line—a chair—that crosses the river about three-quarters of a mile upstream. It's how we provision the ranch. We keep an ATV hid on the east side to cover the twelve miles to the nearest road. We could cross at the chair, head upriver, and cut back across at a similar line three miles up. We'd be back on their side of the river then. We'd have a shot at them. At the girl."

"We've got to do it."

The sheer rock face at the turn grew closer. Kevin realized there would be little time for more discussion or planning. The river was dictating their moves.

"We have the one chance," the cowboy said, "and the currents are mean. Once we're out of this raft, that's it. We make the shore or we're thrown back into the river without the raft."

"Then we can't let it wrap," Kevin said. "If we miss the shore, we have to have at least a chance of catching back up to the raft."

"Dump the cooler," the cowboy said.

Kevin did as he was told. The cowboy maneuvered the raft expertly, holding to the center of the river. He simultaneously tied a line to the cooler's handle and knotted it tightly.

"The cooler floats," the cowboy explained. "But it can also fill up with water and act as a kind of anchor, maybe slowing the raft down and giving us a chance to catch it. But I gotta tell you, with no vests, no helmets, this is not to be taken lightly."

"We can't leave her," Kevin said.

"There's a fine line between nobility and insanity, son. Don't let your balls speak for your brain. This is no video game. If the eddy wins, we lose. And that eddy has won more often than not."

"I get it."

"Water's cold enough to steal your breath. You gotta be ready for that. You gotta swim harder than you know how. Got that? The eddy curls counterclockwise toward the rock, then back upstream. You fight it, you lose. The trick is for us to start high, to make it to the far current and let it carry us to the base of the falls. You fight that current, you'll tire out. You've got to work with it, not against it. Understand?"

He threw the cooler overboard. The raft lurched, and Kevin nearly went over the side.

"If we're doing this, it's now or never," said the cowboy, pulling off his boots and slipping out of his jacket. "Strip down, boy. You want to be as light as you can get."

Kevin pulled off his sweatshirt but left his sneakers on.

"If you end up in the river," John said, "you'll want your feet aiming down-stream—"

"And your hands covering your head," Kevin completed.

In the glow coming from the sky, he saw fear in the old guy's face for the first time.

"You don't have to do this," Kevin added, "I can do this by myself."

"I'm in no mood for four days on the river," John said, working the paddle to steer the raft closer to a current. "Okay . . . You first . . . Go!"

Kevin hesitated, judging the distance, marking the location of the small waterfall in his mind's eye.

"GO!" the cowboy repeated.

Kevin swung his feet over the side of the raft and slid down the rubbery fabric into the cold river water.

78

The water was icy cold. Walt was in up to his knees, wading across a small tributary that fed the Middle Fork, leading his gelding by the reins, the creek bottom too uneven to risk riding across.

"How far?" he called ahead.

"The ranch is one-point-two miles due west," Brandon answered. "It's closer to three miles, if we turn south and head for the put-in."

"Keep it down!" his father called out.

"Shut up," Walt called back to him. "We're working this out."

His father had been acting the taciturn,

grumpy old man all night, preferring to ride ahead and keep to himself, believing, no doubt, that riding ahead meant he was the leader. He hadn't been out in the field for nearly twenty years. Walt could understand it if his father were reliving the manhunt for D. B. Cooper, which had both defined him and limited his advancement at the Bureau. He'd gone on to do great things, was considered a leading expert on counterterrorism, but bringing home Cooper and the money would have turned him into a legend. He'd been churning inside over it for thirty years. He'd been taking it out on his family the whole time.

Garman continued his overflights of the ranch, at an altitude and in a flight pattern that kept him invisible from the ground. But soon the rising sun would catch the plane. There was time for only a few more passes.

Walt had made several calls to Kevin's phone, left three messages. Then Garman had flown in a pattern that allowed Kevin's phone to be logged on to the repeater for a full fifteen minutes. That, in turn, let the GPS track the cell phone. The coordinates placed it at Mitchum's Ranch.

Garman was continuing to make calls to Kevin's phone each time he flew over the ranch. Kevin had not answered any of the calls. And he hadn't returned any of Walt's messages.

The good news was, they had confirmation of the cell phone's location. The bad news was, that information would be impossible to keep from the FBI. Mitchum's Ranch would be the target of an aerial-and-ground assault by noon.

They had as few as three hours and maybe as many as six to locate and rescue Kevin ahead of an FBI Special Forces intervention that Jerry was convinced would result in a body count.

Brandon had discovered an unnamed dotted line on the map crossing the river near Mitchum's Creek that intrigued Walt but would require a detour to investigate. Jerry openly objected to any delay. He was currently trailing the pack horse and favored making for the upriver put-in and floating down to Mitchum's Ranch. Their arguing had continued for the past forty-five minutes, ever since Brandon's discovery. A call to the office hadn't helped. No one could find out what the line on the map indicated.

"There are no power lines in a wilderness area," Jerry reasoned. "The dotted line could mean anything. A dam? A culvert? Whatever it is, it's not worth the delay to find out."

Now on the far side of the creek, Jerry remounted his horse and, taking the pack horse's lead rope, headed due west.

"Dad!" Walt called out after him.

Jerry spun around in his saddle.

"There's no time to play hunches. We know we can float in. We go with the given."

"It's on the map for a reason," Walt said. "Going onto the river will cost us an extra two hours."

"No. The waste of time is heading for a dotted line that doesn't mean anything, doesn't get you anywhere. Kevin doesn't have time for this."

His father couldn't handle the raft alone and all three men knew it.

"Okay. You and Brandon will get the float gear to the put-in. We have radios. I'll ride ahead and see what I can see. We'll stay in touch."

"We're not waiting for you," Jerry said. He turned and rode off.

79

The river had appeared languid, even tranquil, from the raft, like a single sheet of molten gray glass sliding past the dramatic landscape. In the water, it revealed its power and speed. Its cold paralyzing Kevin's lungs, its unrelenting energy flinging him headlong downstream, the river revealed his attempts at swimming as perilously slight and ineffective. He pulled and kicked against the deceptively strong current while attempting to keep an eye on his destination, some tumbled rocks at the base of a gap in the rock face oiled by a small silver waterfall.

Kevin swam with all his strength. There was no time to think. He swam for his life.

Taking a breath midcrawl, Kevin managed to lift his head above the coils of current. The cowboy, who'd let Kevin go first, was caught in the river's main current heading straight for the Widow Maker.

Kevin put his head down and took several powerful strokes toward the waterfall. He was in the slack water between the two opposing forces of the counterclockwise current. If he could catch the current ahead of the waterfall, which was where he was headed, and swim strongly enough to punch through it, it might deliver him exactly where he wanted. He'd swum hard and had chosen a good line.

A flicker of optimism charged him.

Just another few yards . . . I'll be home free.

One last look back convinced him John was in serious trouble. He was heading into the Widow Maker where he'd be slammed up against the rock face and held there by the force of the current.

Separated by a mere twenty yards and yet with entirely different circumstances, he and John caught sight of each other.

"Go!" John hollered.

In that instant, no more than a split second between strokes, Kevin changed direction.

He pulled himself through slack water at the eye of the eddy, his strokes sure and confident, heading for a point in front of the cowboy. He arrived in a matter of seconds.

"Fool," John bubbled.

The cowboy's energy was spent. Kevin grabbed him and tried to kick, but John was sodden deadweight. The two of them picked up speed, rushing headlong toward the boiling white water at the base of the cliff. Kevin steered for shore, dragging John behind him, but it was no use. The river owned them.

The two opposing forces of the eddy, one upstream, one downstream, met at the Widow Maker, now only yards away. Kevin had started them out by swimming for shore. Only now did he see his mistake.

"You've got to work with it, not against it. Understand?" the cowboy had told him.

Kevin lurched back, kicking wildly *away* from shore.

"What the hell?" asked the cowboy.

"It was your idea!"

"Shore!" John called out.

"No! Hold on!"

Kevin pulled at the water with his one free hand and kicked his weary legs as hard as he could. Finally, the cowboy feebly contributed to the effort. Together, they managed to move to the left of the rock wall as the powerful push of the river drew them ever closer to it.

"We're going to hit," Kevin said. "Hold your breath!"

He felt the ferocious tug, the phenomenal power, of the current. It was as if they were being sucked down a drain. They were fully immersed in a wild, boiling froth.

Kevin's lungs burned, his chest felt like it might burst. Then he felt the change: the current was no longer pushing them downstream but was briefly neutral. For the moment, they didn't have to fight it, they could rest.

And then, while fully submerged, as if snagged by a hook, they were wrenched farther to their left, and jettisoned *upriver.* Their heads surfaced and they gasped for air.

Kevin continued to swim hard. The cowboy kicked, finding renewed strength. But the current was their friend now. It moved them upriver, nearly to where they'd jumped from the raft, now long gone. Kevin changed course, pulling John across the slack water and joining the downstream current. With one final pull, he delivered them to the broken rocks at the base of the waterfall. Here, the current turned neutral again.

They clutched the rocks, found their footing and staggered toward shallow water.

Kevin now sat in knee-deep water. John dragged himself up next to him. His large, callused hand reached out for Kevin and slapped him on the cheek. Once, twice, three times.

The cowboy was nodding and smiling, his false teeth having fallen out in the struggle, leaving a hockey player's mouth grinning back at Kevin.

80

I'll have the rope cut and we'll both be free-climbing," Cantell called up to Summer. They were thirty or forty yards off the ground, McGuiness in the lead, then Salvo with his wounded hand, then Summer, with Cantell last. The route had started out quite easy, the rope for safety only, the physical act of climbing requiring little technical expertise.

But Cantell soon realized they'd been lied to: the route the cowboy had suggested grew increasingly technical the higher they climbed. McGuiness, a human fly, had no problem with it. It was child's play for him. Matt Salvo overcame his lack of technical prowess and his broken finger with sheer guts and muscle. It was Summer who was slowing them down, and it had taken Cantell too long to realize it was intentional on her part.

"We'll all be far better off once we're at the top," Cantell called out. "If you want to escape, why don't you try then. Now is not the time. We'll haul you up if we have to. But if you force us to do that, we'll punish you. We'll strip you naked and let the sun get you."

Icy terror raced through Summer. The man knew which buttons to push. The idea of being stripped drove her to reach for the next rock and pull herself up.

The little guy was above her, and he'd mentally undressed her every time he'd eyed her ever since back at the plane. Even now, he would glance down at her and seem to be leering.

Those looks of his paralyzed her. He was the reason she was in no hurry. The copilot had it all wrong. She wasn't scheming. She just didn't want to be close to the little guy.

But she was terrified. She was afraid of

reaching the top, of heading off into the wilderness as a hostage of these men, wondering what they had in mind for her.

"Last warning," the copilot called from below.

81

With the cowboy in stocking feet, the going was slow. Kevin and John followed Mitchum's Creek out of the gorge to the elevated plateau that included the grassy field surrounding the lodge nearly a mile to the north. It was familiar territory for John, after years of maintaining the property, and he led the way through a dark forest, the creek to their left. He displayed a surprising amount of energy, now moving as if his unprotected feet didn't bother him in the least.

Within thirty minutes, they crouched at the edge of the clearing around the lodge.

John pointed out the dangling ropes in the distance, the sky now brighter, the stars all gone. Kevin followed the ropes higher and could make out four tiny figures. They looked like insects dangling on spiderweb threads. They were very near the top.

"That's all of them," John said, the relief in his voice palpable.

"Will we climb? I'm not great when it comes to heights."

"No. As I said, they'll have taken all the ropes with them, if they're any good, and they're good. They'll pull them up behind them. If we're going to catch them, we've got to get across the river and head upstream to that next zip line. That'll get us across the gorge and, I imagine, just about even with them, depending how fast we can travel." He looked again at the top of the cliff. "They won't be running after all the energy they've wasted climbing. If we hurry, we've got a fool's chance at it."

"Is there any food in there?" Kevin asked.

"They could see us cross if we move now. For the girl's sake, I don't think it's worth it. We'll sit here a minute and let them all get over the top. Then we'll provision in the lodge. I have a hunting rifle up in my room they won't have found. It's a beautiful gun and will outshoot anything they brought with them."

Kevin felt the hairs on his arms stand up. There was a tone to the cowboy's voice that said any possibility of forgiveness was gone. Whatever it took, he was going to free Summer. He'd kill them, if necessary. Kevin understood he was now party to that. They were going to hunt these men down.

John sensed Kevin's reluctance.

"You don't have to come along," he said. "You've more than earned your keep, son. You've done good. I can handle this last part on my own. They're in my country. This is my ranch—or that's how I feel about it—and they're about to learn what it means to do what they've done. You saved my life. I will get your friend back for you."

"I'm coming," Kevin said.

The cowboy smiled.

"How did I know that? But you and me, we have an understanding. I'm in charge. You do what I say. *Exactly!* And if it comes to killing, I'll be the one doing it. It's not falling to you, boy."

"I want her back," Kevin said.

"I know that. But you're going to have a life after this. I'm not leaving you with memories you can never shake."

"You make it sound as if you've done this before."

John wouldn't meet his eyes.

"Some men," he said, "live in isolation because they enjoy it. Others, because they deserve it."

The cowboy leaned back against a tree trunk and closed his eyes.

"Ten minutes," he said, "and they'll be over the top."

Sometime later—it felt like half an hour or more—the cowboy was in dry clothes and wearing a pair of lace-up boots. *Army boots,* Kevin thought. Both he and John wore backpacks, and John carried a military-looking rifle over his shoulder. He offered Kevin a nickel-plated snub-nosed .38 revolver. Six shots in it, and a box of rounds for his pocket. John showed him how to reload it, and he warned him not to use it unless his life depended on it. "Not hers, not mine, just yours," he'd emphasized. And Kevin had agreed.

Amid chirping squirrels and singing birds, they jogged up the narrow path to the top of the canyon wall north of the airstrip. Here, as the path continued, there were amazing views to the right of the river sixty feet below and of the forest to the left.

The cowboy ran effortlessly in the high-altitude air, unencumbered by incline or load. Kevin labored to keep up. The older man had come alive, either because Kevin rescued him or he wanted to settle with the hijackers. One thing was clear: he wasn't going to wait for Kevin. He was on his own mission.

It was only a matter of minutes before they reached the zip line spanning the canyon walls. It was antiquated, with a galvanized-steel tower on either side supporting a thick cable from which hung an improvised chair. Two ropes were attached to the chair, one allowing the passenger to pull himself across, the other allowing the chair to be pulled back to the other side.

As planned, Kevin went first. The chair sagged, feeling feeble and dangerous. He tried not to look down as he pulled on the rope across. The cowboy pulled the chair back and followed.

Another ten minutes gone.

Until that moment, Kevin hadn't realized how tired he was. He felt like he couldn't move.

"You said there's an ATV, right?" he said.

"There is," said the cowboy, "but there's no trail between here and Morgan Creek, so it's no use to us. We'll go on foot. Don't drop behind. If you do lose me, just hold to the river as best as you can and you'll eventually reach the zip line about three miles upstream."

Kevin eyed the cowboy. How dare the old man suggest he might actually fall so far behind that he'd need directions.

Just then, John took off running and quickly disappeared into the woods.

82

Ten minutes after they had separated, Walt heard a horse coming up behind him and knew who it was without looking. The horses were lathered and exhaling steam by the time Walt picked up the rarely used trail. He climbed off his horse then and studied the condition of both the dry, dusty soil and the nearby vegetation. Jerry had passed the packhorse off to Brandon in order to catch up with his son.

Walt hadn't yet told his father about the call about Sumner's confession. He kept that in his back pocket.

Jerry had seen his son work his tracking

magic before. For once, he withheld the usual cynical comments that perhaps really concealed his pride. Walt had few equals, if any, on the trail.

"It's the same tire tracks we saw back at the creek," Walt said.

"Okay . . ."

Jerry clearly hadn't seen any tire tracks back at the creek.

"Three weeks, maybe four. The most recent tracks are headed for the river." Walt, kneeling on one knee, looked that direction. "They don't float in their supplies, it's too much work. We should have thought of that." Excitement in his voice, he added, "The dash on the map, it *is* man-made. It's a cable crossing."

As they reached the zip line a quarter of a mile later, Jerry failed to acknowledge Walt's expertise.

"That's Mitchum's Ranch on the other side, isn't it?" Jerry said it like he'd expected it. He consulted the map. "There's two others south of here. Now, here's what we're going to do," Jerry said, interrupting himself. "Tell Brandon to do an about-face and get his butt over here. He can leave the packhorse behind. We won't be needing any of that river stuff, and if we need food, we'll get it at the ranch. We'll go across first and establish the perimeter, which means . . . What?"

Walt was back down on one knee again, shining a flashlight into the half inch of pale dust at the end of the zip line.

"The chair's on this side," Walt said.

"So?"

"Let me see the soles of your boots."

Jerry obliged, balancing against a metal tower.

"Two people . . ." Walt said, training the flashlight toward the woods. "You see this pickling of the surface? A rain shower. These tracks are recent, the past day or so. One's big, wearing combat boots. The other's a kid, Dad, a running shoe, size eight, eight and a half. Any guesses who that might be?"

"If you're trying to stop me from going over there, forget it."

"The chair is on *this* side," Walt repeated. He walked carefully to the nearby trees and studied the ground in the glare of the flashlight. "The bigger guy took off at a run." He touched several spots. "These are fresh, incredibly fresh."

"Why is it you don't want to cross, don't want to get this thing over with? Are you holding out some kind of hope that the Bureau takes this off your hands? Is that what's going on here?"

"Yeah, that's what's going on here. That's why I turned off my phone, abandoned my team. Why I'm looking at a recall vote if this all goes south." He pointed to the tracks. "Size eight and a half, maybe nine. It's Kevin. That's why the chair is on *this* side of the river: Kevin crossed over with one of the hijackers. Not the girl. There's only one set of running-shoe tracks. The combat boots took off at a run. Kevin's at a walk. So maybe Kevin escaped, came across alone and was followed."

"Let's cross to the ranch, look around, find out what we can find out."

"And we waste maybe an hour doing it," Walt said. He pointed toward the woods. "Kevin went that way."

"A *hunch,* that's all it is."

"No, an educated guess . . . Big difference."

"We need to collect data, follow the most promising lead, and find the plane. We are *this* close!" He pinched his fingers to half an inch apart. "We'll start at the crime scene."

"Not me," Walt said, coming to his feet. "You go if you want. We're on comm. You can call to tell me how wrong I was. But wherever these two are headed—and I think it's Morgan Creek Ranch—we can have them bookended. I can move Brandon back up that same trail we came in on. We'll squeeze them."

"And if you're wrong?"

"We know the girl called her father from the plane."

"What?"

Walt nodded.

"We won a confession from the father. The idea was his, the insurance scam. He'd met Cantell while making a film. He cut a deal with him to steal the Learjet and ransom its location to the insurance company. If his daughter hadn't been on the jet with your grandson, if the pilot hadn't sucked in a couple geese over Baldy, it might have all worked out."

"The girl's father?"

"Correct."

There was a long pause.

"Okay, so I'm impressed."

Of all times not to have a tape recorder.

"According to her," Walt said, "no one was injured in the landing. Including Kevin."

"And you were going to tell me this when . . . ?"

"Maybe they're holding the girl at the ranch. Maybe only Kevin escaped. But this is Kevin," he said, pointing down, "and I'm following him."

His father's face hardened and his fists clenched.

"Another way to look at it . . ." Walt proposed. "But you won't like this."

"You keep it to yourself."

"Think about this for a second, Dad. They don't need Kevin. What do they need him for? They've got the plane, they've got the girl. They let Kevin go. It'll be a day or two before he reaches people. But it's a lie, of course. They just want him far away from the ranch so no one ever finds his body."

"Shut your face."

"The combat boots are running because he has a job to do. Maybe he enjoys the hunt."

"I said shut up."

"We have a decision to make here."

Jerry looked across the abyss of the river canyon, clearly seeing that the chair was on their side.

Then something occurred to Walt. He climbed up the tower far enough to reach out and grab hold of the chair's pulley.

"It's not exactly warm," he said, "but it's nowhere near as cold as the rest of this metal," feeling the surrounding frame. "Thirty minutes, maybe less."

"You're talking yourself into this, do you see that? You're making it work nice and tidy like and nothing's ever nice and tidy. I can't play it the way you say," Jerry continued. "Ground rules are, you start at the scene—the ranch—and work your way out from there."

Walt saw his father's rigidity, his unwillingness to let the evidence dictate his next step, and he wondered how much of this resistance stemmed from thirty years ago. A river surrounded by forest, much like this one only bigger. By all estimates, D. B. Cooper had parachuted into the Columbia and drowned. There were never any tracks to follow. Jerry's task force never had a chance to find Cooper yet Jerry still shouldered it as a failure, his failure.

"Surveillance only," Walt said. "You report back to me. Don't engage without some kind of backup—me or Brandon."

"Yeah, yeah," Jerry said, already working with the suspended chair.

"I need you to agree to that. No engagement. We lost Bobby. I can't lose you too."

"Or Kevin."

"Or Kevin," Walt said.

"Okay, so I'll wait for backup."

"Keep your radio on. No excuses."

"No excuses, agreed," Jerry said. "You're going to wish you'd come."

Father and son stared at each other.

"Don't go rogue on me," Walt said.

"We're burning daylight," Jerry said.

He climbed into the chair and secured the chain across it.

"Shit," he said, "I've never liked carnival rides."

83

The cowboy moved with a speed and agility that stunned Kevin. In the past few minutes, John had been transformed, as if by donning combat boots and slinging a rifle over his shoulder he'd dropped thirty years. He was a dog trailing a scent—a junkyard dog at that. Kevin struggled to keep up.

"Wait up!" Kevin called out.

"You fall behind, you stay behind," John called back to him, his missing teeth causing a lisp that might have been comical had the reason behind it not been so chilling.

Kevin got it, then: it was personal. The cowboy wasn't doing this for Summer, he was doing it for himself.

They ran for forty-five minutes nonstop, reaching the second zip line and crossing back over the river, without John ever saying a thing, as if words cost energy. They left the faint trail, forsaking the easier terrain for a cross-country route.

John knew where he was going. And he had a clock ticking in his head: he was constantly checking his watch.

He was going to ambush the hijackers.

Twenty minutes later, over an hour since they'd crossed the first zip line, John finally stopped running. He wasn't even breathing hard, though his shirt was soaked through with sweat. He offered Kevin some water, and Kevin drank eagerly.

The cowboy reminded Kevin of old westerns the way he checked the position of the sun in the sky. Then he led Kevin out of the forest to the top of a pillar of rocks white with bird droppings. They were twenty feet above a rarely used trail bordering a marsh full of knee-high bog star. Beyond was a forest, charred lifeless, the trunks of fir and lodgepole pine standing sentinel, a hundred thousand witnesses to the destructive power of wildfire. The deadness, the blackened bark, made it feel like a graveyard.

Nothing good will ever come of this place, Kevin thought.

The cowboy used binoculars to scout the trail below and to their left.

"No tracks . . . we beat them," he said proudly, his lisp distracting.

"How do you know they'll come this way?"

"It's the trail to Morgan Creek, what there is of it. These guys want the quickest way out. The trouble with having a plan is, you usually stick to it."

"And what's *your* plan?" Kevin asked, unable to contain his concern. "You can't just shoot them."

"You think I'm going to negotiate?"

"In cold blood?"

"Their blood's the same temperature as yours and mine. That's the choice that has to be made."

"But Summer!"

"Same temperature as hers too."

Despite the rising sun, the light breeze ran cold, and Kevin shivered.

"She comes first," he said. "We don't do anything until she's safe."

"You can't put the cart before the horse, son."

"She comes first."

"You listen to me. They have no use for us. And we've seen their faces. We know their names. We're expendable to them, and that'll soon include the girl. Right now, she's valuable to them, but it won't last. We want to focus on what they'll do to her *before* they kill her."

"They won't kill her."

"Of course they will."

"Then why didn't they kill us? Why put us onto the river?"

"We're going to get one chance here," John said, not answering Kevin, not wanting to hear him. "You'd better bone up, son. I need you . . . Summer needs you. You go thinking there's some other way out of this and you'll do this half-assed, and that's unacceptable. Where'd all the John Wayne in you go?"

"Who?"

"Oh, Christ." John surveyed the route again. "You know anything about human nature?"

"I suppose . . ."

"We go taking potshots at them, what's the first thing they're going to do?"

"Shoot back?"

"What's the second thing?"

"Seek cover?"

"You said earlier you're a policeman's son?"

"My uncle's the sheriff."

"You see? It's rubbed off. Yes, seek cover. And if somebody is throwing shots from up here, then what?"

"Down there, I suppose . . . in the rocks."

The cowboy studied the boy's face.

"Have you figured it out yet . . . how we're going to do this?"

"I can't shoot anybody. I mean, maybe I could, but I don't know for sure."

The cowboy's expression revealed his missing teeth.

"I told you before, it's not coming down to you."

"Then what am I supposed to do?"

"The over-under's only good at close range, and it's doubtful these guys are good enough to make the handgun count. Besides, if they go for their guns, they can't be holding the girl. Intelligence and preparation wins here."

"You want me to be your scout, is that it? I can do that."

"No. The intelligence part is this: that shotgun is loaded with bird shot, but they don't know that. It'll sting like a mother, could even blind a person, I suppose. But it's not going to kill anybody, and it's certainly not going to kill me."

"What's *that* supposed to mean?" Kevin said, sizing up the cowboy. "You're not planning on getting yourself shot."

"This kind of thing . . . You can't plan what's going to happen."

84

Deputy Stratum did not prevent Fiona from entering the interview room as Fiona had expected she would. Positioning herself behind the video camera, Fiona decided to record the second interview as a pretense for being in the room. She wasn't going to miss this.

Teddy Sumner had aged in the past hour. Bags had formed under his eyes—the man had been crying—and a gray pallor had replaced the tanning-bed bronze. He reminded her of a piece of fruit ripened too long and left on the countertop.

She didn't want to feel sorry for him, didn't understand how she could. But his remorse had a contagious quality: it begged to be shared, as if others' pity might lighten his load.

"The insurance company received a call," Stratum told him.

"And . . . ?"

"They gave them forty-eight hours to make a wire transfer of eight million dollars to a bank account—"

"In Bishkek, Kyrgyzstan." Sumner nodded. "Well, at least they're sticking with the plan."

"Not exactly," Stratum said. "At least, not the plan you detailed for us. You were right about the GPS coordinates. If the money arrives on time, the coordinates will be sent. But there was mention of 'a package.'" Stratum drew quotation marks in the air. "They said it will be returned when the deposit is confirmed."

"Summer." It came out as a moan. "Oh . . . dear . . . God . . ."

"Can you reach him . . . Cantell?"

"I tried before, remember? He didn't pick up."

"We'd like you to try again."

"I'll do anything, of course. But I don't see what good—"

"If he answers the satellite phone, we'll get a GPS fix," Stratum explained.

Sumner's sagging head snapped to attention. His eyes widened with hope.

"Where's the phone?" he asked.

"It has to be yours," she said, "in case of caller ID." She slid his BlackBerry across to him. "We'd like it on speakerphone, please. Take the position that the ransom call has come in and you've been told it's going to be paid."

Sumner held the BlackBerry in his hand, briefly looking at it as if he'd never seen it before.

"God, what a mess," he mumbled.

He looked up a number on the device.

"This wasn't part of the agreement . . . a call from me. The idea was, no contact."

"You're concerned about your daughter, plans have changed. Be strong with him. Remind him you're holding a card nearly as strong as his. If you turn yourself in to the police, there'll be no money."

"But why would I do that? That puts Summer in the middle."

"She's already in the middle. If you can

negotiate her release ahead of the ransom, maybe they'll take it. It's all we've got."

In Fiona's opinion, Sumner wasn't up to it.

But he punched in the number and hit the green button.

85

First came a radio call from his father. He'd located the camouflaged Learjet, ignored Walt, and entered the lodge without backup, and found evidence of a fight, some wet clothes, and no people. A radio had been destroyed, and there were signs that a room and a closet had been sealed up.

"Given that we found only two sets of prints at the zip line," Jerry said, "they must have split up. That means they went with the river, as far as I can tell, but I'll scout the woods."

"You were going to wait for backup, Dad."

There, he said it.

"Woulda, coulda, shoulda . . . he's my grandson."

Jerry ended the call.

Within minutes, Walt's phone interrupted his chasing scuffs through the pine straw.

The call was the second from the office in the past fifteen minutes, this time re-hashing Sumner's contact with Cantell, a conversation that had gone poorly but which netted them Cantell's lat/long coordinates, putting him less than a mile due west and moving in the same direction as Walt, south-southeast. Summer clearly was part of the ransom package. Cantell hadn't budged from his demands.

Walt marked Cantell's position on the map, being no pro when it came to the handheld GPS in his backpack, and determined he had a fighting chance of intercepting the hijackers. Cantell's refusal to negotiate with the girl's father, his original partner in the Learjet theft, sent up a flare. There would be no negotiating ever.

The position on the map seemed to imply that their destination was Morgan Creek Ranch as Walt had guessed. The Middle Fork ranches were all accessible by plane, and with the ranches being open during the summer, there likely was a plane on the property.

Given the remote location, the plan no doubt was to scout Morgan Creek Ranch and then escape by plane.

He couldn't rule out the possibility that they might try to cross the river at the next zip line, in which case he was being handed an ideal setup for an ambush. But, then, why hadn't more of them used the zip Kevin had?

The contradiction confused him. A possible explanation was that Cantell had split up his team and hostages to circumvent capture. Two different teams, each with a hostage, each with a different route out.

Was that it? Or was Kevin being lured to his grave in the woods.

The only solution was to keep following the tracks. Kevin's rescue came first. Sumner's daughter's would have to wait.

Walt radioed Brandon, got his location.

"You left a dirt trail half a mile back," Walt said, consulting the map.

"Affirmative."

"Turn around and find that trail again. Follow it east to Morgan Creek Ranch.

Cross the river however you can. Incapac-
itate any aircraft or ATVs, then evacuate
the ranch. If there are any horses, take
them."

"Copy."

"If you've got time, change into civvies
and head out on horseback, north-
northeast. Maybe there's a trail you can
pick up. You want to make a line for
Mitchum's."

"Got it."

"If you make contact, play dumb, and
do your level best to stall them. Kevin will
recognize you, so signal him if possible.
Buy me some time to come up behind
them, but don't overplay your hand."

"I'm with you."

"If we have to hit them—and likely we
will—then we're going to hit them hard.
You'll have to turn off and hide your radio
once you are on the trail, so this is our last
contact. Hopefully, I'll see you on the trail
somewhere. If not, we go back on air in
two hours."

When Walt popped out of the forest, he
was looking at another old zip line. The
tracks led to the edge of the gorge, and

the wobbly-looking chair on the far side was empty.

Walt glanced down at the roiling water some fifty feet below. Pulling on the rope, he moved the chair toward him.

86

The morning sun was beginning to bake as Kevin lay back in a crevice in the rock. With only the most minimal of movement, he lifted the binoculars for the umpteenth time and surveyed the lightly trod trail.

There!

Sounds of the forest came from behind Kevin: pine boughs sighing, magpies cawing, obnoxious squirrels chattering—all underscored by the river's timeless advance. As the birds' whitewash coating of the rocks warmed in the sun, stench surrounded him, overpowering the sweet smell of sage nearby and even the bitter trail dust at the back of his throat. All around, insects alighted, wings abuzz. Up ahead, blackbirds darted in and out of the boggy marsh across the trail, the red chevron on their wings a designation of rank.

The cowboy lay on his belly hidden in the waist-high grass at the edge of the marsh. Even though Kevin knew where to look, he couldn't see John with the naked eye. He had to use the binoculars to work from one landmark to the next until he found the place. When he did, he saw John's binoculars trained back at him. Kevin held up three fingers, and the cowboy nodded. Kevin held up his fingers again to make sure the message was clear.

Three people, he had signaled, not the four they had expected. The small guy— crazy, unpredictable—was nowhere to be seen.

The cowboy fashioned his hand into a gun and squeezed the trigger, then nodded. *Game on.* Kevin was to go ahead with the plan.

Kevin practically shit his pants. His mind suddenly cluttered up with all the stuff the cowboy had told him, all the stuff his uncle had told him, all the stuff his mother had told him—half a dozen voices competing for his attention.

Where was Matt? Had he been left behind following a climbing accident? Had he gone elsewhere? Or was he out there just waiting for him?

Strange things happened to time when Kevin was like this. Summer and her two abductors were a hundred yards off, now they were just sixty. Adrenaline charging through his system would not allow him to focus.

Forty yards.

His mind clouded. He wasn't up to the challenge, didn't deserve the trust the cowboy had placed in him. It was just him, after all, *just* Kevin.

He reached for the revolver. The cowboy had warned that its nickel plating might spark in the sunlight, so Kevin wrapped it in a handkerchief with only the dark hole at the open end of the barrel showing.

Yes, now he had it. It all came back to him. Not so hard, not so much to remember. The cowboy had kept it simple for him.

"Can you do this?" John had asked.

"Yes."

"Say it. I want to hear it."

"I can do it."

Focus.

They were now within thirty yards of him, close enough to hear scuffing of weary boots on the trail. One of them coughed lightly.

The copilot was in the lead. He carried the shotgun in both hands. Next came Summer, a two-foot length of climbing rope tied around both calf muscles like a horse's hobble: she could walk but not run. The pilot was last, three yards behind her, carrying the handgun in his left hand and watching her ass.

Kevin wondered if Summer being hobbled like that affected the cowboy's plans. He lifted his binoculars: John was watching the three, his body flat and still.

A pair of magpies burst from the woods and swooped toward the marsh. Kevin followed them, rotating his head very slowly.

And there was Matt, to Kevin's left, at the edge of the woods. He was paralleling the three on the trail, playing scout, slipping in and out of the shadows.

He also carried a handgun. Had John

accounted for all the possible weapons? An occasional snap of a twig gave him away, but he was trying to be quiet.

Kevin dared not move his head. Racking his eyes to the right, he barely glimpsed the three below.

Twenty yards away.

And still ten from reaching the cowboy's mark, a stick by the trail.

Did Salvo's approaching change the plan?

With every step, Matt drew closer.

If Kevin did as John asked, he'd be an easy target for Matt. Wedged in the rocks like he was, he was a sitting duck.

Kevin caught another glimpse of Summer. He had a choice to make, the same choice he'd made in the river when John was being pushed toward the Widow Maker. Only this time it wasn't Mother Nature he was facing but a madman out to get him.

Kevin understood the importance of the element of surprise. He understood that this was the place for an ambush. He understood that everything came together here. Saving Summer came down to this one last chance. If he failed, Summer would be lost. And maybe John.

Kevin had to change the timing.

He would do as the cowboy had instructed, but he had to do it now, before Matt saw him. He should try to get a shot off at Matt, but he knew there was no way he was going to shoot a human being. John was right about that.

Kevin had been the one who found his father. He could never do that to another human being, not for any reason. Not even for Summer.

So if he did what the cowboy asked—and he had only seconds to decide—he knew the shooting would be in one direction only: his.

Kevin began to shake. His muscles locked up. He felt impossibly cold. The revolver slipped from his hand, thudding six feet down in a dirt-filled, cup-shaped indentation in the rock ledge below him.

Summer and her captors reached the stick, then walked past it.

Too late . . .

He glanced down at the gun. There was no way to get it in time. He couldn't fire the rounds to attract attention as John planned.

But Matt had stopped when he heard the gun fall. He'd spotted Kevin.

Matt raised the pistol and took careful aim.

Kevin realized his being shot would create the same diversion the cowboy wanted from him firing the revolver. He didn't have to shoot, all he had to do was make damn sure Matt fired.

Kevin stood up and held out his arms.

Impossible to miss.

87

The crack of a gunshot echoed off the rocks. In the confusion, it sounded as if a second round had been fired. Then a third.

"KEVIN!!" Summer screamed, spotting him atop the rock face, Christ-like, arms outstretched.

Kevin felt a searing jolt to his right shoulder—not exactly pain but the presence of something foreign and frightening—the impact of the bullet spinning him a quarter turn, speckling his face with his own blood. Losing his footing, he fell to the ledge below.

He opened his eyes. He was still conscious.

The pilot and copilot had stopped dead in their tracks, their weapons raised in Kevin's direction.

The cowboy came out of the bog at a sprint from behind the three, their attention being on Kevin, reaching them in four or five long strides. John hit the pilot in the ribs and sent him to the ground. A gun discharged, but Kevin couldn't tell whose. John then scooped Summer off her feet, cradling her in his arms, angling himself in such a way so as to shield her, anticipating the shotgun blast from the copilot. He took the hit, went down on one knee, then somehow managed to stand back up, still holding Summer tight. He continued toward the rocks.

The copilot tracked him with the shotgun, took aim.

The revolver's nickel plating sparkled not five inches from Kevin's face on the ledge.

Without thinking, he reached for it, his finger finding the trigger, and, extending his arm, aimed it.

Red spray erupted from the center of

the copilot's back, directly behind his heart. He didn't move. Still standing up, he was already dead. Instead of falling, he wilted to the ground like a marionette having its strings slowly released. His knee struck his chin, throwing his head back, and the shotgun discharged. A waft of gray smoke rose into the morning sky.

The pilot placed his hands on his head and spread his legs, making a dusty angel in the soil. Deathly silence followed, with not a bird or squirrel or even the wind announcing itself. For Kevin, gun still in hand, it was as if the whole world were holding its breath. He hadn't even realized that he'd pulled the trigger. But there was blood and there was the man, and he most certainly was dead. Kevin was marveling at the accuracy of his shot when his stomach suddenly erupted and he vomited up bile.

Recovering, he couldn't see the cowboy or Summer and didn't know if they'd made it to the rocks.

He released the revolver from his hand, its barrel brushing his forearm as it tumbled to the dirt. The barrel was cold, not hot. The gun hadn't been fired.

Had the cowboy shot the man?

Footfalls came running toward him. In that instant, Kevin realized he'd lost track of Matt. Kevin grabbed the revolver, sensing he was a fraction of a second too late already. He rolled on his side and aimed where the rock horizon met the sky, his finger finding the trigger.

The footfalls slowed. Then a silhouette appeared.

Kevin closed his eyes and squeezed the trigger.

There was a pop, followed by loud ringing in his ears. The smell of cordite hung in the air.

He opened his eyes. The silhouette was gone. Only rock and sky remained. No Matt.

"Put down the gun, Kevin!"

Kevin heard the voice of the man he wished were there instead of the man who wished to kill him. He heard his uncle's voice, not Matt's. Were his ears playing tricks on him?

Before leaving this earth, Kevin was determined to summon up the defining moment of his short life: his finding his father's body. But he couldn't do it like he usually could. Instead, he only saw peaceful blue sky and pristine white clouds.

"Kevin!"

No mistaking it this time: it *was* his Uncle Walt. There was no way it could be but it was.

In his mind's eye, Kevin replayed, videolike, the shots striking the copilot's chest. His uncle could hit a matchbook at a hundred yards.

"Kevin, is the gun down? Put the gun down!"

"Okay," Kevin muttered, releasing the revolver, "it's down." It tumbled off the ledge and landed in the sage.

Kevin heard something and stole a look at the pilot. The man was now facedown, his hands still over his head. The cowboy, five yards away, his rifle trained on the man, was missing his shirt. His back was bloody.

Walt's face appeared cautiously over the edge of the rocks. He reached out a hand and pulled Kevin up.

Matt lay awkwardly on the ground ten yards away, his eyes blinking, his legs twitching, with two holes in his chest. Kevin had to look away.

"Good thing you're a lousy shot," Walt said.

"I thought it was—"

"That arm okay?"

"It's felt better," Kevin said. Then he shouted: "Summer?"

His uncle smiled.

"Down here!" came her voice.

For Kevin, it was all that mattered, it was all he'd wanted to hear. But then purple orbs loomed at the periphery of his vision. He felt faint.

"Morgan Ranch," Walt said into his radio.

"Is he okay?" Summer cried out in panic.

"He's going to be fine," Walt answered. "Just fine."

Kevin felt his uncle's arms around him. He felt a sense of peace he had not known in a long time. And then the world went dark.

88

Using a first-aid kit, Walt cleaned Kevin's wound and wrapped his arm—the through shot that was no longer bleeding too badly—before boarding Garman's four-seater. Garman had transferred the cell repeater, which was about the size of a briefcase, to the plane's small cargo hold, allowing Summer to occupy the front passenger's seat while Walt sat with Kevin in the back. Walt held Kevin's upper arm firmly, keeping the compress on the wound. Despite the pain, Kevin didn't complain.

The FBI was reportedly on their way in a helicopter to Morgan Creek Ranch to "establish supervision." A Life Flight chopper out of Boise was coming for Salvo. While Cantell was dead, Salvo was critically wounded and needed medical attention. But who had decided the evacuation of Kevin and Summer took precedence over Salvo.

Summer, now wearing a headset, listened to radio traffic and communicated with Garman. She checked over her shoulder every few minutes to assure herself that Kevin was still there. She seemed to be in surprisingly good spirits.

"What on earth possessed you to just . . . stand up like that?" Walt asked Kevin, raising his voice to be heard.

"I don't know," Kevin answered.

"You could have gotten yourself killed."

"I guess."

"John said the plan was for you to fire a couple shots, create a distraction."

"Did he?"

"Was that your idea of a distraction?"

Kevin shrugged, then winced with pain. He wouldn't be shrugging again anytime soon. "Plans change," he said.

"You were lucky it was John. Not many like him."

"Do you know him?" Kevin asked, thinking it sounded like he did.

"I know him professionally. He's a good guy who got himself in a bad situation maybe eight or nine years ago. Two men dead. In Lemhi County, not my case. Way I heard it, it was self-defense. That's the way the judge saw it too. Trial was in Hailey, to get a fair jury. John couldn't seem to get it right after that, even though he was acquitted. He took to drinking, got himself in more trouble. Then there were these men in Challis and Salmon, relatives and drinking buddies of the two who were killed, and they'll never see it the way the law sees it. It'll never be safe up there for John. So he just dried up, went to work on Mitchum's Ranch, and has been a hermit ever since."

"Without him—" Kevin started, his throat constricting. He hung his head, not wanting Walt to see.

Walt tousled the boy's hair with his free hand, an intimate, fatherly, forgiving gesture that Kevin couldn't remember anyone doing for years.

"Listen, he said the same thing about you. Said how you saved his life back there at the river."

That gave Kevin another reason to keep his head down. He didn't want Summer to see him. After a minute, he dragged his left arm across his eyes.

"Don't hold that stuff in," Walt said. "You've got to just let it out. We'll get you and Summer some help, some counseling. It'll get better, you'll see."

"Grandpa was ticked he couldn't come with us in the plane."

"Grandpa," Walt said, "has issues."

Kevin laughed out loud. Summer somehow heard him through her headset and turned to make connection once more.

Walt wasn't about to wander farther into those waters and held his tongue. He noticed that the wound had stopped bleeding. He eased his grip on Kevin's arm.

But Kevin immediately reached up and covered his uncle's hand with his own, reapplying his own pressure. Then the fingers of his bad arm twitched, and they sought out and joined the fingers of Walt's free hand.

The two rode out the rest of the flight hand in hand. Nothing more was said. And just before Garman circled the Hailey field to land, Kevin's head slid onto Walt's shoulder and he fell into a deep sleep.

89

It was such a Jerry thing to do: organize a family dinner on the same night his grandson was rescued from the backcountry. He was obsessed with the public's impression of his family. Walt believed Jerry's neurosis could be traced back to Robert's death. Jerry had to show everyone that the Flemings were okay, that they could rebound from adversity with the best of them. If Norman Rockwell had been alive, Jerry would have commissioned a family portrait.

Things were already getting back to normal.

Jerry's bad timing was matched by his choice of bad location. He'd insisted on the Pioneer, all the way up in Ketchum, rather than any one of the good eateries in Hailey. But the Pioneer was Kevin's favorite. And Kevin wasn't about to fight it. Not now, anyway.

Kevin was stitched up at St. Luke's and moved to a private room, where he slept six hours before being discharged to his mother's care. Myra had been uncommonly quiet throughout the ordeal. It had taken Walt several hours to realize she'd been praying.

For his part, Walt spent most of Sunday on the telephone and in meetings. Dog tired, he finally called a joint press conference with the FBI, emphasizing the success resulting from cooperation between his office and their agency. In a strange, almost surreal, twist, the FBI fielded nearly all of the questions. In the end, according to the wording of the official statement, it was a "well-choreographed, jointly operated raid that had resulted in the safe recovery of assets." By assets, he meant the two teenagers.

The dinner itself was painful. Forced but

enthusiastic conversation through the salad course when Myra, fueled by white wine with ice, made a reference to Bobby that had silenced the table.

"I am so done with that," Kevin said.

Walt didn't know if it was his nephew or the painkillers talking.

"Excuse me?" Jerry said.

"My dad, the family's inability to get past his death and remember his life. I don't want to remember that day, I want to remember all the days that came before it. I mean, come on, people."

Kevin caught his grandpa's startled expression and turned his attention to a baked potato the size of a football. But then something happened that Walt definitely attributed to the painkillers: Kevin lifted his head and bravely entered into a staring contest with the senior Fleming.

"The thing is," Kevin said, "I was the one that found him . . . suicide or no suicide—"

At this, Jerry rose several inches in his chair.

"Oh, yeah, I know all about that," Kevin said. "But I don't care how he died, I care how he lived. He was a good dad. Maybe not as smart as Uncle Walt or as brave as

you, but that only made him different, not
bad."

Myra had buried her face in her napkin
and her shoulders were shaking. Walt
reached over and placed his hand on her
back, and she sagged toward him.

"And I'm sick of no one ever talking
about him. You all act like he never existed, and that's just not going to work for
me. He was there with me today."

He stabbed at the potato, then set down
the fork.

"I dropped that gun because of him, and
I don't know if that was a good thing or a
bad thing. But I'm not pretending anymore
that he never existed." Kevin looked around
at each of them. "So *all* of you had better
get used to it."

Definitely, it was the painkillers, because
his statement was followed by a devilish
grin that he fought to conceal but couldn't.
And then, inexplicably, he began to laugh—
a small laugh, at first, a chuckle. But it
grew inside him and then spread like a
virus around the table until everyone,
including Jerry, was laughing. The uncon-
trolled group laugh drew the attention of
the crowded restaurant. They were laugh-

ing about a dead man and everybody was watching them, noticing them. It was a laugh that made Jerry proud.

Before heading back down the valley to the now-open bridge, Kevin asked if they could stop by work for a minute, meaning the Sun Valley Lodge. Walt knew damn well he had no intention of talking to the boss, who wouldn't be there at eight o'clock on a Sunday night anyway. But Walt dropped Kevin off while he and Myra waited silently in the Cherokee, Myra not knowing what to say and for once not trying to.

Then her shoulders began shaking again, and she reached into her purse and fished out a tissue, cleaning herself up.

"Thank you," she whispered hoarsely.

"No problem," Walt said, looking out the windshield at the hotel's reddish façade, thinking briefly of Hemingway as he always did no matter how many times he visited the lodge. He pushed his anger over Teddy Sumner back, having no idea how or even if the law would ever catch up to him. Cantell was dead, and quite possibly so was the connection between the two. Walt had a couple of interview tapes he needed to decide what to do with.

Kevin came out of the lodge a few minutes later. Despite having his arm in a sling, he seemed to be walking taller. He had a confident, almost smug expression on his face as he climbed into the back.

"Everything okay?" Walt said.

"We're good," Kevin said.

"We're good," said Myra, unable to control her tears.

"Mom, get over it," said Kevin. "She's just a friend."

Myra's shoulders continued to shake but now with laughter. She was laughing into her tissue and looking over at Walt, her teary eyes filled with utter amazement.

90

—hwz it ging?

sme. u? WYCM?

Kevin responded to the "Will you call me?" by immediately dialing her number.

"Hey," she said. She sounded so close all of a sudden.

"Hey," he said. "How's the tennis?"

"Haven't played."

"You should."

"You sound like my father."

"How is he?"

"The same. In big trouble. I may have to

live with my aunt, or something. It sucks."
A silence crossed the line. She filled it.
"No big deal."

"I . . . I think about you all the time."

"Yeah. Me too," she said. "My shrink
says that's part of it."

"Mine says I'm supposed to move on.
Right . . . Not going to happen."

"We're coming up there."

"Here?"

"Yeah. Some kind of hearing or something."

"I don't think I'll ever fly again," he said.
"That's what I dream about: those flames."

"My dad, he cried like a baby," she said.
"Apologizing. As if *that*'s going to change
it. Said how he screwed it all up. I said:
Duh!"

"My uncle says people do weird stuff
when they're cornered."

"Don't go defending him," she said.

"You've got to forgive him," Kevin said.

"No way."

"Way," he said. "So he goes to jail, so
what? Maybe you could live up here or
something. Maybe it all works out."

"Yeah, like that's going to happen."

"It might," Kevin said.

Silence.

"So, will I see you when you're up here?" he asked.

"If you're looking for me," she said.

He tried to follow the shrink's advice and just say what came to his mind, but it wasn't as easy as she made out, and he heard himself whisper, "The thing is . . . I think about you all the time. I feel like—"

"Shut up," she said. "I love you too. BFF."

Best friends forever.

Kevin swallowed, trying to regain his voice. "No . . . not for me. It's more than that, more than BFF."

"Yeah, I know," she confessed.

He felt good all of a sudden. Incredibly good. "I'm going to see you when you're up here."

"Duh!"

He thought he heard her crying. Only a few seconds later, mumbling some excuse about needing to be somewhere, she hung up.

Kevin held the phone in his hand, staring at it. He remembered calling his uncle from the back of the jet as it took off. He remembered leaving the phone by the chimney of the lodge and his uncle telling him how it had helped track him to the ranch. He considered calling the cowboy and thanking him for everything he'd done. He'd been invited to spend time at the lodge and to fish or white-water raft, and he thought maybe that would be a fun thing to do with his uncle. But he wasn't going to fly in. If they ever went back there, they would have to hike it.

91

What's to become of her?" Fiona asked. The view from Walt's back porch included a dozen hummingbirds battling for control of the feeder. Shadows from the aspen trees slanted across grass that needed mowing. It was almost nine P.M. He'd made them a dinner of microwave lasagna, peas, and coleslaw from the deli. He was sipping Mexican beer. She preferred red wine.

"A white-collar guy like Sumner, he'll win multiple extensions. He'll push the trial back at least a year, maybe two. Days before the court date, he'll cop a plea and get eighteen months in minimum, where he can get home visitations and play volleyball. She'll be in college by then, immune from a lot of it."

"I feel bad for her."

"Yeah." He worked on the beer and watched the hummingbirds duel with their long bills, their wings going a million miles an hour. He felt like that more often than not: insanely busy but just hovering in the same place. "We caught the woman. Reno, at the tables. We have the phone records connecting her to Cantell, and our visual of her here. She'll do time along with the others."

"But months, not years. That's what you said, right?"

"Way of the world. She'll do less time than either of the other two. They're in for kidnapping. Big difference."

"Kevin?"

"Doing better. I owe him a night of fishing. Maybe you could guide us on Silver Creek."

"Love to do it. Just name a date."

They took Bea for a walk around the block, the smell of barbecue lingering, windows lit blue with the glow of televisions.

Crickets buzzed loudly, mixing with the sound of lawn sprinklers. A jet flew overhead, its wheels down for landing. Walt thought back to all the walks around the block he'd taken with Gail, surprised and comforted that those memories didn't land in the center of his chest. He looked over at Fiona a couple of times and knew she was aware of him doing so, but neither said anything for a long time.

"You don't talk much about your life before coming here," he said.

"This was—*is*—a place for me to start over," she said. "The past is better left where it is. You know?"

"I'm not sure I know, but I'm learning. Yes."

Kids, playing in a tree fort, cried out. The tree fort had a stained-glass window and an asphalt roof. Walt wondered if this was the right place to bring up kids. The private jets. The tree houses.

"It's not the same place it was ten years ago," he said. "This place."

"You're tired. You need a break."

"The girls will be back from camp tomorrow."

"You must be looking forward to that."

"Big-time," he said.

Bea raced out ahead of them, then circled back and came to heel on her own. Fiona reached down and rubbed her head, and Bea jerked up to lick her hand; Fiona laughed.

Walt nearly said, *"I could get used to this,"* but held his tongue for fear how she might take it. *Baby steps,* he thought.

"We could go over to Henry's Fork," she said. "It's fishing really well. With Kevin, I mean."

It would mean motel rooms. Three or four days at least. Meals together. A five-hour drive each way. That was the subtext, and it wasn't lost on him.

"I don't think I'm good enough to fish Henry's Fork," he said, "but Kevin would love it."

"I can teach you," she said. "It's what I do, remember?"

"With the girls getting home, we couldn't do it right away."

"But you'll think about it?" she asked.

"Absolutely."

Beatrice ran to the base of a tree and barked up at a pair of crows. Walt called her back to his side.

"You're probably buried with work, anyway," she said, giving him a way out of such planning.

"I am. But I always am. I can get away. It's got to be coordinated with Kevin's schedule. He's back at the lodge. Lisa would have to watch the girls."

"They could come, couldn't they? We could take turns with them. They'd love the park. We could do a day trip." They walked another half block. "Too pushy?"

"No. Not at all. It's me and work. That's all. I love this job, but it owns me. I have to prepare for the hearings. There's a ton of paperwork to get done. There will be pleas. I don't always see eye to eye with our prosecutors. I don't want to be away and miss something."

"If the kids hadn't been on the plane," she said, "do you think they would have gotten away with it?"

"I suppose the insurance would have paid out. If they hadn't, then the plan was to go back months later and fly it out and sell it out of the country. A jet can hide for a long time in the Nevada desert."

"So in a way Kevin and the girl . . . they're the ones who stopped it."

"And the bird strike—the plane going down. But, yeah, they did. It's true."

"Young love," she said. "Chalk up another one." Bea licked her hand again, causing Walt to reach down and tug her collar. "I didn't mean to lessen your role in it," she said.

"I didn't take it that way."

"But you're okay. Right?"

"With wounding a man and killing another? Is that the question being asked?"

"I shouldn't have said anything."

"You have every right to," he said. "I don't have an answer. That's the truth. I don't know what to say. He'd fired and hit John. Was aiming for a second shot. You don't think at times like that. You just do what you do and live with the consequences."

"I didn't mean—"

"So here we are," he said. "Do I think about it? Yup. Can I do anything about it? Nope."

"It's past," she said.

They looped around the block and headed back toward the house. What was at first an uncomfortable silence settled away to the sound of Beatrice's paws on the asphalt and the rustle of their clothing. A neighbor waved and called out to Walt, and Walt called the man by name returning the greeting.

Walt's hand brushed Fiona's, and for an instant he considered hooking her fingers with his, and maybe she was having the same thought the way her eyes looked out straight ahead, but nothing came of it.

"Beautiful night," he said.

"Someday I'll tell you," she said, surprising him.

"No need. You're right about the past. I like what you said."

"Easier said than done, like everything else."

"Looks like the Dalai Lama's coming to town."

"Are we changing the subject?"

He chuckled.

"What?"

"Nothing. Well . . . not nothing. Gail and Brandon."

"What about them?"

"Just before the auction dinner, she ripped him a new one. Made him heel like a bird dog." He rubbed Beatrice's head.

"Because?"

"That's the beauty of it. That's why I can laugh about it. I have no idea. If I had to guess, it was that he missed some appointment with her. She has this real thing about being stood up. But it could have been him taking the wrong car, or forgetting to fill the ice trays or not cleaning hair out of the shower drain. But what got me was how sweet it was not to be on the receiving end of it, how I wouldn't have traded with him for anything."

She reached down for Beatrice as well, and their hands touched. Or was that what she'd meant to happen? he wondered.